If It Ain't One Thing …

Mary Morony

ARCHWAY
PUBLISHING

Archway Publishing books may be ordered through booksellers or by contacting:

Archway Publishing
1663 Liberty Drive
Bloomington, IN 47403
www.archwaypublishing.com
1 (888) 242-5904

Because of the dynamic nature of the Internet, any web addresses or
links contained in this book may have changed since publication and
may no longer be valid. The views expressed in this work are solely those
of the author and do not necessarily reflect the views of the publisher,
and the publisher hereby disclaims any responsibility for them.

Any people depicted in stock imagery provided by Thinkstock are models,
and such images are being used for illustrative purposes only.
Certain stock imagery © Thinkstock.

ISBN: 978-1-4808-4939-6 (sc)
ISBN: 978-1-4808-4937-2 (hc)
ISBN: 978-1-4808-4938-9 (e))

Library of Congress Control Number: 2017916792

Print information available on the last page.

Archway Publishing rev. date: 11/09/2017

Tons of thanks to:
Sara Sgarlet
Lisa Tracy
Kate O'Connell
Denise Hood
John McAllister
Chris Perot
Ralph Morony

1

There! Right there on Free Bridge for God's sake! Mackey sat fuming and feeling anything but free. The red light only added to the traffic congestion, which was even more stopped up than her head, and she was fifteen minutes late for her appointment with a destiny that she already didn't like.

I'm sorry. I'm late. It was the traffic—a wreck I couldn't go around. No need to lie. I can't remember when I have ever come into your office and not waited. Do you think you could …?

If you liked it, then you should have put a ring on it. If you liked it, then you should have put a ring on it.

Isn't it awful about that little girl? Did you hear they're making dolls?

I'm really sorry. I know the value of time. It was the traffic. You wouldn't have believed how bad it was! It was an awful wreck, and the rubbernecking … Don't you just hate that? I do too. It's just so … well, a lie.

You know damn well. Take responsibility. You left late.

Right, I left late. If I hadn't forgotten my cell phone and gone back for it, I wouldn't be late. There are no victims here. No excuses either. If I'm too late, I'll just make another appointment. So what? I'm late, BFD. I'll come back. It's only fifteen minutes. No big deal; they schedule in fifteen minutes for just this sort of thing.

You son of a bitch, move the … Go, go, go! Goddamn it, I missed the light, you stupid … Now I really am late!

If you liked it, then you should have put a ring on it. If you liked it, then you should have put a ring on it. If you liked it, then you should have put a ring on it. All the single ladies. All the single ladies. All the single ladies …

The traffic was so bad. I hate minivans. Have you ever noticed how they are always in the way, always in the middle of some clusterfuck?

Snarled traffic? Traffic jam? I need to clean up my language. Jesus! Gross, dude. Pick your nose somewhere a little less public.

I can't believe this bridge sways so much. I thought they fixed that.

Oh my God, I'm late.

Come on, let's go. You can make it.

God, I hope there isn't a policeman around, or I'm really screwed.

I wish Eric had made me get up. Why does he keep turning off the damned alarm? I probably could have, but then Joey doesn't help either. I hate it when things are so damned crazy in the morning.

If you liked it, then you should have put a ring on it. If you liked it, then you should have put a ring on it. Now put your hands up. Oh, oh, oh, oh, oh, oh, oh, oh, oh … All the single ladies …

I've got to start going to bed earlier. Maybe I shouldn't have had anything to drink last night, or at least not as much. Did I drink last night? Three—too much! Oh my God, the mess. I can't believe I left that spilled cereal there. Does he have to do it every morning? You'd think I'd be used to it by now. I don't know why Eric's logic made any sense—let the cat clean it up.

… put a ring on it …

She's not supposed to be on the counter. I don't want to know how she gets up there. And how in the hell are you supposed to train an animal if you aren't consistent? Maybe it will still be there when I get home. I hope so. What am I thinking?

Oh shit, I left the list. What was on it?

She rummaged through her purse, located her phone, and punched in Eric's name, noticing her hands quaking slightly. "Eric, hi. What was I supposed to pick up at the store? … No, I left the list on the counter … I'm late, so I don't know anything yet. My head is so stopped up, I can hardly breathe. I'll call when I do … Yeah, I'm going to pick up Joey … Milk. Anything else? … Thanks. Bye. Love ya."

Don't forget the milk. Milk, milk, milk. "I can fill out the check while I'm waiting at this light. Oh, right, no check. That's why I pay for medical insurance."

If you liked it, then you should have put a ring on it. If you liked it, then you should have put a ring on it.

She gazed at her reflection in the rearview mirror, brushing down the light brown wisps and adjusting her ponytail. Gray eyes stared back at her. Her father liked to say her hazel eyes were his best barometer for how she was feeling—sort of along the lines of the old saying "Red skies at morning, sailors take warning." For Mackey, her father said it was green eyes, delight; gray, take warning; light blue, ice storm and run for cover!

Who was the dimwit who thought it was better for the little kids to go to school earlier? Trying to get to that damned bus in the dark is impossible. Poor little Joey's so tired when he gets home. It could be colder, I guess. I wish it would snow.

Jesus! Come on! Get out of the way!

… All the single ladies …

Her phone twittered. "Hello," she barked. "Oh, sorry. Hi, Mom. I can't talk now. I'm on my way to the doctor's."

"Are you sick?" Stuart asked as she tried to quell her rising dread. *Stuart, for God's sake, stop. People go to the doctor all of the time. Give it a rest! She sounds like she has a cold.*

"No. Well, I don't know. There was something not quite right with my Pap smear, I guess, because they called and said I need to come in."

Sounding casual but feeling otherwise, her mother said, "I hope it goes well. I guess you won't be able to go with me to see your grandmother then."

"Nope, not today. I'm slammed. I'm at the doctor's now. Gotta go. Give Gran and PopPop my love. Bye."

❦

The tires protested with a squeal as Mackey whipped her car into the space closest to the door. She grabbed her checkbook just in case, stuffed it into her back pocket while clicking the door lock over her shoulder, and raced into the office. With a breezy smile, she greeted the girl behind the counter. "Boy, that traffic!"

Looking up absently, the receptionist pushed a sign-in sheet at her.

She noticed two names ahead of her own. "Whew, I'm not late."

Now put your hands up. If you liked it, then you should have put a ring on it. … Oh, oh, oh, oh … 'Cause if you liked it, then you should have put a ring on it.

Picking up a dog-eared *Real Simple* magazine, she noted that it was last month's issue. She began to leaf through it, only occasionally looking at a picture or an ad as she studied the other patients. One by one, the room emptied. A nurse, as featureless and menacing as a queen's guard, came to the door, issued a perfunctory summons, and disappeared again, closing the door behind her.

Who does this doctor think he is? I can't believe I have to wait this long. The arrogance—does he think he's God? Her supporting foot twitched up and down while her crossed leg swung back and forth, making the magazine in her lap jiggle and bounce. She stole a glance at her watch. *God, I hope he doesn't keep me waiting much longer. I'm going to be late getting Joey from school. Like I need to spend my whole day off here. I'm not going to have time to get to the store or do any of my errands. Goddamn it. Would you hurry up? This is absurd.*

All the single ladies …

"Ms. Buckner," the nurse called from the door, looking around the room with a detached air, her hand resting lightly on the doorknob. "Ms. Buckner?" she repeated, sharpening the command.

Surprised to hear her name, Mackey started and then got up and followed the nurse through the door. "Do you have any idea? Could you just tell me why he wants to see me?"

The nurse cut her off. "In here. The doctor will see you in a moment. Please disrobe and slip this gown on," she said as she shoved a folded paper tunic at her.

Mackey felt and heard it crinkle and crunch as she took the proffered gown from the nurse's outstretched hand. "I thought he just wanted to talk with me. That's all his secretary said; he just wanted to talk with me," Mackey pleaded, pushing the gown back at the nurse. "I don't need this."

"Please put the gown on. The doctor will be right in," the nurse said flatly, laying the folded paper gown on the examining table and leaving the room before Mackey had a chance to protest further.

Okay, Robota. Jesus Christ, lady. Are you human? Do you have to go in for a fifty-thousand-hour tune-up? What a cold bitch! I really, really don't need this. I'm changing doctors. This is ridiculous. She continued to mutter to herself as she pulled off her jeans. She tossed her clothes in a pile on the chair and then rearranged them, tucking her bra and underpants underneath her casually folded shirt.

A soft knock at the door heralded the doctor's arrival. The door swung open before Mackey had a chance to respond. Dressed in her paper garment, she snapped, crackled, and popped on the edge of the chair in the corner. The doctor grabbed his examining stool with his foot, pulling it over to sit next to Mackey. He held a manila folder in his hand. His legs were splayed out on the too-short stool, giving him a toad-like appearance that Mackey decided suited him, half-expecting a *ribbit* to come out of him. Despite the height difference in their seats, they were still sitting eye to eye, and his knees were close enough that she could feel the heat of them, though they did not quite touch.

"Well, hello, Mackey." He took her hand in both of his. "How are you today?"

"Okay?" she said hesitantly, trying to decide if she wanted to pull her hand away. Finally, she just let it go limp. "You wanted to see me?" She glanced down at her body. "I thought you just wanted to talk. I really don't have time for an exam." *Oh God, futile … how ridiculous is this?* She digested the absurdity of it, sitting here before him in her gown of spun paper, nothing needed but the Gorgon at the door to enter for a full examination to take place in less than a few seconds.

"I do want to talk to you. Your tests results were atypical." A cold, clinical clip replaced his warm tone. "I want to do another Pap smear. It happens more often than you would think, and at this point there's nothing to worry about. I'll let you know, but I'm quite sure this is just a typical false positive. Would you get up on the table, please?" With that, he rolled his stool back to the end of the examining table as the nurse entered the room.

The ol' bitch must have been listening at the door. How else would she have … False positive? Positive for what? Atypical? "Is this going to take long? My son gets out of kindergarten at noon, and I have to be there to pick him up." She noticed the desperate note in her voice.

"We're going to test the smear right here. It shouldn't take more than an hour."

"An hour? But I don't need to be here for that. You can call me, can't you, with the results?" Her head shot up when she heard the door move in its frame from the nurse leaning against it.

"We'd like it if you would stay. In case …" His voice trailed off as Mackey climbed on the table and put her heels in the stirrups. The nurse covered her lower half with a sheet.

"In case what?" She flinched as the doctor inserted the speculum.

Looking up, the doctor said, "Hold still please," and then lowered his head again. "I'm sure everything will be fine." Faster than a pickpocket in a crowded mall, he was up and had stripped his gloves off. "I'll be back as soon as I know something." The door shut before she could rise to her elbows.

Before she even had her feet out of the stirrups, the nurse was out the door with a condescending command. "Don't get dressed; he may want to re-examine you." She shut the door with a mechanical click.

Tears gathered in the corners of Mackey's now-blue eyes as she sat cross-legged on the table. Her head felt like it was stuffed with concrete. Fingers held tightly together, she attempted to wipe away the tears without smearing her makeup. *Is he kidding? Goddamn it, I'm not sitting here waiting for an hour. I've got things to do. It's my day off. Hellooo. Who does he think he is?* She looked at her watch, gasped, jumped off the table, and began rummaging through her clothes, fumbling for her phone. *I'll never get across town. I have to wait, my ass.* She scrolled for her husband's name, poked it with her finger, pulled off her crackling cover-up, balled it in a knot, and threw it into the corner with one swift, fluid motion. She then put the phone on speaker, set it on the examining table, and started fastening her bra.

"Honey, it's me. I've been delayed at the doctor's, and I can't get Joey in time. Can you get him?" Picking up the phone and switching off the speaker, she sighed in exasperation. "Oh God, never mind, I'll do it." Dressed now, she slammed her feet into her shoes, tore open the door, and practically ran through the nurse standing just outside. Before the woman had a chance to gasp a response, Mackey was out in the waiting room. She didn't bother to speak to the bored receptionist as she barreled through the double doors and out into the parking lot.

෬

Stuart chided herself as she left the house. *Will I ever get over this blasted dread?* she wondered as she automatically went through the freedom runs her beloved therapist had taught her so many years before. *Ah, Jacob, Dr. J, wish you were here with us now.* "I'm free to feel dread, and I am free not to feel dread," she mumbled as if reciting the rosary—and then she racked her brain to think of another way to be free of this blasted entrenched mindset. She had followed Jacob Berke's teachings since they first met almost forty years before. There was no question that he had made it possible for her to survive the loss of her first family and to start another one. That they had shared so similar a grief just served to strengthen the bond they shared. She knew that Dr. Berke didn't believe there was anything that couldn't get resolved with the right amount of concentrated effort to turn thoughts in a more positive direction. "I'm free not to think about the dread. I am free to think about the dread." But no amount of effort had ever been able to dislodge this quick, kick-to-the gut, heart-wrenching dread that fell on her like so many bricks whenever she thought that her daughter, Mackey, or her husband, Bill, or now her grandson, Joey, was facing any sort of threat or danger.

The wind pulled at her unbuttoned coat, causing her to hastily button up as her thick mane of hair, now streaked with gray, slipped out of the band that held it in a loose ponytail. *It's too cold to walk today.* She stopped, fiddled with her hair as she thought for a minute about going back into the house and changing to warmer clothes, and then decided just to drive the several hundred yards to her parents' house—what she still considered their new house, she thought now with fond amusement. It had already been fifteen years since Ginny finally prevailed upon Joe to build this more "suitable" house for the two of them. Stuart and Bill had then moved into the house Joe had given Ginny as a wedding present forty-eight years earlier. She and Bill had jumped at the chance to move out to the farm and remodel the old house, bringing them and teenaged Mackey closer to her parents.

As Stuart backed the car out of the garage, she scanned her thoughts to see if she could detect any difference from the freedom exercises, wishing again fervently that Dr. J was still alive. *Help me focus, Jacob …* She turned the car toward her parents' house. *Maybe Dad can help. God knows he did enough work with Jacob. I don't know if I've ever talked to him about this dread. How could that be?*

As if he'd heard her, Joe's voice popped into her mind. *Wins! What are your wins?*

In the few minutes' drive to her parents' house, she listed at least a half dozen things that had gone well for her that morning. First win: She reminded herself how extraordinarily grateful she was to have Bill in her life. As a husband, he couldn't be more perfectly suited—smart, easygoing, and funny and possessed of a casual elegance that made him handsome, though few people would think to mention it right off the bat. Sometimes, she forgot to be grateful for it. She laughed when she thought of how funny it was that her man's man of a husband had to live his entire life with women—first with his mother and sister and then with her and Mackey. This had to be why he was so tender, she figured. She was glad that rather than carp about not having a son with whom to share hunting, fishing, and sports, he had just invited Mackey to share his love of the outdoors and sports, rounding her out into a whole human being.

The second win today was the big laugh she and Bill had shared watching Rusty attempt, yet again, to catch the squirrel that regularly raided the bird feeder. They seldom failed to marvel at the dog's complete lack of hunting instinct. Of the two, Bill exhibited more loyalty than Rusty, given that he refused to part ways with his Irish setter despite the dog's inability to perform in the field. Rusty's continued lack of success made his antics even funnier as the squirrel sat on a branch just out of reach, chattering insults at him. She smiled, realizing that even starting her day off with a big belly laugh hadn't ensured protection from her reflexive gut-wrenching reaction to perceived danger.

Dad is going to have to help. It's time to get over this. I really can't stand being such a worrywart. She pulled into her parents' drive. Joe and his two bloodhounds were walking just ahead. "Is this perfect or what?" she called out as she rolled down the window. "Brr, it's cold out there."

"It's what!" Joe shouted.

"I said, it's cold. Can you get in the car? I need some help."

Her dad climbed into the passenger seat. "You said, 'Is it perfect or what?' I was saying it was *what*." His eyes twinkled as Stuart grimaced. Turning to address the dogs, he commanded, "Stay, you two. I'll be back in a minute."

The massive bloodhounds flopped to the ground.

"What can I do for you?"

The car window instantly steamed up. "Wow, you are one hot ticket there, Pops," she said with a laugh before turning somber. "I have been feeling a sense of dread ever since—well, ever since the accident, if I am honest. I've been applying Jacob's freedom exercise to it for years, and I still have it." She looked at her father and fought to hold back the tears. "What do I do?" she all but wailed.

Smiling, Joe reached over, patted his daughter on the knee, and asked, "Do you remember what Jacob said about double-negative goals? Remember, he said that if you think about getting rid of something, you are focusing your mind on what you don't want. The trick was to think of what you would get if it were possible to have your goal. What would that be?"

Stuart pondered briefly, trying to calm the old anxiety. "Mmm. I'd feel safe, secure, and relaxed?"

"There you go." Joe patted her knee again. "You know how to do it. Make those feelings your goal. It is as easy as that. *And* you know that."

"Dad, it is not that easy," she started to protest, before remembering how many things in her life had seemed just that easy. She leaned over and kissed her father on the cheek. "Of course. You are right. I have been focusing on the getting rid of—not the invitation to those other feelings." She sighed and then laughed a little with relief. "Ugh! Thanks, Dad. What would I do without you?"

"You don't need me, kid. You've got all that it takes to have a fantastic life. By the way, from the outside, it looks pretty darn fantastic as it stands."

"I know. I know," she said, laughing again. "But you know what a perfectionist I am, always striving for better."

"Watch that!" He playfully pointed a finger at her, wagging it just the tiniest bit.

"Yeah, yeah. Out with you, before Daisyduke's slobber freezes her to the ground. I'll see you at the house," she said, giving him a playful shove. She watched with a third win in her heart as Joe and the dogs headed up toward the house.

❦

Clicking the unlock button repeatedly, Mackey scurried to the car, the lights blinking with every click. *I'm going to be so late. God, I hate this. Joey already had a terrible morning. I must have yelled at him twenty times to hurry up, and now he's going to be a wreck. I hope they don't make him wait in the office. He hates that.*

She had the key in the ignition and the engine cranking before the door shut. *Why can't Eric ever help out? He is so helpless! It's always on me.* Gravel skidded under the car as she slammed the car into reverse and then drive. As she negotiated the parking lot exit, she scrolled through her phone contacts, looking for the school's number. The phone rang while she pushed out into near-gridlock traffic. *Let me out, you bastard. It's not like I'm keeping you from going anywhere. Some people can be such assholes. Look at this traffic. What is the holdup?* She beat the steering wheel with both fists while still clutching the phone.

"Hello. Stone Robinson School. Can I help you?" The phone's squawk made her jump. The traffic had momentarily taken her mind off the call.

Now she absently held the phone to her ear, still focused on the jam ahead. "Hello, Betty? This is Mackey Buckner. I'm going to be late picking Joey up today. Would you please tell him?"

"No, I'm sorry. Would you like to speak with Betty?"

"No," she practically shouted. "Would you just tell his teacher, Janice Simon in K-1, so that she can tell him? Please?" *Could you be any dumber? Come on, lady, this isn't rocket science.* The traffic began to move. "I'll be there as soon as I can get there. I'm probably twenty minutes away."

"What's your son's name?"

Oh, for God's sake! "Joey Buckner. He is in Janice Simon's K-1 class, room 102," she seethed. *Get up off your fat ass now and waddle two doors down. You can do it. No, go through the light … go, go, go-o-o … oh, goddamn it.*

"And your name was?"

"Janice—no, Mackey. *I don't even know my own name.* Bucker, B-u-c-k-n-e-r." She enunciated each letter with the exacting clipped politeness of a very old spinster elocution teacher. *God, I'm going to be there before this idiot gets the message straight.*

"All right, Mrs. Buckner. I'll give her the message when they get back."

"Get back? Back from where?" Her voice rose. "Where are they?"

"It says here that the K-1s are on a field trip to the planetarium and won't be back until 1:45 in time for a 2:00 p.m. pickup. Didn't you get the note? Well, you had to because he wouldn't have been able to go if you hadn't sign—"

Mackey hung up. *Well, at least I can go the grocery store. Shit, the list. What was … paper towels? Uhh, I can't even think. Uhh-uhh-uhh, coulda put a ring on it …*

The traffic started to move. *I wish I had never heard that damn song.* She turned on the radio and then fidgeted through her purse, found a stick of gum, and popped it into her mouth. She pushed radio button after button, looking for what, she wasn't sure.

"Debit card to buy a filet of fish sandwich … your pet sea lion … the Home Depot has a good taste … we've lowered the cost … more saving, more doing. It's cold out there … chance of snow … want to hold 'em like they … if it isn't rough, it isn't fun … I'll get him high … can't read my p-p-p-poker face … p-p-p-poker face mum mum mum mah."

I hope it snows. I hope it snows, really snows, she thought. She drove around the parking lot twice. Since she couldn't get close to the store, she settled for a space close enough to a cart return. *I hate it when people leave carts out in the middle of the parking lot. Wonder why there are so many people here? P-p-p-poker face … p-p-p-poker face mum mum mum mah.*

Oh great, another dumbass song stuck in my head, she thought as her phone rang. She stole a look at the caller ID. It was her cousin Virginia. She groaned but took the call nevertheless. "Hey, Virginia, hi! Ay yi yi, have I had a day …"

☙

Joe's words from their conversation over breakfast continued to swirl around in Ginny's head. Wasn't he just being selfish? *Sure, he is old and tired. Sure, he is bored and ready for a new adventure. But don't the family's feelings matter, just a little?* When she allowed herself to think about it, though, when was it a good time to die? Ginny worried over the thought like a canker sore you can't help touching with your tongue as she slowly got ready for Stuart's visit.

Flinching just the tiniest bit as she caught sight of her new hairdo in the mirror, she wondered if she'd ever get used to it. It had taken twenty years to get accustomed to the snow-white hair that had replaced her beautiful blonde locks. She wasn't sure that she would live long enough to get used to this new style, shorter and sort of breezy. It was certainly easier to take care of, but … She took extra pains this morning, pinching her cheeks to add a little color, putting on a little more lipstick, and making herself stand up straighter. At least her sapphire eyes hadn't lost their sparkle, she reassured herself; that was something. She bent in close and looked into them. *Are you still there?* She smiled at herself. "You old fool," she muttered. "Where else would you be?" She understood at least a little why Joe wanted to leave. *Old age, not for sissies*, she thought grimly. She understood all too well. *But not at Christmas time, Joe, not over Christmas.*

She had to laugh. Stuart was coming over to work out Thanksgiving plans. Ginny knew what Stuart wanted, and she easily could have called. After all, what was there to work out? It wasn't like Ginny was going to cook. Ginny was tired too. Joe wasn't the only one. She was happy to let Stuart take care of all of it, run the show, make the plans. She supposed that Stuart was just being kind, trying to include her—which made sense because when she honestly thought about it, she was pretty sure that if Stuart had just announced her plans, it would have made her mad as hell. Passing the torch seemed such an awkward affair, yet passing it was necessary. Ginny, no matter how much she wanted to, could no longer run the show. God, she missed Ethel.

The whole holiday drill, why was it necessary? Of course, Stuart wanted her mother to come over to their house to "help" with the dinner that day, to give Ginny the respect Stuart felt she deserved. Ginny knew this but still resented it—and Stuart for it. The damned predictability of it all was irritating. Stuart wanted to run the show and would also spend a good chunk of time trying to manage Mackey. "Why couldn't she just phone the whole visit in?" Ginny grumbled. Funny, she thought, and really a little ironic—here was her oldest daughter, her Stuart, a practicing psychologist and a good one at that, a daughter she could be very proud of from what she'd heard. *And yet when it comes to her own family … Tolerance, Ginny. That's what you need, tolerance*, she reminded herself. She acknowledged that yes, she needed the reminder.

Gravel crunched on the drive, announcing Stuart's arrival. Ginny groaned inwardly, wishing for a simpler, easier anything and everything. *Maybe Joe does have the right idea*, she thought as she laboriously pulled herself up from her chair and slowly walked to the door, grateful that—at least for now—she knew she appeared more graceful than she felt on the inside, which was more like Boris Karloff's Frankenstein.

The two women hugged. Stuart held on tighter than usual, tighter and longer. "How are you feeling today?" she asked, giving her mother a look of intense scrutiny. "Quick, get in the house. It's cold out here. I don't want you to catch a cold."

"Still kickin', though to hear you talk, you would think I'm at death's door. Stop it," Ginny laughed. "I guess the cold is why you drove?"

Stuart acknowledged her mother's question with a nod as she picked up the bowl of leftover Halloween candy by the door. "When did you start getting trick-or-treaters? We didn't get any. We never have."

"We haven't. I just felt like I needed to be prepared. Besides, your father likes that stuff."

"At the rate he eats it, it will turn to dust before he finishes it," Stuart chuckled. "Speaking of Halloween, do you remember that darling Dutch girl costume I had with those adorable wooden shoes? It was so cute. Remember, Ethel took me around the neighborhood, and when people looked out and saw her, they wouldn't open the door? When I started to cry, Ethel said, 'Now don't' you give it a second thought, honey. Dey musta run outta candy is all.'" Stuart mimicked Ethel's dialect. "I remember the shoes were hell to walk in. She carried me from house to house and put me down at the door before ringing the bell. I swear, only two or three people in the whole neighborhood opened their doors to us."

"No, I don't remember. That's terrible."

"Mother, it happened all of the time. Your children experienced racism firsthand every time we went anywhere with Ethel, which was a lot, as I remember it."

"God only knows where I was during all of that time," Ginny replied sadly, remembering it only too well. "Clearly not aware of the goings-on." She shrugged and shook her head. "Do you want something besides that to eat?" She looked down at the bowl of weeks-old candy. "God, I'm beginning to sound like Ethel."

They both laughed. "I don't know that you ever didn't sound like Ethel. You have for at least as long as I've known you—and she, you," Stuart said with a laugh. "This is our first Thanksgiving without her. I don't know … It's going to be hard. I don't know if I can do it."

"Don't be silly. Ethel hadn't cooked in years. Seems to me, you've been cooking Thanksgiving dinner for at least the last five," Ginny observed.

"I don't mean cooking it. I mean having … not having Ethel around for Thanksgiving. I will so miss her."

"God, I miss her every day," Ginny lamented. "Every single day. It's funny that we were such good friends. It sure didn't start off that way." As they talked, they made their way into the kitchen. Ginny's mind flew back to the day Ethel found her in the barn with Cy. *Thank God it was Ethel*, she thought. *If it had been anyone else …*

"I thought, if it's okay with you, that we'd have Thanksgiving dinner here this year. I'll do it all. Your dining room is so much more elegant than mine. We can take your good china out for a spin. It's been a while since you've used it, I bet?"

"I'll have to get the silver polished," Ginny protested, trying to hide her surprise. "And …"

"Leave it to me, Mother. I'll take care of it," Stuart interjected.

"I am not an invalid. I want to help, so let me at least get the house in order." This was the last thing she'd expected, Ginny acknowledged inwardly, and she tried to lighten the moment with a little laugh. "It's not like I'm going to be lifting bales and toting barges or anything! I think I am still able to ask Verna and Nina to do a little silver polishing." She patted her daughter's hand. "Did I ever tell you about the time Ethel attempted to teach me to cook? After several attempts on her part, she finally concluded, 'Miz Ginny, best you let me do it.' I was sure it was as easy as she made it look. Turned out it wasn't. It also turned out that I wasn't ever going to be a good cook—certainly not when I had Ethel around to do it for me!"

While listening to her mother reminiscence, Stuart made tea and opened and closed cabinets as she looked for something to eat besides the candy. "How do you and Dad manage?" she asked. "There isn't enough food in this kitchen to keep a gerbil alive."

"We do just fine, thank you," Ginny said, bristling again. "Neither of us has much of an appetite these days. I don't know whether you know this, but we're both well into our nineties."

"I know. Believe me, Mother, I know. I'm just saying that Ethel would take a dim view of the contents of this refrigerator. Seeds?

And what is this?" Stuart screwed her face up and laughed, holding up a bag of green slime.

Ginny waved toward the trash can. "Do you remember the time we first saw your and Bill's house? No, of course, you don't. You were away then, already at college. Ethel came through the house as the children were ooh-ing and ahh-ing over this and that. It was so important to me, at the time, that everyone like it. I was holding my breath because I could tell Ethel was doing her utmost not to say what was on her mind. That was a herculean task, as you can well imagine. Finally, she couldn't take the strain and said, 'Miz Ginny, dis a fine house, but you won't be needin' me no mo'. This house ain't set up for no maid.' I like to have died on the spot." Ginny laughed. "Talk about a deal breaker. And you know the payoff? This kitchen we're in right now was designed for Ethel to have her own sanctuary, even though at eighty she wasn't working. She never liked the idea of an open kitchen. She needed her privacy—maybe more than the rest of us."

"She was a character, Ethel was," Stuart agreed. "I think she actually always hated that house. She did say it was the kitchen when I asked her to come live with us after Early died. 'Couldn't abide the kitchen!'" Both women laughed hard. "Can you imagine?"

"I can, actually," Ginny said, remembering both Ethel and her older husband. "Ethel was extremely private and very proud. She was keenly aware of her space—and others' as well. I couldn't have imagined her ever living anywhere but on her own on their little farm, even after Early died. It couldn't have been easy at the last for her. If she hadn't had that stroke, there is no question in my mind that she would have died in her bed at home alone and would have preferred it."

Stuart jumped in quickly to add, "Well, don't ever say I didn't try! I don't suppose you want to come live with us?"

Ginny shook her head vigorously.

"I didn't think so. But you know the offer stands. It's not like we don't have the room. Whenever you are ready, Bill and I would love it." She walked over and wrapped her arms around her mother. "You know I love you?"

"I know, and I love you too. You don't think I appreciate your offer and what you do for your father and me, but I do. I really do. Who knows, maybe one day I'll take you up on it. Won't you be sorry then!"

They laughed as they sat down at the breakfast table. Ginny purposely sat in the sunshine, allowing the sun's rays to soak into what seemed like her constantly cold frame.

Ever attentive to the nuances of her mother's body language, Stuart asked, "Are you cold? Would you like me to start a fire? I hear they are calling for snow. It feels like it—you know, that raw damp cold? Does Daddy still start fires?" She got up and started fussing around the fireplace. "It doesn't look like the fireplace has been used for a good while. Maybe we should get you somebody to live in," she said, half to herself.

"Enough," Ginny snapped. "Enough! Joe and I do just fine on our own with Nina and Verna coming a couple of days a week. Besides, I think I might be able to throw a stone at your house. It certainly isn't as if you are far away. I know you mean well, Stuart, but it gets a little tedious to hear you constantly fret over our supposed failings. I assure you, we are quite aware of what we can do and what we can't. It might appear to you that we're suffering. I promise you we're not. Neither Joe nor I forgo anything we feel strongly about. You're just going to have to trust me. And you're also going to have to stop this worrying about us, please!"

Stuart acknowledged her mother with a nod and changed the subject. "Speaking of designing the kitchen so that Ethel had privacy, it makes me laugh whenever I think about you and my Bill designing this house together. How you are able to speak even now is a mystery. I can remember him grumbling about you not knowing the first thing about designing a house. 'Post and beam—Jesus, she wants post and beam construction and then wants to separate the space with walls!' He'd shake his head, remembering that he was talking about my mother, too polite to say that he thought you were a damned fool."

"Did he really think so?" Ginny asked. "I do remember how adamant he was about that ridiculous, what did he call it, bird's nose …?"

"Bird's beak dormer," Stuart said.

"Exactly. I must have told him a thousand times I didn't want any of those silly gewgaws on the roof, just a plain cedar-shake hip roof with extra deep eaves. I didn't want the place to look like a motel." She laughed. "I don't think I'll ever forget how furious I was when the roofers had finished and that stupid window was perched up there in the middle of the roof. To give the devil his due, I am fond of the light it puts in the hall. I hadn't realized that those deep eaves were going to make the house as dark as they did." She pointed a thin gnarled forefinger at her daughter and laughed. "Do not tell him I said that."

"You aren't the only one that ended up giving the devil her due. Just recently even, I heard Bill say to a client, 'You know, I thought my wife's parents' house was going to look like a barn designed by Dale Evans or, worse still, Roy's horse Trigger, all rustic stone and rugged timber—but I swear I think it might be one of my best designs. And the way she uses the element of surprise to such advantage on the inside, with her beautiful antiques and rugs. That mother-in-law of mine has mighty good taste.'"

Despite the compliment, Ginny was tiring and starting to feel a bit peevish. Time for the visit to come to an end. She knew her limits these days, so she pushed what she believed to be Stuart's agenda to the fore. "You are inviting us for Thanksgiving dinner at our house, this house, are you not? We would love to come. Thank you so much for thinking of us." She laughed at herself. "And what about your brother Gordy—um, make that *Gordon*?" She corrected herself with a roll of the eyes, stressing the last syllable. "I'll never get used to that. He'll always be Gordy. My brother was Gordon. More change, and for what? Just for change's sake."

"Okay," Stuart said, reading the push. "I'm sorry, Mom. I love you, and I do worry about you. It seems to be a habit I've gotten myself into. I need Dad's help to get me out of it—the habit, I mean. Mackey has gotten me so riled up. You know, I really think she is suffering from a serious mental health issue. Mackey is a big worry for me. And I don't know what to do about her. That's not entirely true. Dad helped today by reminding me where to focus. So forget what I just said. But grown children are harder than younger ones."

"Don't you know I know that?" Ginny agreed.

"Why didn't you tell me?" They both laughed.

"Would it have made a difference?"

"I wouldn't have had any!" Stuart said, laughing again.

"I know that's not true," Ginny said, patting her oldest child's arm reassuringly.

"So I worry. Then I start worrying about everybody and everything. You know how the old mind works."

"Yes, I do, darling. Yes, I do. You know the only thing you can do for Mackey is love her."

"I do love her. What if that's not enough?" Stuart asked.

"Then love her more," Ginny said with certainty. "Stuart, look at you and me. There were times in our lives that nobody would have bet we'd make it. And we did, and our lives aren't so shabby. How do you suppose that happened?"

Stuart shrugged.

"Somebody loved us. And when we were the most unlovable, they loved us more. We are poster children for 'love us, love us more.' You've just got to trust life, honey."

Stuart changed the subject, jumping back to her brother. "Gordy … uh, Gordon and Susan have plans, it seems. She actually sounded pretty good, considering that the last time we talked, this past summer, she was six sheets to the wind. It is such a shame. She is such a sweet woman. Alcoholism is a dreadful disease."

"Yes, it is," Ginny agreed, "and it's a hard one to get hold of.

Hitting bottom is so painful for everyone, as you well know," she added ruefully.

"We both do," Stuart agreed.

They were silent for a moment, both recalling times in their lives that were now so long in the past—Ginny's struggle with alcohol, Stuart's brief fling with something harder.

Stuart sighed. "Maybe I should ask Gor … *don* about Thanksgiving. I wonder if I will ever get used to it either? Otherwise, it will be just us seven—you, Dad, Bill and me, Mackey, Eric, and Joey."

"Sounds good to me. I don't see any point in asking Gordy. There is no reason to undermine their already frail marriage. You know, Susan has always reminded me of a titmouse, pretty in a plain and simple way, same coloring, that pale red hair turned to gray so young. I remember my surprise when Gordy first brought her home years ago. I wonder if they would have married if she hadn't been pregnant … so young they were." Ginny sounded long ago and far away as she drifted closer to the fire that Stuart had started. "Not that I'm criticizing. I think she's lovely—a little jumpy, a little tentative, but such a sweet, kind, austere nature. It is as if he wanted somebody the polar opposite from the women he grew up with. That, I suppose, is probably not all that odd. But I am sorry she has to suffer so. I don't think she's ever had a particularly happy life. Dear Lord, her mother was dreadful." Ginny shuddered, moving her chair still closer to the fire.

∽

Customers were lining up for grocery carts. *This cannot be because of the "possibility" of snow. Please, God, tell me that people aren't this ridiculous. What was that …? Oh right, I need drain cleaner. Umm, paper towels, orange juice …* As she constructed the list in her head, she absently pushed her way through the frozen food section, tossing in dinners and vegetables. *Could you not leave your cart right in the middle of aisle?* She nudged the offending cart to the side with her own cart, picked up ice cream, and moved on.

"Sorry!" she said as she bumped another cart, though she wasn't sorry at all, actually. Then she had to wait to get the next-to-last jug of milk as the woman ahead of her held the cooler door open, perusing the contents like it was her closet and she couldn't decide what to wear.

"*Excuse* me." Mackey gritted her teeth as she ducked in past the woman like a prizefighter with a killer left hook. "I just need to get this ..." She grabbed the jug of milk and wheeled away, avoiding eye contact as if she had pulled a fast one on somebody instead of just, for Christ's sake, getting some freaking milk.

As she rounded the corner to the cleaning products aisle, she noticed that the checkout lines had started snaking around the displays and up the aisles. Foregoing clean drains for the immediate future but grabbing some paper towels, she moved to the least populated line. She was still chewing her gum, which by this time was completely tasteless. *Remember to buy gum.* She looked over at the express lane and started counting the items in her cart. *One, two ... damn, fifteen. Let me see, is there anything I can ... It's not going to make much difference anyway. This line looks shorter, only one of the carts crammed beyond capacity. What is she thinking? That she'll be snowed in for the winter? It was only a chance of snow, lady, a chance.*

A cart bumped up against Mackey's hip as she leaned over her own. "Excuse me," both women muttered as they smiled weakly at one another. Mackey's head spun a little as she straightened up. *When was the last time I ate? Did I eat lunch?* She noticed some protein bars on a nearby shelf and sidled over to grab a pack, eyeing her cart like a mother bear. She tossed them into the cart and looked around, daring anyone to comment. *I hate it when people do that. When you are in line, you ought to be in line. However, desperate times call for desperate measures.* She shrugged her shoulders at a woman who appeared to be glancing her way and smiled again, more weakly even than before. The line inched its way to the checkout counter.

The radio was playing over the store's speakers. *"California dreaming on such a winter's day. I stopped into a church along the way …"*

"Price check! Produce, price check," the PA screeched.

It was as if the whole store heaved and groaned. Mackey checked to see if the shopper who had committed the offense was in her lane. A woman two aisles away was looking around sheepishly. *Thank you, Jesus.* Mackey's line lurched forward. *Poor woman. I wouldn't even think about buying something today that didn't have a price tag. Only two more carts to go before I can … hey, you ahead of me, you can put your stuff up now. Now! Could you stop reading that trash and pay attention? There are people behind you who have lives and places to be. Hellooo! What time is it anyway?* She pulled out her phone and checked. *Great, if I'm not out of here in a half hour, I'm still going to be late picking Joey up. Why didn't I tell him to ride the bus? Oh right, we were going to do something fun on my day off. Right, some fun.*

A store clerk scurried past with the mystery produce. The woman two aisles over had a waxen smile plastered on her face. *Yeah, I bet you are really sorry!* Mackey put her foot up on one of the grocery cart support bars and leaned forward over the handle, stretching her back. The cart jerked forward and smacked the man in front of her on the butt.

"Oh my God, I am so sorry. I don't know how that happened. Are you all right? You're not hurt?"

"No." He turned to empty his cart.

"I am really, really sorry." *Okay, fine, don't respond. Just go ahead and empty your damn cart. I didn't mean to, really. I am sorry. Stop it, stop. You didn't do anything wrong. Give yourself a break, for God's sake. Nobody was hurt. Stop making such a big deal out of everything. Stop!*

Her phone rang, and she pulled it out of her bag. "Hello."

"Mrs. Buckner?"

"Yes."

"This is Dr. Strother's office. Your tests came back negative. Have a nice day." The phone went dead.

Well, there's that.

The radio continued playing over the store speakers. *"Sittin' on the dock of the bay, wastin' t-i-m-m-m-e ..."*

Feeling a little faint, she took the box of protein bars out of the cart and opened it. Wrapping her gum in the foil she'd taken off the bar, she shoved the wrapper back in the box. As she started to take her first bite, the line moved ahead, and it was her turn to disgorge her groceries onto the conveyer belt. She stuffed the bar into her mouth and unpacked her cart while trying to chew.

"Sittin' here resting my bones. And this loneliness won't leave me alone. It's two thousand miles I roamed. Just to make this dock my home ..."

A sob welled up in the back of Mackey's throat, but like the protein bar, she stuffed it.

Finally, it was her turn. She smiled at the cashier, who just glanced back. "How are you today?"

"Just fine. You?" the young woman chirped.

"Good, thanks. How long has it been like this?"

"Ever since I came in this morning. You know they are calling for snow. It always gets ... paper or plastic? Any coupons?"

"Plastic, thanks. No. Here, I'll do it." Mackey took a plastic bag from the stand and wrestled it open. But by then, the girl already had the last of her items in a bag.

"I got so much honey the bees envy me. I got a song—sweeter—than the birds in the trees. I guess you'd say, what can make me feel this way? My girl, my girl, talking 'bout my girl. Hey hey hey."

"That's 130.62. Credit or debit?" The cashier's voice had long lost its chirp. She stared at Mackey expectantly.

"Uh, 130.62, really? How did that happen?"

"Ma'am, debit or credit?"

I don't think I have that much in my account. A hundred and thirty dollars—how did that happen? I can't use my debit card. What if it doesn't go through? I'd die. Oh God. "Um, check?" she said. *A check would take at least a day to process, right? And it won't snow, so then I could get to the bank and make a deposit.* Mackey hastily scribbled a check and handed it to the clerk.

"Your supermarket card, ma'am." The clerk was looking at her like she had two heads.

Duh. She had been so preoccupied, she hadn't even thought about it. Mackey dug for her wallet again and pulled out the supermarket card.

The clerk switched on her light and rested her arm over the register while she waited for a manager to respond, her other hand on her expansive hip.

"What's the matter?" Mackey practically shrieked as she noticed the people in the line behind her exchanging glances with one another. She mouthed, "I'm sorry," to the woman just behind her and smiled that sick smile people smile when they don't know what else to do.

"It's not our card."

"*My girl. I've even got the month of May with my girl.*"

She fumbled through her wallet, finally finding the correct card. As she tried to control her shaking hand, she offered the clerk the new card. The light went off. A receipt spewed from the register. She hastened out of the store with just ten minutes to get to Joey's school. The store's parking lot teamed with circling cars looking for a place to park. She ran to her own as another stalked behind her. Once she was inside her car, she gestured at the woman in the waiting car to move back. "If you don't get out of the way, I can't back up. Don't glare at me, lady. You gotta move. Where do you want me to go? Aww, a light dawns dimly, finally. Okay, I almost feel like staying here so that you can't get in and that other car—"

Before she could finish her thought, that was exactly what happened: another car slipped into Mackey's space before Mackey was able to move on. She chuckled as she left the lot to the sound of a very irate woman's horn blaring. *Serves her right.*

"Sittin' in the morning sun, I'll be sittin' when the evenin' comes, watchin' the ships roll in, And I watch 'em roll away again …"

That's such a great song, she thought as she turned the car toward Joey's school.

2

The phone rang several times before announcing, "Call from Barstead, Peter."

"When did you get that phone," Stuart asked, "and who programmed it for you?" Her shock was apparent in her voice.

Completely ignoring her eldest child's remark, Ginny walked slowly over to pick up the phone, willing herself to stand up straight and hold in her tummy. *I eat like a bird. How is it possible to have this enormous belly?* Ginny mentally thanked Joe for insisting that she take that yoga class decades earlier and for his constant insistence ever since. Had she not done yoga, the way things felt now, standing might have broken her in two. Glancing in the mirror, she reassured herself that all was still in one piece and said, "Oh, that's Sallee. Wonder what she wants? Hi, Sallee. To what do I owe the pleasure of this call? Stuart's here. Is it all right if I put you on speakerphone?"

"Hey, Stuart," Sallee chirped, though she resented the fact that every time she called her parents, her older sister seemed to be there. "How are things going?"

"Same old, as Ethel would say—sixes and sevens." Stuart laughed, thinking about how much Ethel had influenced her speech and actually her very being, now that she thought about it.

"Good ol' Ethel. I miss her so much," Sallee rejoined, "and I didn't see her every day for years. Still, the finality of her death is so shocking. It drives home her absence so much more than just being a distance away."

"You two need to talk to your father," Ginny interjected as she pulled the throw around her, sinking into the sofa cushion. "Our resident guru has a very clear sense of how wrong you both are. Ethel is still as available as she ever was," she giggled, "according to his all-knowingness, Joe Mackey."

"More of his mind-over-matter stuff? Sri Joe-annda does indeed go on at that topic hammer and tong," Sallee chuckled, knowing full well how her words were landing on her sister. "I think I had half-hoped he would grow out of all of that."

Like an old trout that should very well know better but can't resist the lure, Stuart rose to her sister's bait, not bothering even to stop and wonder why Sallee was taking shots. It was just what Sallee did.

"Don't knock it until you've tried it," she replied sweetly. "The man knows what he believes and lives it. That's more than some of us do." Tit for tat—she did not refrain from throwing that little zinger in. It wasn't like Sallee hadn't been offered the benefit of Dr. J. It was too bad for her that she had rejected the help, but she might have profited from Dad's and an older sister's experience if she hadn't been so bloody stubborn. "You've got to admire that. And it seems to work for him too."

"How's it working for you, Stuie?" Sallee shot back.

"Ooh, playing without gloves, are we, little sis?"

Ginny broke in. "Now, girls, be nice. The point was not to start a riot, but to let you know that Ethel is gone only if you think she is. Before you jump all over me, I just want you to know I have a hard time with it too. But your dad swears by it."

Sallee muttered, "Some things never change."

"Speaking of which," Stuart said, "Mother is sporting a new hairstyle. Very attractive, I might add."

Ginny grunted but smiled at her.

"Do tell," said Sallee.

"It is short, very short, with soft curls. Well, actually a little spiky. It's very attractive and very hip—not like we would expect anything else from our mother." Stuart gave her mother a warm smile, and Ginny couldn't help but laugh.

Much to Sallee's dismay, she heard herself jumping in eagerly, with mock seriousness. "I just got a new haircut too, and it's short and spiky, just like my mommy's." She was taken aback at just how eager she had been to share that piece of information—*what was up with that?*—but she swiftly rallied. "How 'bout you, Stuart? Still sporting the Mackey long hair?"

"Yep, still sporting the Mackey long hair. Not ready to give that up yet." Stuart chuckled. "Change still comes slowly in some quarters."

"Changing the subject and back to Dad, where is he? I have some news."

Right on cue, the door opened in a cacophony of canine panting and sliding claws. The bloodhounds hustled in, tails wagging, with Joe in the rear.

"Daisyduke, Gomer, *down*, sit," Ginny barked sharply, making a preemptive strike before the dogs could slime her. "Sallee is on the phone," Ginny said to Joe before he could greet Stuart, as he always did, with "How's my favorite girl?"

"Aw, I hear him. Hi, Daddy," Sallee called out.

Joe winked at Stuart and called back, "Sallee, my favorite girl."

Sallee responded primly—but willing it to be true with every fiber of her being—"Daddy, you know you're not supposed to have favorites." That would be the day. Weren't he and sister Stuie so invested in their superior psychological hoopla?

"So what's the big news?" Joe asked, not even remotely interested in having it drawn out. "I hear you have some."

"Yes, I do. Big happenings up here," she said, trying hard to sound enthusiastic and positive. "Virginia is getting married."

"How wonderful," Stuart replied enthusiastically while her father crossed his eyes and Ginny tried to suppress a giggle.

"Tell us more," Ginny said and then fired a series of questions, one on top of the other. "When did they meet? Who is he? Do you like him?"

"Did you have to ask that question? Did you really?" Sallee whined.

"In a word," Joe translated, "not so much?"

"That's not a word; that's three," Stuart said.

Sallee answered haltingly. "I … it … yes, I suppose. I wish he weren't an out-of-work actor and that Peter and I didn't just happen to be lawyers in the entertainment business. It seems awfully convenient. And he seems awfully transparent."

"Transparency is good," Joe asked, "yes?"

"Not when you're dumb as a box of rocks, and you think you're pulling the wool over your soon-to-be in-laws' eyes," Sallee answered.

"Honey, nobody would ever think they could pull the wool over your eyes, nobody," Joe assured her.

"That's the thing, Dad—he thinks he is."

Ginny jumped in but would soon wish she hadn't. "Honey, Virginia is no fool and has so much to offer. I'm sure he loves her."

"Love is blind, Mother," Sallee reminded her, "and she has her own agenda."

Every self-preservation alarm in Ginny's head was going off— red alert, don't go there, stop, turn around. Sallee was as protective as a cave full of mother bears. The standard rule of engagement with Sallee was never, never participate in her criticism of her children, no matter how enticing she might make it. In case she needed the reminder, Joe sent Ginny a warning glance that spoke volumes, and she heeded it, concluding neutrally, "Well, it's wonderful news. I hope they'll be very happy."

"Did you hear what I just said, Mother?" Sallee asked just a little too confrontationally.

Ginny shot Joe and Stuart her deer-in-the-headlights look and shrugged as Stuart dove in to save her.

"What are their plans for the wedding?" Stuart asked.

"Actually, that is why I called. Virginia would like to have the wedding over Christmas at your house."

Three sets of eyes rolled. Joe hastily asked, "Can we have some time to think about it?"

"Absolutely," Sallee said. "That is the reason I called, to give you all some time before Virginia called to ask you. I didn't want you to get blindsided."

"Thank you for that," Ginny said as she attempted unsuccessfully not to roll her eyes again. "Does she have plans beyond having it here? Is it going to be a large wedding?"

"Well, that's the thing. Alex, her fiancé, has next to no family."

"What does 'next to no family' mean?" Ginny asked.

"His mother's dead, he has no relationship with his father, and his sister wouldn't be able to come."

"That's too bad," Ginny said, meaning it.

"So the plan is to have a small wedding with possibly a few friends and just our family a few days after Christmas. Please don't feel like you have to do it. I understand it's a massive inconvenience."

"Darling, if we can, we will," Ginny assured her. She looked over at Joe, who was shaking his head vigorously side to side. "Your father and I will talk and get back to you as soon as possible."

"No, that's not necessary," Sallee said, responding way too fast for anyone's comfort. "Virginia plans to call, so you can tell her what you think."

"Oh" was all Ginny could think to say as she thought, *Thanks for that.* It had become suddenly a very long day, and it was only early afternoon. "Okay, well, we will talk later. Love to Peter, Gord, and Virginia. Got to go. Love you. Bye."

She clicked the phone off, fleeing the lion's den before Sallee had a chance to say another word. "Dear God in heaven, protect us," she murmured as she rested her head on the sofa back and stared at the ceiling.

❧

Three-year-old Virginia had caused a rift that had never entirely healed between Ethel and Sallee—and between Sallee and her mother, for that matter. It had happened some twenty-five years earlier, when Sallee and Virginia came to visit for Thanksgiving. The plan was that Peter would follow for the weekend, after taking care of a few things at work.

This would be their first visit home since Sallee and Peter had married seven years earlier. Though Ginny and Joe had gone to Connecticut to visit on several occasions, it did seem that for two New York lawyers with a small child, travel was just too difficult. But now little Virginia was old enough to travel easily, and Sallee was so excited to show her off. Ethel and Ginny were beside themselves in anticipation. Ginny, practically giddy, couldn't wait any more than Sallee for Ethel to see her darling little granddaughter.

They were coming in on the train, and it was assumed that Ethel would go with the family to greet them. But she decided against it, stoutly maintaining that "Sallee an' that baby girl gon' want time t' settle in 'fore meetin' new folks."

Ginny tried to convince Ethel that she hardly constituted new folks. "You're more family than anybody," she exclaimed in amazement. "Even if little Virginia has never laid eyes on you, she'll know you. I think it's like Joe says—'It's an energetic thing.' Sallee knows and loves you, and the baby will pick up on that."

"Lord, Miz Ginny. I don't' wanna be creatin' no problems he'ah. I jes' think it's better t' wait til' de mornin' t' see 'em when ever'body's fresh, dat's all. You know good as me, li'l ones can be hard t' predict. And I knows Sallee is goin' t' want dat baby girl t' be perfect."

"That should be easy," Ginny laughed, "since we know she is! I'm sure Sallee will be disappointed. But you know best, and I'll be sure to tell her your reasoning. She has spoken of little else since she told me they were coming for Thanksgiving."

Ginny chattered on, changing the topic to Virginia and Stuart's young daughter, Mackey. "She is darling. I can't wait to see how the two cousins play. It's such a treat that they are so close in age. I'm sure that the sisters are happy about it as well."

"Dat li'l Mackey is bright as a new copper penny," Ethel chuckled. "I swear 'fore Jesus, I ain't never seen a child as wise as she is. If I di'n' know better, I'd swear she kin read yo' mind. An' sweet-natured, ain't none t' beat it."

"Hold a little love over for Virginia now," Ginny laughed. "Not like I think you would do anything else. I know how big your heart is, and especially for all our rascally Mackey children."

Ethel glowed from the compliment Miz Ginny had bestowed. There was no question that the Mackey children and grandchildren were every much hers as they were Miz Ginny and Mista Joe's. It felt real good to have Miz Ginny acknowledge it.

When Sallee got off the train, Ginny exclaimed, "My goodness! Sallee, congratulations. Why didn't you tell me that you were pregnant? When is the baby due?"

"Hello, Mother." Sallee hugged Ginny while Joe stood by, trying to catch his granddaughter's eye. "I wanted to surprise you with the news. Needless to say, we are over the moon about it. Hi, Daddy." She kissed and hugged Joe.

Virginia tried to push them apart, but Sallee continued, ignoring the child's shoves. "I'm due in January. That's why I came for Thanksgiving rather than Christmas, like you suggested."

"No, Mommy, no hugs for him!" the little girl shouted, pushing and scratching at Joe as hard as she could.

As Ginny had predicted, Sallee was disappointed that Ethel hadn't come with her parents to meet the train. "I was hoping that our arrival would be a bigger draw. I mean, I know it's past her normal working hours. But somehow I didn't think that would have mattered to Ethel."

"Honey," Ginny explained, "she is beyond excited. She wanted you and Virginia to have time to get settled before Virginia had to meet a stranger."

"Ethel, a stranger?" Sallee scoffed. "Who is she kidding? I talk to Virginia all day long about Ethel this and Ethel that. She knows as much about Ethel as she does about you and Daddy."

Ginny felt just a little pang of jealousy that must have showed on her face. Joe came up beside her and wrapped an arm around her, pulling her close. "Don't worry, Granny. You will always be tops with me," he whispered in her ear.

Ginny laughed as she held out her arms to her sleepy grand-daughter, who burrowed into her mother's neck.

"Let's get you two home," said Joe. "Somebody looks a little like a sleepyhead to me." He winked at Virginia, who was peeking out from her mother's collar.

"No, I'm not sleepy," she announced. "I'm Virginia, and I'm not going home. I am going to my mommy's old house." Much to her grandparents' surprise, she didn't stick out her tongue, as her tone indicated that she might.

"On our way to your mommy's old house, then." Joe saluted, gathered up four bags, and led the way to the waiting car. Ginny picked up three more bags while Sallee pushed a stroller ahead of her and Virginia watched imperiously from her mother's arms.

Joe went back for the rest of Sallee's things. Once everything was in the car, he closed the trunk and climbed into the driver's seat. "Traveling with children, you practically need movers on retainer," he laughed.

Sallee snapped, "I packed lightly. I'm sorry."

"Oh, your dad is just fooling. You know how he likes to tease," Ginny said and mockingly glared at Joe.

They arrived back at the house without further incident. "You must be exhausted," Ginny remarked as they climbed the stairs for the third time with armfuls of bags on each trip. "I know I am," she laughed. "Can I get you anything?"

Sallee shook her head. She was still coaxing Virginia out of her coat when Ginny came into the living room and collapsed in a chair.

The child was not shown her bedroom until far past Ginny and Joe's bedtime. As Ginny struggled to keep her eyes open, Sallee prattled on about Virginia's many accomplishments and the new baby while the child played havoc on the piano and her grandparents' nerves. When she wasn't banging on the piano, she was picking up and playing with Ginny's collection of jade figurines.

"I'm sorry. I didn't even think to put these things away," Ginny said as she lunged to catch a toppling antique china vase that Virginia had just brushed by. "Darling, would you like to play with the dolly?" Ginny held a rag doll, shaking it as she would for a puppy to entice the child away from another round of piano playing. She noted that their two bloodhounds, Fred and Ginger, were nowhere to be seen. *Would that I could be so lucky*, she thought.

"No, Virginia wants to play some piano," the child protested, not pausing in her foray on the keyboard.

Ginny couldn't help but groan. Relieved to see Sallee hadn't noticed, she made a big show of checking her watch. "Oh my, no wonder I am so tired. Look at the time. It is almost midnight. Virginia, can I show you where you and your mommy are going to stay?"

"No!" Virginia pounded on the keys, not looking up.

Sallee jumped in. "If you need to go to bed, go ahead. Virginia and I are going to stay up a while more. She slept almost all the way down here, so I don't imagine she's very tired. We're going to stay in my old room, right?"

"Ethel made up the crib in Helen's room. We didn't know if Virginia still slept in a crib. You can move when Peter comes. Or if you want, we can move the crib into your room."

"That won't be a problem. She sleeps with us at home too. We don't need a crib."

"Oh" was all either parent thought to say.

On their way to bed, Joe muttered to Ginny, "It's going to be a long Thanksgiving."

Ginny tried to smile. "Oh Lord, I am glad Ethel had the good sense to wait until tomorrow to meet Little Miss ... I don't know what."

"Yeah, that's going to be a ... umm, I don't even think I have a word for what it's going to be. But whatever it is, you can bet it's going to be a doozy."

❧

Joe had hit the nail smack on the head. Ethel nearly bit her tongue in two when, on her first meeting with Virginia, the child hauled off and kicked Sallee in the shin. "You didn't tell me that she was fat," she shouted, taking refuge in her mother's skirts.

Sallee never acknowledged the kick or the insult to Ethel as she blithely chatted about how great it was to see Ethel after all of these years.

Ginny asked at breakfast if Sallee might like to go shopping. "I'm sure Ethel would be delighted to watch Virginia for you. Wouldn't you, Ethel?"

"Yes'um, you know I would," Ethel gamely replied, though she was not at all sure she was up to taking care of this undisciplined monster. Then she admonished herself for her less than charitable thoughts. "I'd be happy t', Sallee. Give you an' yo' momma a chance t' catch up."

"Oh no, Ethel, that's just fine. Thanks, though. Peter and I don't leave Virginia with anyone. We never have. We both feel it creates such deep and abiding emotional scars to be separated from your parents when you are young, and since Virginia is going to have a little brother soon, we especially don't want to leave her," Sallee said breathlessly as she patted her tummy.

Ethel, Ginny, and Joe's glances shot from one to another like so many balls in batting practice. Dear God, this was going to be a very long ten days.

"Virginia, you wanna come help ol' Ethel in de kitchen?" Ethel bent over and held out her forefinger for the child to grasp. "We kin bring in breakfast fo' yo' Momma an' Granddaddy an' Gran'momma. How 'bout dat? Yo' momma used t' love helpin' out in de kitchen."

"Nooo!" Virginia looked Ethel up and down with utmost disdain and buried her face in Sallee's skirt.

No one could foresee that Sallee would go into labor the day they were supposed to leave to go home to Connecticut and that she would be restricted to complete bed rest in order to keep her from delivering for as long as possible. No one could have foretold that Peter's approach to his son's attempt at early arrival would be to bail at the first opportunity, citing crises at work and leaving Ginny, Ethel, and Joe to cope with his fractious family—or that he would have what Ginny later fumed was the audacious arrogance, as he was departing, to tell Sallee that under no circumstances were his children to be left alone in the care of any of her relatives.

When Sallee informed Joe of her husband's edict, Joe asked calmly, "How do you suggest we deal with the minor problem of the delivery? I don't suppose you want Virginia there, do you?" He could see that Sallee was quite caught off guard by that eventuality, so he offered, "Let me see if we can work out a solution."

Sallee appeared grateful for her father's offer. "I'm glad I told you rather than Mother. I'm not so sure she would have been as helpful." She smiled.

Joe thought as he smiled at his daughter, *Truer words have never been uttered.* The Israelis and Palestinians would have a better chance of a lasting peace if Ginny ever got wind of this.

Peter made a big show of how much of an imposition coming back would be, but rather than allow his child to be sullied by the likes of Sallee's family's care, he managed to get back before young Gordon Barstead, named for his uncle, made his appearance on December 20.

Stuart—presumably the safest of Sallee's family members, at least in Peter's mind—was pressed into service when it became obvious even to him that he couldn't be in two places at the same time, not that he wouldn't have been happier to stay with Virginia while his wife labored through his son's difficult birth.

While Peter was at the hospital attending to Sallee, Stuart

brought Mackey and Virginia over to the house to enlist Ethel's patience and aid. "Virginia is more than a handful on her own. I feel like I'm putting fires out all of the time. She bullies Mackey, stamps her daintily shod little foot, and shrieks, 'Mine,' whenever her cousin picks up a new toy. They are cute shoes, though, aren't they?"

Ethel grunted a dismissal of the shoes and then patted Mackey on the head. "Doan you mind, you sweet girl. Ethel'll take care o' it fo' you. Come here an' sit on Ethel's lap."

In fact, her girth guaranteed very little in the way of a lap, but the child was well accustomed to perching on Ethel's forearm, pressed up against her ample bosom. She rested there for a few minutes and then slid down to the floor and toddled over, green eyes sparkling, to a stack of toys near her cousin. Shrieks ensued.

Stuart watched and wearily shook her head. "Mackey can't have a thought that Virginia doesn't want to pounce on and take away. Poor Sallee, I don't how she's going to cope with two little monsters like this."

Ethel scowled deeply. She might not have agreed with every one of their choices, but she was not one to gossip about Ginny and Joe's children, their spouses, or their offspring. Peter, however, had exceeded the bounds, and in Ethel's mind it was open season on "dat no-count fool Sallee done married." Hands firmly planted on each hip, she scoffed, "Sallee only got one monster t' deal wit', an' if she asked me, I'd tell 'er throw him out as fast an' as far as she kin throw. He is ruinin' dat child, an' I 'spect he'll ruin de new one too. Whoever hear tell o' such a thang? Not lettin' yo' own family take care …" She sputtered to a halt. "I never. Dat man ain't right in de head is all I got t' say." She stood up, eyeing the two girls as Virginia snatched yet another toy. "An' I kin tell you what else. I don't' think he is what he say he is, neither. He wouldn' know de truth if it bit him on his BO9. Ever'thing dat come outta his mouth is a lie."

"Goodness, Ethel, you really don't like him, do you?" Stuart laughed. "What's a BO9?"

"You do? You like 'im?" She stared up at Stuart and then added dismissively, "His backside."

"I don't dislike him. Hmm …" Stuart contemplated her brother-in-law for a while. "He certainly is good-looking with those dark curls and startling blue eyes."

Ethel gave Stuart a disapproving sideways glance.

"And he isn't without charm. When he wants to, he can charm the pants off of you."

"Not me! No sirree!" the older woman countered,. "No way dat rascal is charmin' me." She bustled over to the two little girls to give Mackey back the wooden lamb she had been playing with before Virginia snatched it away. As sweetly as she always spoke with the children, she said to Virginia, "You got dem dollies over he'ah. You don't' need dat lamb. You let Mackey have de lamb back now."

Virginia let loose a bloodcurdling shriek. "Nooo! Go away, you." She marched up to Ethel and started to push her. "Go away."

Ethel looked over at Stuart and said, "Ain' natural fo' chil'ren t' act like dis." She came closer to Stuart, out of earshot. "She done seen dis he'ah behavior. I 'spect Sallee is puttin' up wid a worl' of 'buse an' I ain't got no idea why."

"What's to be done?" Stuart asked. "She won't listen to anyone making a contrary statement about Peter or Virginia. Everything you say is considered an attack."

"That's wha's got me so riled up. You kin lead a horse t' water all de day but if dey won't drink, dey ain't nothin' you kin do. I is so frustrated, I could spit nails."

❧

Two days of unrelenting labor, a caesarean section, and a jaundiced baby whose vital signs plummeted dangerously during the birthing ordeal left Sallee and the baby with an extended stay in the hospital and too weak to travel afterwards. Shortly after baby Gord made his arrival, Peter was called away on supposedly important business, leaving Sallee ensconced in her old bedroom with Virginia and the new baby, at the mercy of her odious relations.

The young family's child-rearing philosophy didn't involve much compromise on Peter's part. As Ethel noted, "It's all well 'n' good for Sallee to be the only one to mind the chil'ren. Don't' let him be put out on 'count of havin' to do it his own self. He out the door 'fore it has a chance to open good."

Ginny and Ethel remarked to each other that despite all of Peter's derisive talk about Sallee's family, both children had Sallee's family names. "What do you think that means?" Ginny asked Ethel.

It was becoming apparent that Ethel did not like not knowing. "Ain't got no idea. Jes' like you, I is findin' dat mighty peculiar." She shook her head as she resisted the urge to pull out a cloth and dust a spotless table. "Dat man is a hard one t' pin down. I'll give 'im dat."

After several days of watching Sallee, who was nearly delirious from lack of sleep, struggle with an overindulged three-year-old and a colicky newborn, Ginny decided to intervene. She coaxed Virginia to follow her out of the bedroom by offering a new dolly as way of bribe while her mother indulged in a rare few moments of sleep. As Ginny passed the crib, she decided to take a huge risk. She whisked the fretting baby out of his crib, and with a cartoonish tiptoe and overly exaggerated finger to her lips, she managed to get Virginia to quietly follow her into the kitchen, where she handed Ethel the little bundle. "Don't hurt him," she hissed with a wicked giggle as the absurd parade continued into the dining room.

As the child played with her newly won payola, Ginny set out a child-sized tea service around the room. She then went around to each tiny plate and put down a raisin or two; she poured not more than a thimbleful of milk into some of the cups and a few pieces of cereal into others to entice the child to eat. "I hate myself for doing this," she said to Ethel, who stood swaying in the kitchen doorway, caressing the baby and watching her employer tiptoe around the room, silently but furiously working to maintain the unstable calm.

"You ready fo' yo' breakfast?" Ethel asked as Ginny slumped into a chair and Virginia prowled from treat to treat.

Ginny nodded, resisting the urge to shush Ethel. Bribing children was not a policy she had ever supported, but she couldn't stop herself from trying to help Sallee. Desperate times called for desperate measures, she told herself, assuaging her guilt. Maybe Peter was right, she found herself thinking, but she quickly dismissed the thought with a shake of her head.

The two women were so close that despite Ethel's beatific smile as she stood in the door cuddling the baby on her shoulder, it was clear to Ginny that Ethel was not on board with corrupting Virginia any further.

"What would you do?" Ginny said, throwing up her hands.

Ethel shook her head. "I wisht I knowed. I 'spect you doin' jes' fine. I really cain't say, Miz Ginny."

Ginny started a hushed rant. "It is the most frustrating thing in the world to try and ascertain what someone else is thinking. I can't ask her outright; she gets defensive. If I try to pry information out of her in a conversation, I sound like a bad shrink, and she shuts down. I am at my wit's end." She was about to jump up in exasperation when Virginia suddenly appeared in her path.

"Virginia wants more." The child climbed into Ginny's lap and stared up at her grandmother, her light gray-blue eyes irrevocably melting Ginny's heart. "Please," she added, and that sealed the deal.

Ginny was besotted. She and Ethel looked at each other in utter astonishment. Shrugging, Ethel powered into the kitchen to fetch both cereal and milk.

Returning, she presented the newly gentled Virginia with both, only to be spurned, albeit politely. "Raisins, please?" When Ethel returned bearing raisins, the little girl slipped off her grandmother's lap, took the bowl of raisins Ethel had offered her, and carried it over to the dolls' feast on the floor. "Dolly says thank you." She and her new dolly spent the remainder of Ginny's breakfast chatting happily among themselves.

Joe happened on the scene midway through breakfast. "Good morning, Virginia," he said as he kissed Ginny on the cheek, whispering, "How did you manage this?" Not expecting a reply, he pulled his chair up to the table and tucked into his usual hearty breakfast.

When Ethel appeared with a coffee pot in one hand and the baby on her other hip, Joe stopped eating altogether and sat gapmouthed. "Did something happen I don't know about?" he finally asked.

"I took matters in hand," Ginny offered, "sort of. Honestly, I don't know what happened."

Just then Virginia looked up. "Hello, PopPop," she said.

Joe nearly choked on his toast.

She stood and walked over to him with her new doll in tow. "This is my friend Mackey," she announced, kissing the doll on its lips.

"Well, hello, Mackey," Joe said. "It's so nice to meet you. I have a granddaughter by that exact name."

Virginia giggled and went back to her doll-sized breakfast.

"What did you do, wave a magic wand? Is this Virginia?" he murmured to Ginny, who lifted her hands in an exaggerated shrug.

Gordy—now officially Gordon—and Susan came by later that day, bringing sons Trey and Andy and laden down with gifts for the baby and the boys' little cousin Virginia. Sallee, up and a bit refreshed from her short respite, had chosen to ignore Ginny's infraction. She sat by the fire with the baby asleep in her lap, basking in the glow of her family's loving attention. Truthfully, she was delighted that Virginia had other human beings to be with. Peter didn't need to know. He was, after all, absent. He didn't need to know that the whole family was gathering to see her and that she couldn't be happier about it.

Stuart and Bill arrived with a fretful Mackey. "I don't understand," Stuart said as she allowed her daughter to slide out of her arms. "She's been like this all morning."

Mackey toddled over to Virginia, who was having a tea party with her new doll, Mackey.

"No, only one Mackey," Virginia announced in what had become known in the household as her imperial voice. She grabbed her new doll up in her arms to protect it from this interloper. Stuart and Ginny exchanged covert glances. It was going to be one of those days.

Ethel had bustled all morning, preparing for the boys' visit. Fifteen-year-old Trey, one of her favorites, made a beeline for the kitchen to greet her.

"Lord, look at you. I swear you done growed another foot since I last laid eyes on you." She gave the boy a hug and then held him at arm's length, peering up into his young face and admiring what she saw. "Where's dat Andy?"

"Nope, Ethel, I still only have two." Trey smiled, looking down at his feet. "He's with Mom, as usual."

Ethel looked at him quizzically until the foot joke finally dawned on her. "Git on outta here, boy, wit' yo' smart self." She chuckled, playfully smacking him on his backside with her ever-present dish-towel–cum–dust cloth. "I hopes he might come on in he'ah an' say hey."

"He probably will after he makes sure Mom doesn't snag a drink somewhere. Ya know, he's her self-appointed keeper."

Ethel shook her head and clucked, wiping a clean counter. "What's he, twelve now? Too young t' be worryin' 'bout such thangs." She shook her head. "Seems sometimes like it jest never ends."

Trey answered with a nod. "What's cookin'?" he asked, lifting lids and looking under trays draped with dishtowels. Being in the kitchen or anywhere with Ethel had always been a safe haven for Trey as long back as he could remember. Early, Ethel's husband and a great friend of Trey's dad, also shared the safe-haven designation, not an honor Trey bestowed lightly or regularly.

"Never you mind. Did you see de baby? He's a cute little thang. Dat Virginia, she migh' be de first chil' ever that I ain't been able t' …" She let it drop. "It so good t' see you, boy." She gave him a big toothy smile. "Early been askin' me why you an' yo' daddy ain't been comin' round like you used ta."

Trey's bright face instantly clouded over. "Mom's been drinking a lot lately. Dad doesn't seem to have much time for fun, I guess. Tell Early hey for me, would you?"

"Sho' as you born 'e be glad t' hear from you. Sorry 'bout yo' momma. Dat drinkin' is a hard devil t' get loose of. I know. Don't' be too hard on 'er. I 'spect she bein' hard 'nough fo' de lot o' you."

Trey sighed, "I guess." As he heard his father bluster a hello to Ethel, he said, "Gotta go. Just wanted you to know I love you." He gave her a quick hug and passed Gordy on his way out.

When Trey entered the living room, Virginia—to everyone's utter amazement—ran up to him, demanding that he pick her up despite the fact that she had never laid eyes on him. He complied and shrugged to the slack-jawed adults.

❧

Twenty-five years later, Virginia was not much more predictable.

"V. A., where did you put my scarf? I need it now. I've gotta go. I told you, I got a callback." Alex had begun to be more demanding. Virginia found this vexing especially since it forced her to play the aren't-I-just-the-cutest-little-thing card so often these days. Truth be told she would sooner chew him out but some concession had to be made, she supposed. Besides he generally caught himself before she had to turn on him. "Sweetheart, where is my scarf?"

She took her sweet time looking around the room. He was good-looking, it was true, but what a slob—and vain, oh God, was he vain. She supposed that was the price you paid for falling in loving with a model. *If he weren't so needy*, she thought, *he'd be perfect.*

"I don't know why you think it's my job to take care of your things," she grumbled. "Don't call me sweetheart. I've told you before I hate it." She stood in the middle of the room, turning slowly and scanning the room. "If you can't be bothered to hang it up, how do you expect me to know where you dropped it? I'm not your mother, you know. You do know that, don't you?" She looked up at him with her big gray-blue eyes, feigning interest in his answer. When no answer came, she resumed her search. Finally spying the scarf on the floor, half-hidden by an empty pizza box, she picked it up as if it were a snake. "This," she said with a smirk, holding it out in front of her with two beautifully manicured fingers, "is this what you're looking for?"

He snatched the scarf, whipping it around his neck in one seamless motion while checking himself out in the mirror, and then air-kissed her goodbye and left without a word.

"What a fucking prima donna," she snarled to herself as she straightened the picture that had been knocked askew when he slammed the door. "Why do I put up with him? Oh right, I forgot—I love him, and he's good-looking. Or was it the other way around? I forget," she said, looking at her reflection in the nearby mirror.

Wandering into the kitchen of her minuscule apartment, she opened the fridge and peered in, hoping for inspiration and finally opting for a mango Yoplait. She absently took a few spoonfuls and then stuck the container back in the refrigerator, spoon and all. With a back kick to the fridge door, she dialed her cousin Mackey on her ever-present cell.

"Hey, what's up?" Virginia said. In her postage stamp–sized bathroom, she fumbled through the drawer, looking for an emery board as she pretended to listen to Mackey's dull, painstaking rundown of her latest day of drama, all the while waiting for the moment when she could turn the conversation toward a more pleasing subject—namely, Virginia and her wedding plans. Damn, she had to remember not to ask Mackey questions, since she was such a conversation hog.

When Mackey stopped for a second, Virginia dove in. "I went to this cute little boutique today and picked out the most adorable bridesmaids' dresses. You are going to look so cute in it," she gushed, as if Mackey had said nothing at all. "Have you decided how to wear your hair? Never mind. I'll get a stylist to come out to Gran's and do everybody's hair."

Mackey said, "You know, I have been trying to figure out since I first saw his picture on Facebook who Alex reminds me of. It came to me today. Don't get mad at me when I tell you. Promise?"

"Why in fuck would I get mad at you?" Virginia lay back on her bed and glanced at a picture of Alex.

"Well, because … you know he has almost white woolly hair. You know, it's kind of nappy," Mackey said.

"Yeah, so?"

"Do you remember when we were little kids? I'm talking really little kids. There was a toy at Gran's. It was an antique pull toy. Do you remember?"

"Yeah, we fought about it. It was … a lamb!" Virginia trumpeted.

"That's it. Gran gave it to Joey a few years ago. I thought it was so cute. I just put it up on the shelf in his room as a decoration, so he couldn't break it. Anyway, I bumped into it the other day. I swear, it reminds me of Alex. I think it's the wool—the color and texture of Alex's hair. Pretty funny, yeah?"

Virginia hooted. "Totally, he totally looks like that lamb. I've been racking my brain ever since we met, knowing that he looked like somebody I knew. That's it. That's totally it." She pushed aside her irritation at Mackey's having gotten the lamb. "That's really funny. Hey, gotta go. Alex is calling. Talk later. Bye."

Clicking over to Alex, she said, "What?"

"Just wanted you to know I'm probably going to be pretty late. There are a lot of people here." He apologized, even though he hated himself for doing it.

"Whatever," she said, her voice dripping with contempt. "I've got lots of wedding plans to work out anyway." She clicked off and pushed her mother's number. The hard edge entirely disappeared from her voice as she bubbled sweetly into the phone, with no trace of her previous rancor. "Hey, Mom. What's up? … Great. How's

Dad? ... Heard from my little bro? ... Maybe we could meet for lunch this week?" Butter would have had a short half-life in her sweet mouth.

"By the way, you know I've been shopping, and it's so awkward to have to pay for everything and then have to send the bills off to you." She lay back on her bed, twirling her foot and admiring it from many angles. She got up from the bed and rummaged around the closet. With the phone tucked under her chin, she searched around until she found the shoes she had been thinking of. "I was wondering, could you possibly just get me my own American Express card? ... No, on your account so that I can charge stuff that has to do with the wedding." She put the shoe on and lay back down on the bed to admire it. It was a stunning shoe, she thought; she particularly liked that it was a sling-back, so sexy.

"Stuff, you know. I promise it's just ... no, it's just to get my wedding stuff. It would make everything so much simpler this way. You know, you could pay the bill, and I wouldn't have to pay and then bill you. It would be so much cleaner and simpler. Besides, they do such a good job of keeping track of everything ... Okay, thanks so much. Do you think I should wear sling-backs or pumps? ... On my wedding day, of course ... A pump, huh? I was thinking a ..." She kicked the shoe off, replacing it with a stiletto.

"Well, things are good. I found a really cute dress today for the bridesmaids ... There are five bridesmaids ... What do you mean, you thought Mackey was going to be my only bridesmaid? That doesn't make any sense. I never said that ... I thought you were going to tell Gran that it was a small wedding? Hello, a hundred and fifty people is pretty damn small ... What do you mean that's impossible? After Christmas, what?"

She felt her eyebrows knit and put her fingers up to feel that she wasn't creating that crease. "People get married after Christmas all the time." Finding the crease, she attempted to relax her forehead. "For Christ's sake, Mother, you can hardly say my grandparents' house is a destination wedding. It's not like they live in the islands or in a French château." She sighed heavily and sat up. "I can't say that it's a destination wedding, and I can't—I can't imagine that anybody else would either. Sure, people have to travel. So what is new about that?"

The contempt she'd felt earlier with Alex began to creep into the conversation. Was everyone in the world actually living on some other planet? "What on earth do you mean, I should be prepared to have most people not come? … For God's sake, Mother, people are used to going far afield for weddings nowadays, and they'll think it's just so quaint that I'm having it at my grandmother's house out in the country. Rustic is so in right now … Why do I want the wedding there? I would have thought that was obvious." She stood up and started pacing, gesturing wildly with her free hand. "I did go to UVA, remember? … What do you mean, what does that have to do with anything? … I did go see them once. Besides, my friends also went to UVA. A lot of them are from Virginia. A lot of them still live there, so you don't need to worry about people having to travel."

She rolled her eyes in exasperation. "No, I haven't talked to them yet. I thought you were going to do that. You could call and feel them out anyway … Yes? Great, so I'm supposed to call up your mother, your parents. Please, at least see what they think … All right, all right, I'll call them … I'll let you know. Don't forget to get the American Express card. Black would be best, okay? Love you. Bye."

After bringing the call to an abrupt end, she moved on to her e-mail and then to social media. What would be more awesome for the wedding invitations, paper or electronic? Rustic—get a photo of the house. Either way, it would just be so cool, Christmas in the country with the New York–to–Richmond set. *Destination with a twist*, she thought. *I like that. Oh, I know the perfect invitation: über huge, traditional calligraphy, engraved … Mr. and Mrs. request the honor, yada yada … I wonder, do you spell out 'Mister'? And what's Mrs. the abbreviation for anyway? Mistress? So much fun!*

3

Mackey rolled into the school with just two cars ahead of her. A quick glance in the rearview mirror showed three more after hers. Perfect timing.

"Hum, hum, hum hum, hum, hum … Sittin' on the dock of the bay, watchin' the tide roll away. I'm just sittin' on the dock of the bay, wastin' time."

As he stood beside his teacher in line, Joey waved to his mother while brushing his brown curls out of his eyes with the other hand.

Mackey grinned a goofy grin and waved back maniacally. *He looks so big, so cute. Look at how much he's grown. The clothes I just got him already just barely fit!*

She called out to his teacher as he climbed into the car. "Hi, Janice. How was the planetarium?"

"Joey's got lots of stories to tell, don't you?" Janice smiled down at him as she fastened his seat belt. "See you tomorrow, Joey, if we have school."

"Really? No school?" Mackey was astonished.

"You can't tell these days. It doesn't take much for them to decide it's too dangerous. You know, the buses, with snow in the forecast … they might just call a two-hour delay. You just can't tell." The teacher stopped. "What am I saying?" she laughed. "Tomorrow is Saturday. Bye! See you Monday!" She gently shut the door, and Mackey pulled away as Janice moved to the next car.

"Hey, little bud. How're you doing? Did you have fun today?"

"Mom, the planetarium was so cool. It was like there were stars inside a building, a building! When they turned out the lights, there were jillions of stars. It was so cool." His light brown eyes sparkled with excitement.

"What did you like best?"

"I liked everything but the talking. It was boring."

"Like what was really good?"

"Like when he turned the sun on. And then he sped up time and made the day go really fast."

"Because you were having fun?"

"No, because the guy could speed up time. We saw the sun rise and set and then the moon and snakes and triangles. Oscar got to shine a pointer at a planet. I'm hungry."

"Here, I've got some gum. Oh no, never mind. I forgot to get it. You'll just have to wait. We'll be home in a minute, and I'll get you something there. Did you hear it was going to snow? Maybe …"

"Snow, yay. I hope it snows. I hope it snows. Can't we stop? I'm really hungry."

"No, and don't whine. You know that never gets you what you want."

"Oh, puh-leeze? Please, please hurry, Mom, I'm really hungry."

❧

They had just walked Stuart to her car in the early twilight, and the door had barely shut behind them. Ginny leaned up against the door. "Whew, Joe. I didn't think she'd ever leave. It terrified me that she was going to offer to fix dinner. About the wedding—"

Joe jumped in. "No. No, no, and no. Don't even think about it. Absolutely not, Ginny. It will kill us."

"Isn't that what you want anyway?" she asked, laughing. "How convenient would that be? You go out with a bang, achieving your goal, and nobody could blame you or accuse you of being selfish."

"But they could blame Virginia."

"Good point. Keep that in mind. That does put a monkey wrench into your plans, doesn't it?" She shot him a knowing glance, throwing in an arched eyebrow to make sure he didn't miss it.

"Ginny, I would've thought you of all people would understand. It's time." He hobbled over to the sofa and flung himself down.

She rolled her eyes, knowing that the hobbling was just an act. Daisyduke and Gomer looked up, mildly concerned. Then, reassured that all was well, they threw themselves wholeheartedly back into snoring.

"Joe, I understand. I understand completely. I'm selfish. I'm not ready to let you go. I know what you say—that you won't be going anywhere. But I'm not as sure about that as you are. And I know the children aren't. Dying is a big deal, particularly on this side of the grave. Holidays are a big deal. When you put them together, you have increased their significance exponentially. And oh God, the drama!" She laughed. "We are absurd. How ridiculous can we be, sitting here talking about your ultimate demise, as if we had any choice in the matter."

"Ginny, that is my whole point. We do have a choice." He reared up like a palsy victim and then flopped back down, adding to the image.

"You are ridiculous," she sniffed. "Do you want dinner?" Then, feeling a bit nostalgic, she asked, "Do you remember our wedding? The first one, before you ask. Remember how many things went wrong? Bertha dropped the cake after she burned the first one. Ethel spilled punch on my mother's dress. I was never sure whether she meant to or not. You know, we're not really sure how much she liked my mother. That was the beginning of the whole cake debacle as I remember it …" Ginny could hear Ethel's soft cadence in her mind, and she imagined how Ethel might have remembered the day.

⌘

"Ethel, git on in he'ah. You gotta press Miz Bess's dress. Have you finished makin' de punch?" Bertha was shooting out questions and orders like a drill sergeant.

Ethel knew this was not the time to be takin' nips from the punch bowl. But how was she supposed to make a decent punch, a punch worth drinkin', if she didn't taste it as she went along? Ethel practiced asking her mother that question, sure that the question was bound to come up shortly. Besides, she needed somethin' to calm her nerves. The house was all sixes an' sevens. Miz Ginny musta whirled in an' out o' de kitchen a dozen times dis mornin'. "Where's dis?" "Can you press dat?" "Did you pack my blue shoes?" Enough t' drive a soul to drinkin' if dat soul hadn't already started on her own.

I had to admit the house was lovely. Miz Bess done a beautiful job makin' it so, usin' her many talents wit' flowers. Ol' man winter hadn't helped none. Frost 'bout kilt every bloom in d' garden. But Miz Bess cut magnolia leaves, turnin' 'em every which way. 'Til then I didn't know magnolia leaves had so many colors, green an' gold an' copper. I think she mighta even painted some o' them leaves wit' real gold, as shiny as dey was. It was a right beautiful sight what she did wit' 'em. Somehow she found roses, an' she musta paid a king's ransom fo' 'em too. Dey was de prettiest things I ever seen an' made Miz Ginny's bouquet jest beautiful.

You know, I felt such a fool when I spilt punch on dat dress of Miz Bess's. Well, truth be told', I didn't spill anythang on it as much as I used it t' wipe up de rum I had spilt. Lord, I about fell out tryin' t' git de stain out an' de dress pressed 'fore Momma o' Miz Bess found out. It's not like it could be helped. She did brang de dress right int' de kitchen where I was makin' de punch. Momma tol' her t' put down dat dress, an' I'd get t' it. I wasn't payin' no mind t' what dey was sayin' as I was devotin' most all o' my attention t' tastin' the punch. I wanted to get it just right. So when I spilled a goodly 'mount of rum on the counter, I jest took the first' rag I could lay hands on to mop it up. How was I s'posed to know it was Miz Bess's dress?

Dat weren't all, neither. Mista Joe showed up all a flutter. Why people think de kitchen is where dey gotta be when thangs go wrong is beyon' me. De kitchen is where work gets done. Don't need mo' folk in dere dan de ones dat be doin' de work. Least ways, dat's how I sees it. Mista Joe come in sayin', "Bertha, Ethel, I forgot de ring."

Momma say, "You gots time. Go on home an' git it. If you leaves now, you be back in plenty o' time."

"Dat's just it; I forgot t' buy a ring," he said, like we was gonna pull one out o' the air fo' 'im.

"Lord, Mista Joe. What you want us t' do?" Momma asked.

I piped up, "Here you go, Mista Joe. You can use dis." I handed him a cigar band dat Early give me as a reminder dat one day he was goin' t' get me a fo'-real weddin' band. "Dis here works fo' me. I 'spect it'll do 'til ya can git de real one."

He hesitated for a second like he was thinkin' it might not do. Then he like t' scare de pants off me—he bent down an' give me a kiss an' a hug. "Thank you, Ethel. You have saved de day."

Momma was so flustered she dropped de cake. Since she hadn't started icing it, we was able t' piece it t'gether so hardly a soul could tell.

Thank de good Lord nothin' else went wrong dat day, an' Mista Joe an' Miz Ginny had a right' fine little weddin'. Ever'body enjoyed de punch.

℘

When they got home, Mackey gave Joey the key. "You open the door while I get the groceries. You can do that, right?"

Joey raced off toward the door with her keys.

"It's the gold key," she called after him. "Put it in the lock with the flat part on top, remember? Like Daddy showed you."

Well, he seemed to manage that all right, she thought as she approached the house. *Shutting the door, I guess, will be the next lesson.* The door was wide open with the key still in the lock. "Joey, you gotta take the key out of the door, remember? Where are you? I thought you were hungry."

"I am, but I had to pee," he said as he made his way out of the bathroom, zipping himself up as he went.

"Did you flush? Joey?"

"Yeah."

"Joey?"

"I did."

"Okay. If you said you did, you did. Did you put the seat up before you went?"

"Mom."

"Okay, but you don't always, so I gotta ask. Sorry." *Why are you apologizing? He doesn't, and he probably hasn't this time.* "I'm going to make some popcorn. Okay with you?" she said. She started to swing the bags up to the counter and then stepped back before they reached their full arc. Ugh, there were white sticky cat paw prints everywhere. She let the bags slip to the floor. The bulk of the morning's spill lay in a congealed blob, looking like anemic scrambled eggs from so many paw imprints. *Christ, how many times could the damn cat have walked through it? Well, at least she ate the cereal. Oh shit, cereal. I forgot the damn cereal. Shit! Shit! Shit! Shit!* Her eyes fell on the list still on the counter. At the very top was cereal, all caps, underlined three times, with two exclamation marks after it.

"No, I want cereal," said Joey.

Of course you do. "We don't have any. It's popcorn or nothing … and don't even think about fussing about it. Got it?"

"Yeah, but can I have an apple too?"

"Sure. They're in the bowl on the table."

"No, they aren't. Daddy ate the last one this morning."

"Then it's popcorn. Sorry, bud," she sighed. "I'll make it right after I get this stuff put away. If you help me, it won't take as long."

He sat down at the table, leaned his elbow on it, and held his head in his hand. "I'm too tired." Then he laid his head down on the table.

"Most of it can wait. Just let me get this frozen food … K? Honey, are you okay?"

Joey was asleep. She left him there while she hurriedly put away the frozen food and then scurried over to him and checked his forehead for fever. Scooping him up, she thought, *Gosh, I forget how little he is still. He's so light. My sweet little guy. I love you so much.* She kissed him on the neck, burrowing in between his neck and shoulder and savoring his little boy smell as she carried him to his bed and tucked him in. She lay down next to him outside of his covers, intending to stay for just a second, and fell fast asleep.

An hour later, the phone woke her. She lurched up out of a deep sleep and stumbled to the hall phone. "Hello?" she murmured, half asleep still and not wanting to wake Joey.

"This is First National Bank and Trust. I would like to speak with Eric Buckner."

"I'm sorry …" She rubbed her eyes and forehead. *What on earth?* "He's not in. Can I take a message?"

"Is this Mackey Buckner?"

"It is."

"This is just a friendly reminder from your neighborhood bank that your mortgage payment is past due." The bank officer's voice was prim. "We understand that things are tight these days and want you to know that our new policy is not to assess penalties for a full ten days after the due date. Thank you."

Great. I was sure I paid the mortgage. Didn't I? I must have. I didn't have enough money to buy groceries. Wait, no, I didn't think I had enough. I better check. "Uh … I'm sure we submitted our payment last week. I'll check. May I call you back?"

She sat down in front of the computer, typed in the online banking address, and waited. *Damn, this thing is so slow.* A few seconds later, the page finished loading, and she typed in her password. A few more seconds passed. *We need a new computer. There must be something wrong. Why is it so slow? Come on, come on. Hmm, I must not have paid the mortgage. How could I not have?* She scrolled down and checked to see when the last payment had been made. *You idiot. How could you be so stupid, stupid, stupid?* She clicked all of the appropriate buttons and then double-checked to make sure that the mortgage was paid. She decided to activate the automatic feature on the mortgage payment and carefully set it to pay the day before it was due. *We don't need your largesse. Thank you for nothing, you friendly neighborhood robber barons.* With a dramatic flourish, she clicked off.

Raising her hands in the air, she danced into the kitchen to start dinner, singing as she went. "Talking 'bout my girl, my girl, my girl. Hey hey, hey my girl, my girl." *Oh damn, the cat mess.* "Dinner will have to wait," she said out loud as she started in on the counter. "You bastard cat, you." She playfully shook her sponge at the self-satisfied cat licking herself at the window.

"Hey, sweetie. How was your day?" Eric asked as he plopped his armload of papers onto the counter, took off his coat, and casually draped it over the nearest chair. "Man, it's gettin' cold out there." He stamped his feet like people do after they say things like "It's getting cold." "The kids were impossible in physics lab today. Too close to the holidays. I don't know why I even assigned these papers."

"How'd it go at the doctor? Did you hear we might get snow tonight? Pretty cool, huh?"

"It was okay. Yeah, cool. Apparently, I'm going to live. Test results were negative." She held her cheek out for his peck while continuing to peel a potato. "Still have a stopped-up head."

Oblivious to the pile of mail and papers that had started slipping off the counter in ones and twos, he turned toward the door as Joey bounced into the room.

"Daddy, Daddy, guess what?"

"Hey, bud. What, what, what?" He bounced up and down in time with his son. The glasses on the already-set table bounced too. A few more papers slipped onto the floor.

"No, guess! You didn't guess."

The bouncing stopped. Eric, looking like a larger but exact version of his son, put his finger to his chin and pursed his lips as if in deep thought. "You, uh, um, let me see … you won the lottery … no, you kissed all the girls on the … no, you drove Mommy home from … uh, you got a job? I give up. What?"

"No, silly," Joey said, rolling his eyes. "I went to the planetarium today. It was so cool. We saw constableations and stuff. Like Oren."

"Really, did he give you a ticket? Pull you over for speeding? Officer Oren … do I know him?"

"No, Dad. They are stars." He screwed his face up in a question. "Tickets?"

"Oh, Orion the archer, not Oren the officer."

"Yeah, that's what I said."

Eric looked over at Mackey a little guiltily. "Sorry, honey. I forgot to tell you. I signed the permission slip last week. It wasn't a problem, was it?"

"Come on, Dad," Joey said as he tugged on his father's arm. "Let's go watch *Planet Earth* again. I wanna watch the one with the bugs. K?"

"K, but let me see if Mommy needs help." Eric moved quickly over to kiss Mackey's neck.

"No problem," she said with a smile, shaking her head as she peeled another potato. The last of Eric's papers slid to the floor. *"Talkin' bout my guy, hey, hey, hey, my guys."*

With the potatoes at a boil, Mackey stuck her head into the family room. "Eric, dinner is going to be a while, so I'm going to go for a run. I'm hoping it may clear this congestion. Back in twenty. Would you turn the potatoes down in five minutes, please?"

"To what?"

"Just low. Thanks. On second thought, just turn them off, but make sure to leave the top on." *Even he can handle that, I'm sure. I think Joey could even do it.*

Twenty minutes later, the smell of burned potatoes greeted her as she came back in the door. *I knew it. Why in the world would I ask Captain Space, airhead extraordinaire, to do anything so concrete as turn down the potatoes?* "Oh, Eric," she sighed, "you are such a goofball." She took the rag out of his hand. "Good God, Eric. Don't you know water conducts heat? I thought you were the scientist in the family. The nutty professor is more like it." She laughed. "You could've gotten a bad burn, you id—" She stopped herself as Joey came in "You silly goose," she laughed.

"Sorry," Eric said, definitely looking sheepish as he moved toward her, preparing to hug her. "I forgot."

"I know. I shouldn't have asked." She turned, picking up the smoking pot and holding it between them. "You were doing something else. I shouldn't have gone running." *I should have stayed home and followed through. I can't expect Eric to pick up the pieces. But I don't know why not. I pick up for him all the damn day. Why do I have to be super freak?* "Just a quick shower, and dinner will be on the table, ten minutes at the most. Okay? And hey, do you think you could run to the store after dinner and get some cereal? I forgot it today."

"Sure. I can do it now if you want, but it was on the top of the list."

"Right, it was. Later would be better." *Stupid me. If you don't want to go, just say so, damn it. What's the matter with me? He's right. It was on top of the list. The man doesn't have a devious bone in his body. He'd do anything I asked—maybe not very well, but he'd try. It's what I love about him.* "Thanks, honey."

"I'm hungry," Joey announced. "When are we going to have popcorn?"

"No. It's dinnertime. We are going to have chicken casserole and …"

"You said you were going to make popcorn," he whined.

"That was then. This is dinner."

"I want popcorn." He folded his arms across his chest and pouted. "I hate chicken!" The whine rose to a wail as he collapsed in tears on the floor.

"Let's eat now. He's hungry. I'll shower later." She pulled plates out of the cabinet and started piling food on them. "Can you do something about him?" She poured milk into a cup and replaced the jug in the fridge in one continuous motion. With both hands full, she shut the door with her hip.

Eric was vainly attempting to coax Joey off the floor. "Come on, bud. Dinner is ready. Let's eat."

"I hate chicken," he roared and refused to budge.

"Let's just sit down and eat." Mackey pulled out her chair and sat down. The two of them pushed food around on their plates while Joey wailed and thrashed on the floor.

"Don't you think we ought to do something?" Eric whispered. "We can't just let him continue like this. Can we?"

"Go ahead. I haven't a clue." Mackey speared a piece of chicken without looking up. "I know what I'd like to do, but I think they arrest people for that. He's your son too. Don't ask me. You don't need my permission. Man up."

"Joey, get up right now and eat your dinner. Look, it's really good." He put a big forkful of the beige casserole in his mouth and mimed enjoying it. Joey only wailed louder. Eric looked at Mackey and shrugged his shoulders as if to say, *Well, you try.*

Mackey pushed her chair out, slammed her napkin on the table, got up, picked up the suddenly boneless child, and took him to his room, thrashing, kicking, and screaming.

After cleaning up the dinner and the rest of the morning breakfast mess, Mackey checked to see if it had started to snow.

Eric joined her at the window, wrapping his arms around from behind and snuggling into her neck. "I love you, you know. I appreciate all of the things you do for me. I wish I were better equipped to live in the world as you do, but I don't seem to be wired that way. And I think I've actually been worse since I got tenure. Thank God they haven't asked me to chair the department."

She reached up and patted his hand as they gently swayed back and forth at the window.

"You have no idea how terrified I was that you might have been gravely ill. It is such a relief. I honestly don't know how I would live without you."

She turned around, melting in his embrace.

☙

Alex tore into the apartment as if pursued. "V. A.!" he bellowed like a castaway seeing a rescue plane. "V. A.!"

She emerged from the bedroom, disheveled and groggy. "Something wrong?" She rubbed her eyes and ran her fingers through her champagne-blonde hair.

"Did I wake you up?" He looked puzzled. "It's not that late. You look perfectly adorable, though." He came over and wrapped his arms around her, kissing her on the top of her head.

"Cut it out!" She peered at the kitchen clock. "It's one thirty—I'd say pretty late. Where in the hell have you been? You left way over twelve hours ago."

"Sorry, but listen—I got it! I got the gig." His voice rose with excitement as he gathered Virginia up in his arms and spun her around. Then he kissed her hard. "I got it. Look." He waved a paper in front of her face. "Now I can get you the ring. They are going to give me an advance, pay me during filming, and give me a percentage. How's that for negotiations?" He beamed with pride. "I don't even think your parents could've gotten me a better deal. And I'm going to be a star. They're going to make me the star of this movie. I am so excited. I got it! I got the part. My big break! I knew it was going to happen soon." He had let Virginia go but continued cavorting around the cramped room, shouting, "I got it!"

"Shhh," she hissed. "Shut the fuck up. The neighbors."

"Fuck the neighbors! I have something to celebrate," he whooped.

Virginia shot him a scathing look that brought him back to her sense of reality.

"Okay, I'm quiet. But do you get what this means?" he asked, looking earnestly at her.

With both feet now firmly back underneath her, Virginia took the contract from his hands, perusing it as she crossed the room and flopped onto the sofa. "That is so great. Honey, I am happy for you. When do you start?"

"We already did, tonight. We have another shoot tomorrow. They loved the way I looked. Said I was perfect for the part. Finally, my looks are going to pay off." He checked himself out in the window's reflection. "It's great. Do you get how great this is?"

"So great," she chimed absently as she peered at the contract. "My husband-to-be a movie star. I like the sound of that. I wonder what I will wear on the red carpet."

"Whatever you wear, you'll look fabulous. We'll be the best-looking and best-dressed couple there."

"I guess this is a pretty small production company, FlyBy Productions. That's a funny name, like by the seat of your pants," she commented before tossing the contract on the table, having already moved on.

"What? What are you saying?" Alex looked confused. "Well, yeah, it is pretty small ... yeah, pretty small." He suddenly sounded to Virginia like he was hedging, like he was hiding something. "We have ... we mostly ... actually, I have to go back tonight because the filming has already started, and they were really, really happy with me."

Virginia glared at him. "This is legit, right? What's the name of this picture?"

"Yeah, I just came home to get some stuff and to tell you how excited I was that I got this part. Um, the name of the movie ... I'm not sure that it has one yet." He was beginning to fidget.

Knowing how much V. A. hated fidgeting only increased his nervousness. *Maybe I shouldn't have taken that last line of blow.* He tried to suppress his need to twitch.

Her voice started off as controlled as she could make it, until her suspicions got the better of her. "So you are telling me that some production company is paying you big bucks to act—to star, no less—in a movie that just starts filming the minute you walk in the door."

He nodded his head eagerly. "Cool, huh?"

"Let me get this right." Her voice was rising with each word. "They are taking a completely green actor—"

"I'm not completely green. I've done a few commercials," he protested.

"—and putting him in the starring role in their production? Tell me, Alex, does this gig entail taking your clothes off?"

"Damn it, Virginia. Come on, give me a break."

"That better not be what you're doing is all I have to say. It's embarrassing enough that you've been an out-of-work actor. How much of a cliché is that?" Her face relaxed. "I guess I've just allowed myself to get too stressed about the wedding. I have to go to bed. I noticed I'm getting frown lines. Are you coming?"

"I don't know. I was supposed to go back; it was just meant to be a short break. You go to bed. I'll call and find out." He pulled out his phone, but then thinking better of it, he said, "But I don't think I should be trying to get out of it the first night, do you?"

She stomped into the bedroom. "Suit yourself!" She slammed the door and then reopened it. "Don't forget we are supposed to find your suit tomorrow"—she slammed the door again—"for the wedding!"

Later, as Eric and Mackey spooned in bed, she said, "It's the rush that really gets me." She looked back at him to make sure he was still awake and then continued. "Like a heroin hit."

"You've taken heroin?"

"No, but I imagine that it's like a heroin hit. Like tiny little pinpricks of sensation, pleasurable sensations spreading out all—"

"Why heroin? Why not an orgasm? Or chocolate?"

"I don't know. It just seemed like how I imagine heroin would feel. Really, never mind. This is just too damn hard." She moved away from him.

"I'm sorry. Don't go. I want to understand. Really, I do. I'll try to just listen and not analyze. Promise." He pulled her up on top of him and held her there. "I love you. I want to know all about the you that is you. I want to know what goes on inside. Honestly, I'm not judging you. It's the way my damn brain works."

"Okay." She kissed him and slid back onto the bed beside him. With her arm on his chest and her chin resting on her arm, she continued. "I guess I used heroin as a metaphor because I know it's a lie. My brain lies and tells me how good the drama feels—how good it feels to be alive and that this drama is alive. It's like that first drag off a cigarette or a triple espresso."

"Does this happen whenever you talk to her? What if you hung up the phone?"

"She gets me so churned up that I can't concentrate on anything but. I've got to know. I might be missing something. But then I feel so used up."

He picked up a piece of her hair and traced the outline of her hand and then picked up her hand, covering it with little kisses. *God, I wish I knew what the hell she is talking about. Shit. I feel like Schrödinger's cat, and truth be told, I hope I'm dead when I get out of this box.* "I love you. You know that, don't you?"

"I do." *Let me just finish*, she thought. *I've got to get this off my chest.* "Then I find myself rushing, rushing to brush my teeth, rushing to get where? Get it done, I suppose, whatever *it* is." *Oh my God, rushing sweet moments like this so that I can talk about the fucking drama. What is the matter with me? Rushing for the sake of it, as if I even liked the rush.* She rolled over on her back and covered her eyes with her hands. "Make it stop," she moaned. "Make it stop." *It hardly takes a moment before the rush is all there is, and then I'm the slave. I'll sacrifice my child, my marriage, my health, and my peace for the story. Some stupid damn story, any story.*

"Do you think you ought to maybe see somebody about this?" *You're on shaky ground here, buddy. Better make sure she doesn't think you think she's nuts.* "Dan Tuner really helped me get it together after I nearly starved myself to death. It's not like I think you aren't able to cope. It just that …" *I think you aren't able to cope.* "Somebody outside of me or you might be able to give you some insight that you don't have, something more helpful than what I can provide."

She patted his hand as he continued.

"I know I irritate the hell out of you because I'm so linear. It's not like I don't want to help. I just don't think I can."

"Whatever is in the way, whatever makes it so that I can't be right at that moment, can't drop the drama … I guess I need help because I don't know what it is. I am compelled like a drug addict to find the next fix, to find out what's going on. How is she? Has anything happened? Did they make a decision? I rush to pass judgment on the powers that be. I'm always rushing to find fault, rushing to bitch, rushing to commiserate over the injustice of it all," Mackey lamented. "Lucky for me, I've had a lot of it—injustice—but you see, I know that's a lie. You see, it's not any old drama that hooks me, although if there isn't anything going on in my life, I can be distracted for a minute or two by someone else's whirlwind, but it is only momentary. That's why I endure Virginia's endless tale of 'my wedding.'" She rolled over, staring at the ceiling in the dark.

"Oh God, what a horrible affair that is going to be," she continued. "But the drama—the real attraction—comes from my own drama. I can tell it and tell it, adding flourishes upon flourishes and casting myself as the heroine or the victim depending on my audience." She turned to see if Eric was still listening.

He gently stroked her cheek. "Your mother and Joe have something that works for them. Have you ever talked with either of them about these feelings? They might be able to help. Whatever it is that they believe, it seems to work wonders for them," he offered.

"How do you know? How do you know it works for them?"

"Look at them," Eric said. "Look at how your mother was able to get over having her family killed and move on with her life. People don't do that. I don't think they do anyway. That kind of stuff can screw you up for good, and your mother is hardly screwed up."

"Do you know how much she worries?" Mackey asked.

"So maybe it's not perfect," Eric admitted, "but she's a hell of a lot healthier than most people I know. And your grandfather—just look at him."

"I don't know. Maybe I'll ask him about it. I am sure as hell not going to say anything to Mom. She'd freak out," Mackey said as she looked at the clock radio. "Look at the time. Got to get some sleep."

☙

The promised snow never came. Eric checked first thing after he crept out of bed. Saturdays were his favorite. He could spend real time with Joey, and more importantly, he could give Mackey some help. Though he didn't like to admit it, he knew that as brilliant as he was, he couldn't function without someone to look after the details of life. In grad school, he had fainted at his desk and had to spend a week in the hospital from dehydration and lack of food because he had just forgotten to eat. *A lot of damn good a genius IQ is if you aren't smart enough to keep yourself alive—so smart, yeah.* Mackey made living in the everyday clean-socks, food-on-table, bills-paid world possible, and he loved her for it. Rare as it was, when he saw an opportunity to help her, he took it. And he flat-out loved his son.

"Hey, bud. You awake?" he whispered, tucking his head into his son's room. "Want to get some breakfast? I thought we could go to that diner—you know, the one that makes those pancakes you love so much. How 'bout you get dressed?"

Joey, groggy from sleep, rubbed his eyes and tried to focus on his father.

"Did I wake you up?" Eric stole a look at the clock. "Oh God, I'm sorry. I didn't realize it was so early." He stepped fully into the room and shut the door behind him as quietly as he could. The latch clicked softly. "Go back to sleep," he said as he crawled under the covers with his son.

Three hours later, the phone rang, startling them both awake. "Wow, look," said Joey. "We really slept late. It's nine forty-seven. Can we go get some pancakes at the diner now?"

"Yeah, let's just get dressed."

"Dad."

"What?"

"You are dressed. Did you sleep in your shoes? Dad, you are the craziest." Joey laughed as he rolled on top of his father.

"Oh, right. Okay, well, let's go then." Eric hugged his son, holding him for as long as the little boy would allow, and then raked his fingers through his own hair, patted it down, and rubbed the sleep out of his eyes. As he ran his tongue around his mouth, he thought about suggesting that they should probably brush their teeth but dismissed the thought. "I'm ready. How 'bout you?"

"Since I don't sleep in my clothes"—the little boy giggled at his father—"you gotta wait a minute. You know Mom gets mad if I go out in my jammies." He crawled over his father and scrambled to get dressed.

Eric lay on the bed with his arms behind his head, gazing absently at the ceiling while Joey opened drawers, pulling out too many clothes and leaving what he didn't want in a heap on the floor.

A few minutes later, as he attempted to exit the room without stepping on any clean clothes, Eric remarked, "Seems to me that there was more order in this room the last time I looked. Maybe we could help Mom a little by picking this stuff up?" He leaned over and scooped up a pile of previously folded clothes and handed them to his son in a bundle. "Here, put these back in the drawer."

Joey stuffed the clothes in the drawer and shoved hard to close it.

"Let's ask Mom if she wants to come with us."

Joey ran into his parents' room and leapt on the bed. "We're going to get pancakes. Wanna come? Wanna?"

"Hang on a second, Virginia," she said into the phone. Putting the phone down on the bed, she hugged Joey, combed his hair with her fingers, and kissed him on the top of his vaguely straightened hair. "Hey, sweetie. Did you sleep well?"

"Yeah, we're going out for breakfast. Want to come?"

Eric sat down on the bed. "Yeah, wanna?" He smiled at his wife.

"You guys go ahead," she said, indicating the phone. "You know Virginia. Wants to tell me all her news," she said with a laugh. "And you know me—I gotta tell her mine. So we could be on the phone for a while."

Joey had already wrestled free of her embrace and was out of the door and struggling with his jacket. "Come on, you guys. I'm hungry."

"We'll miss you. Want anything?" Eric asked as he was leaving the room.

"Yeah, bring me a latte? Please," she said, smiling. "But I want it hot, so don't order it until you are ready to come home, okay?"

"Hot latte. Got it."

When Eric reached the front door, it was already open, and Joey was headed toward the car. "Come on!" he yelled, waving his arm behind him to speed his father along.

"Okay, okay, I'm coming." Eric ran to catch up with his son. "Jeez," he said putting on his seat belt. "You'd think you hadn't eaten in a week. You okay back there? Zero minus three. Ready for takeoff, Captain?"

"Ready!" Joey adjusted himself in his car seat so that he could see behind as they backed out of the drive. "Don't want you to run over my bike again."

"Well, if somebody didn't leave it right behind my car, it probably wouldn't have gotten run over." Eric laughed. "You want to fly this ship?"

"Nooo!"

"Don't let me forget a latte. Got it?" He looked in the rearview mirror.

Joey gave him two thumbs up, giggling.

"Okay then, we have liftoff."

Eric carefully made his way out onto the road. He wasn't exactly a bad driver. He just had to remind himself to concentrate on the task at hand, constantly. Joey had brought along a Lego truck that he busily applied himself to dismantling and reassembling between checking to make sure that his father was paying attention.

"Sure is a pretty day, huh?" Eric said, looking back at Joey. "The sky is so blue. I'm glad those clouds finally blew out of here."

"Dad, the road. You know we're not supposed to talk while you're driving. Mom says …"

"I know. We're almost there. I'll maintain radio silence, sir." *I need two keepers*, he thought.

They pulled up into a spot right outside of the silver fifties-era diner. Eric turned the car off, opened the door, started to climb out, and stopped dead.

"What's the matter, Dad?" Joey called.

"Nothing. I just forgot to undo my seat belt." He laughed. *Smart but can't seem to function outside of the playpen. Don't forget the latte.*

҂

Joey banged the door open. "Mom, we're back. I had dinosaur pancakes, and Mom—"

"Back here!" she called. "I gotta go, Virginia." She put down the phone and looked up as her son ran into the room. "Wow, I can't believe you're back already. Dinosaur pancakes? How does that happen?"

"They make 'em in the shape of dinosaurs. It's so cool." He kicked off his shoes and turned on the TV.

"Why don't you go watch that in the other room? I need to get dressed. Gosh, look what time it is." *Could you have spent more time on the phone? It's not like you don't have things to do other than listen to your cousin bitch all day long.* "Hey, Joey. Where's my latte? Did he forget?"

"No, I didn't," Eric said as he entered. "Here it is. I brought you a croissant too."

Father and son winked at each other and then high-fived as Joey left the room.

4

The night after Stuart's visit, Joe lay in bed, working every bit as hard as the fairy-tale stepsisters to stuff himself into Ginny's shoes. He'd been so sure of himself and the decision to die consciously, to take fate into his own hands—not suicide, just making the choice and willing it to happen. She knew that, didn't she? How would it feel if he reversed the situation? If Ginny were ready to go, and he wasn't, what would that feel like? Tough question. What would old Dr. Berke say? Yeah, the GOALS formula. *Oh, Jacob*, he thought, fondly remembering his mentor, *where are you now when we need you?* Jacob Berke had been a lifesaver more than once, for him and Stuart and a whole lot of other people—that was for sure.

Joe quietly sat up in the early morning light. Ginny was already up, probably in the kitchen. It was their usual routine: she would putter, and he would take most of a half hour to meditate. He pulled up the old formula. First, there was the goal: to die consciously, soon. Nothing new there. He certainly had organized the situation so that Ginny was well aware of his wishes and had given her tacit, if reluctant, agreement to his plans. That had been in place for months now—although, he reminded himself, she still had some issues with the timing.

Goal … organization … awareness … let go … GOAL, there you had it. Sometimes it almost seemed too easy, but that was deceptive, which Joe knew only too well. What was that story Jacob told about the gates, the dragons, and the warriors? He wasn't sure, but since it had floated to the surface of his awareness, he was quite sure it was important. Dredging deeply into his memory of the time he had spent with Jacob Berke, he managed to bring most of the story back to mind, although its meaning was eluding him at the moment.

The first gate was Blindness, and the dragon that guarded it was Dreams—no, Sleep, that was it. He knew well that the warrior needed for that gate was the Listening Warrior. That was the irony. When confronted with blindness, you had to learn to listen. Joe knew that well because he had been listening his entire life. He felt quite sure that by virtue of how long he had been listening, he was at the second gate, although most of his family was still outside that first gate.

Still, he paused. If indeed he'd passed through, then what had he heard in all that time? And what had blinded him? He had puzzled with the two issues for most of the previous night, waking up this morning disappointed that he had no resolution. "Wait, if I'm 'dis-appointed,' Jacob would say I 'missed my appointment.' Or who have I appointed and to what task? More puzzles," he groaned. "Get a grip, old boy. Conscious dying is not a casual pursuit. Of course, you are going to have questions. You should worry if you don't." *It's not the questions I have a problem with; it's the dearth of answers*, he mused in response.

He knew, as well as anybody could know, that death wasn't the end. But he also knew that Ginny didn't know that. Since he couldn't forget what he knew, he found it difficult to put himself in her shoes. He also found it impossible to explain how he knew what he knew, other than to say he just *knew* it. He resolved to continue to seek answers and open himself up as much as he possibly could for what came next.

When Ginny brought in his breakfast smoothie, Joe was meditating, eyes closed. "Oh, heck, I didn't time it right this morning," she grumbled. "I thought you'd be finished by now."

"Usually, I am," he said. "My timing is off."

"I'm glad you finally realize it," she said, with mock seriousness. "I didn't want to point it out again."

Joe took his smoothie from his wife with some surprise. *How on earth did she know?* Then he had to laugh. *I love the way things work.* "You will be glad to know I've been thinking about what you said, and I think you're right," he said, patting the edge of the bed for her to join him. "The timing is off. So don't worry. I won't be pressing my agenda on the family—well, at least not during Christmas or the wedding."

Ginny took his invitation, sat, and reached over to give him a little hug.

"But," he said, affectionately waving her off, "you know that I have made very specific instructions when the time comes. You won't have to make any awful decisions like when your mother—or Frank and the twins—died. It's all taken care of." He hugged her back, pressing his cheek against hers and then looking into those deep blue eyes of hers with a big smile. "Who knows, I might outlive you all!" He downed the smoothie triumphantly and handed her back the glass.

"Thanks so much," she said wryly.

"You know, Jacob in so many ways was my deus ex machina. He showed up in my life at the perfect time and solved myriad problems almost instantly. Well, he didn't so much solve them as he taught me how to reframe my situation so that I could solve them. I shudder to think what would have become of Stuart had he not appeared when he did."

Ginny shrugged. It was an old disagreement between them. "She probably would have been all right. I don't think she was anywhere close to being a hard-core drug user."

"Of course she wasn't," he acknowledged, "but she had more than her fair share of issues and a whole lot of anger that could have consumed her had she not found Jacob."

"You know I am no Jacobite," she said firmly. "Yes, he helped, but I don't think you give yourself or Stuart enough credit." As always, she found Joe's worship of his old mentor a bit tedious. "I managed to pull myself up by the bootstraps without the aid of Herr Doctor."

"True," Joe acknowledged, restraining an old impulse to retort, *And you got a whole lot of help from your support staff, who got a whole lot of help from Jacob.*

"And Ethel," Ginny hurriedly added to shore up her case, "completely cleaned herself up without his aid."

He rose from the bed and started heading for the shower. "Right again. No argument there. I was just saying that the timing was perfect." He changed the subject. "I want a church service. I like the liturgy, and I think funerals that don't have some liturgical bounds can go off track in a hurry. Is that all right with you?"

Ginny got up, followed him into the bathroom, and glared at him, shaking her head. "Would you just stop with this?" Then she registered what he had said. "What? You haven't set foot in a church in how many years? Thirty?"

"I was in church just the other day. I go pretty regularly, actually. Mr. McCue and I have had some exhilarating conversations about life and death and all that lies between."

With a sigh, Ginny rolled her eyes at him. "How long has this been going on?"

"The way you say it, you'd think I was having an affair," he laughed. He pulled off his pajama top and tossed it in the hamper. "That would be some miracle," he snickered as he flexed his biceps and then reached in to turn on the shower. "It would have to be for my rugged good looks."

"Or a gold digger," she said, and they both laughed. "How long have you and Mr. McCue been meeting?" She summoned her best glare. "Why don't I know this?"

"It never occurred to me to tell you. How long has he been at the church?"

"I have no idea. Why don't you go on Sundays?"

"Hard to say." Joe bit his lip. "It didn't occur to me. But I do want a service in the church, and I want Mr. McCue to officiate. He knows all about it," he said as he shut the shower door.

"I wouldn't have thought Jacob's Eastern philosophy would sit well with Mr. McCue's Presbyterian orthodoxy." She raised her voice over the sound of the water.

"What?" Joe shouted back. He opened the shower door and grinned. "I can't hear you!"

Shaking her head, she turned to leave the room. "Never mind."

❦

Alex grabbed his coat and scarf and left. "Who the fuck does she think she is? Nobody treats me like that," he muttered. *If she wants to treat me right—and be married for that matter—she can fucking change her ways.* Shit, he was beginning to hate this whole fucking wedding thing. That was all she thought about, talked about, or did. *Fuck her. She can call me up and fucking ask me to come back. Otherwise, I'm at work.*

He closed the door behind him, fully intending not to come back until Virginia called and begged. He played the scenario over several times as headed to the movie set, aware that similar scenarios had been playing out with too-frequent regularity. As he walked along the deserted streets, he thought about his future and this excellent chance to make something of it.

Hell, what did he have to worry about? Nobody would know. They had already worked out his stage name: Angus LeBoeuf. He liked that. It had real class. Okay, maybe "class" wasn't the word, but he did like the sound of it. Shit, most of his friends would be jealous if they did find out anyway. Who wouldn't be?

The contract was for three films. That would give him enough money to buy Virginia the biggest fucking ring she could ever want and set him up with a great talent agent. It was a dream come true. It certainly wasn't like he was signing up to make a career out of porn. *I don't know what the big fuss is. The sex scenes in most major pictures are as explicit as most porn anyway. I'll just get really good at sex scenes. What could be wrong with that? I still don't think I'll tell her, though. Skirts can be so strange. But when she sees the Benjamins, whoa! Those babies'll get her attention and keep it.*

The Brooklyn L train finally came. *Late night, should've thought of that. I'll be a little late.* Still lost in thought, he sat in the empty car for the short hop from Manhattan. *When I have my pockets stuffed with big ones, her old man is going to stop playing this high-and-mighty role with me. Hell, he'll probably even start a campaign to recruit me into his stable of clients. Sorry, Pops. I think I'll hire your competitors just to make you …* Shit, he didn't care. Alex just didn't like the son of a bitch and his attitude, as if Alex wasn't good enough for his daughter. *The son of a bitch, I'll show him.*

He was so hyped that he hardly noticed the drunks or their smells littering and perfuming the street as he emerged in the warehouse district. It all made perfect sense to him as he tapped in the code, swung the industrial door open, and charged up the steps. Even the lines of blow made sense. He was glad to see there was more; that last hit had pretty much worn off. Who expects you to work all night without something to help you stay up? *This might well be the perfect job*, he thought as he helped himself to a line. *Free drugs, sex, and I get paid for it. Who could ask for anything more?*

ை

"Alex, where are you? We have to shop for your suit today. Remember? Call me back. Did you come home last night? Are you all right?"

Virginia called Alex every five minutes for the next two hours. Each call served to heighten her anxiety and irritation until she was downright panic-stricken. Maybe something really had happened during … Holy Christ, what if he was dead? *I can't believe they made him work last night*, she thought. *Did he go back last night, or did he leave early this morning?* She started to cry and willed herself to stop. "I hate free time and crying."

She was just about to call 911 when Alex stumbled into the room, pale and haggard, eyes flaming. "Oh my God, what happened to you?" she wailed. "You look terrible. Did you get something in your eyes?"

"Thanks a shitload," he responded with a snarl.

"Look at yourself. Holy fuck. You look like you've been up for months without sleep and using lye for eye drops. Are you sick?"

"No, just exhausted. I feel like shit, though."

"Well, you look it too. I made an appointment for us to meet the tailor this morning for your suit."

"Change it ... and not for later today." He threw himself on the couch.

"Alex—" She started to protest but stopped in mid-whine when she saw the expression on his face. She was panicking on the inside. *Maybe he doesn't want to get married. Oh my God, how embarrassing would that be after all of the plans I've made?* "Can I get you something? Make an appointment with a doctor?" She plunged on. "Honey, I'm sorry about last night. You know how grumpy I can be when I first wake up. I love you." It sounded more like a question than a statement.

"Yeah, me too," he croaked as he shut his eyes and pulled a sofa cushion over his face. When his phone rang, he dug into his pocket, pulled it out, and threw it against the wall without bothering to look at it.

Virginia decided today was a good day to go to work even if it was Saturday. She dressed quickly and left the apartment as quietly as she possibly could. Barely out in the hall, she punched in the number of one of her five bridesmaids. She recounted the latest wedding plans, deftly dropping a derogatory comment or two about Alex between discussions of hairstyles and heel heights as she made her way to the subway. Finally, having made plans for lunch and an appointment to shop for bridesmaid shoes and having further denigrated Alex for good measure, she rang off and hopped aboard the uptown train.

At about four o'clock, as she was getting ready to leave work, Virginia called Alex, turning on her most velvet and compelling tones to ask him out to dinner. "Let's go out and talk over the wedding plans over a delicious red. We can go to that new Italian restaurant you wanted to try, just the two of us. Doesn't that sound like fun?"

"Fuck no!" was his immediate and unequivocal response. He backpedaled swiftly with a lie. "Sorry, I was just practicing a scene when the phone rang. Yeah, sure, but can we do it tomorrow night? I'm working tonight."

"Sure, I guess. You must be a real badass in the film." She laughed, not quite sure she bought his little subterfuge. There was something about all of it that didn't add up. "I just got my new Amex—black, mind you—so we could really have a night on the town."

"Tomorrow night, K? Love you."

"Yeah, me too," she responded before clicking off.

Virginia was sure that Alex's reaction was more about the excitement of a new job than about them—that and his exhaustion at having to work all night. But just for insurance, she decided to cement the wedding deal. "I'll call Gran," she said out loud. "It's the perfect thing to do under the circumstances."

Looking at her contact list, she realized that she didn't have her grandmother's number, so she texted her mother. "Hey mom can you send me gran's #? ILY."

Sallee texted back with the number immediately. Virginia punched in the numbers and waited for her grandmother to answer.

A few seconds later, Ginny's voice came on the line, sounding frail. "Hello?"

"Gran, hi. It's Virginia," she shouted into the phone. "How are you? How's PopPop? Mother tells me that she's already given you my great news. It's just like her. She's always stealing my thunder!

I don't blame her. I know she's very excited and couldn't wait. Isn't it wonderful? ... Thank you." She hailed a cab and jumped in, handing the cabbie a card she had made up with her address for just such occasions. "He can't wait to meet you either. I've told him so much about you. What I'm calling about is to ask if we could have the wedding at your house ... Oh, I don't need to shout, sorry. Like I was saying"—*before you interrupted me*, she thought—"is it's so beautiful, and I have so many beautiful, wonderful memories of the place. I just think it would be the perfect place to get married. We could have the wedding in a tent ... No, they have heaters and things. I was hoping we could come down for Christmas and stay with you. Then the wedding'll be right after."

At a key intersection, the cabbie looked back for confirmation. She shook her head no and pointed straight ahead, holding up two fingers and then pointing east. The cabbie nodded and plowed on into the early Saturday evening traffic.

"We haven't done that in years, and we think it would be so much fun. You and PopPop would have to do nothing but show up as your beautiful selves. That should be pretty easy for you two," she laughed. "The whole thing would be catered. Flowers too, all brought in. Guests would stay at other places, except for the family. I was hoping we could all stay at the farm. I know you have lots of room. Mother told me years ago about your idea to have spaces for all of the family—like the way you converted the barn and Aunt Stuart's place and everything—so we could all visit. I just think it would be so much fun for the family to be together. Don't you?" As the cab drew up in front of her apartment building, Virginia whipped out her credit card and ran it through the machine, ready to jump out as soon as the cab came to a stop.

"No, you don't have to make a big deal about Christmas either. We can have all of that taken care of, Christmas dinner catered. The catering crew will clean up, and I can even have a maid service come to take care of getting everything ready for guests—cleaning and taking care of all of the extraneous work of having so many people there—so honestly, there would be nothing that you two would have to do … Do you really think so? Do you think … Oh, thank you so much! Oh, Gran, thank you so, *so* much! Please give PopPop my love. Ask him to give you a hug and a kiss from me, and give him both for me. I'll be seeing you soon. Thank you, thank you, thank you!"

She blew Ginny her best air kiss—"Mwaah"—and then clicked off and texted her mother. "Called Gran, she's down with it."

It wasn't until Virginia's key was in the door that she remembered to worry about the home front. What was up with Alex anyway? She was beginning to think that he didn't want to get married. She carefully pushed the door open.

Alex—showered, shaved, and rested—descended upon her immediately with apologies piled on apologies. "Hey, hon. I am so fucking sorry for being such an asshole. I … just the hours … I'm just not used to those kind of hours. I'm so sorry that I took it out on you. I called in an order for Thai. That okay for you? I got it hot, level 5 hot. Right?"

She nodded. "I am so glad you're feeling better. I was beginning worry that you didn't want to get married."

He pulled her down on the sofa and onto his lap and held her down as he proceeded to kiss her all over.

She squirmed and giggled. "So can we talk about the wedding soon?"

"In a little bit," he said. "I have some business to attend to first." He started on her neck and kissed her down to the top of her blouse, gently unbuttoning it before pulling it off. Then he proceeded to kiss her all around her bra. Just as he unfastened and slipped it off, the doorbell rang. "Wow, that was fast. I just called it in."

He stood up and dug around in his pants pocket, looking for his wallet and to adjust himself. He opened the door, which barely missed hitting the sofa as it swung open into the narrow living room.

These renovated Lower East Side tenements—great style, right price, but never mind privacy.

Virginia had scrambled to put herself back together before he opened the door, and it was only after paying for the dinner and turning back to her that Alex realized he had exposed her to the delivery boy. "Oh man, sorry. Want to eat now or later?"

"Yeah, now," she said, stuffing her bra between the sofa cushions as she moved to make room on the sofa for him and the bag of dinner.

He opened the tom yum soup with chicken, gave it a big sniff, and then proceeded to take a bigger swig from the container. "Hey, share," she said as she got up to get some plates. "Save me some. You could wait for a bowl and a spoon."

"I haven't got cooties, if that's what you're worried about," he laughed.

"Just would like to get you into the habit of using your table manners. You know we have a wedding coming up, and people care about that shit. At least my grandmother and parents do."

"Really, a wedding? Who's getting married?" He laughed as he pushed her down on the sofa and snatched off her blouse. He took another swig of soup and then dribbled it between her breasts. He proceeded to lick it off, and she giggled. He looked up to flash her a lascivious grin. "It's so much better this way."

"Don't use it all up. I still want some."

Before she knew what hit her, he had stripped and was lying on the couch, and she was sitting astride him, drizzling soup into his belly button until it streamed to points south.

"Be my guest," he said.

She was slurping up the soup between fits of giggling when the peppers started to take effect on his most sensitive parts. He began to writhe, and not from pleasure.

"Stop, you gotta get off. This shit is burning like hell," he screeched between laughing and grimacing. "Last time I fucking order a five."

She rolled off of him, laughing until she got the hiccups. Between hiccups she gasped, "Alex Boyd, I love you."

☙

On her way to work Monday morning, Virginia giggled every time she thought about Alex and the soup. Just as she was about to call her mother, her phone burbled.

"Hey, Mama. What's up? The funniest thing happened the other night. Alex and I had Thai for dinner and—" It occurred to her midsentence that this might not be the most appropriate story for her mother, and she quickly amended it to give it a G rating. "I knocked over some tom yum soup, and it fell in Alex's crotch. It was super hot, not burning hot—like hot, hot—but you know, spicy hot. I didn't know that boy could dance like that," she laughed.

She turned the corner of the hallway into her office. "No, he's all right. I think he'll live. I don't think those peppers are so hot that they can actually burn you … I don't know. Do you want to check? … Yes, cool, we'd love for you two to join us for dinner tonight. Hey, let's go to Masa. You know, it's over near you on Columbus Circle. I've been trying to get a reservation for weeks now, but I'm sure your peeps can get us in … Okay, meet you there around seven? Looking forward to it. See you soon. Bye."

She quickly clicked Alex's number. It went immediately to voice mail. "Hey, we're going to Masa with the 'rents tonight. Call me. Supposed to meet them at seven. I hope you finally cooled off," she giggled. "You sure were hot Saturday night, in more ways than one. Love you. Bye."

☙

Sallee was the first to arrive at Masa, followed shortly after by Peter. "Hi, honey!" Sallee said, kissing him on the cheek. "Happy we got a moment or two before the newly affianced arrive. Should we sit?"

The maître d' showed them to their table.

"It is a lovely little spot," Sallee said. "Look at the flowers. Breathtaking."

Peter looked around. "I guess the flowers are always breathtaking in these little dives. The biggest bang for the buck." He ordered their drinks—single malt on the rocks for him, pinot grigio for her—and then looked for the menu and whistled. "Shit, it's a sushi bar, minimalism, and you pay extra for the minimal. Christ, will you look at the prices. Let me guess. Virginia picked the restaurant." He laughed. "That girl has a talent for spending my money."

Sallee laughed too but thought, *Excuse me, but it is my money too, big guy. Nothing like the wife's little law firm salary to help support your high-finance show biz dealings. The big stars think you are all that, since you schmooze with the best of them, but I know who does the bulk of their work.* She thought about saying something but decided to drop it. She was looking forward to a nice meal, not a fight. "This little at-home wedding is turning into quite a pricey affair, so I'm glad you're still laughing."

"Are you surprised at that? Has anything Virginia done not been expensive? I hope this husband of hers doesn't turn out to be the most expensive thing she's ever done."

"They're not married yet. He's still just her fiancé. Please don't call him a husband—there's still time. And stranger things have happened. Ah, and here's Virginia now." Sallee discreetly acknowledged her daughter. Virginia had admonished her mother years before that nobody waves or looks excited when greeting a friend in a restaurant. *It is so gauche*, she had said. Once again, Sallee was reminded of her mother's etiquette rules of so long ago. It was easier to go along with the program than to protest, and so she did—continuing, she thought now, to lose bits and pieces of her soul along the way. But what the heck. It was too late to fix it now. Living in the Big Apple meant being on top of the world—and if that meant it took a little bite out of everybody, well …

"Hi, honey," Peter said as he jumped up and kissed his daughter.

"Long time no see. How are you? Where is that good-looking man you're planning on wedding?"

"Hi, Daddy. Hi, Mom." Virginia gave her dad a big kiss and hug. She air-kissed Sallee across the table and sat down. "This is a swell place," she said, looking around.

"Looks to be," her father said. "How are all the plans coming along?"

"They are coming. Because Gran took so long, I had to pay extra to get the invitations fast-tracked."

"*Mother* took long?" Sallee asked.

Peter's glare said, *Leave it. It doesn't matter.* "We only have one daughter," he laughed, patting Virginia's hand. "So the invitations are on schedule?"

"They have the coolest service. Not only are they the best engravers in New York, but for only a hundred dollars more, they do the addresses by hand—calligraphy, of course—and stuff the envelopes and mail them with a stamp made from a picture that I send them. Isn't that cool?"

"All that for a hundred dollars," Peter said knowledgeably. *Maybe the kid is getting a little money sense after all.*

Virginia spotted Alex and jumped up to greet him.

"Look at that," Peter said to Sallee. "She actually found a deal in the wedding vendors racket."

Sallee smiled grimly. "Hate to bust your bubble, Daddy," she said, drawing out the "Daddy" much longer than was necessary. "But that's a hundred dollars an invitation, on top of the cost of the engraving. Mucho dinero!"

"Oh. The girl does have a talent," he said and took a big long pull from his single malt. Sometimes Peter thought Sallee was jealous of Virginia.

5

The day before the invitations were meant to go out, Ginny spent another in a succession of mornings on the computer, looking for her old friend Rebecca. "Please don't send them. Don't send them until I find Rebecca," she begged Sallee over a Skype call.

"Mother, you're being unreasonable. We can send out the invitations, and if you find Rebecca, we can send her one. We don't have to hold them up because you can't find Rebecca."

"I guess that makes sense. What's your Facebook password?" Ginny demanded.

"Why in heaven's name do you want that? I didn't know you even knew what Facebook was."

"I thought I would look her up on Facebook. Of course I do. I don't live in a cave, you know. What is it?"

Sallee laughed. "Sometimes I think you do. Do you honestly believe Rebecca has a Facebook account? And even if I gave you my password, would you know how to look for her there?"

"Well, no. I guess you're right. It was a stupid idea. Besides, she didn't have any children who would lead me to her on Facebook."

"That's right. Her daughter Charlie died before Rebecca even married Dad's doctor buddy, right?" Sallee asked.

"Yes, she never really got over that bout of pneumonia that she had. I think she was always in poor health. She died in her early teens."

"Mother, she was in her early teens when I met her. She just didn't look or act it."

"Well, anyway, I'm going to keep looking for Rebecca. If she's out there, I am bound and determined to find her. She might well be my only friend."

Later that afternoon, Joe came into the den to find Ginny still sitting at her desk, surrounded by ancient address books. "What are you doing?"

She sighed. "Still looking for Rebecca. What does it look like?"

"That you're awash in address books," he chuckled. "Something I've always loved about you, Ginny—once you get something in your head, there ain't no stopping you."

She leaned back in her chair and waved a dismissive hand at the desk with a sigh of resignation. "Every one of these numbers is a dead end, as is any reference to Jacob Berke, doctor or otherwise. Mount Sinai Hospital is just sorry as hell that they can't give out that information," she said defiantly.

She stuck her cheek up to Joe for his kiss and then made a face at him. "One thing's for sure—I've used more of my brain today than I have in a month. I even called up the *New York Times* and asked if I could hire somebody to go over their obituaries for the last thirty years and see if Rebecca was in them. No dice." Pressing both lips hard together, she sat pondering the situation. A new thought struck her. "You don't remember Rebecca's father's name, do you? Or where he lived?"

"What good would that do you?" With a smile, Joe shook his head and sighed.

She gave him an I-don't-know shrug. "I pestered Sallee for the last week to look in the New York phone book. Do you know that she swears there isn't one anymore? Says that it doesn't exist. I don't believe it. How about a private detective?"

"No, absolutely not. Ginny, I know this is hard for you, but you have to give it up. No doubt, Rebecca is long dead."

"I refuse to believe, Joe, that she's dead. I just refuse." She raised the pencil she had been twiddling and threw it at the pile of address books on the desk. "I hate that I lost touch with her after Jacob died. I remember how devastated she was. She was as devoted as you and Stuart to that man."

"Honey, I don't see how there's anything else you can do. She's disappeared, off the map, out of your radar. If you can't find her online and you've checked everybody that you knew in common, I don't see that there's anything left to be done. You are going to have to let this go," Joe insisted.

"I don't know why Sallee can't just go over to her apartment and check. It wouldn't take twenty minutes," she grumbled.

"Ginny, listen to yourself. You checked out their old apartment the last three times we went to New York. You know she hasn't lived there in years. Besides, Sallee has a thousand things to do other than chasing after your friend. Seems like a lot to ask considering she has a business to run, clients to deal with, and a difficult daughter's wedding looming on her horizon. What is behind all of this?"

"I would have thought you of all people would understand wanting to find a connection. I hate the idea that I am alone, all by myself out here."

"Hello, what am I—chopped liver?" Joe pulled a chair up beside hers and took her hands. Looking deeply into her blue eyes, he whispered, "I'm still here."

She started to cry. "But only begrudgingly. You don't want to be. Joe, I don't want to be alone."

He leaned his head against hers. "I know. I think it's just the way it is—you and me, the last ones standing."

༼

Gordon, at sixty years old, was a much-respected and successful dairy farmer. Never a slave to fashion, he looked much the same now as he had as a boy, slightly disheveled in plaid shirts or T-shirts, blue jeans, and boots or sneakers. His hair was still close-cropped but graying, and there was less of it. The only noticeable additions were a paunch and his hat. He was the kind of man who felt undressed without his hat, and if he could have his way, he would never take his Virginia Tech ball cap off. His wife, Susan, had given up the no-wearing-hats-in-the-house fight long ago. Ginny, however, was unrelenting on that score. Gordy and Susan hadn't moved far in their adult decades—their very neat clapboard farmhouse at the southern end of Greene County was barely fifteen miles north of his parents' place. Ginny never visited their house without suggesting that Gordy and Susan should enlarge the windows to take advantage of the magnificent views of the Blue Ridge Mountains. "This is so glorious!" she would say, turning around and spreading her arms wide.

Susan had long since ceased to hear the suggestion, while Gordy patiently responded each time: "Every day when I walk out my door, I take in the sight—one to behold, to be sure. I'm outside all day long. I see this all day." At this point he'd wave to encompass the entire view. "And I don't come into the house until dark, so I can't see this"—another sweep of the arm—"from here anyway. So I ask you, why go to the bother and expense?"

Today, returning from the post office, he fumbled with the back doorknob until he finally got the catch loose and then banged the door open the rest of the way with this foot. He had several Amazon packages stuffed under each arm and letters tucked in and around the bundles. Trailing him were the dogs—the bloodhound Lance Six, known simply as Six, and Burt and Early, the two Jack Russell siblings. Whistling, he dumped his load on the kitchen counter while the dogs scrambled over to their beds, the two smaller ones circling three or four times before settling down. Seeing his wife and, for her benefit, displaying a big chagrined smile, he dramatically backtracked, stepping precisely in each footprint until he got to the mudroom, where he took off his barn boots. Shuffling back into the room in his slippers, he picked up a large, magnificently addressed envelope and opened it. "I never have understood why they put these things into two envelopes. Do you know?"

Susan shook her head. "So is that the wedding invitation?" She came over and peered around her husband's shoulder. "It's lovely! It's very exciting, and I think it's good for Joe and Ginny, you know that?"

He finished reading and then handed her the two envelopes and the invitation. "I suppose," he grunted. "They do seem to have a little more spark in their step. Dad even looks livelier. More engaged, I think. I'm not quite sure I know how I feel about this whole family-together-for-Christmas-and-wedding thing, though. It is hard enough just having our own kids at Christmas, when they do come." He wrapped his arms around her and whispered in her ear, "It's going to cut down on the afternoon delight, you know. With all the grandkids running around the house, we won't ever get a moment to ourselves." He nuzzled her ear before he let her go.

"I wish you wouldn't do that," she said, reflexively rearranging her hair. "You know how ..." She pulled away. "Do you think the boys will come?" she asked, half-hoping they wouldn't. *Some mother I am*, she chided herself. *But there it is.*

"Oh," Gordon laughed, "I suppose Mr. Oh-So-Fancy will have to be there, and if he comes, so will Mr. Jesus-Come-Lately too."

"Gordon, I don't think that helps. Calling the boys names is not going to help."

"Sometimes I can't help myself. It helps me feel better about things if I can laugh at them. It's not like I call them that to their face."

"You know better than that." She lifted the cast-iron skillet onto the stove and stood staring at her husband, both hands on her hips. "Gordy—excuse me, *Gordon*, though I can't for the life of me understand why you have insisted on this change—do you honestly have nothing nice to say about your sons? When we were growing up, you know they used to say, 'If you haven't got anything nice to say, don't say anything at all.'"

"I didn't change anything. It's the name I was born with," he replied, ducking the issue.

Susan, not to be placated, raised an eyebrow.

"Okay," he replied, "but what I said is true. Trey is oh-so-fancy, and didn't Andy come to Jesus lately?"

"You know what I mean." She managed a mock scowl but was having a hard time not laughing, up until recently a rare occurrence. "Sometimes you can be just so stubborn." She tossed the potatoes into the greased pan and turned down the gas.

Thumbing through the rest of the mail, Gordon said absently, "That new guy that we have in the milking shed reminds me so much of Early. Did you ever meet Early?"

Susan looked up, puzzled.

"Ethel's husband. I swear, he was the smartest man I ever met."

"I do remember you telling me about how he helped you out. The new guy, is he smart like Early?"

"That remains to be seen," Gordon sighed. "He sure made me think of Early today. I can't put my finger on how. No, I doubt he is anywhere near as smart as Early was. I know one thing, though. Early would be able to help me figure out how I feel about these sons of mine."

"Well, if that's the case," Susan said knowingly, "he can still help you figure out how you feel about those sons of yours. All you have to do is ask."

"Jesus, you're beginning to sound like my father." Gordon chuckled and looked at his wife a little nervously. "Do you buy all of that mind stuff he talks about?"

"Actually ..." Susan walked over and sat down at the table next to Gordon, primly holding herself up straight and folding one hand over the other. "He has been helping me stop drinking. You had noticed, hadn't you?"

"That he was helping you," Gordon asked, shooting her a grin, "or that you'd stopped?"

"The latter, smarty!" She tossed her head and went back to her potatoes. "After dinner I'm going to call those sons of yours and see if they plan to come to the wedding and for Christmas. Has the family ever all been together?"

"With all the grandkids and great-grandkids? Well, no. Joey is the youngest, I think, or maybe Andy's girl, Sally."

"Joey is five, Sally is seven, Potts is almost six, so let's see …"

"Who calls their son Potts, for God's sake?" Gordon demanded without heat.

Ignoring his interruption, she continued, "Didn't all of your siblings come to our wedding?"

"Yeah, we got married before Helen went to California. Or did we? I don't know. I remember Stuart's first husband, Frank, came, and they brought their twins. I remember they weren't as big as my fist."

"Maybe a little bigger than that," she laughed.

He shook his head emphatically, waving his fist in the air. "That big! Together." His eyes twinkled.

"That whole thing was so tragic. How Stuart got on with her life, I can't even imagine——a husband and twin babies mowed down by a drunk driver." Susan shook her head with a pang of guilt over her own drinking, as if all the unrecovered drunks in the world were responsible for taking Stuart's first family away. *That kind of thinking doesn't serve you*, she reminded herself.

Later that evening, she called Trey, an infrequent occurrence. As she listened to his voice-mail message, she debated whether she would leave a message of her own. Finally deciding that she would, she said, "Hi, it's Mom. Just wanted to know if you got your invitation to Virginia's wedding? I hope you're planning to come. I would love to see you and Potts. This is your Christmas this year, isn't it?"

She hung up and immediately dialed son Andy's much more called number. "Hi, Andy. How are you? Did you get the invitation to Virginia's wedding? Are you going to come? I know your grandfather will be so happy. Bringing the children? … Oh, they're with their mother. That's too bad. I don't suppose there's any chance she would let you bring them? It is a once-in-a-lifetime sort of event. Your dad and I were talking about it just at dinner. The whole family hasn't been together since he and I were married, at least. That leaves out a whole lot of people … You don't think so? Would you ask her, please? Virginia must be a very sweet girl to come up with the idea. Everything else going well? … Work? … Okay. It was good to talk."

While Susan talked on the phone, Gordon sat in the TV room, intermittently dozing and thinking about the upcoming wedding. Maybe for the first time ever, he actually asked himself what exactly had come between him and his boys. It felt like it had happened so fast. He suspected, however, that it had taken a very, very long time—like watching yourself grow, one little increment, one little decision, one little misplaced word at a time—until they found themselves here, as far apart is any three people could be, and for no apparent reason.

What you thinkin' 'bout, puttin' a garden on dat dried-up, weed-choked piece a hardscrabble? It be easier on all y'all if you move on over a hair where de ground's a little softer, where you can see little sprouts growin'. I ain't sayin' you can't build a garden on dat ol' weed patch. Jest sayin' it be might near easier plantin' where de ground is willin' t' help. Powerful lot easier on yer back, an' you knows how I likes t' keep it easy.

Gordon flinched awake. He could've sworn that Early had been standing right there in front of him, talking. "Guess I musta dozed off," he muttered. He looked around just in case. "Or maybe I'm going crazy."

෪

Bill put the mail on the breakfast room table and gave Stuart a shout before trotting upstairs to take a shower. His perfect eight-mile Saturday morning run had included a stop at the post office, and while he ran, Stuart had busied herself making his favorite Saturday breakfast. The fact that she not only was accomplished in her profession but also was a fabulous cook and delighted in cooking for him was among the things he loved and admired about her. He counted himself one of the luckiest men in the world, having Stuart as his wife. Though her sweet and tender heart, her amazing attention to detail, and the fact that she was stunningly attractive even in her early sixties didn't hurt, possibly the most important thing was her sense of humor. Stuart wasn't a clown, but she had an innate sense of timing and irony that made Bill laugh often, quite a change from the world he'd grown up in. Every time he thought of his dour, long-suffering mother slogging from one day to the next, nurturing every tragedy that befell her and talking about ones that hadn't as if they had, he was filled with gratitude that this remarkable woman had consented to be his wife. He held her parents in as high regard as well. The three together and separately had taught Bill that life was so much easier when you could laugh. Her life, he would reflect— possibly a thousand times more tragic than his mother's—had given her ample opportunity to hone the skill to find humor in everything, humor and acceptance.

By the time he came back downstairs, the breakfast table practically sagged with delectables. Stuart sat backlit by the morning sun, and he noticed that her blonde locks, like everything about her, were gracefully transforming into the next phase of life. Looking over the invitation in front of her—the much-awaited invitation—she glanced up and said, "It's really beautiful. Look." She held it up for his perusal.

"I guess," he said with a shrug. "It looks pretty traditional to me. You know how I feel about that."

She giggled. "I. M. Pei, I forgot! Yes, something more innovative, I suppose, would suit you better. I love the traditional look and feel of this—the weight of the cream-colored paper, the calligraphy they chose, and the fact that they achieved this extraordinary thing in less than two weeks. Certainly helps to be connected, *n'est-ce pas?*"

"I can't a resist a woman who can lay a little French on me," he joked as he handed the invitation back to her.

"That sister of mine certainly is that—connected. Coffee?" She poured him a cup, draining the French press. "I have to say, I am really excited about this. We haven't gotten together as a family since I don't even know when. Do you remember?"

"Not on my watch, we haven't, and that's … twenty-eight years?"

"Try thirty next week. It's a big one. Good that we had this chat."

"No! Are you sure?"

She nodded. "I know these things."

"Hmm, will dinner and a movie do?"

"Not on your life," she laughed.

"Warned."

They sipped coffee without speaking for a while.

Bill picked up the invitation and looked at it again. "I know it must have been a disappointment to your mother over all these years. Her idea for renovating the barn into guesthouse suites was brilliant. Clearly, she had—actually, I know she had—family get-togethers in mind as a regular occurrence. I wonder why it never happened?"

"I guess you did know," Stuart rejoined, "since she hired you to design it. I can still hear Ethel telling me about you."

"Stuart, honey, it been a time now. You best be gettin' on wit' it. Can't be sittin' out yo' whole life mournin' over what done happen. For sure it was a terrible thang havin' yo' babies an' Mista Frank swept away like dat. I ain't gonna lie t' you, I is proud as can be how you handled yo'self, but it's time. Yo' momma done found a right smart-lookin' boy here wit' dis renovation she been doin'. We think you should come fo' lunch tomorrow just like you do, an' yo' momma will invite him fo' lunch too."

"Ethel, no, I'm not ready. You two old ladies—"

"Who you callin' old, girl? Get on outta he'ah."

"Okay, well, what I'm saying is you guys need to find something better to do than to try to run my life."

"We ain't tryin' t' run it. Jest helpin' you along. We know a thing or two 'bout life now. And yo' momma an' I both know de worst thang you can do is t' mope for too long. It ain't got nothin' t' do wit' not havin' a reason t' mope. Jest ain't good fo' you is all."

"And the rest is history," Stuart chortled.

"I love the image of Ethel playing Cupid, flittering around, all God-only-knows-how-many pounds of her adorable self, on little wings with her tiny bow and arrow," Bill said. They both laughed hard.

"You know the reason I think it didn't happen—why the family didn't share my parents' vision? Here, I'll read a quote I came across the other day that I think sums up the answer beautifully. It's from Erich Fromm. Wait a minute … it's here somewhere. I liked it so much that I copied it. He said, 'If I am what I have, and if I lose what I have, who then am I?'"

Bill's eyebrows went up. "Fromm? That's good. Umm, Fromm … remind me."

"Oh, for goodness' sake, my dear nonliterary architect!" She rolled her eyes affectionately. "Best-selling psychological guru? *The Art of Loving*? He was a really good friend of Jacob Berke's in New York."

Bill's decision to help himself to seconds of her freshly baked scones at just that moment precluded any response from him, so Stuart continued. "I suspect that some of our family, probably including my siblings, are afraid to lose what they have. I don't think they believe they could get anything better. Sad, I think. That sort of attitude creates such a sad existence. It's always surprised me that I was the only one who was able to embrace Jacob's teachings besides Dad. That they couldn't see the changes that were wrought in our lives is a mystery and probably always will be."

Bill, mouth still full, merely nodded agreement. Stuart's touchstone, for sure, was Dr. Berke, a man he'd never met but about whom he knew so much—probably the biggest single influence in his accomplished wife's life, including her decision after college to go on to grad school in psychology. And from there, he was a major influence in her lifelong practice, which had perhaps sustained her through the grief of losing Frank and the twins. His face clouded at the thought of all she'd been through and how her relentless, determined optimism had pulled her through most of it. When he finished chewing, he said, "I've always been sorry that your two sisters never wanted to avail themselves of your mother's brilliant idea and my fantastic job of bringing it to fruition. They really missed out. I'm glad Ginny will finally get her wish, if only once."

Stuart acknowledged Bill's words with a smile. "You know," she said, "the other day when I was at Mother's, and Sallee called to tell her about Virginia getting married, Sallee took shot upon shot at me, and I just don't understand why."

"Darling, there's every chance it had nothing to do with you. People in general don't like other people who seem to have more than they do."

"How in the world could Sallee believe that I have more than she does? That's ridiculous."

"Last time I checked, you were happy." Bill laughed, reached out, and squeezed her hand. "How happy do you think Sallee is? That is certainly something to want, and if your mindset is all about what you have, like you suggest, then what in the world gives you the right to be happy when she has so much more?"

"Beats me. Except for Jacob's teachings."

"Exactly. And nobody is going to go there. That would be terrifying; you know it would. Speaks to that quote you read me."

"Yeah, I guess. I'm going to make an attempt over Christmas to reach out to Sallee in a way that she can feel and understand, so it won't frighten her away."

"This may not be the time. She's going to have a lot on her plate. You might want to rely on that perfect timing of yours, whenever you decide to do it."

"But hey, when she has a lot on your plate might be the perfect time! We will see. But whatever happens, I'm excited about this. I really am. I think it's wonderful that Virginia came up with this idea. She must be some kind of insightful girl."

"That's not what I hear from Mackey," Bill said, thinking of how close their daughter and her soon-to-be-wed cousin seemed to be these days. *Lot of frantic phone calls from the Big Apple, from what I hear*, he thought. "But who knows, maybe she is," Bill said. "Like you said, whatever happens. And me, I'm happy for you and your parents that y'all will get to sit on the sidelines and watch this unfold. It'll be good for all of you not to be the center of attention but the supporting players for a change."

"You think that we hog the spotlight?" Stuart was pushing her chair back to take dishes to the sink but paused with a slight frown. "You don't think we elbow other people out of the way, do you?"

"No, I just think that you three are all natural leaders. People gravitate to you and expect you to lead—and then resent you for it."

She sighed.

⁊

At fifty-five, Helen was a handsome woman, albeit thin and a trifle severe. The youngest of Joe and Ginny's children, she'd long since ceased to surprise them with her business acumen, having created a thriving business as a graphic artist with twenty people now in her employ. Feelings of inadequacy were foreign to her in her professional life, and she greatly resented these vestiges of a past life as she stood on the veranda of her bougainvillea-covered adobe in Santa Barbara. She opened the envelope as she walked into the house.

Sitting down next to Janice on the sofa, she gave her mate a quick kiss before saying, "I told you one day it was going to happen, and here it is." She held a large envelope in her hand, her name magnificently inscribed across both envelopes. "I think I told you, my sister Sallee's daughter, Virginia, is getting married." She held the invitation up for Janice's inspection. "It just arrived. Looks so East Coast, doesn't it?" She laughed. "I think we just might have to go." She paused, thinking and frowning as she turned the envelope over in her hands. "The whole family is invited for Christmas and the wedding. It will be at Mother and Dad's house, naturally." She shuddered.

"What do they know about me, Helen?" Janice asked, biting her lip.

Helen shrugged and shook her head emphatically.

"You never told them anything?"

Helen shrugged again, apologetically. "It's one of the saddest parts of my life, that I haven't had the courage to share you with my family." Turning defensive, she added, "You don't know these people, Janice. They would make the Supreme Court justices question their ability to pass judgment. I just …" She stood up and then sat down again. "I just wasn't up to it. It has nothing … honestly, it has nothing to do with us. It's just the remains of them and me and a lot of stuff from a very long time ago."

"Do they know you're a lesbian?"

"Hell no. Well, shoot, Sallee for sure was always a genius at ferreting out information. So who knows. But I just couldn't …" She let the sentence die and then picked it up again. "I was never up to telling them. And so if I told them about you, they'd … I … I would be out. I just couldn't take any more rejection. You don't know them."

"Do they know about our children?"

"They know about Dennis. I never said anything about Leah because it would … I would have had to explain too much."

"Do they know that Dennis is black?"

"Yes, they do. That seems to be one area where my mother has an amazing degree of acceptance. I've sent her pictures of Dennis all along. But remember, that's not a lot of communication—possibly a picture in a Christmas card. She called a week or so ago to tell me about the wedding, which was highly unusual. She almost never calls."

"That's it for sixteen years? You sent pictures of Dennis in a Christmas card. And for twelve of those years, you've neglected to mention that you are in love and living with the person you love?

And that you have a stepdaughter? Helen, I am finding it hard not to get my feelings hurt here." Janice looked like she was about to cry. "Nor did you bother to mention until now that you spoke with your mother last week!"

Helen was torn between leaning over to comfort Janice and running screaming out of the house. "Suit yourself, but I'm inviting you to come to the party with me. I'm inviting you to come to the wedding and meet the family. Maybe it's too little, too late. If so, I'm sorry that I'm such a coward. My family scares the hell out of me. I couldn't wait to leave. I have not talked to my sisters or my brother since I left. And my parents ... I've only talked to them when they call, which isn't often. I might add, none of my siblings have reached out to me either."

"Did something happen before you left, something that caused this rift?" Janice asked.

"No. I just don't think, other than sharing the same womb, we had anything in common—that and the horror of our childhood. I am no more interested in rekindling a relationship with them than I am in shooting myself in the head. But this invitation seems like a perfect time for you to meet the people who were so instrumental in forging all of my peculiarities. I'm only sorry that I waited so long because you won't be able to meet Ethel. And her I did love."

Helen looked down, picking at a thread on her sweater. "Ethel ... she died two months ago, and I suppose her passing is part of the reason I'm feeling so compelled to go to this wedding. I need to put that part of my life behind me permanently."

"How do they feel about Asians?"

"I don't think they'll have a problem with Leah. Ethnicity doesn't seem to be an issue. But I can guarantee you that my sexual orientation will be a humdinger."

"Do you think the children should go?"

"You are actually considering coming with me?" Helen suddenly was not sure whether she was excited or horrified.

"Well, if you want me to meet the family, I don't know how else to do it. And I think the children should come too."

"The invitation is for Christmas and the wedding—do you think you can actually stomach that? I know how you feel about the crass commercialism of Christmas. I assure you, this will be Christmas on steroids, as crass and commercial as it gets." She laughed.

"Helen, I love you. I have no doubt I will find things to love about your family. They are, after all, a part of you. I promised to take you with the good and the bad, and just because it's inconvenient and unpleasant doesn't get me out of that promise. Who knows, maybe it will be fun."

Helen rolled her eyes. "That I sincerely doubt," she said as she sat down at her desk and filled out the reply card with a plus-three.

✌

"Eric, the invitation came today. Look at it. It's really pretty. You can say one thing for Virginia—she's got good taste. Crazy as a bag of badgers and quite possibly as mean, but she's got great taste, except in bridesmaids' dresses." Mackey laughed. "I am—really am—kind of looking forward to this affair." She handed her husband the envelopes.

He gave them a brief uninterested glance before placing one envelope neatly into the other and then setting the invitation back on the counter.

"Wouldn't it be fun if it snowed?" Mackey said. "We could all go sledding, like we did when we were kids. It will be so much fun for Joey to meet his cousins. Yes, I am looking forward to it—not so much to that bridesmaid's dress, though. Did you see it?"

Eric shook his head and looked at his wife hard. "You're asking *me*, who just barely remembers to put clothes on? You think I'd notice anything about a bridesmaid's dress other than it's a dress?"

"Good point," Mackey laughed. She went into the bedroom and brought it out. "Well, take a look. It is hideous. Eric, this is a hideous dress. You can program that into your mega-IQ mind. I think Virginia subscribes to the idea that no one should look even remotely as good as the bride." She laughed again as she hooked the hanger over the kitchen door.

If you liked it, then you should have put a ring on it … If you liked it, then you should have put a ring on it.

"Duly noted," Eric said. "I will not endeavor to buy a dress like that for you ever, not that I would ever be so bold as to think about buying a dress for you. What's so awful about it?"

"We could start with the color—puce. She says it's lavender, and if so, it is one butt-ugly shade of it, if you ask me. Guaranteed to make any skin tone go gray. And then we could move on from there."

… All the single ladies …

"Never mind," said Eric. "What are we going to eat?"

"We're going to Gran and PopPop's for dinner tonight. I told you this morning. I don't suppose you remember that I'm going to talk to PopPop about our discussion the other night? I don't hold out much hope for his being able to help me, but who knows? I suppose stranger things have happened."

"That's really great, honey," he said, racking his brain to remember what they had talked about and then deciding it might not hurt to ask. "You mean about the …" He let it drop and changed to a more immediate question. "Are they cooking? I didn't think your grandmother cooked. Do you want me to get Joey ready?"

"Sometimes …" She shook her head. "Yeah, that would be terrific. Gran has a lady, a relative of Ethel's, I think, who comes in to cook for them a couple times a week. I suspect Gran could poison us all."

If you liked it, then you should have put a ring on it … If you liked it, then you should have put a ring on it .

"Joooey!" Eric called, bumping the dress off the hanger as he passed.

Mackey bent over to pick it up and sighed. "It's only one night, and it's for Virginia. She likes it. Sooo … I hope I don't kill myself

with the shoes, though. I don't think I have ever worn heels that high. Hell, I didn't know they made heels that high. That would make the party: bridesmaid falls down and breaks her neck. Great headline. 'Bridesmaid tumbles to her death, clad in puke—er, puce!'"
Mackey looked around to see why Eric wasn't laughing and realized he had left the room.

He reemerged with Joey in tow. "He says he doesn't want to go to his great-gran's."

"Tough, big guy." She tousled his hair. "You go with us, or you stay home all alone with no food. What do you think?"

Joey pouted as he resisted a proffered jacket. "They're just so *ooold.*"

Eric laughed, gently teasing him as he attempted to get his son's arms into the sleeves. "What if they said that about you? 'Oh no, not Joey, he's just so yooooung!' Here, you do that thing you learned at school. I don't know why I am trying to put it on you anyway. You're big enough to put your own coat on."

"Give it here." Putting the coat on the floor, Joey stood next to it and somehow had it on and zipped up before either parent could figure out how he'd done it. "People like kids," he added. "Nobody likes old people."

"Joey!" both parents snapped.

"That's a terrible thing to say," Mackey said. *All the single ladies … Ugh, too much radio. Time for a talk with PopPop for sure. Got to break this insane constant chatter.*

"Or think," Eric added. "You don't think that, do you?"

"Nah." Joey shrugged impatiently. "Let's go. I'm hungry."

᳄

The first-grade family tree project was impossible. Potts's parents were too hard to pin down about what they did. That's when Potts and his best friend, Elliot, figured out that his dad had to be a spy. He looked the part, wearing tuxedos all the time, driving fancy sports cars, and accompanying pretty women to things called "premieres" and "screenings." Other kids' parents were doctors and lawyers, real estate developers and dentists—real jobs. Elliot's dad was a stockbroker. Elliot put pictures of ticker tapes, banks, and a Wall Street sign on his poster. Potts brought a picture of his mom since there were so many pictures of her in their apartment and since she was so beautiful. The boys had concluded she was a model. His Russian grandfather, Potts was pretty sure, must have been a soldier since he was dead, but his mother said he was a farmer. He put a small picture of a Russian soldier on the poster and then took it off. There was no reason to give the kids any other reason to make fun of him. His grandfather Gordon had a farm where they made milk, so he found a picture of a cow and glued that onto the poster board.

Potts had never met or even seen a picture of his grandfather Gordon or his grandmother Susan. He was looking forward to it since being on a farm sounded like one of the most fun things a kid could do—and for Christmas too! Besides that, he had a whole family to meet, including cousins he had never heard of before, even cousins his own age to play with. It was too bad his mother wouldn't be able to come, just like it was too bad that his parents didn't live together anymore. The new apartment was big, and it had a lot of light and lots of pictures of his mother—nothing not to like except that his dad didn't live there with them. Elliot's big brother and his friends all said Potts's mom was sexy. He didn't know about that. It wasn't something he and Elliot thought about. Girls their age were basically bossy and impossible.

What he did think about was why his parents couldn't have come up with a better name than Potts. His mother explained that it had been her father's name. When he thought about it, he decided that Potts was better than how his mother pronounced it, saying the full name: *Pattaub*. When she snuggled with him at bedtime, calling him her little *malysh* and *moya sladkaya*—her darling baby—he hated it. He asked her please not to say those things when Elliot spent the night. His friends laughed at her accent. He liked the way she talked. He liked that his mother seemed younger than his friends' mothers and prettier. Elliot's brother said she was *exotic*.

Elliot said that Potts's dad must be rich, since Potts and his mother lived in such a nice apartment and Potts could go to private school. Whatever. The only thing they couldn't figure out was, how do you get rich if your father's just a farmer? Elliot had overheard *his* mother saying to his dad that there were only two ways to get rich: "To inherit it or …" Potts and Elliot concluded the other thing must be illegal since she whispered it, and then she and Elliot's dad laughed like parents do when they talk about naughty stuff around each other. *Is being a spy illegal?* Potts wondered.

He'd seen the big fancy invitation on his dad's dresser when he spent the night last week. He wouldn't have dreamed of asking his father about it had he not seen his name on the envelope: *Master Stephan Pottaub Mackey.* He could just barely make it out because the writing was so fancy. And now here he was going to see his grandparents, his great-grandparents, his aunts and uncles, and most unbelievable of all, these cousins he hadn't even known existed. As exciting as the prospect was, he wondered what his mother would do for Christmas all alone in New York. He was sorry that his father had said no when he asked if she could come too. She said she hadn't been on a farm since she left Russia.

❧

They had a cousin named Potts? "Wow, what kinda name is Potts?" Sally asked.

Andy sat for some time, lost in his thoughts, before answering this child, who at seven was already able to run circles around him and any other grown-up within range. He didn't know what kind of name Potts was, and it had never occurred to him to ask.

Andy was Susan and Gordon's second son and a modest, down-to-earth man who had given up his childhood dream of working alongside his father on the farm for what he had been told was a better idea—something more, well, professional if not prestigious. Desperate for his older brother Trey's approval, he'd chosen managing a feed store over "letting shit-assed cows run his life." *That was what Trey had said, wasn't it?* He'd asked himself that question way more than once. Andy had been married unhappily for enough years to produce two children whom he adored. His wife had just recently divorced him, on the heels of running away with a much more interesting guy—of whom, in her mind, there were many.

"Potts's mother is Russian," he said to Sally, reaching out to rumple her hair. "I think he's named after his grandfather. Potts is a nickname for some kind of Russian name that no one can pronounce," he added, editing out the multiple unkindnesses he had heard from his father on the subject.

At nine, Josh, a true ginger-white redhead with orange freckles and cornflower-blue eyes, knew these things. "If he is Uncle Trey's son, then we have the same grandfather, and his name is Gordon," he pointed out. "And I don't think he is Russian."

"Is he?" Sally asked as she twirled her long strawberry locks, forcing herself not to suck on the ends, as her mother reminded her on a daily basis.

"No, just like you two had Scottish grandparents on your mom's side, Potts had two Russian grandparents. And I think, just like your Scottish grandparents, Potts's grandparents are dead. You are very lucky to have two grandparents who are still alive," he said.

"We have Gran and PopPop too," Sally added. "Does Potts have a Gran and PopPop?"

"Yep, they are the same as ours," Josh said. "That's how we are related. He is our cousin, just like Joey has the same Gran and PopPop."

"He and Uncle Trey are going to stay with us for Christmas?"

"No, we are all going to stay at Gran and PopPop's for Christmas. All of us." Andy sighed, not at all sure he was looking forward to this family adventure. At least he would have the kids for Christmas.

There was that. He prayed that his mother wouldn't drink this year. *How many Christmases have been ruined by drink?* he wondered.

"Not Mom," Sally said. "She said something about wild horses. I don't know, but I don't think she wants to come for Christmas or the wedding." After a short pause to consider, she asked, "Does Gran have wild horses?" Her blonde eyebrows knitted together over light blue eyes.

"No, Gran does not have wild horses. It's okay. Your mother doesn't have to come. But she did say you two could. It'll be fun to meet your whole entire family, don't you think?" He wasn't sure about it but was going to try for the children's sake to make the best of it.

Sally quickly corrected her father, her pudgy little face screwed up in an earnest need to right her father's statement. "Not all! Mom won't be there or Uncle Cam and Aunt Mora, or Mom's other brother," she said, trying to remember her uncle's name.

"Right, *my* whole family." Andy sighed again as he ran his fingers through his thinning mouse-brown hair. *This kid has a legal mind if anybody does.* She made him laugh, though he knew the Lord had sent her to test his patience. Patience, he prayed, would be in short supply this Christmas season. He knew this holiday was going to test him. He dreaded the idea of spending time with his brother after all of these years. Trey had a way of making him feel small and stupid. It wasn't like he ever said so, but Andy could tell he thought so.

6

Mackey found that talking with her grandmother a few weeks earlier after dinner had focused her attention on the need for a change. Her lack of patience at the slightest perceived upset and her increasing irritation with everyone around her were undeniable. When an article on the detrimental effects of noise pollution on the human psyche popped up a day after her conversation with Ginny, it had seemed like a cue—with suggestions for how to alleviate the symptoms of her discontent. Since it was her day off, she decided to turn the alarm off just to see if she could wake up without benefit of any noise or outside stimuli, as the article suggested. To her surprise and delight, she awoke at exactly the time the alarm would have rung. She gently nudged Eric awake. After a few minutes of tender lovemaking, they got out of bed, amazed at what a difference such a small change could make. "Luxurious!" Eric proclaimed, grinning from ear to ear. "Better than any alarm clock. Let's throw that sucker out and find other ways to reduce noise. I am all over this idea."

It was amazing to discover how much noise she had automatically programmed into her day. Now, as she got Joey up and fixed breakfast, she caught herself in the habit—so ingrained that it had been completely unconscious—of turning on the television as she entered a room. While making coffee, she counted three times she had to stop herself from clicking on the TV.

Getting Joey ready for school, she discovered, was far easier without the distraction of the tube, even if it was just the news and seemingly of no interest to a little boy. Breakfast was awkward since the local morning show had previously filled what now appeared to be a vacuum. When Eric complained, she reminded him of their conversation and their little interlude that morning.

"Yeah, I know. I just hadn't counted on it being so hard. I guess that's pretty telling, isn't it?"

Joey's complaints were bitter and not nearly as easily assuaged. "I don't know why we have to give up watching TV. It seems stupid to me."

"Only for a week," his father reminded him. "We just want to see what difference it'll make in our lives."

As Mackey backed the car out of the garage, a news flash grabbed her attention, announcing the probability of a large snowstorm over the weekend. Sitting at the bottom of the driveway, waiting for the school bus, she zoned out as a commercial for pest control rambled on about the benefits of green, year-round vigilance against roaches and other vermin. Only when Jocy shouted from the back seat, "Here comes the bus," did she realize that the radio had come on automatically and just as automatically had sucked her in. Horrified at the insidious nature of the level of noise that she'd been accepting as normal, she quickly snapped it off before jumping out of the car to help her son out of his booster seat.

She stole a quick kiss as she lifted him out from the car. "I'll pick you up today, okay? There's a note in your lunch box telling your teacher. Bye, honey. I hope you have a great day." She stood at the car and watched as he climbed onto the bus. They had a pact that she wouldn't kiss him on the bus steps.

"It's too embarrassing, Mom," he had explained shortly after the school year started.

As she pulled the car back into the garage, she decided that once she was inside, she would try the second recommendation the article had suggested: to sit quietly for fifteen minutes.

As the morning continued, Eric seemed to be taking forever to leave the house. "Don't you have an early class today?" she asked, eager to have the house to herself.

"I don't have office hours until ten. Is there something you want me to do for you?" He looked up from some notes for his seminar.

"Well ..." She hesitated, feeling a little awkward. "I was hoping to try to meditate for fifteen minutes, and I guess I thought it would be easier if I was alone."

"You go ahead. I've got stuff to do, and if the phone rings, you won't have to worry about having to answer it. You sure have embraced this elimination of noise pollution in a big way. I'm impressed."

"If you had spent the last few years in my head, you would too," she replied, a little defensively.

"I'm not criticizing," Eric reassured her. "I'm as big an offender as anyone. I'm thinking these kinds of changes might help me be less ditzy, actually. I've been thinking for a while that I might try meditation. How about we try it together?"

"Okay, but if the phone rings, then what?" She'd already embraced the idea of his taking that noise distraction off her plate.

"We can take it off the hook for fifteen minutes. Okay?"

Mackey found herself resisting the very suggestion of unplugging from a key source of noise. *This is harder than I expected*, she thought. "Umm, where do you want to do this?" She caught herself looking around for a quiet corner in order to claim it first. *Man, you have got it bad, kid. No use beating yourself up, though.* She tried a new tack. "What I've read about meditation is that just sitting quietly with no agenda is the best way to start. Can we try that?" She was surprised at how vulnerable she felt sharing this with Eric.

"Sure, we can sit on the sofa if you want, or I can go in the other room if that would be more comfortable. Whatever you want."

"Are you nervous too?" she asked.

He nodded. "I feel like it's the first time we're kissing or something. It's odd." They laughed. "I think I'll go in the other room, okay?"

For ten of the fifteen agreed-upon minutes, Mackey sat quietly, casually checking in with her breathing while steering clear of too many thoughts. When she opened her eyes to find that only ten minutes had passed, she was profoundly disappointed. The next five minutes were torture as she berated herself for so little self-control. Finally giving up at fourteen minutes and twenty seconds, she got up to check on Eric. Finding him on the sofa in what appeared to be a blissed-out state totally infuriated her. It took every bit of will-power she had not to interrupt him. She eased herself into a chair and watched him for the remaining minutes.

Even before his eyes blinked open completely, she was on him with questions, trying to ascertain his secret. "I knew you would be better at this than I would be."

"This is not a competition," he reminded her. "Besides, I'm not sure I was doing it right. I sat there getting lost in my thoughts just like I always do. I think you aren't supposed to think. What were you doing?"

"For the first ten minutes I was sort of just there, aware that I was there but not thinking so much. When I opened my eyes and found out only ten minutes had passed, I jumped all over my shit. I started listening to the noise in my head—you know, the 'I'm stupid, the can't get it right' on-and-on drill that I do."

"Maybe we should just keep trying and see if it gets any easier. I'm not sure anybody reaches enlightenment right away." He sat on the arm of her chair and let himself slide down next to her. "It's a start." He kissed her tenderly. "San Jose wasn't built in a day."

She laughed. "No, I don't suppose it was."

He put the house phone back on the hook and then picked it up again to check for any messages. There were three from Virginia. "It could be worse," he laughed as he handed the phone to Mackey.

⁓

Ginny and Joe snuggled in the sitting room, lit only by the Christmas tree and a roaring fire, watching snowflakes swirl outside. Gomer came over to them, put his giant head in Joe's lap, and whined. Joe patted his wrinkled brow. He was about to pat the cushion when Ginny shook her head. "Let's not share the sofa with the dogs tonight. He can go lie down next to Daisyduke at the fire."

Joe pointed toward the fire. "Go lie down." The big dog lumbered away.

"I love this room when it snows," Ginny said. "The wall of windows, it's just perfect for snow watching."

Joe nodded in agreement. "It was brilliant on your part."

"I wasn't tooting my own horn," Ginny said, stiffening.

"I didn't think you were," he answered. "I think you have an extraordinary eye for this kind of detail. You know what you like, and you know how to get it."

"That tree is some kind of spectacular." Ginny gazed up at the fifteen-foot spruce that Virginia had had installed by a cavalcade of tree trimmers the day before. "Now there's a girl who can get things done. Easily a hundred people decorated the tree." She laughed. "Hope they are going to stick around to take it down. I can't even imagine how much money that girl is spending. And I am glad I don't have to."

She leaned into Joe's shoulder, pulled the throw over them, and listened to his beating heart. "Honey, I don't want you to die. I love you. I love the life we have together. I love being with you. And honestly, I don't think I could stand it if you left without me."

Joe pulled her closer. "I know, sweetie. It's not time. I was wrong. It was arrogant of me to think that I had that kind of power or that it was even possible. And I can only imagine how hurtful it was for you to hear me yammer about wanting to move on. I'm sorry. Last thing in the world I'd want to do is hurt you." They kissed a long, slow, sweet kiss and then sat in the silence, watching the snow fall and the crackling fire.

After a while Ginny said, "The snow is beautiful, and it's very romantic, but I'm heartbroken that because of it Helen can't come."

Joe nodded in agreement.

"I didn't realize airports closed down in anticipation of bad weather."

"Apparently, this is being billed as the storm of the century," Joe said. "Talking about feet of snow in some places and in others multiple yards of it. I think the entire city of Chicago has been closed down already. This squall we see is just the beginning."

"Well, anyway, it was wonderful to talk to Helen tonight. Can you imagine that she honestly didn't think we knew she was gay? And she thought we'd think less of her because of it! That hurts. It really does. To think she stayed away that long. It's so sad, really. But I'm glad that she has Janice. She seemed very sweet. I enjoyed our chat."

"It's funny that Helen chose a black man to father her child. Things really do go full circle," Joe said thoughtfully.

"You mean since my first love was a black boy?" She started to laugh. "Even if he was my brother. What a life we have led."

Joe got up to poke the fire and throw another log on. "I could get used to this—fires laid and extra dry wood stacked nearby, meals magically appearing and the remains disappearing just as magically. Virginia has anticipated our every want."

"It'll all disappear just like in the fairy tales once Bridezilla turns into the wicked wife from the north," Ginny cackled. "It's too bad that Gord can't get out of Chicago. I imagine you heard Virginia this afternoon *talking*—I use the term loosely—to the airline people about her brother's flight. Good God almighty, she could have made a stevedore blush. Do they still have those?"

"Blushing stevedores?" Joe laughed and shook her shoulders lovingly. "We need to be nice. We are talking about our granddaughter." Joe snickered. "Speaking of whom, She Who Must Be Obeyed has gone to the station to meet Alex's train. I hope she can drive in this stuff—although I venture to say, there is nothing that girl can't do. However, she would do well to remember Ethel's axiom: you catch more flies with honey than vinegar." They both laughed.

"She is a firebrand!" Ginny giggled. "God help that hapless

husband of hers. And she certainly runs roughshod over Sallee. Never could I have imagined that Sallee would turn out to be so servile. She always seemed so independent and strong-minded as a child. It's good that they came down today. I'm not sure they would have been able to come tomorrow, private jet or no. Though I imagine Peter would be happy to miss this whole affair. I don't get the impression that he is particularly taken with his daughter's choice, or having a wedding in the bosom of Sallee's family. He makes such a strange show of belonging while pushing us away with hands and feet."

"Virginia probably wore Sallee down," Joe said. "And as far as Virginia's choice is concerned, I doubt this is the first time Peter's had to adjust his opinion to suit his tiny tyrant. It's cute that she's so tiny—it makes her a little less draconian. As far as his attitude toward us, I don't even bother."

"Yeah, but Virginia didn't get that way in a vacuum, size not withstanding."

"I think Sallee couldn't stand up to Peter. He does spoil the kid rotten. You remember what it was like that Thanksgiving, don't you? I guess she decided it was better to go along and get along. Otherwise, there would have been a constant fight."

Ginny shook her head. "That was quite the holiday, with Sallee in childbirth and both of them insisting no one else could baby-sit their delicate daughter. Virginia wanted every toy Mackey had. I would have loved to have seen Ethel with 'grown-up'"—she put the last word in air quotes—"Virginia. That would have been a sight." Ginny laughed.

"I forgot to tell you of the latest drama," Joe said. "The tent people were supposed to put the tents up today but didn't and wouldn't because of the storm."

"I can't even imagine what kind of hell rained down on them."

Joe sat up with twinkling eyes. "Well, at least as of now, the caterers and the bartender are still on, and it's a good thing. You know, we could get snowed in with our beloveds for quite a long while, in which case let's skip the scotch and take some hemlock together."

"Deal," Ginny laughed.

❧

Spurred on by the changes he saw in the tiny bit of meditation he and Mackey had tried, Eric applied his academic research approach to the problem of learning to meditate. After asking everyone in the physics department and everyone he knew in the psychology department, he came upon a meditation practice that centered on the heart. It seemed like the perfect approach for the two of them. A friend in the psychology department was doing experiments in heart-centered meditation and happened to be looking for volunteers. Eric signed the two of them up without even pausing to ask Mackey if it would interest her, so sure he was that she would embrace the idea.

This behavior was such a departure from his usual mode that Mackey, rather than react with anger, decided at least to listen. After all, what did they have to lose?

"One of the advantages is that we're going to be taught a specific type of meditation, and besides having a baseline test done at the beginning of the study and another at the end, the only requirement is to be there—and oh, to keep a diary during the whole thing." Eric was bubbling with an enthusiasm Mackey hadn't seen in years, and she couldn't help but go along.

After having their baselines checked and learning the technique, they plunged into the project like explorers on a new planet. Each stage of the experience was shared and marveled over. Mackey discovered that she was afraid of her heartbeat. "It creeps me out," she told Eric after a meditation session. "It's something about being conscious of how important the organ is to me, I guess. I'm not sure what it is, but I am afraid of it. I think in a way I always have been— when I think about it, I never wanted to listen to it *or* for it." She sighed. "I guess this isn't going to work for me if I am afraid to get in touch with the major focus of the study. It's odd—I always thought I was so heart-centered, and here I am looking for my heartbeat while trying to avoid it at the same time. There's a contradiction for you!"

"Don't give up," he countered encouragingly. "Haven't you noticed big changes? I know I have."

"Yeah, but how do I know it isn't because we've turned off so much of the outside noise?"

"I don't know. I guess the best way to find out would be to turn the outside noise back on and see," he suggested. "You can do it. I don't want to. I didn't realize how much all of that noise made me retreat into myself—and not in a good way," he hastily added, "like in meditation. More like I crawled into a cave and came out only when I had to. Haven't you noticed that I'm more present? Not so much of an airhead? I have." He looked so earnestly at Mackey that she had to laugh.

"I don't care if it comes from less outside noise or from meditation," he continued. "I am not going to jeopardize my progress to find out, despite how it might be skewing the study."

"And you a scientist too." Mackey mockingly shook her head. "I get what you're saying. I don't guess I mind where the peace is coming from either. Besides, this kind of irrational fear probably needs to be confronted, not avoided." She stopped, bit the side of her lip, and then asked, "Don't you think?"

He looked perplexed.

"I mean," she said, "don't you think that it is an irrational fear? And that it needs confrontation?"

"Absolutely! Let's just keep at it and see where it takes us. You can ask my friend. She said if you have any questions, to ask."

☙

The next morning brought a cloudy Christmas Eve, but the snow had stopped, leaving less than three inches on the ground. At breakfast, the chatter was all kinds of congratulatory bravado. Peter laughed.

"All of that gloom and doom for this." He waved his arm toward the window as he snickered. "Even weather is entertainment these days."

"I wouldn't count those chickens just yet," Joe said. "I don't think we have seen the last of this storm."

Sallee walked in, having just gotten off the phone with Gord. "I think Dad's right. If we get anything like a third of what Chicago got, we'll be here until spring."

Peter groaned loudly. "Please, God, no."

Joe didn't say it, but he seconded Peter's lament.

Sallee began to fuss. "Do you think we should call this whole thing off?"

"If only we could," Peter muttered under his breath, but audibly. Aloud, he asked, "What would be the point? We are all here now."

"What if the electricity goes out?"

Peter shook his head. "Sallee, stop it. Have you seen the fleet of generators Virginia has out there? I think she could power the Pentagon for a week if need be," he grumbled. "Weathermen can be wrong, and storms can change course. All due respect, Joe, maybe this is all we're going to get."

Joe laughed and said, "Maybe. Sallee, the whole house is wired to our generator, and there is plenty of oil in the tank and the barn too. You don't need to worry. We'll be fine. Hopefully, it won't come to that. But it does appear that we need a fallback position for the tent."

"Virginia has already taken care of that," Sallee said. "I don't know how. Put the bartender in a corner of the living room, for starters. And the caterers are still aboard ... I can't imagine how much it's going to cost, but Virginia says she's got it all worked out. She is still working on trying to get Gord here. I tried to tell her that the airports were closed down. There was no way anybody would by flying in or out of Chicago, but as usual, she wouldn't listen." Sallee ended with a sigh.

Just then Joey raced into the room and jumped into his great-grandfather's lap.

"Hey, big man!" Joe gave his namesake a big hug. "Where are your mom and dad?"

Joey pointed outside.

"Do you know who these people are?" Joe asked.

Joey buried his head in Joe's sweater. "No" was his muffled reply.

"Of course you don't. That was a silly question. Turn around and look! This is your great-aunt Sallee and your great-uncle Peter. Can you say hello?"

A tentative hello and a head duck was all the greeting they got.

"He is adorable! Mackey's?" Sallee gushed. "Though I hate being called a great-aunt. That seems so old."

"You are," Joey stated flatly.

The room broke into laughter.

"Thanks for that, kid," Sallee chuckled, tousling his hair.

☙

Later that afternoon, Sallee and Peter sat working in front of another fireplace where a fire had been laid, only awaiting a match to be struck. Peter had been perusing his e-mail when all of a sudden he took his glasses off, laid them on the table in front of him, put his elbows on his knees and his head in his hands, and groaned.

"What's the matter? Has something happened?" Sallee's voice rose in panic as her husband stared dumbly at the floor. "What?" She had to keep herself from shouting.

Finally, Peter sat up, pinched the bridge of his nose, wiped his glasses, put them back on, and asked, "Do you know who G. S. Mackey III is?"

"You mean Gordy's son? Did something happen to him?"

"Yes, I mean Gordy's son. Gordy's son—your nephew—G. S. III, a.k.a. Trey Mackey. I can't believe I didn't put this together before. It just kept niggling at me, so I asked that new kid at the office—what's his name? Nat, I think—to do a little digging. I remembered that Virginia said that Ginny had told her he was some sort of producer." He stood up and starting opening cupboards. "There's got to be some booze here somewhere."

Sallee pointed to a cabinet. "I think it's there. Would you please tell me what has happened?"

He found the scotch, poured himself a big glass of it, downed it, poured another one, and brought the bottle and another glass back to the chair with him. "Nothing has happened. Do you remember the name of the production company that supposedly hired Alex?"

"No ... I don't know ... some ridiculous name. Seat of the Pants or something absurd like that. Why?"

"Yeah, it is an absurdly ridiculous name all right. FlyBy."

Sallee nodded in agreement. "That's it. What the hell is going on?"

"Do you know who owns FlyBy?"

"Would you stop asking me these asinine questions and tell me what's going on?" she snapped.

"G. S. Mackey III is the sole owner of FlyBy Productions, which just so happens to produce pornography. Our soon-to-be son-in-law, employed by said production company, goes by the stage name Angus LeBoeuf."

It was Sallee's turn to put her head in her hands and groan. "Do you think Virginia knows this?"

"I certainly hope not." He enunciated every word precisely as he offered her a full glass of scotch. She took it and made a major dent in it before they both leaned back against the sofa and laughed until tears streamed down their faces. They'd stop to gasp for breath, then mutter, "Angus LeBoeuf," and burst out laughing again. When she was finally able to speak without cracking up, Sallee asked, "What in hell are we going to do?"

"Murder comes to mind," Peter deadpanned. Then more seriously, he said, "I don't think we should do anything just yet. I, for one, am not interested in blowing your nephew's cover, although I would love to string him up by his slimy little balls. With as many shell companies as G. S. III has set up, it is obvious FlyBy is on the down-low."

"I would certainly hope so," Sallee sniffed. "It makes me sick. Gordy and Susan, particularly Susan, will be mortified."

"Exactly. So let's keep this on the DL ourselves for the time being. We have a few days before the wedding. This storm might actually be a blessing. You might suggest that we postpone until after the holidays, when the weather is more cooperative."

"It would sit better coming from you," Sallee said. "She's not all that responsive to me. I'd say more reactive, actually."

❧

In his usual I-own-the-place manner, Trey sauntered into the living room—mere *walking*, after all, was so pedestrian. The tiniest bit undone that no one acknowledged his arrival, he went over to the bar, ordered a Dewar's neat, and then turned around to discover Virginia at his elbow.

"My mother tells me—" She stopped and smiled. "Wait, let me back up. Hi, I'm Virginia." She laughed. "I don't think we've seen each other—actually, I know we haven't seen each other—since I was a little tiny kid. I don't remember it."

He glanced down, correcting his automatic dismissive response as he recalled that Virginia had the starring role in this production, not any of his. "Oh, hey, good to see you." He air-kissed her upturned cheek. "What a great idea, this"—he waved expansively with a perfectly manicured hand adorned with a gold crest ring—"getting the family together." He assayed his younger cousin's physical attributes and then abandoned work mode, but not before thinking, *Pity you have to get married*. He chuckled. "I haven't seen these people since I was teenager. I think I remember what you're talking about. Even happened here, as I remember. No, not here exactly—this house is new—but somewhere around here?"

They both shrugged.

"Somehow I was roped into babysitting. I guess Ethel … no, Ethel was here. So I guess I really wasn't in charge. It had something to do with … well, Sallee—I mean, your mom—was clearly running the show somewhere." He tried to imagine himself as a babysitter and laughed.

Virginia continued, "Mom tells me that you orchestrated quite a production with Andy, Mackey, and me. It must've been over Christmas. I think Gord was Jesus?" She laughed. "I hear you're still in production."

Trey puffed up reflexively, glad to know that he was known. "Oh, that's right. Your parents are both in the entertainment business."

"Well, yeah. They do not entertain. Believe me." She giggled. "Mostly they just keep everybody in the business from hurting each other." They both laughed.

"It's a pretty brutal business," he agreed. "Where is the lucky man?" he asked as he surveyed the surrounding family clusters.

Virginia stood on tiptoe, casting about until she found Alex. "He's over there," she said, pointing, "next to the window, see? Mackey and I call him my little lamb. See his fuzzy head?" She smiled. "His hair reminds us of that sheep. You probably know. You must have played with it too. Remember? It was wooden and had white curly wool …" She stopped, seeing that Trey was not at all interested in a long-ago play toy. He was much more of a current player. She didn't like the way his eyes narrowed as he watched her fiancé.

Finally, he asked, "Do I know him?"

"I don't know." Virginia was baffled. But then, they all did live in New York. "Where would you have met him?"

"What does he do?" Trey asked uneasily. Meeting an associate in his line of work could be awkward at the best of times. He made an effort to keep himself away from the sets for just that reason.

"He's an actor. Actually, since you own a production company, you really ought to keep him in mind."

"I would think your parents could give him lots of contacts."

"My parents are very strict about one thing—truth be told, only one thing. They do not believe in nepotism. I had to get my own job. Couldn't work for the family firm. Gord got his own job too, in Chicago. That why he's not here."

Trey looked at her quizzically.

"The snow. Gordon, my brother—he's in Chicago and can't get out. So anyway, Alex is on his own. Stupid, really."

"It is certainly a shame," Trey sympathized. "They must have a hell of a Rolodex."

"Oh well. Daddy says we'll thank him one day. I guess. Come on over and meet Alex." She waved to her fiancé across the room just as a waiter approached.

"Excuse me, miss. My boss asked if you would come to the kitchen for a minute." Turning to Trey, he asked, "Can I get you another drink?"

Trey nodded, put his empty glass on the proffered tray, and ordered another. He spied his grandmother and made his way over to greet her. Giving Ginny a hug, he said, "Gran, it's lovely to meet"—he quickly corrected himself—"to see you again." He meant it, despite his rather stiff demeanor. Turning on his charm, he continued, "You look phenomenal. No one would ever guess that you were a day over fifty-five. I know that can't be the case, since I'm close enough to fifty myself."

Ginny laughed. "Trey, you are as charming as ever and no better at telling fibs. Do you remember the time that you wrote your name in the table and blamed it on Andy? Who might have been two at the time. Ethel caught you red-handed, and you still …"

Time melted away for Trey as the memory came flooding back.

"Honest, I didn't do it. I don't know who did. Andy, it was Andy. I'm sure it was Andy!" Trey flinched reflexively, desperate not to get hit.

"Trey, honey, you best not be tellin' me no tales." Ethel found it hard to glower down at the boy—hands on hips, head shaking— since she adored him. "You know good as me Andy can't write, an' from what I can see, you got de pen in yo' hand. You's in enough trouble. Why you go an' do such a thang?"

The boy looked up at Ethel and began to cry. "Ethel, don't hit me. I didn't do it."

"Darlin', I ain't gonna hit you." She shook her head, deciding not to ask him who did.

"Yo grandmomma ain't goin' t' be happy when she gets home an' finds dat you been tellin' tales, not t' mention somebody done wrote yo' name on her dinin' room table. Now is she?"

"Does she have to know? Promise, Ethel, I didn't do it."

"I don't' see how she could miss it. But you tellin' stories dat ain't true' 'bout it gonna make thangs go worse fo' you." She chuckled. "So how 'bout we start wit' tellin' de truth an' den we can see what we can do 'bout dis here."

"Okay, Andy didn't do it," Trey admitted. "But neither did I."

"Who did den?" Ethel asked, her head tilted to the side, one eyebrow cocked, lips pursed.

"This robber came into …"

"Honey, dey ain't …"

"Okay, maybe I did, but I didn't mean to," he hastily said. "Please don't tell Granny Morga. She gets awful mad when …"

"Don't' you worry none 'bout dat. I ain't tellin' her nothin'. Let's see if we can fix dis," she said as she took the child by the hand and led him down into the basement. "I 'spect it's gonna take some work. You is gonna have t' help." She looked down at him.

He nodded his head, eager to do whatever she wanted.

"I don't think I'll ever forget that." Trey laughed nervously, striving to conceal the fact that he not only had forgotten it but now was shaken to his very core by the memory. He'd worked hard to stuff his past away and had been sure his efforts had paid off, or he never would have risked coming back for this, never. "Ethel did a pretty good job of fixing the table, as I remember."

Ginny nodded. "She did. You can hardly tell. And look at you now—very distinguished, those little touches of gray in that gorgeous copper mane of yours. You don't dye it, do you?" she added, with a mischievous twinkle in her eye. "That reminds me of the time when Joe and I were on an extended trip to Ireland. I asked a girl who had fantastic copper hair, much like yours, where she got it done. Can you imagine?"

As his grandmother blathered on, Trey felt a tension take hold of his gut and start to rise. He ceased listening as he tried to will himself to breathe normally. What was "normally"? Was he in fact breathing?

Ginny meanwhile was chattering on: "... sure that her colorist must be phenomenal to have achieved such a magnificently flawless shade—it couldn't be natural. She gave me the name, and I made an appointment for the very next day, to have this obvious artist work her magic on me."

His heart pounded against his chest wall. He took out his hand-kerchief to wipe his brow, trying to concentrate on his grandmother's words and curb the desire to gasp for air. His lungs refused to function in their usual manner, and each breath felt more labored than the last.

"So eager was I that the grubby exterior of the shop didn't put me off. You know, true artists and all that. The long and short of it is, my hair was fried. The women had no more idea how to color hair than I did."

They both laughed. Seizing the clue his grandmother had left at the end, Trey jumped on it, hoping that whatever he said would make sense. "I didn't know you colored your hair. I assumed it was always that beautiful color naturally." He smiled and gave her a wink, surprised that no one could hear his heart racing and also that he was able to put together a coherent sentence.

"This," she said, touching a lock of her newly shorn hair, "is all me, as if you paid attention to such things then. When was it that we last saw each other, anyway? Oh, and where's Potts? Didn't he come?"

"Maybe my graduation from Woodberry? Potts is in our room. I didn't know what the protocol was."

Ginny shot him a confused look. "Protocol?"

Trey was stammering to explain when Susan appeared from behind. "It is good to see you, son," she said in her usual understated way. Trey hadn't had time to steel himself for her. She reached out as if to hug him, and when there was no reciprocation, she withdrew. "You look well. Where is Potts?"

Quick to see this as an exit strategy, he announced, "I was just on my way to get him. Back in a sec." He forced himself to exit the room as casually as possible, fighting the urge to run. Once out in the cold, he leaned up against a column, squatted down, and put his head down between his knees to stem the rising panic. Gulping in the cold air, he felt he couldn't get enough. *I can leave now. I can tell Potts that something's come up, totally unexpected, and we have to fly back tonight.* He straightened up, pulled out his phone, checked his e-mail to be sure of the airline before dialing, and waited, more anxious than he could remember feeling in a very long time. *Damn it, what was I thinking, coming here? I must have been out of my mind.* The call didn't go through, nor did the subsequent twenty-one.

He had taken to pacing in a circle while running his fingers through his hair, when he wasn't clutching at his chest, where his heart still pounded against the chest wall. He was so absorbed that he didn't notice Andy's approach.

"Hello, big brother."

Trey jumped at the sound of Andy's voice.

"Are you all right? What are you doing out here?"

"Something's come up. I've got to get back to New York tonight," Trey stammered. "Hey, good to see you." He willed himself to act as normal as possible, though he felt transparent as glass. "Who are these little guys?"

"I hope whatever you need to get back to can wait. There's a blizzard out there, and it's Christmas Eve. I don't see anybody leaving here anytime in the near future." Andy turned to the children.

"Kids, this is your Uncle Trey. Trey, this is my son, Josh, and my daughter, Sally."

Both children stepped up and offered their hands to their uncle. Trey reached down to shake each hand, still struggling in vain for his accustomed big-man-in-town composure.

The little girl, bold as brass, pumped his hand vigorously. "Hi, Uncle Trey. I'm Sally with a 'y.' Where's Potts?"

"Uh, he's in our room. I was just going to get him when I got the call that …"

"We'll get him." The children were off before either man could protest. All Trey could do was groan.

Andy was now truly concerned. "Man, are you okay? You look terrible. You are standing out here in a blizzard without a coat, sweating like a pig."

"Thanks, I feel like it too." His mind immediately latched onto this as his next best exit option. "Yeah, it must have been something I ate. I gotta go lie down. Tell them I'm a bit under the weather, would you?" Trey made a motion of feeling his forehead for fever.

"Sure," Andy said. "Be … glad … to." *Didn't you just say you had to go to New York? Mm-hmm. Up to your old tricks, I see.* But rather than confront his older brother, he took the cue and went with it. "Can I get you anything? You don't need to go to the hospital, do you?"

Trey shook his head and then thought, *If we can get to a hospital, then why not the airport?* He immediately dismissed the idea. The airport would be shut up tighter than a tourniquet. He came back to real time to find his little brother cooperatively taking charge.

"Well, don't worry about Potts. We'll keep him out of your hair. I'm pretty sure I'm going to be asked, so I'll make the offer. He can stay with us tonight. Okay?"

"Yeah, sure." *Might as well not ruin his Christmas.* Trey's mind and heart were still racing to come up with his next move. He certainly couldn't stay in his room forever, and the growing wall of snow beyond the porch roof didn't offer much hope for an early retreat.

It looked as if indeed they might all be here a long while. Or at any rate, it might feel that way.

҂

Back in his room, Trey paced a route defined and peppered by his son's belongings, absently picking up the child's toys or clothes and then dropping them again as he berated himself for his feelings and for thinking he could pull off this family visit. "Jesus, what was I thinking?" he muttered. "I don't belong here. These people and I don't have anything in common. I am almost positive that kid has a part in our latest film. I know I've seen him. It would be just swell if he recognized me, and shit, his parents are in the business. How could I have missed that? No, get a grip, not his parents—her parents. Christ …" His heart really felt like it was about to explode. He lay down on the bed and then jumped to his feet, reeling from vertigo caused by the head rush. He grabbed for the edge of the table until he recovered his balance. If he hadn't brought Potts, he could have just let himself crash. Couldn't let his kid find him dead on the floor in a pool of blood, though. Couldn't let his son know what he really was.

There was no choice. He had to keep moving. His pacing resumed, as did multiple variations of his previous thoughts. He picked up his phone, dialed the airline again, and held his breath again, this time to disappointment when a recording came on the line. The obnoxiously smooth female voice informed him that due to a severe winter storm, all flights had been canceled. No flights were scheduled until further notice. The recording invited him to check back periodically for any updates and thanked him for "choosing us as your airline." He fought the primal urge to scream.

And then, just like when he was a kid, that sinking feeling started to engulf him. It had always happened when he heard the footsteps approaching, the dread threatening to swallow him up whole or to suck him down into its depths—like before he'd quite learned to swim, when he saw the shore's edge so near, excited and reaching out, only to find that it was too far away. Did he have enough air? Would he make it? Did he have the strength? The more space fear occupied, the lower he had sunk. His arms and legs had flailed impotently. Water washed over him as his wild struggling forced him down—too far, too, too far. But this time it wasn't the water. This time it was so many questions feeding the fear. Unknowns—the water, the depths, the unknown. But this time was different—never had his heart figured in before. Had it just skipped a beat? Did it always make that drub-dub? It was a heart attack; it had to be—nothing else it could be. What were the symptoms again? What were you supposed to do? In swimming, they always said if you got in trouble, all you needed to do was relax and you'd float to the surface. *How the fuck do you relax when your heart is threatening to beat through your chest wall?* he wondered.

7

Virginia strode out of the kitchen looking like a gunslinger hoping someone would cross her. After much searching, she found Ginny, Stuart, and Sallee chatting together. "Just the people I'm looking for," the younger woman said, practically snarling. "The caterer has to leave. It's Christmas Eve, and apparently the storm is raging." She gave a dismissive eye roll. "And *they* are worried that they won't be able to get home. I offered to pay them more if they would stay"—by now she was pouting in disbelief—"but nobody took me up on the offer."

Sallee sighed pointedly, and Stuart cut in. "Well, it is Christmas Eve. I'm sure people want to get home to their families."

"I'm sure," Virginia agreed as she tried to get a grip on her irritation. Had her mother been the one to say that, she would have snapped her head off. Aunt Stuart was a bit of a different matter, not so easy to manage. "Anyway, they are going to put dinner out on the sideboard in fifteen minutes, and we are going to have to take it from there," she grumbled. "Could anything else go wrong?"

"Darling, that's not so wrong. I honestly believe we can manage to feed ourselves," Ginny chuckled. "Most of us have been at it for years. And as far as cleaning up, how hard can that be?"

Mackey, coming in from the hall, chimed in. "I couldn't help overhearing. But really, that isn't a big deal. Caterers have containers for everything. You don't even have to wash the plates—just scrape them, put them in their bins, and stack the bins outside. I'll be happy to do that. Have you seen the snow? It is amazing. It might actually be too deep and dangerous to go sledding tonight in the dark. It's really coming down. But if anybody's up for it, I'm in."

God, I feel like I am trapped at Sunnybrook Farm, Virginia fumed inwardly. *Golly gee, shucks, so much for my fabulous country wedding.* Then she rallied, congratulating herself privately on her good humor. "This reminds me of that Katherine Hepburn movie, remember? You know, where they're marooned in a snowstorm. They had a horse-drawn sleigh? Does anybody know what I'm talking about?"

"I think it was called *Holiday*," Ginny said. "I always thought she was so glamorous."

Virginia smiled. "Me too. Yeah, let's go sledding after dinner. Maybe Uncle Gordon can pull us around in the inner tube. Do you remember that?" she said to Mackey.

"You have the most amazing memory," Mackey commented. "You couldn't have been more than three at the time."

"How on earth do you know how old I was? I had no idea."

"Because, you ninny, you were only here that one time when Gord was born. I don't remember it from that time, but I do remember later when Uncle Gordy would pull Mom, Dad, Gran, Pops, and me around on a huge inner tube. But you weren't here." The two went off happily reminiscing over the good old days, leaving the older women to resume their conversation.

"Mackey seems happier these days, I'm glad to say," Stuart said. "And you know who else does? Susan. She looks fabulous. And I don't think she's drinking."

"She's not. She and your father have been seeing each other regularly for the last few months," Ginny replied. "You know how he leaves a path of saved souls in his wake."

"Has he been talking to Mackey too?" Stuart asked.

"No, I have," her mother admitted with a wry smile. "You know—Joe and I, just like Oprah and Dr. Oz."

They all laughed.

"Mother, you are absurd," Stuart declared. "All of this time …
and you are teaching Jacob's methods!"

"Don't rush in too quickly, darling," Ginny cautioned. "How
do you know I was teaching any method? I am not a Jacobite." She
couldn't resist her favorite joke.

Sallee chuckled. "That's good, Mom, really good."

"Mackey asked me if she could talk, and then she did," Ginny
continued. "All I did was listen. There is a lot to be said for listening.
More times than not, people have the answers they need without
anyone else's fixing. I think that was the secret to Ethel's success. She
was a great listener—not that she didn't try to fix everything with
food, but still, she was a great listener."

Stuart started to cut in. "I listen—"

"You don't need to get defensive, dear," her mother interrupted
gently. "I know you listen. I also know you are a terrific mother.
This isn't about you. We were talking about Jacob and his training.
Right?" She took Stuart's hand. "I know how much he and his
training helped you. But he and it weren't the only ones. And there
were times when it was plainly not appropriate for the situation. Like
when you were in mourning. You needed an ear, not a fix."

Stuart thought she saw Sallee smirk but decided to ignore it. "I
guess you are right. Ethel was a good listener, and I remember she
said she 'didn' hol' no stock in dat mind bidness o' Mista Joe's.'"

They all laughed; Stuart's evocation of Ethel had lost nothing
over time.

"Hello, Susan!" Ginny called out to greet her daughter-in-law,
who she noticed was standing a discreet distance away, near the arch
into the next room. "Join us. Stuart was just remarking on how well
you look."

"Thank you." Susan walked over to join them. "I feel better than
I have felt in years, thanks to your father. I wish I hadn't resisted
him for so long. I feel like he has given me my life back. It is odd
that I would say 'back,' as I am not sure I ever had one until now."

"Chalk another one up to Dad and his mind control," Sallee said, sounding more bitter than she meant to.

Stuart countered, "*You* gave you your life back, Susan, and I am so happy for you. You do look so happy, and so does Gordy—I mean Gordon. What is this *Gordon* foolishness, anyway?"

"I don't know." Susan rolled her eyes. "I would say a midlife crisis, but he's way beyond that."

All but Sallee laughed.

Ginny put her arm around her second daughter. "Honey, are you worried about the wedding? It will be fine. Everything will work out just perfectly. He is a very nice young man, I think. I've only just talked with him, but if Virginia picked him, he couldn't help but be a lovely guy. He certainly is, as Ethel would say, easy on the eye."

"I hope you are right, Mother," Sallee sighed. "I hope you're right."

❦

In the living room, Virginia flopped on the sofa in front of the fire while Mackey went over to the tree and rooted around in the stacks of presents before picking up a gift. She brought it back to the sofa and handed it to Virginia. "This is for you." She chortled, so chuffed she was with her idea.

"Thanks," Virginia gushed. "But don't I have to wait? Until Christmas?"

"Nope, this is just our own private little one." Mackey sat down next to her cousin, eager to see her reaction. "Ever since I thought of giving you this, I have been so excited. Go on, open it."

"Okay," Virginia said as she carefully untied the ribbon.

"I never would have thought you were one of those gift dissectors. I figured you for a rip-into-it present opener like me. I can't get the paper off fast enough," Mackey laughed.

"I am a real attention-to-detail sort of girl," Virginia giggled. "I like everything done just so. I think that's why I was so good at wedding planning." She left the package sitting in her lap and turned to Mackey. "You know, I think I want to be a wedding planner—I mean professionally—and an event planner. I think I'd be really good at it. What do you think?"

Mackey kept her immediate first thought—*God, help the poor soul who hires you*—to herself. Instead she insisted, with mock impatience, "Go on, would you just open my present?"

"No, really, what do you think of the idea?" Virginia picked up Mackey's gift again, turning it around as she inspected the wrapping. "I like to have my seams match up. You know, end to end? I'm sort of Martha Stewart-ish that way."

Uncharitable thoughts began to stack up in Mackey's mind. She forced a laugh, silently ordering her eyes not to roll up into her head. "Just open the present!" she commanded with less humor than before.

Using her thumbnail, Virginia carefully peeled the tape off the paper. As if unwrapping a rare artifact, she gently removed the paper from the box. Before opening the box, she rolled the paper up into a tube and tied it loosely with the ribbon.

Doing her level best not to shout, *Jeez, open the damn box already!* Mackey instead asked sweetly, "Are you actually going to use that paper again?"

Virginia didn't bother to answer. Finally, with the unwrapped box in her lap, she painstakingly removed the top and placed it on the cushion beside her before she peered inside. Gently, she moved the tissue paper aside to see the wooden lamb from their childhood. She squinted at her cousin, as if to ask, *What is this, a joke?* and then picked up the toy to look under it into an empty box. "I don't get it," she finally said.

"There's nothing to get," said Mackey. "I thought, since we talked about how much this reminded us of Alex, that you would like to have it. I guess I was wrong. It's okay if you don't want it." She was disappointed but not devastated, since giving away the precious toy had felt like a bigger sacrifice than she had expected. This way, she'd get credit for the gift and get the lamb back as well, kind of a big win in her mind.

"No, it's okay. Thanks. I'll keep it," her cousin said with little conviction. "It was a sweet idea." Running a finger over the toy's woolly body, she said, "It does sort of have Alex's hair." She put the toy down by the side of the sofa before jumping up to get a gift for Mackey.

Brushing off her failed effort, Mackey threw herself into unwrapping Virginia's present with lots of gusto. "Oh, nice!" she exclaimed as a box of electric curlers came into view. "I've always wanted some," she lied.

"I thought they would be helpful for the wedding," Virginia said. "You know, I couldn't find anyone to do our hair. If you ever have a daughter, make sure she doesn't get married around Christmas. People just won't do anything. I'm certainly going to steer my future brides away from weddings around the holidays."

❦

As the dinner started to wind down, Ginny pulled out a piece of paper and tapped her spoon on her glass. "I have a letter—actually, an e-mail I printed out—that I want to read. It is from Helen. I hope I can get through it without dissolving into a puddle of tears. Here goes:

"Dear All,

"To my utter surprise and delight I am completely grief-stricken that I am not there with you all this Christmas. Thank you, Virginia, for having such a wonderful idea. I have to admit when your gorgeous invitation first arrived, 'a wonderful idea' was not my first thought about it.

"I have the great joy of having the most fantastic mate in the world. Janice helped me see the opportunity that your invitation provided to heal so many old and painful hurts. I don't know if you know this. I am a lesbian. When I left home, I didn't know it. I just knew I hated myself profoundly. Discovering and accepting my true sexuality has been a lifelong process—one I was quite sure I had accomplished. That is, until your invitation showed up in my mailbox.

"To make a long story short, what I discovered with Janice's help was that I had stockpiled a whole bunch of self-hatred back east. I knew if you knew who I really was, you would hate me, so I made you guys responsible. Guess what—you're not! The relief that knowledge brings is exquisite. Not only do I feel like a million dollars; I look like it too. Always a good thing when you are in sales in California.

"This blasted snowstorm ruined my plans to bring my family east for the wedding. Janice, my wife, our son Dennis, and our daughter Leah are not to be deterred. Our plan is to come visit for spring break. Hopefully, you will still be snowed in so we can be with all of you! Just kidding—but do plan on a visit from the Simmon-Mackey bunch, wherever you are.

"I love you all so very much and miss you more, so much so that it hurts. Thank you, Virginia, for this fabulous idea, and Alex, for asking her to marry you to get this ball rolling. If you two are half as happy as Janice and I are, you will have way surpassed the odds, but go for broke and be as happy and then some!

"Much love,

Helen"

When Ginny finished reading, her face hurt from grinning. As she tapped her spoon again, she stood and raised her glass. "To Virginia." There was a rather long pause before she hurriedly added, "And Alex!" As she raised her glass again, she continued, "May they live happily, lovingly ever after." She sat down only to bounce right back up again. As everyone laughed, she added, "And to all of my family."

While the dishes were being cleared, Joe asked Gordon where Trey was. "Andy said he saw him outside just as he was coming in," Gordon replied. "He said that he wasn't well."

"Oh, that's a shame. I presume the little blond boy is his?" Then, remembering his great-grandson's name, he added, "Potts?"

"Yup, let me bring him over to meet you. I'm sorry. I thought someone already had."

"Let 'em play. We'll have plenty of time to get to know each other. It looks like we are in for it. How are you able to leave the farm with all of this weather?"

"I told Fred, my herdsman, that I would stay and help. He drew the Christmas straw this year. But he wouldn't hear of it. Said to go on and have some time with my family. He and the girls will make out just fine. They are in good hands. He's a hell of a man and the best damn herdsman I have had the good fortune to know. I'm lucky to have him."

Gordon was warming to his subject; he loved to talk about his "girls" and the dairy operation. "Though this weather isn't as bad as you might think on milking," he continued. "We have a loafing barn big enough for the entire herd. The hardest part is getting to and from the barn. I imagine Fred'll sleep in the apartment at the barn.

I would if I were there. It's all about having the right equipment to manage these sorts of situations." He leaned back in his chair, beaming proudly.

"I'd say," his father agreed.

"That letter from Helen sure was good to hear. She always did hold herself back, I remember. Do you think it was because she was a lesbian way back then? It doesn't surprise me that she is. I'm sorry that she thought we wouldn't love her if we knew."

"We all do a good job of keeping ourselves locked in our personal prisons," Joe replied. "I'm glad that Virginia's wedding gave Helen the key to unlock her door." He glanced out at the snow, still falling steadily. "Want to come out and check on the storm?"

"No-o-o," Gordy said with a mock quiver, "thank you. You go right ahead. I'm not even sure I'm going to make it back to my room tonight. That fire and sofa are awfully inviting," he laughed.

Joe smiled his agreement, quietly scraped his plate, and placed it in the dirty dish container before slipping out of the room unnoticed.

⁊

Rather than dampening the Christmas mood, the storm excited the children to fever pitch. "Santa is really going to have to use Rudolph tonight," young Sally insisted. "Look, you can't even see outside. It's all white."

"No," Josh said, with the voice of authority available only to the most seasoned of white Christmas veterans and snow-gazing experts. "You have to turn all of the lights off, then turn the outside lights on like this!" He raced to the light switch to demonstrate. "Watch," he commanded as he clicked off the lights in the room and ran to the window—where he found that Sally was correct: all he could see was white. Various adults in the room shouted for him to turn the lights back on before someone got hurt.

Andy hurried over to the switch and quickly restored the lights. "Josh, Sally," he said in his sternest tone, "don't ever do that again.

Someone could trip and fall in the dark. Your great-grandparents are far too old and frail to be put at risk like that. Don't do that, do you hear me?"

Ginny rolled her eyes at his remark. *Thanks for that, bud,* she sniffed to herself

"Yeah, Dad. Sorry," Josh mumbled.

Sally smirked and shot her brother a practiced *you-think-you-know-so-much* look.

Meanwhile, five-year-old Joey and his just-older cousin Potts were scrambling under furniture—hiding, then popping out, and screeching with delight when anyone happened to walk by, only to slither off on elbows and knees to reposition themselves for another foray.

Virginia took a dim view of their shenanigans when they appeared just under her feet and almost knocked her akimbo. She let everyone know about it at top volume. "Jesus, Mackey, can't you control that little brat of yours? You two, stop it right now. Do you hear me?"

Eric swooped in and grabbed both boys, whisking them out of the room before his wife's cousin could create an even bigger scene. On the way past Mackey, he said, "Kiss your mom goodnight, Corporal Joe. Captain Potts, you're with us. Your commanding officer is out on patrol, and he left orders for you to bunk with the corporal here. We gotta set up camp in the den. I think we are going to have to stay here tonight, so we might as well stake out a good place to sleep before someone else claims the space." Eric gave Mackey his *I've-got-this* wink, but Joey resisted, wriggling.

"But what about Santa Claus?" he demanded. "Will he be able to find us?"

Sally reported that she had it on good authority that Santa Claus knew not only who had been naughty or nice but also everyone's exact location. He would be sure to find them no matter where they might spend the night.

"How do you know?" Joey asked suspiciously.

"My mom told me when I was worried about it one year. You see, my parents are divorced, and that means that Josh and I have to spend Christmas one year with my dad and one year with my mom." She patted Joey's arm in earnest. "Don't worry," she assured him with a shake of her long hair. "Santa had it all sorted out."

Eric buried his face in Joey's neck to keep from laughing out loud.

☙

Joe stepped outside and immediately realized that the conditions were far too severe for him to make it the two hundred yards to the barn without a coat. Back in the house, he checked to be sure that nobody was watching and slipped his coat off the hook before heading back out into the blizzard. Standing on the porch, he struggled against the wind to zip his coat as snow gusted around him. The snow came at him sideways from all directions. He felt like he was being pelted with shards of glass. Tucking his head, he steered toward the barn. In the few hours since the snow had started, at least a foot of the stuff had fallen. Coupled with the wind—easily gusting at forty miles an hour—and the still falling snow, what was underfoot made for difficult going. It was a good thing Ginny had insisted on lining the path with trees years before; he'd argued against it then—an obstacle to mowing—but he was grateful now, certain he'd have lost his way without them. He cursed his stupidity for neglecting to check for his gloves or put boots on before setting out. *What was I thinking?* he chided himself. *This is the kind of stupidity that gets people killed.*

Beyond the halfway point, his heart started beating so hard that he worried he was having a heart attack. His breathing became increasingly labored, but with little choice but to continue, he dismissed his anxiety and moved forward, until he tripped on the steps and fell face-first into the snow. His bare hands stung from the cold. He struggled to lift his head and quell his rising panic. For a fleeting second, he actually thought he might drown. With a tremendous effort he was able to get himself under control and drag himself to his feet, although his head was swimming. His hands and feet ached from the cold. The relentless wind made it impossible to gauge where he was. Worried that stuffing his hands in his pockets might cause him to lose his balance, he rubbed them together in hopes of staving off frostbite and forged feebly ahead. By the time he reached Trey's room, his breathing was so labored that he had to bend over with both hands on his knees and gulp what little air his burning lungs could accept. His heart felt as if it was going to explode from overexertion or fear—he wasn't sure which. He fell against Trey's door hard as he gasped for breath.

Hearing the fall, Trey rushed to the door, pulled it open, and just barely caught his snow-encrusted grandfather as he fell into the room. "My God, Pops, are you all right?" Trey held his grandfather upright. Seeing that the older man was unable to stand on his own, he lifted him gently over his shoulder and carried him to the bed. "What in hell are you doing out in this weather?"

His grandfather gasped, "Coming to check on you." He dug at his coat collar, wheezing like a leaky pipe organ. "Loosen my collar," he croaked.

Trey laid his grandfather on the bed, unzipped his coat, unbuttoned his shirt collar, and took off his wet shoes. "I'm going to have to get some help. You don't look good."

Joe attempted to raise his arm to dismiss him but could manage only a feeble flop of his hand on the bed. "I'll be all right as soon as I catch my breath," he gasped, just loud enough to be understood.

Not knowing what else to do, Trey ran to the sink, filled a glass with water, and then reconsidered and canvassed the cabinets for some whiskey. Finally finding some bourbon, he dumped out the water and poured a big glass full before bringing it back to his grandfather. "Here, take this. It might help." He gathered Joe up in his arms, propping him up with pillows so that he could take a sip, and then sat on the bed next to him and held his limp hand. "Pops, Pops, what …? Why would you do this to yourself?"

The liquor burned the old man's raw throat all the way down. "I was worried about you, son," he managed, sounding a bit more like himself. "Let me be for just a minute. I'll be all right."

"Shouldn't I get some help? You don't look so good." Trey, much to his surprise, was fighting back tears. "I don't think I've ever told you this, but I love you, Pops. God knows, I don't want you to die."

"I don't think I'm going to die. The ticker's just not as young as it used to be." His heart had stopped racing, and his breaths were coming more evenly now. He took the glass from his grandson's hand and downed half of its contents on his own. Flinching, he coughed, "I'm better now. Thanks."

"Jesus, you scared me … scared the hell out of me, in fact. Let's not do that again." Trey shook his head and laughed.

"I heard that you were not well. Look okay to me. Too much family, too many memories?" Joe asked as he attempted to sit up against the headboard, poking and prodding pillows out of the way.

"You could say that," Trey acknowledged. "Feelings sort of sneak up on you. I just wasn't prepared."

"I know what you mean," Joe said with a smile. "Family is a multiheaded hydra. When you least expect it, one of those heads comes out of nowhere and bites you in the ass."

Both men laughed.

Joe put his feet back down on the floor. "That was scary. Thought I was a goner there for a minute. And here, I thought I was ready to die. Let's not tell your grandmother about this little episode. Okay by you?"

"I'll be as quiet as the grave, as I believe Ethel often said."

Joe grunted. "Hmm, I don't think I ever heard her say that."

"I don't suppose you asked her to keep your secrets. I did, and often. She was too—quiet as the grave."

"So anything you want to talk about?"

"Nope, I've got to work this out for myself."

"Good luck with that. Do you mind if I stay for a while? Actually, I don't think you have much choice. I might die on the way back." He chuckled and then thought about his sudden arrival. "I'm not interrupting anything, am I?"

"Only a panic attack, and I'm glad to have that stopped."

"Panic attack, that sounds pretty serious. Not your everyday pesky memory then?"

Trey shook his head. After a while he muttered, half to himself, "Family is serious shit."

The two men sat looking at each other, one on the bed, the other in the room's wingback chair, for a good while. They attempted a little small talk and then gave up and stared at the floor. Periodically, Trey would stand up and go to the window to peer out. "Doesn't look like it's slowing down any. Somebody is going to come looking for you any minute." The words weren't yet out of his mouth when there was a knock at the door.

"Son, you in there?" It was Gordon. "You haven't seen Dad, have you?" The knob turned, and the door eased open. "Okay if I come in?" Gordon yelled, swinging the door wide as a pack of snow-covered dogs raced into the room and shook all over Trey.

While he looked on helplessly, Gordon's terriers Burt and Early jumped up on the bed and pawed the pillows, scratching to make a nest for themselves. Daisyduke and Gomer—whining, tails wagging furiously—went straight for Joe on the bed. Joe stopped them with a hand command before they leapt up. They leaned up against the edge, checking to make sure he was all right, before slumping into two snowcaked heaps on the floor. Gordy's bloodhound, Six, followed suit.

Gordy started to come in and then stopped, walked back out into the hall, and stomped his feet to remove the snow. Joe looked down at the puddle around his own wet shoes. Gordy stepped into the room while stamping and flapping the remainder of the snow off his boots and coat. "You guys having your own private party or what?" he demanded.

"Pops heard I wasn't feeling well and came to check on me."
Trey's voice had hardened considerably. "Do we really need all of
the livestock?"

Joe looked up from his shoes and smiled at Gordy. "Yep, I didn't
realize how bad it was out there when I started out. Just gathering
my strength to make the trip back."

Gordy's three dogs whined. "It's a bitch, I'll tell you that," Gordy
asserted. "Wind will cut you in two. Lose your way, which is easy to
do considering you can hardly see your hand in front of your face,
and you are a dead man. But Mom's worried about you, Pops, so
I'm going to have to take you back. Do you want me to carry you?"

"God, no. I can make it under my own steam. But I would appreciate your coming with me—both of you, if that's all right with
you, Trey."

Trey sighed. "Okay, I got to see about Potts anyway."

Gordy said, "Between Andy and your mother, the kids are under
control. Santa Claus is making plans as we speak."

"Shit, I forgot all about that," Trey mumbled.

Gordy took another look out the window. "I'm not sure we
ought to even try to get to the house. It must be coming down at
about a foot an hour. I think I'll call up there and tell them we're
going to spend the night out here."

Trey groaned. "Perfect."

❧

While the elder Mackey men searched out and found whiskey to
while away their Christmas Eve, the younger Mackey women were
fixing for a blockbuster of a fight. Having discovered that the storm
was far too fierce for anyone to go out to play, they sat on the sofa
in front of the fire, chatting. As it turned out, the bride was doing
most of the chatting.

Bless Eric's heart, Mackey thought. *He does come through in the
clutch.* With Andy, he had indeed taken the "corporal," the "captain,"

and the rest of the younger set to the den to settle in for the night, leaving Mackey no other recourse than to listen to Virginia's unceasing complaints, while quelling the urge to smack her for calling Joey a brat.

"That caterer will never work again if I have anything to do with it," Virginia was now carping. "The wedding will be their absolute last job." As she complained, she absently played Tetris on her cell phone, cursing whenever she lost the game.

Mackey attempted to be the voice of reason, reminding Virginia that there was a blinding blizzard raging outside, that it was Christmas Eve, and that you couldn't reasonably expect people to abandon their homes and families at Christmas.

"Hey," Virginia shot back, "I didn't put a gun to their heads and force them to take the job, you know? Nobody had any qualms about working Christmas Eve when they took the job and the large retainer I gave them."

Mackey forced herself not to take a shot. "Well, it's not exactly like it put us out. So what? We had to do a few dishes. Gran has a dishwasher …"

Virginia made a show of rolling her eyes to the back of her head as she interrupted, "You don't *have* to wash the dishes." The contempt in her voice shocked Mackey. "You don't *wash* rented dishes. Do you live under a *rock*?"

Doubly stung by Virginia's vitriol, Mackey was finding herself a little afraid of her cousin and responded lamely, "Slip of the tongue, for heaven's sake. We just stacked the dishes like Aunt Sallee said. I don't know as much as you do about these things, but I do know how to treat people. And I think you could take a lesson or two, if not from me, from somebody."

"What the fuck is that supposed to mean?" Virginia demanded. "You don't treat people in this business like they're your best friends. They'll take advantage of you. Just like the fucking caterer did."

"I am pretty sure that woman was clear that you were no friend of hers," said Mackey. "Virginia, do you remember Ethel?"

"Sure, why?" Virginia snapped, smarting from Mackey's earlier comment.

"She used to say to me all the time, 'You can get more flies with honey than you can vinegar.' I understand that you want to be taken seriously. You don't want anybody to take advantage of you. But basic common decency goes a long way, and—excuse me for saying this—you are mighty low in that department. Why are you so angry?"

Virginia sat up ramrod straight on the sofa, turned toward Mackey, and all but spit in her cousin's face. "*You* try being civil when all the plans that you slaved over for the past month unravel through no fault of your own. You try putting together this zoo of a wedding on your own, without any help from another soul …"

"Wait a minute! Wait just one minute, you. I bet you I asked you at least a hundred times what I could do to help. Knowing this family, I am willing to bet I wasn't the only one either. All I ever got from you was a breezy 'This is fun, this is easy, I love this'—just before you would spend the next forty-five minutes complaining about what a pain in the ass all of this or that was. You've got a serious attitude problem, Miss Fancy Pants. I'm sorry your wedding isn't coming off the way you wanted it to. But it's not my fault. Or my son Joey's or Potts's."

"Potts!" Virginia exploded. "Potts, what a stupid name for a stupid little—"

Mackey came close to smacking her but continued instead. "Or Josh's or Sally's. You have been perfectly miserable to those children. You seemed to want to ruin their Christmas Eve. The fact that you tried to tell him there wasn't a Santa Claus was about the cruelest thing I've seen anybody do lately, and I don't understand why you would be so hateful."

Virginia glared at her cousin as tears began to well up in her eyes. "You don't understand …"

"Maybe you're right. Maybe I don't understand how it goes for you. Maybe you had a miserable, horrible childhood. Maybe your parents beat you and molested you. You didn't have a roof over your head or clothes on your back. Maybe they locked you in a closet, didn't feed you. Whatever it was, it doesn't give you the right to ruin—"

Drawn by the shouting, Ginny, Stuart, and Sallee appeared. "Girls, girls!" Ginny cautioned. "It's Christmas. How about a little of the spirit?"

"Fuck you," Virginia screeched as she gathered up her phone and ran from the room—followed closely by Sallee, who was remembering that she too had yelled exactly the same words to exactly the same woman years earlier.

❧

"Ethel, before I got sick and had to go to the hospital ..." Sallee squirmed around in fresh sheets, kicking up the covers to try to make room for her feet. Ethel always pulled the sheets so tight that it was hard to get into one of her freshly made-up beds. Finally adjusting the bedclothes to her liking but exhausted from the effort, she continued. "I yelled something at Mom, something real bad. I don't know if I should bring it up and tell her I'm sorry or just leave it and not say anything." She lay quietly, watching Ethel change the sheets on Helen's bed.

"Honey, it all depends on how you feel 'bout it," Ethel said as she lifted the mattress to tuck in the corners of the bottom sheet. "Does you feel like sayin' yer sorry will make 'er feel better, or will it jest remind 'er o' somethin' dat's better off bein' left in de past?"

Sallee rolled to her side as she followed Ethel's movements,. "What it was ... it was such a terrible thing I said. I sort of feel like I need to tell her I didn't mean it."

"Darlin', I 'spect she knows you doan mean it. She knows you love her."

"But it's such a terrible thing I yelled." Sallee rolled on her back and looked up at the ceiling as she debated whether she wanted even to say that word in Ethel's presence. Finally, throwing caution to the wind, she said, "Ethel, I yelled, 'Fuck you.'"

At that Ethel whipped around like a spinning dervish. "Say what? Where on earth did you hear such a word as dat? Who you been talkin' t'?" she spluttered. "Doan you ever let me hear you say dat word again. Do you hear me? Dey won' be 'nough soap in this he'ah house t' wash yo' mouth out." To herself she quietly said, "Lord have mercy, no wonder Miz Ginny was mad as a nest full o' hornets … No, Sallee, doan say 'nother word t' yo' momma 'bout it, hear? Jest let dat be."

"I feel terrible about it," Sallee whimpered.

"Right, you should too. I can't 'magine what would cause a soul t' say such a thang t' dey own momma. Sallee, you jest best be leavin' it alone." Ethel fussed with the sheet as she fumed. "What is this here world comin' to?"

"I'm sorry, Ethel," Sallee said, hoping Ethel would find a way to forgive her for both of them.

8

Mackey jumped up from the sofa and ran to her grandmother. "Are you all right, Gran?" she asked as she put her arm around the old woman and guided her back toward the sofa. "Come over here and sit with me. I'm sure Virginia didn't mean to say that to you." *I bet Gran doesn't even know what "fuck" means.*

Ginny sat down next to her granddaughter, leaned over, and patted her on the knee. "Don't fret about me. That's not the first time somebody has yelled that at me, and I'm here to tell the tale." She laughed and then turned serious. "But I am concerned about Virginia. She seems to have an awful lot of stress on her. I'm sorry things aren't going the way she wants them to. If the storm keeps up, I think the wedding will be a complete nonevent. I'm sure that won't make her very happy."

"You know," Mackey said, shaking her head, "I'm not even sure she wants to get married. But that's not what I want to talk to you about right now. What I want to say is how much I appreciated our chat a couple of weeks ago." She pulled her legs up under her, put a pillow in her lap, and turned toward Ginny. "I took your advice and unplugged. Haven't even been listening to music in the car. Eric and I are learning to meditate. We do it together, and I sit for a few minutes by myself too, several times a day. I gave up playing games on my cell phone, and I've limited social media to once a day at night. I also don't stay up late and watch movies like I used to. It's made such a difference. The noise in my head has all but disappeared. It's like I completely unhooked from the drama. The only time I actually really get keyed up is when I talk to Virginia—not that I do much talking. It's mostly just listening. Otherwise, things have calmed down so much, and I'm so much happier." She leaned over and gave her grandmother a kiss. "And it's all because of you."

"Honey, I didn't tell you to do any of those things. I didn't tell you to do anything at all. I just listened. You came up with your grocery list of things to do or not. But I'm so happy for you! You know the world we live in is a crazy-making place these days. There're just so many distractions. It's hard to keep up. As Ethel used to say when she'd put the children down for a nap, and one or another would protest, 'A soul needs a little peas and quiet.' Except it wasn't really Ethel who said 'peas and quiet'; Gordy did. He asked me once, 'Why does Ethel say, *I need quiet little peas?*'"

"Oh, that's great!" Mackey laughed. "The things kids say. It never stops, does it?"

Ginny nodded and then reached out for her granddaughter's hand. "Mackey, I envy you your relationship with your Joey. When I was your age, I didn't have anything close to that with my children." She glanced down at her watch. "Oh, good Lord, look what time it is. I hope Gordy made it to the barn all right. I'm going to find the number down there. I call it so seldom, I can't remember it. I don't even know why I didn't think to call earlier rather than send Gordy." Ginny scooted forward on the sofa cushion. "Would you mind giving your old granny a hand? This sofa is too low for me to navigate in any sort of ladylike fashion."

Hopping up, Mackey extended one hand while gently pushing on Ginny's back with the other. "Please, let me find the number and call."

"That would be wonderful. Thanks. The number is in my telephone book by the phone."

"Nobody has one of those anymore, Gran," Mackey laughed. "You are on the verge of being a fossil," she teased as she hustled over to the phone.

Ginny stuck her tongue out at her. "Cheeky brat." She laughed as she arched her stiff back. *She doesn't know how close she is to the truth—or does she?*

Mackey dialed the number only to get a busy signal. She hung up and dialed again. Seconds later, Gordy picked up the phone. "Uncle Gordy? Uh, Gordon, sorry," Mackey stammered. "Gran asked me to call and check if everything is okay. PopPop is with you, right? … Uh-huh … Uh-huh, yeah, that's a good idea … Okay, I'll tell her. Y'all stay warm down there, and Merry Christmas!"

Ginny was trying again to get up from the sofa. "They're fine?"

"Yep. Here, let me help. Uncle Gordy said that it was too dangerous to try to make it back to the house. He said we should all stay here tonight, and they'll be back first thing in the morning." She took her grandmother by the arm and strolled with her down the hall to her room. "He said that PopPop sends you his love. And PopPop said to put you to bed and make sure you stay there—no nocturnal wanderings! Do you do that?"

"What?"

"Wander around in the night?"

"Me? No."

"Eric and I will just have to sleep with you to make sure then," Mackey declared, laughing.

"Humph," Ginny snorted with mock disdain. "But would you mind finding my cane? I'll likely be up before all of you, and I can't remember where I left it. It's definitely way past my bedtime."

❧

Stuart caught up with Sallee just before she reached the door to the guest room where Virginia had sequestered herself. "Come on in here. We can talk," she said, guiding her younger sister toward their mother's room with an arm around her shoulders.

Sallee flopped down on the big bed and put her hands over her face to cover her tears. "That girl … I just don't know where I went wrong."

"Did you ever consider the thought that you didn't go wrong, that she is just perfectly Virginia?" Stuart asked.

"I'm not sure that it doesn't feel better to think I went off track than to accept the fact that my daughter is a horribly self-absorbed brat," Sallee snuffled.

"Maybe just a little harsh," Stuart said soothingly as she sat down on the bed next to her sister and put her arm over the younger woman's shoulder again.

Sallee shook it off, leaning away from her sister. "What gives you the right to judge me or my daughter?" she snapped.

"Sallee, I'm not judging you. I don't think Virginia is a horribly self-absorbed brat, and I don't think you made her what she is. I think there are lots of things going on for everyone tonight, not the least of which is the huge blizzard raging outside. The fact that Virginia put together this family Christmas is testimony to her expansive view, in my mind."

"Humph," Sallee sniffed.

Ginny and Mackey entered the room before Sallee had a chance to tell Stuart that she could get along just fine without her sanctimonious observations and to just butt out of her relationship with her daughter.

Ginny's remaining good humor was fast dissolving. "Do you mind if I get in bed? I am done in," she managed to say with a smile on her face, although it took an effort. "Your father said that you should all stay here tonight. The storm is too fierce even to attempt a trip to the barn in the dark. Can you girls sort that out? I am just too tired to think. I suppose Susan can stay in here since Gordy is at the barn with Joe and Trey."

"Susan is sleeping in the den with Andy and the kids. Eric and I can sleep on the floor anywhere," Mackey offered. "Aunt Sallee, why don't you and Uncle Peter stay in the guest room? Mom and

Dad can sleep on the pullout sofa in PopPop's office, and Alex and Virginia can sleep in sleeping bags on the sofas in the living room."

"Sounds like a good plan," Ginny agreed. "There are sleeping bags and extra linens and blankets in the linen closet in the hall."

"We'll take care of it, Mother. Don't worry," Stuart assured her. She rose and cuffed her sister lightly on the shoulder. "C'mon, sis. Let's find the linens and get started on this."

Sallee, amazingly, rose without protest and followed.

℘

Ginny had lain down on the bed without even bothering to take her clothes off.

Mackey lingered, gently working to extricate her from shoes, sweater, and whatever else could easily be removed. "Gran," she asked, "how can Aunt Sallee let Virginia be such a brat? I think I might smack Joey from here to the end of next week if he even considered acting the way Virginia does."

Tired as she was, Ginny had to smile inwardly. *Ahhh ... sounds just like Ethel.*

"It just boggles my mind that anybody can go about life that way," Mackey persisted. "That she said what she said to you ... I just don't even know what to think about that."

Ginny slithered under the covers and pulled them all the way up to her chin, clothing notwithstanding. "It's cold," she shivered. She then lay back on the pillows and sighed. "Honey, Virginia has a very strange life, really, a hard life. And we can't blame Sallee." In her heart of hearts, Ginny wasn't sure she believed that. Sallee didn't have to let Peter bully her as much as he had. "Children turn out the way they do, not necessarily because of what their parents do or don't do."

Mackey crawled under the covers next to her grandmother, moving close to Ginny to impart some warmth. "I'm sorry, I don't see how you can even think that. How in the world has Virginia had a hard life? She's gotten every single solitary thing she's ever wanted handed to her. How can that be a hard life? Isn't that everyone's dream?"

"It's precisely because she's been handed every single thing she has ever desired. The fact that she has never bumped up against *no* is what makes her life so hard. Her every desire is a command in her mind, every wish an edict. I know a little bit about that prison that she is in. I found myself in a similar situation, although I was much older and more entrenched than she. It took losing a baby, the dissolution of a marriage, and abuse heaped on my children to get me to see the pernicious nature of my thinking. Life, like a black-and-white photograph, needs white-whites, black-blacks, and all the shades of gray in between."

She nestled a little deeper into her pillow, turning to Mackey. "Fortunately for Virginia, nothing has gone right for her since she arrived here. Sooner or later, life has a way of forcing you to pay attention, and I believe that is what's happening now for Virginia." She paused, looking around at her room. "Maybe it's the effect of this old house or of invoking the family, I don't know. Be careful what you wish for, eh?"

Ginny laughed quietly and then continued more seriously. "It's easy to judge her. Try to see the beauty behind her behavior, the calling out for love and connection. She knows it's not right. Deep inside, she knows that her behavior is dreadful. She wants someone to apply the brakes. I suspect that is why she is especially awful to Sallee. Sallee was a dedicated mother ..." *In fact*, Ginny thought, *whether Sallee was a good mother is up for debate. But maybe Sallee really did believe all that malarkey she used to spout about motherhood. God knows I wasn't such an outstanding role model.* Ginny shook her head, dismissing her inner reservations. "Virginia just wasn't ready for what Sallee had to give her. And I hope you know all of this is an oversimplification and just my thoughts."

"Sorry, Gran. I'm not buying it. Mom's told me your story.

There's no way you had everything handed to you. If anything, you had everything taken away."

"The story doesn't count," Ginny responded. "It's attitude that I'm talking about. She has the same 'I deserve this because I am X or Y or Z' attitude that I had. There is no *deserving* in it. You are who you are because you won't settle for anything less. You work for what you want and at who you want to become. I didn't, and Virginia hasn't yet, but I suspect she will soon."

Tired as she was, Ginny now propped herself up on one elbow, turning to Mackey again. "And when she does, my dear grand-daughter, she's going to need a friend. You can be that friend—and a real force for good in her life. Look at the good inside her. She singlehandedly brought this family, long estranged, together. She's like … the Grinch!"

Mackey looked at her grandmother quizzically, wondering where she was going. "Well, heck yes, I'd say! She's trying to steal Christmas."

"No, remember the story. She just has a heart two sizes too small. But it's growing and growing. Isn't that what happens? I'm sure, well, pretty sure, it is. And *you* are her Cindy Loo Who."

"I guess." Mackey had to laugh, although a bit grudgingly. "Well, Gran, you're bound to be exhausted, and I gotta go play Santa Claus right now—and quickly, before kids start waking up. You don't happen to know if Andy brought any Santa presents, do you?"

Ginny shook her head as Mackey got up and slipped on her shoes.

"I love you so much, Gran. Thank you for sharing your wisdom with me. You sure have given me a lot to think about."

"Thank you for letting me, sweet girl. I love you too. Sweet dreams and Merry Christmas." She gave her granddaughter a kiss and rolled over. "I am going to sleep well tonight."

✧

Bill and Peter stood on the porch stomping, hopping from one foot to the other, and smacking their coat sleeves, trying to warm up. Alex, out there somewhere in the darkness between the house and the barn, had insisted that he would keep on digging for a while more. "You'd think we'd have created a little body heat with all that shoveling," Peter complained. "Man, it's cold as hell out here. And it seems like a pretty useless effort"—he waved his gloved hand expansively—"this digging. It's coming down faster than we can move it and blowing over all our pathetic progress. You can't even tell we did anything."

He had a point. In the forty-five minutes the three of them had been out there, they had made little progress in clearing any path to the barn. Bill, meanwhile, had completely given up the notion that he, Stuart, and Mackey's family would be able to make it back home for the night. "We're going to have to stay up here tonight," he said. "I actually think it's too dangerous just to be outside, let alone try to get ourselves home or even to the barn. Let's hope the power …" At exactly that moment, the porch lights flickered three times before going out altogether, with a loud crack in the near distance. "Doesn't go out. Damn. Good thing they have a generator." He stopped and listened, looking up at the still-darkened porch light. "That's weird. It should already be on. Just great, what a night. I'm off to the basement to see what's up with the generator," Bill said. "You want to call Alex off?" he yelled back over his shoulder as he pushed back into the house, searching his pocket for a small penlight he had attached to his keys long ago for just such emergencies.

Peter shouted over the wind, "Yeah. Happy as hell you're here, Bill. I don't know the first thing about generators. What was that crack? Did you hear it?" But Bill was already gone, so Peter headed gingerly out into the wall of white to fetch Alex.

I ought to leave you out here, Monsieur Angus LeBoeuf. It might just cool you off a bit. He snickered to himself as he made his way downhill in the dark through the drifting snow, following the track they had only recently cleared, now all but filled in again. A big blast of wind and snow blinded him for a second, causing him to stumble into a drift. As he tried to correct his forward momentum, he stepped into what he later could only surmise was a drainage ditch. For the second time in only a few minutes, he heard a crack, this time as his ankle snapped and a shock of searing pain shot up his leg. He fell face-first into a snowbank. Writhing in white-hot pain, he fought for purchase with his arms and one good leg. Finding none and seized by terror and pain, he willed himself to stop the panic and think. Arching his back, he was able to pull his face a fraction out of the snow, enough to take a breath, and he then rolled in the direction he could only hope was downhill.

Alex, finally admitting to the futility of his efforts, found Peter shortly after he had passed out. Without a moment's hesitation, the younger man discarded his shovel and scooped up the injured man. He made his way toward the house, following the now almost invisible path and cradling Peter in his arms as if he were a weightless rag doll. When he reached the porch, he leaned against the door and pounded with one fist, hoping to roust someone from the dark house, and then began kicking at the door. Eric, coming into the living room with a pile of bedding, dropped his armful and rushed to open the door and help him into the house.

"Mackey," he yelled, disregarding the sleeping house, "get in here quick! Hurry!"

Mackey ran as fast as was possible in the dark from her grandmother's room, with Stuart and Sallee not far behind her.

"Eric, stop shouting!" Stuart hissed as loudly as she could. "Damn it all, why aren't the blasted lights on?" she cursed as she bumped into the corner of a chest of drawers and Sallee slammed into the back of her. "What's wrong with the generator?"

Bill emerged from the basement in time to collide with them in the hall. "The starter battery must be dead. I can't find another and won't be able to fix it until tomorrow." With the two women, he stumbled into the living room. "Jesus, what's going on?"

"Mr. Barstead is—Peter's hurt," Alex said. "I found him in the snow like this." He gently laid the unconscious man on the carpet near the fire, which now provided the only light in the room except Bill's small penlight.

Sallee gasped. "Oh dear God, he didn't have a heart attack, did he?"

Alex was busy unzipping Peter's coat and checking his vital signs. "We need to call 911," he said over his shoulder. "I can't imagine that anyone can get through in this weather, but maybe they can talk us through what needs to be done."

Sallee stumbled through the dark toward her husband, ready to elbow *that creature* out of the way. She stopped short when she saw how tenderly Alex was ministering to him. She moved to Peter's other side and took one of his icy hands in her own.

Mackey was at Peter's feet, removing what she thought were his boots, only to discover that his feet were clad in low duck shoes and encased in a thick layer of snow. As she scraped away the snow, she noticed that one of his feet seemed to be turned. "Dad, can you bring that light over? I think he might have broken his ankle."

Bill, who'd been searching the cabinets for batteries, turned his penlight's thin beam on them.

Mackey continued, "Look at this—it looks bad. See how swollen it is? And that's even considering that it's more or less been on ice since it happened." *Who goes out in this kind of weather in these?* she wondered as she tossed the dripping duck shoes out of the way, but she had the presence of mind not to ask.

Eric groped his way to Joe's office, where the reception, such as it was, had proved to be best. He hastily punched in 911 on his cell phone and waited for what seemed whole minutes for an operator to answer. He then did his best to streamline the explanation. "Yes … I'd say in his late sixties, not sure, I'll ask. We found him in a snowbank. It's not clear if he's had a heart attack or a stroke or what. He's still unconscious. His ankle appears to be broken. Hold on … uh …" He groped his way back into the hall, making a mental note to find flashlights as soon as possible, and shouted, "Aunt

Sallee, how old is he? And they want to know if he has a history of heart problems."

"Sixty-five, and no, not that we know of." Sallee didn't even look up into the darkness as Eric gave the dispatcher the information, bumping into a chest of drawers as he shuffled back to the office and the window by Joe's desk.

Mackey crept over to position herself on a chair outside the office door, and as Eric told her what the dispatcher was saying, she acted as go-between. "Pulse?" she called into the living room. "How's his color? They say they will send out a crew—fire, ambulance, police, whatever they can find—but have no idea how long it will take to get to us."

Alex reported that Peter's pulse was just over 110 beats a minute, adding that he thought that was pretty near normal under the circumstances. No one in the room could dispute what he said, and since he spoke with such authority, Mackey just passed on the information.

The 911 dispatcher confirmed Alex's conclusions. "Keep him warm, don't leave him alone, and call back if there are any changes. We'll get someone out there as fast as we can; it's just tough right now."

Mackey dutifully relayed the information as she wondered, *What kind of idiot would think of leaving an unconscious man alone?*

"He seems to be coming to," Alex reported.

Eric waved at Mackey to indicate that he had heard, but she repeated the news anyway, and he realized that she probably couldn't see the gesture. "Got it," he replied.

With both hands, he felt his way carefully out of the room. Finding his wife perched on the chair outside of the door, he helped her to her feet and carefully moved toward the living room and firelight, keeping one hand on the wall to steer himself.

Stuart, seeing that she couldn't be of any help as far as Peter was concerned, cautiously made her way to the kitchen cabinets, where she knew Ginny kept candles and matches stashed. She started setting them up, using empty wine bottles as emergency candlesticks.

Less than twenty minutes later, they heard a fire engine laboring up the drive, changing the wall of snow outside from red to orange and back to red.

Eric's phone lit up. "Hello?"

"I tried to tell them the barn, but I see the truck is headed toward the house. Tell them he's down here in my room. It's the first one on the left when you come in the near door."

"Who is this?" Eric demanded.

"Sorry. This is Trey! I tried the house phone, but I guess it's out. Pops fell down out in the snow, and I don't think he's doing so hot. I called 911 just a few minutes ago. I can't believe they're here already."

"Okay, got it. I'll get back to you in a minute," Eric replied, hanging up without waiting for an answer. He raced to the door and threw it open to greet two firemen before they could step into the house. He moved out into the cold, carefully shutting the door behind him and quickly explaining the situation out of the earshot of the rest of the family.

One fireman retraced his steps to the chugging engine. He slipped it into gear and headed in the direction of the barn, dimly visible in the headlights. The other followed Eric into the house and over to Peter, who by now was struggling into consciousness. Setting down his emergency kit, the fireman checked Peter's vitals and then looked at his ankle and whistled softly. "Ouch, that's nasty-looking." He searched his bag for a splint. With careful haste he wrapped Peter's ankle before beating a swift retreat to the hall, looking for guidance from Eric.

Eric walked him back to the front door, pointed out the direction to the barn, and shut the door after him as the fireman switched on a headlamp and plunged into the darkness.

"Well, I know these are extraordinary conditions, but you would have thought that he could have said, 'Call me in the morning' or something," Sallee grumbled.

∽

With Peter stabilized, Bill, Eric, and Alex descended to the basement, armed with candles and multiple flashlights, to look for a generator battery.

Alex let out a slow whistle. "Look at the size of her," he said, admiring the generator. "Shit, this thing could light Times Square."

The three pulled open every drawer and cabinet and were ready to throw in the towel when Alex said, "Wait a sec, I just thought of it—we can get one of the generators they were going to use for the tents. Aren't they still out by the kitchen door?"

"Oh!" Bill was obviously impressed. "Yeah, that might work. 'Course they're under a foot or two of snow."

"No problem. This is just like home, except back there it's more like five feet of snow. Come on, Eric. Grab a shovel and let's find 'em. They probably have the same starter configuration as this, and we can get one wired up in no time." He ran up the steps, with Eric not far behind. "Hey, man, who was on the phone? Do rescue people in the South have to announce their arrival?"

"No, it was Trey. Seems Joe took a tumble out in the snow. Trey didn't like how he looked, and he'd called 911 right after I did."

"Man, if it ain't one thing ..." Alex didn't bother to complete the saying.

"I know, and I didn't want to get everyone all stirred up. That's why I hurried out to meet them and why the guy that looked at Peter's ankle ran off so fast. There should be more EMTs arriving soon, I imagine."

"Good call. Let's get these lights on." From the top of the stairs, Alex called back down, "Hey, Bill. See if you can find some wire, some wire strippers, and some electrical tape in case I have to jerry-rig this baby. Back in a few."

By the time the lights in the house were on, an ambulance had arrived and taken Peter away, accompanied by Sallee. What the rest of Peter's caretakers didn't yet know was that another emergency vehicle had already whisked Joe away, with Trey in attendance.

Meanwhile, Gordon and the five dogs were following the tracks left by the rescue vehicles back to the house. Fueled by a little too much bourbon and a good portion of concern for his dad, Gordon carefully made his way as the blowing snow again began to cover the path. Along the way, he practiced what exactly he was going to say to his mother, even as he held onto the unlikely hope that she might already have gone back to bed.

Some yards short of the house, he stopped, thought, and turned around. The snow was letting up a bit. No question Ginny needed at least one good night's sleep before whatever shit hit the fan tomorrow, and so did he. "Screw it," he said to the dogs. "Come on." Together, they made their way back along a band of boot tracks and fast-fading paw prints to the barn doors. "Right, guys. Good work. Let's get us some sleep. Tomorrow is already lookin' like a looong day."

❧

Not until Mackey awoke the next morning on the floor in Joe's office did Eric tell her that PopPop, too, had been taken to the hospital. They held each other while they talked over what Ginny had said the night before.

As his hands started to wander, she said, "Not now. Too much, just too much going on. But not because I don't want to or love you." With a quick kiss, she pulled herself up and headed for the kitchen to make coffee and spend some time with her own thoughts before the house came roaring to life again.

Four children crept out into the living room at what seemed like the very crack of dawn to check first for signs that Santa Claus had not forgotten them and then on the snow accumulation. Potts had worried that the snow might have disappeared over the course of the night.

Sally assured him that that would have been impossible. "We

had more than a foot of snow before we went to bed last night. It can't go away that fast, even—"

Joey interrupted his cousin. "How do you know? How do you know we had a foot of snow?"

"Simple." Sally led her younger cousin to the window and pointed to a yellow yardstick just barely poking out of the snow a few feet beyond the house drip line in front of the window. "See, Daddy put that out last night so we could see how much snow we got. It's almost three feet. Wow! Let's go sledding."

"Whoa there, miss," Andy cautioned as he emerged from the den, rumpled and sleep-worn, his light rust-colored hair matted on one side of his head. Tucking in his shirttail, he shushed them. "Quiet down. People are still sleeping. You can't go out yet. It's too early, and besides, it's still pretty blowy. You don't need to worry—nothing is going anywhere anytime soon. Look at the temperature." He pointed to the thermometer on the edge of the big window. "It's twenty-three degrees, way too cold to go out there without lots of protection. The snow would be up to your chin, Josh, and probably over the rest of your heads."

"Cool!" the two younger boys exclaimed in unison.

"Over our heads, wow!" said Potts.

Sally crowed, "We can make tunnels and play Eskimos."

"Aw, Dad, come on. Aren't we going to be able to go sledding?" Josh asked.

"Yes, when the storm is really over. Look at how the wind is still blowing."

As the children stared out at the winter white, Sally caught her father glancing around the room. She exclaimed, "I think Santa musta had a hard time getting his bag down the chimney. He had to move furniture and everything. I bet Gran is going to be mad when she sees what a mess he made."

"Yeah," Andy said, wondering what had gone on last night. He was glad to see that some elf had taken care of filling all of the stockings, since he hadn't counted on falling asleep and hadn't told anyone where he'd hidden his trove of stocking stuffers. *So much for thinking ahead and bringing the stuff up from the barn before the snow got to be such a big factor*, he grumbled to himself.

Mackey emerged from the kitchen with a cup of coffee, which she put down before whisking Joey off his feet. "Merry Christmas, everybody! Look, Santa found you. What do you think of that?"

The little boy squirmed out of his mother's embrace. "Yeah, look, he even brought my stocking over from home." A cloud of worry passed over his face. "Does that mean he didn't leave me any presents at home?"

"It probably does. I don't think Santa has time for double visits. One visit per kid," his mother said as she took a big swig from her mug.

"Yeah, but when I went to Granny Kate's last year, Santa left me stuff there too."

Mackey hid her face behind the mug, suppressing a laugh as she tried hard to match her son's earnestness. "You just can't tell what Old Whiskers will do, can you?"

Joey leaned in to Potts and Sally and conspiratorially confided behind his hand, "She calls Santa 'Old Whiskers.'" He shook his head. "I don't know why."

"'Cause he has lots of whiskers," Sally said, pointing out the obvious. "He probably doesn't mind."

"I hope not," Joey remarked. "He is not the kind of guy you want to make mad."

Mackey and Andy turned away and ducked into the kitchen, laughing.

"Hey, what happened here last night?" Andy asked in a hushed voice as he poured himself a cup of coffee and offered Mackey a refill. "Sorry I left you guys to do S. C. duty."

"Eric and I found your stash. Thanks for wrapping and labeling. That was a huge help. And thanks for considering all of the children. I wish I could say I had been so smart," she whispered. "Fortunately, after we divvied up all of your goodies and all of the things I brought for Joey, it turned out pretty even. I hope Sally won't mind a few boy toys." She shrugged. "I hope you didn't have any particular things for anyone."

"Nope, all very general. It's all good. Thanks again. But what happened?" Andy asked again as they wandered back to the living room, where the kids were impatiently prancing with excitement.

"Can we open our presents now?" Josh asked.

"Wait a few minutes. We have to wait until everyone is up."

Groans rolled through the younger ranks.

"You know they will all want to be here to see you guys," Andy said reassuringly.

Mackey held up a hand. "That's right, guys. Just hold on a sec. Josh and Sally, I want to talk to your dad for a second. Then we'll let you wake everyone up." She looked up as Alex walked into the room. "Oh, hey, Alex. Merry Christmas."

As Mackey quickly went to pour a cup of coffee for Virginia's fiancé, Andy noticed that she seemed much friendlier with Alex than she had the night before. Alex and Andy followed her into the kitchen.

"How 'bout you fill Andy in on what went down last night while the kids and I roust the troops?" she said as she offered Alex the coffee.

"Sure," Alex agreed, accepting the steaming mug from Mackey and taking an immediate big gulp. "Virginia said she'd be out in a bit, to go ahead without her."

"Okay, I'll get Eric and Mom. I think that under the circumstances, we should let Gran sleep."

"What circumstances would those be?" Ginny asked as she suddenly appeared at Mackey's side.

"Um, uh, that we had such a late night!" Mackey surprised herself with how quick she was with the lie, though it was pretty lame as lies went. "Let me get Mom and Bill. Andy, you want to wake your mom? Oh, never mind—here she is. Merry Christmas, Susan! There's coffee made. Merry Christmas, Gran." She bent down and kissed her grandmother's cheek and hurried off before Ginny could ask any more questions.

In the hall Mackey bumped into Eric emerging from the office. "Merry Christmas, honey." She fell into her husband's embrace. "God, I almost let the cat out of the bag. Gran walked into the kitchen and overheard me say we should let her sleep under the circumstances. Have you heard how PopPop is?"

"No, but I told Stuart and Bill. I hope you don't mind." He whispered in her ear, "Stuart is on the phone to the hospital now. You don't know Trey's cell number, do you, or Sallee's?"

She shook her head. "No on both counts. Sorry. As for my folks, are you kidding? God, no, I don't mind. I'm grateful I didn't have to tell them. How did they take it?"

"They're great. You know your mother is all business when it's time for the rubber to meet the road. It's only afterward that she loses it. I'm heading to the kitchen to get them coffee."

Mackey handed Eric her almost-full second cup and said, "I'll do it. How 'bout you get the kids organized? They are chomping at the bit to open presents. Being pretty patient too, I'd say." As she turned, Bill stepped out from the basement. "Hey, Dad. Merry Christmas! Just on my way to get you and Mom some coffee."

"I need it," he said. "I gotta find Gordy. He's not up here, is he?"

She shook her head no.

"I didn't think so. He's not answering his cell, and we've got to get to the hospital."

"Oh, no. Do you know something? Not PopPop—is he okay?"

Bill put up his hand up to stop her. "Whoa, I don't know. We have to get Sallee and Peter home—and I imagine Trey too. That was all I was thinking. I didn't mean to alarm you. Your mom is trying to get information now. It would be helpful if we could get some cell numbers."

"On it," Mackey announced.

Rejoining her father a few minutes later in the living room, with two steaming cups of coffee, she had more thoughts on how the day was shaping up. "Knowing Gordy, he is on some tractor already, plowing us out. Alex is out shoveling the path. Andy and Eric are going to help him as soon as we get the kids and stockings sorted. The snow looks like it's finally letting up. It's just shy of three feet."

She turned to the under-ten set. "Okay, kids, let's get 'er done. On your mark, get set, go!"

As the children dove into their stockings, Mackey gave Andy and Eric two thumbs up and nodded her head in the direction of the door: she had this covered, and they should head for the shovels. She joined Ginny and Susan on the sofa brigade for the obligatory *oohing* and *aahing* as toys and spent wrapping paper began to litter the floor and happy children shrieked with delight.

"Has anyone heard from Sallee?" Ginny asked, having been apprised of Peter's portion of last night's drama. Before anyone could answer, Virginia entered the room. "Does Virginia know about Peter?" Ginny murmured.

"I don't know," Mackey whispered. "Alex didn't say." She waved across to Virginia, who gave a wan smile in return.

"Merry Christmas," said Mackey. "There's coffee in the kitchen."

Susan stood up. "Can I get anyone anything? I'm going to see about feeding this crowd."

"Do you need help?" Mackey asked.

"If I do, I'll ask Virginia. You have your hands full here."

Mackey rolled her eyes. Just loud enough for Ginny to hear, she whispered, "Good luck with that."

Her grandmother playfully admonished her, "Now, Cindy Loo, it's not easy to grow a heart that's two sizes too small. Leave her be."

☙

Gordon hopped out of the tractor cab, turning to lift the waiting terriers down to the snowy walk. Spotting Alex, he said, "Nice job clearing the steps and walk. You do this?" The three bloodhounds loped up to him, having followed the track he had carved out of the snow. "Come on, guys. Let's go get you fed."

"I was just about to help clear the walk to the barn when I saw you coming up the drive," Alex said. "I don't suppose there's any point in clearing it today."

"I don't think so," Gordy agreed. He looked over at the progress Andy and Eric had made and laughed. "They're not much help, are they?"

"No, but they mean well," Alex laughed.

"That's right—you're from out West. I don't guess this even counts as much snow from where you come from."

"You know, I figured something out as I was clearing the steps. It's not so much about the amount of snow as it is about the tools you have to deal with it." Alex held up a cheap, lightweight snow shovel. "Something like this isn't worth a damn. You can't shovel heavy snow with this. So if you haven't got the right equipment, a foot of snow is a big deal."

"I think we got more'n a foot. I'd say closer to three. What's going on inside? Any news about Pops?"

"Peter? I think he just has a broken ankle."

"No, Pops. Wait, what? Peter broke his ankle? When?" Gordon asked.

"Last night. They sent a fire engine out, and later an ambulance took him off. Who's Pops? You mean Mr. Mackey? He went to the hospital last night too? I don't know if they even know about him in there."

"Well, great! I always love being the bearer of glad tidings," Gordy grumbled. "On Christmas too! I better get inside and see what's up." He moved in the direction of the house. The dogs were hungry and didn't need any more coaxing as they scrambled out in front of him and up to the door, where all five started whining to be let in. "Okay, I'm coming," Gordy snickered. "Sheez, patience!"

Josh swung the big front door wide open before Gordy could get to it, and all five dogs swarmed in, nearly knocking the boy down in the process. "Happy Christmas, Granddad," he called as he ran to give Gordy a hug.

"Would you get yourself back in that house, boy? It's cold as all get-out out here." He grabbed the boy in a big sweep of one arm and carried him back into the house, kicking the door shut with a snowy boot.

Susan greeted him at the door with a tentative kiss and a sigh as she looked down at the mound of snow that had fallen from his boot.

"Okay, sue me," he said with a grin. "It snowed, for God's sake."

She laughed. "Merry Christmas to you too, you old grinch. Here, drink this." She shoved a steaming cup of coffee at her husband. "Is everybody ready for breakfast? It's ready for you. Will you go out and tell the boys to come in before you take your boots off please? I'll get the dogs fed. C'mon, guys," she told the dogs, who immediately gathered around her.

Virginia had tossed napkins and utensils haphazardly around the table. As everyone began to claim seats, it was obvious there were some people missing. The children were buzzing with excitement. Virginia scowled at them, and Mackey bit her lip, trying her damnedest not to call her cousin out.

"Where is everybody else?" Virginia demanded. "Are Mother and Daddy still asleep?"

"Oh, honey, didn't anyone tell you?" Ginny said.

Virginia shot Alex a withering look. "No! Tell me what?"

Alex grimaced and shrugged.

"Your father broke his ankle last night and had to be taken to the hospital," Ginny said gently. "Sallee went with him."

"Oh great. Poor Daddy. That pretty much puts an end to the wedding taking place."

Everyone looked stunned by her reaction.

"There is no way you could go ahead with a wedding anyway," Gordon informed his niece. "There's three feet of snow out there. Nobody is coming or going for a very long time. I've plowed down to the road. A snowplow hasn't touched it. You can't even tell that a fire engine and two ambulances have passed in the last few hours."

"Two?" Ginny asked, suddenly aware that Joe had not come in with the others. "Who was the other one for?"

Stuart slid into her seat at the table. "Dad," she said. "I've just been on the phone with the hospital. They say he is all right. He might have had a mild stroke last night, probably brought on by his exertion in the snow."

"What was he doing in the … ohhh." Quickly replaying the night before, Ginny silently vowed to give him a piece of her mind when he got back.

"They've run tests. There doesn't seem to be any damage. We can pick all four of them up whenever we can get there."

"Who else is at the hospital?" Ginny asked.

"Trey," Gordy said. "He went in the ambulance with Dad."

"Father is in the hospital?" Potts asked, mildly concerned.

"No, darling," said Mackey. "He went with PopPop last night to keep him company. Don't worry, he's fine."

"So my father is a hero," Potts beamed.

"Boy, this looks delicious, Aunt Susan," Mackey exclaimed, shoveling a big spoonful of something custardy-looking onto Joey's and Potts's plates. "You are going to like this, guys." Looking over at her aunt, she asked, "How did you have time to do all of this?"

"I just followed the caterer's instructions. Everything was done. All I had to do was heat it up. Thanks for your help, Virginia."

Virginia didn't hear Susan. She was too busy bawling Alex out for not telling her about her father's accident. "How could you have not told me?" she hissed just barely under her breath, leaving no one out of the drama.

Ginny debated stepping in but decided that the prudent course was just to pretend to eat her breakfast. It wasn't like she didn't have her own annoyance at being the last to know pertinent information. *Best to deal with that first*, she thought. Her granddaughter offered up an excellent example of how she didn't want to come across, but she certainly did appreciate Virginia's outrage. How dare they not tell her that Joe had gone to the hospital! She sat quietly as she felt her anger escalate. *Joe promised me. He promised me he wouldn't die.* She had to will herself to remain composed.

Determined not to let Virginia set the tone for the day, Mackey praised the serving plates filled with bacon, egg, and cheese. "Is this a strata or a frittata? Does anybody know the difference?" she asked a little too cheerily as she passed a plate down the table. Moving on to the plate of warm cinnamon buns, she said, "Boy, these smell just like my idea of Christmas! Try one."

Susan, realizing what Mackey was up to, jumped in with a discourse on strata versus frittata that caused Gordy to stop shoveling his food in long enough to say, "It's cheese and eggs. Who cares? And it is good."

Determined to keep the focus away from the quarreling young couple, Susan offered, "I made some hot chocolate for you non-coffee drinkers. Does anyone want any?" She raised a large china coffee pot. Four children and several grown-ups raised their empty mugs and were especially pleased to learn there was a bowl of sweetened whipped cream to go along.

Susan's distraction worked. Virginia and Alex sat side by side, brooding but quiet. Ginny was also brooding, until she suddenly remembered something Ethel had said some years earlier.

Miz Ginny, did I ever tell you 'bout de time jest afore Early died? He'd jest come home from seein' de doctor. Dey tol' 'im he had de cancer, bad. I like t' cried my eyes out when he say dey didn' give 'im more'n 'bout six months t' live.

"Early," I said, "darlin', I doan think I could stand t' see you sufferin'."

He say, "Like ya gots a choice?"

I cried me some more—like de old folks say, cried me a river.

After I got finished cryin', I got mad. Early was so acceptin' o' what de doctor say.

"Why ain't you fightin' dis?" I axed 'im. "Why you gotta lie down an' take what he say?"

"Whatta I gonna do? Who I gonna fight?"

"Maybe you oughta go see 'nother doctor. You know, dat doctor you see coulda been wrong."

"I knows, Ethel. I knows. It doan change much. I can drop dead tomorrow an' not suffer a wink. Only one be sufferin' is you, wastin' all dis he'ah time cryin' an' fussin' today. You knows, I don't give one wit fo' buttermilk. You's de one dat likes it. Put a glass in front o' me, an' I won' touch it. Same fo' lard. I would 'spect you'd lost yo' mind if you put a hunk a lard on a plate in front o' me. But when you mix dat stuff up wit' flour an' whatever else you puts in, I will eat dem biscuits all de livelong day. That's how I see it is wit' de Lord. He give' me a little somethin' I don't like an' little some else I don't care fo'. I don't know what He got cooked up, but I 'spect it be every bit as good as dem biscuits o' yours."

What he say make me so mad, I couldn't talk t' 'im, an' den he up an' died de very next day. An' you know, he was right. I has suffered more 'bout wastin' de last minutes I had wit' 'im bein' mad dan I can say.

9

"Think we'll able to get out?" Joe grumbled from his bed, if you could call the contraption he was lying on a bed. "I can't believe we are going to be stuck in this damn hospital all day long." He leaned up against the pillow with his hands behind his neck and his feet crossed at the ankles.

Trey lounged in a green Naugahyde chair, his feet propped up on the foot of Joe's bed. "I don't think you need to worry about it, Pops. Knowing Dad, he's already plowed out the drive and is on his way, dogs and all." He groaned at the thought.

Trey pulled out his cell phone and tried to call his father again. Nothing. "Still no service," he said. "It doesn't make sense that there is no cell service here." He looked through the glass wall of the cu-bicle—*hardly a room*, he thought—past the nurses' station and out through the waiting room window to the snowfall outside. "Do you think it'll stop anytime soon?"

"I don't think it's supposed to go on for more than a few more hours. But that was yesterday, and I don't remember hearing them calling for as much snow as we've gotten, so your guess is as good as mine."

Trey grunted an acknowledgment.

"Maybe the phones aren't working because there is just too much traffic on the lines since the electricity is out in so many places," Joe said with a shrug. "Hey, I really appreciate your coming with me,

Trey. It's been nice to get to know you a little bit. It has been such a long time."

Trey waved him off.

"You didn't have to," Joe insisted. "Did you talk to the doctor, since you are here already, about your panic attacks?"

"Pops, there weren't a lot of people in my childhood that I remember fondly. You were one of them—you, Gran, and Ethel. I don't want you dying, and most especially not on my watch. The rest of it …" Trey shook his head. "No need to talk about. Just too many old, bad memories is all."

"We haven't got anything else to do, so if you change your mind, I'm a good listener."

"It was a long time ago. Don't see any point in dragging it all back out to the light of day. I'll be going back home soon, so whatever problems I had can go back to their little hideaway and leave me in peace."

"Maybe that might work for you. Never did for me," Joe said. "Once my little houses of horrors made their way to the surface, I had to deal with them. It was as if they got a little oxygen and came back to life, sorta like in the horror movies with the mummies. And the only way I could find to do that—deal with them—was to talk about it."

"Think I'll just risk that possibility." Trey was cordially dismissive.

"Okay, suit yourself, but if you need an ear, I'm here. By the looks of things, you're not going to be leaving anytime in the near future. And there is the possibility you will need someone to talk to. I'm not pushing, just making the offer."

There was an awkward silence while Tray mulled over what his grandfather had said.

Joe considered the upcoming homecoming and how Ginny, he was nearly certain, would express her displeasure when she found out what had landed him here in the first place. There was one very good thing that had come out of this, which was that he knew with no uncertainty that he wanted to live. This idea of dying consciously had been just plain hubris on his part. He chuckled to himself. *You are a piece of work, old man.*

Trey looked up, startled. "Did you say something?"

"I was just laughing at my arrogance. I spent the last four months haranguing Ginny about how much I wanted to die consciously. Can you imagine anything more absurd? As if I had the power. Well, there's one thing I now know for certain. Dying is not what I want. I imagine your grandmother will be quite relieved. She's been trying to talk me out of this foolishness since its inception."

"You are a crazy old coot," Trey agreed. "What does *conscious* dying even mean?"

"Just part of the ego trip. Sometimes I wonder how Ginny puts up with me," Joe laughed, "but I'm damn glad she does. I can't imagine how painful the last few months have been for her, listening to me talk about how I want to die."

"You guys are lucky," Trey said." Your relationship …" He just left it at that since he didn't have any idea what he was trying to say or where he might go with it. The last thing he wanted to do was open up a discussion of relationships, having had so many stellar examples from which to choose.

"Luck, son, has nothing to do with it. It has taken a lifetime of hard, concerted work and dedication, let me tell you," Joe said.

Oh, please don't. Trey was looking for a good exit line when he noticed an arrival at the nurses' station just outside of Joe's emergency cubicle. "Wait, isn't that Sallee?" *Saved from the gallows,* he thought. It had seemed certain that his grandfather was just settling into prying his secrets from him. He jumped up and in two steps was standing next to his aunt. "Hey, good to see you," he said. "Is Dad out in the truck? Which door?"

Taken completely by surprise, Sallee didn't recognize Trey at first. "What are you talking about?" she snapped. "I'm sure I don't know where *your* father is."

Trey, glad to have a break from Joe's prodding, chose to ignore

Sallee's less than pleasant attitude. "You didn't come by yourself, did you?"

"No," she flared. "I came last night with my husband." She looked at him like something she wanted removed from the bottom of her shoe.

"You didn't come to pick up Pops?" Trey asked, deciding that this bitch's attitude would just have to be borne, since telling her where she could stick it would not advance his case much with the family.

"What are you talking about?" She'd started looking around for some help when she spotted Joe sitting on the gurney disguised as a bed. "Daddy!" she shrieked as she ran to him. "What are you doing here? What happened?"

"A little tumble in the snow is all. You know, I'm just too old for that sort of foolishness without having to be checked from bow to stern afterward."

Sallee looked for verification from Trey, who stood where she had left him, composed but … she didn't know what. His face, inscrutable as the sphinx, gave no indication of what he might be feeling.

"Do I take it from what I heard you shriek at Trey …"

Sallee flinched and looked at them both in confusion.

Trey smiled. *Atta boy. Stick it to her, the bitch.*

"… that Peter came in last night as a patient as well?" Joe asked in a most pleasant tone.

"Yes, he broke his ankle in the snow. Trying to dig a path to the barn."

"By himself?" Joe asked as he chuckled inwardly at the idea of his pompous son-in-law getting off his ass to do anything resembling manual labor. "Broken ankle, hm? How did he do that in the snow?"

"No, Bill and Virginia's beau were helping. I don't know. I imagine he twisted it or stepped in a hole. He didn't have on proper snow boots," Sallee said. "I'll go get him. He's just down the hall. They have casted his leg," she said with a grimace. "A full leg cast. It was a bad break, poor guy."

She got no disagreement from either man about that, but possibly not for all the same reasons. "Leave him be," Joe said. "Must have been a very bad break—probably hurts like hell. We'll come down there when the doctor comes back and gives me permission to leave. Okay?"

"Is someone coming for you?"

"My guess is Gordy. He knows I'm here. I don't know if he is aware that you two are. But don't worry. Gordy will get us all home no matter what. He's a man who can be counted on to get 'er done." Joe laughed.

Sallee grimaced again. "I was just going to ask the nurses if I could use the phone when he spoke," she said, nodding toward Trey.

Trey leaned against the counter at the nurses' station with his arms crossed across his chest and one leg casually crossing the other at the ankle, staring at Sallee. *Bitch*, he thought, *fucking high-and-mighty bitch.*

"Your nephew does have a name, Sallee," Joe pointed out as evenly as if he were remarking that it was a nice day. "I have no doubt Trey would appreciate it if you addressed him by it."

Sallee took her leave and hustled down the hall. *Like a frightened old lady*, Joe thought. *She didn't get much sleep, but I can't think that that would make her so remarkably disagreeable to Trey.*

As Trey settled back into his Naugahyde roost, Joe asked, "Did you two have some altercation?"

"You were privy just now to every word we have spoken since I was fourteen years old. Your guess is as good as mine why she was acting like such a bitch. Sorry about that—she *is* your daughter."

"No, I do agree that is what she was acting like. It's interesting, though … she's not normally like that. Not overtly anyway. I guess Peter's accident is worse than she's letting on. And then there's this wedding. I can't imagine they are still planning to go through with that."

"Beats me. If I can't get back to New York, my guess is people won't be able to get here either," he said, suddenly realizing he'd left without a word to his son. "I hope Potts is okay," he added.

"My hunch is he hasn't even noticed you're gone," Joe rejoined affably—a thought that did little to ease Trey's mind. He suspected that Potts rarely if ever noticed when he was present.

"Mackey and Eric are good with kids," Joe continued, "and I bet you he and Joey are up to all kinds of mischief. Oh, by the way, Merry Christmas!"

❧

Sallee stormed into the slightly larger orthopedic room where Peter dozed in a wheelchair, his entire leg encased in plaster. "You'll never guess who's here," she exclaimed.

Her abrupt and noisy entrance startled Peter to attention. "Sallee," he said, blinking awake. "What are you talking about? Have they come to get us?"

"No," she said impatiently. "I *said*, 'You'll never guess who is here.'"

"If we're not leaving this place, and it's not someone here to pick us up, then I don't give a rat's ass who the hell is here."

"Dad and that … jerk." She waved a hand in the direction she'd just come from.

Peter glowered at her. "Jerk? What jerk? There *are* so many." His laugh was brittle.

"*You* know—Gordy's son, G. S. Mackey III. Where does he get off calling himself 'the third' anyway? He's a junior. Everything about him is fake. God, he makes my skin crawl. I feel like he's undressing me with his eyes."

"My guess is he is not." Peter smirked at his wife and then chuckled.

"Okay, asshole," she snapped, "find your own way home. I didn't come here with you to spend the night and fetch and carry for poor little you so that you could vent your spleen by taking shots at me. I can go home and let Virginia do that and sleep in a perfectly comfortable bed until she does, instead of this abysmal excuse for an armchair."

"What the hell is the matter with you? I was just kidding." Peter winced, partly for effect and partly because his leg did hurt.

"I'm not in the mood, thank you," she snapped. "Dad says that he's pretty sure Gordy's coming for us. I'm, oh, so looking forward to riding in close quarters with that creep."

"Unless you want to drive Virginia away for good, I suggest you give up your ever-so-sensitive sensibilities and just keep your mouth shut. I have a plan. I think this snowstorm has worked in our favor. It's clear the wedding can't go on now, and I'm pretty sure I'm going to be able buy *LeBoeuf* off. He seems to like cash from what I can gather. If we make a big stink about Gordon's son, the whole thing could come back on us. You know how your family is inclined to circle the wagons."

"You self-righteous prick! Peter, I have had it up to here." She started to hold her hand up to indicate how far and then let it drop in frustration. "Enough of you taking shots at my family. I have put up with your bullshit since we met. I've allowed you to run roughshod over me, dictate how to raise our children, and even tell me what to think and say, all based on the idea that you know better because ... why, Peter? Why do you know better? I forget." Her voice rose until she was shouting. "Oh, I remember—I don't have any idea how to behave because I was brought up all wrong. How in hell did I ever get to a place where that made sense to me?"

Peter tried to cajole her into lowering her voice. "Sallee, come on, sit down. You're tired. It's been a long, hard night on top of a very long, hard day. Lie down on the bed and get some sleep."

His efforts only infuriated her more.

"Shouting at the top of your lungs—do you want to bring your father and the pornographer down here?" he asked, hoping this might get her to see reason.

"I am sick of it. I don't think there's anything wrong with my family—certainly not any more wrong with my family than what was wrong with yours, and God knows there was an awful lot wrong with them."

"We don't have a pornographer in my family, nor was I raised in a hotbed of alcoholism and abuse." Peter feigned control before he started to bluster. "Your father abandoned you to be beaten by your despicable mother, who allowed the help to beat you as well. Then your very pious father finds religion"—the contempt Peter felt for Joe was palpable—"and waltzes back to kiss and make it all better after his daddy leaves him buckets of cash. And you tell me there's nothing wrong with the way you were brought up? I beg to differ. I think you suffer from Munchausen or Stockholm syndrome—one of those mental illnesses. You don't even know what healthy is. Monsters raised you. Look at what happened to your brother's kid. It is a perfect case in point. Your brother raised a fucking pornographer, for Christ's sake. What more example do you need?" He was shouting now.

"You bastard. You have the audacity to point fingers at me and my family when the product of your oh-so-healthy parenting is showing off how magnificently she was raised—as she throws temper tantrums worthy of an infant, shouts obscenities at my ninety-three-year-old mother, and acts like a perfect horse's ass—rather like her father, I might add. How dare you!"

"I am sorry to break up this love fest," Joe said from the doorway. "I assure you, if there had been a way to save myself from hearing the vitriol spewing from this room, I would have gladly taken it. Neither I nor any of my fellow patients, nor the staff, could help but hear." Joe continued evenly, "I have to ask, Peter, why on earth would you allow your daughter to choose such an unsavory place to marry?" He turned to go. "If you don't mind, the rest of us would very much like to be spared any more of your acrimony." The door swished closed behind him.

"A pornographer?" Joe asked his grandson as they made their way back to his room.

"Adult films." Trey shrugged, wishing Scotty could beam him up right about now as he gave his grandfather a sick smile.

"I can see why you are so taciturn."

As Joe and Trey were settling back into bed and chair, respectively, Sallee suddenly came barreling past the nurses' station. "Daddy, I am so sorry," she wailed from the doorway of his room. "Can I come in?"

"Sallee, I can't stop you. I have to say, however, that I would greatly appreciate it if you could give me some space to collect my thoughts right now."

Trey jumped up to leave.

"You," Joe said as he pointed to the chair, "sit."

ᕧ

"You want me to do *what*? Are you out of your mind?" Trey shook his head. "No way, no damned way."

Joe calmly repeated, "I'm going to say it one more time, so make sure to listen. I want you, the producer, to script a play."

"You're crazy. What on earth are you talking about? I'm a producer, not a playwright," Trey protested. "What the hell are you trying to prove?"

"You're going to have to use that talent of yours to rewrite what just happened here. You can base it on …" He thought for a minute and then broke out in a wide smile. "Perfect, couldn't be more appropriate." He paused for effect and then announced, "*A Christmas Carol*. It is the season, after all, and the subject matter is exactly what's called for. Hell, Dickens has already done most of the work for you. You are to write a part for Peter. Sallee will write your part, and Peter will apply his skills to creating a new role, an entirely new role, for his lovely bride."

"I don't understand the purpose of this." Trey stood up and began to pace. "We're not actors."

"Sit down," Joe snapped. "I don't want you wasting any energy. And that last remark of yours, sir, is where you are dead wrong. You idiots have been playing a part your whole lives. You know how the story goes, don't you? Christmas past, future, present. Peter and Sallee were kind enough to show us Christmas past, just now. We can safely infer Christmas future from what we heard. I want you all to write a new Christmas present. I want it believable. I expect to see the performances of your lives. And I expect to see Ginny have the happiest, most loving Christmas of her life."

"What if they don't, they won't do it? What if they just tell you to go fuck yourself?"

"I will go home, I will shoot Ginny in the head, and then I will turn the gun on myself," Joe said, his eyes cold as blue steel. "If you don't believe me, try me. Now get the hell out of here."

✧

Trey might have been the last person Sallee expected to see walking down the hall toward Peter's room. She had been glad to see that the nurses' station was at least temporarily unstaffed and had taken a seat directly across from it, trying to compose herself before dealing with Peter again. She hoped that the staff hadn't heard all that had come before. The fact that her father had was absolutely mortifying to her. Shame couldn't even touch how she felt, but it didn't prevent her from sneering up at her nephew.

"You had better follow me. I have something to tell you," Trey said, immediately continuing on toward Peter's room, not even re- motely interested in her reaction to him. He didn't bother to knock or hold the door for his aunt. He walked into the room, pulled the doctor's wheeled stool over with his foot, sat down, and glared at Peter while waiting for Sallee to follow him in.

Debating exactly what her next move would be, Sallee distracted herself by fussing about Trey's arrogant behavior. *Who the hell does he think he is, that he can me tell me to follow him just like that?*

From inside Peter's room, Trey bellowed, "Now! Sallee, get in here now."

When Sallee didn't respond, Trey went out into the hall, picked up the chair with Sallee in it, kicked open the door, and placed his load on the floor in front of her husband.

From where Joe sat down the hall, it was easy to tell exactly what had transpired from the sound of Sallee's enraged protests. A nurse hurried by his room, and he called out for her to stop. "I apologize for my ill-mannered family. They have been badly brought up, as I am sure you have heard."

"We can't allow this sort of behavior," the nurse protested. "They are disturbing the peace of the other patients. The staff is now on the beginning of its third twelve-hour shift. We need to catch some sleep as best we can. If these disruptions continue, I will have no recourse but to call the police."

"I understand," Joe said, nodding. "I think the histrionics are about to come to an end. Possibly one more outburst—"

As if on cue, there was a loud shriek. "What the hell?"

"I believe things will settle down from here on out," Joe told the nurse. "But if I am wrong, please do not hesitate to call the authorities. And thank you for working on Christmas. I am sorry you are stuck here, and I'm sorry for their behavior."

Sallee, now back outside his cubicle, stood listening to her father talk to the nurse. When the woman left, she was too ashamed to look at her. She ducked her head instead as she walked into the room. "Did you really tell Trey we had better get along, or you were going to go home and kill yourself after killing Mother?"

"Is that what he told you?"

"Something to that effect."

"I don't care if you get along or not, Sallee. You can do whatever you please when you are not a guest in my house. But I don't want that poisonous attitude anywhere near me or Ginny or the rest of my family. What I told Trey, and I'm pretty sure he told you, was that I expect you three to figure out a way to act like human beings for the duration of this storm. Script your parts because if you take this stuff home and act like you did here, I will shoot Ginny and turn the gun on myself. I am not kidding around. I would sooner have your mother dead than have her subjected to what I heard earlier."

Sallee started to protest but realized that Joe was leaving no room for doubt about what he was saying. Overcome with shame, she turned and retraced her steps to the orthopedic room.

ℱ

As Sallee sat listening to Peter and Trey bicker as to how they were to proceed, her mind wandered back to Ethel's room at the beach, the day before baby Dennis died. As she thought about that scene, she felt it had come to mind for a reason, so she began sharing it with no preamble.

"Ethel sat in the rocking chair, giving Dennis his bottle, rocking and cooing down at him. He was such a little thing. He held onto her forefinger like he'd never let it go, and he just gobbled down that milk. Must have been one of his last meals, if not the last. That was how I found them—I'd come in and thrown myself on the bed, looking for Ethel's opinion about something that had bothered me for some time. I knew she would have the answer.

"Carrie and Ben taught in a black high school during the school year and had worked at the beach house in the summer for years, long before my grandmother died. Not only did they take care of the house; they took care of whoever was visiting too, which generally amounted to my Uncle James and his wife Lizbeth and their daughter, Jilly. Mother had brought us down to the beach house that summer for what was really a rare visit there for us. It was the summer after Daddy left us.

"It didn't make sense to me that Carrie and Ben didn't like Ethel. I asked Ben one time why he didn't like her. He just blew the question off—which, now that I think about it, he did often. He was not one to voice much of his opinion. Carrie, on the other hand, would tell anyone except maybe Uncle Jimmy, Aunt Lizbeth, and Mother what she thought. I think I was afraid to ask her. She did frighten me."

Peter said, "She was probably the first black woman you knew that wasn't steppin' an' fetch—"

Sallee cut him off. "Would you shut up and listen?" She looked at Trey, as if for reassurance.

He said nothing but was leaning forward on his stool, elbows resting on his thighs, nodding for her to continue.

"I remember that I asked Ethel that day why it was that Ben and Carrie didn't like her. Her answer didn't make any sense to me at the time.

"She said, 'Some folks only see de brightness of de future, an' dey throw away any gold from de past. When Carrie an' Ben look at de past, all dey see is what dey ain't got. Dey is lookin' fo' de future t' give 'em what dey think dey missed out on. I think I's what we coloreds call an ol' folk. De ol' folks try t' make sense of de past; dey see dat dere was some good thangs 'bout it an' some bad thangs, too. What's wrong wit' me in Carrie an' Ben's way o' seein' is I ain't got no education, so I's stupid, an' I still work fo' white folks.'

"'But so do they,' I pointed out.

"'But de difference,' Ethel said, 'is dey see it as a step t' a better place, not as a restin' place or a way o' life like dey see I do. Ain't nothin wrong wit' seein' life dataway—jest makes it hard t' appreciate what's goin' on in de meantime, an' de meantime is dis he'ah time. It's too late fo' me t' get educated. When I was comin' 'long I had a choice: I could go t' school, or I could eat. I'd been stupid t' choose an education. I still gotta eat an' pay my bills. Dis he'ah is de only way I know I can do dat. 'Sides, I like what I do. Been doin' it my whole life 'cause I like it. Lovin' babies comes easy t' me. Don't matter what color dey is. Y'all's my babies. Ain't jest a job t' me. But takin' care o' dis house an' yo Uncle James an' Aunt Lizbeth an' little

Jilly is a job fo' Ben an' Carrie. Ain't wrong, jest is. I'd take my way o' seein' hands down. I 'spect dey'd take deirs.'"

Peter snorted as Sallee finished. "You could've spared us the Uncle Remus tale. I don't see how that pertains in the slightest to this guilt trip old Pops has foisted on his little girl."

"You really are a dumb fuck," Trey growled. Turning to Sallee, he said, "Sallee, my suggestion to you is to leave the son of a bitch here and go on with your life." Trey glared at Peter, whom he was coming to loathe. "I can't see how he adds one thing to the mix, and we only have a few hours at best, knowing my father, before it's showtime. I don't think Peter cares that Pops is dead serious."

"Ethel could have been describing me, rather than Ben and Carrie, for the last forty years," Sallee said, nodding slowly. "I don't know when I started looking at what was wrong in my life or why I started hoping that things were going to get better in the future. I threw out the gold of my past for a promise of a future that could not possibly be kept. I chased the emptiness of career and success in the hope of finding what was inside me all of the time. Talk about stupid. The picture I painted cast me as a poor little victim, abused and unloved." Sallee looked over at Peter, her eyes brimming with regret and sadness. "I can't blame Peter for believing my tale of woe. I told it so often I convinced myself of its truth." She started to cry. "The heartbreaking part of this is I missed out on so much love—my parents' and my family's and even Peter's, while hating him for not saving me from my own lie."

She took a deep breath. "Maybe Peter's right. What Dad's doing might be a guilt trip. Maybe he is trying to manipulate us. But I don't think so. It's not his style. I can't even begin to talk about the shame I feel to even think that he would rather be dead than be in a relationship with me like I am now. It is a hell of a wake-up call."

Trey hunched over on the stool, listening to his aunt while he debated what he was going to do. He knew the old man would blow Gran's and his own head off in a second if things didn't change in a positive way. That was a fact Trey could take to the bank. Being responsible for one's grandmother's death was bad enough. In addition, as much as he wanted to believe what he had told Joe—that the panic attack was a function of being back here—he knew it was a lie, just like Sallee knew her life was a lie, cast in the starkness of Joe's injunction. In the light of so much clarity, it was hard to hide, but to admit to these assholes what he had been afraid to admit even to himself for his entire adult life seemed to be asking too much. He didn't have the integrity to come clean, nor did he have the stones to stand toe to toe with Joe.

No one spoke for a good fifteen minutes, each wrestling with his or her own private devils. Finally, Trey started. "Shit, the old man has outplayed me. I have turned this upside down and backward, looking for a loophole."

Peter gave a derisive snort. "I bet you did, G. S. Mackey III."

Sallee jumped in. "Stop it, Peter. That's not going to help."

Trey glared at his aunt's husband for a long time before deciding he had no choice but to continue. "The way I see it, I have two choices: I can let you"—he shot another hate-filled glance at Peter—"control the situation by continuing to jump at your bait, or I can come clean. Pops is one of the few remaining people on this planet whose opinion I care about when it comes to what he thinks of me. Gran happens to be the other. So he's got me by the short hairs. If there were another way, I swear to you, you son of a bitch, you'd be toast.

"Sallee had the courage to show the way. I'm going to follow her lead and tell the story that seems to want to be told." He stopped, pointed at Peter, and said, "One fucking word out of your mouth, and I swear I will rearrange your face and be glad to do it. You can count on Sallee seeing you fall out of that chair." He stopped and looked at both Sallee and Peter until Sallee nodded, and then he continued.

"My grandmother Morga, the Scottish one, came to live with us just after Andy was born. I don't know if she had nowhere else to live or if she came to help out my mother, who was a drunk."

Peter moved in his chair. Trey stopped his story and gave him a look that said *don't even think about it, fucker.*

Sallee also glared at him. "You are so despicable. Can't you see how hard this is for Trey? Stop being a bastard."

"Swear to God, I was just trying to get comfortable." Peter hastily raised his right hand. "I swear."

Trey resumed his story. "As I am sure you, Sallee, can imagine, life at home was not much fun. The old battle-ax made it less so. Mom must have gone to treatment or something. She wasn't around. I think I was maybe five or six years old when it first happened. I have a name for her that in deference to you, Sallee, I won't use. I'll call her, to use Peter's word"—he glared at Peter—"a monster, because she really *was* a monster." He directed another pointed stare at Peter.

After a pause, Trey continued. "She came into the bathroom to make sure I was taking the bath that she had commanded—everything from that bitch was a command. I was in the tub playing with boats or something. The monster leaned over like she was going to wash me and grabbed hold of my dick. I got hard right away. I assure you, I couldn't help it. She slapped the ever-loving shit out of me as she screamed that I was a filthy guttersnipe. One time might have been something you could forget, but the monster did it over and over."

He paused, closing his eyes for a moment to collect his thoughts. "I tried to tell Dad. He wouldn't listen. How the fuck does a little kid even have words for that kind of shit? I never could tell when it would happen next or what would bring it on. She'd call me in from outside, stuff her hands down my pants, grab hold of me, and wail away. The only place I ever felt safe was at Gran and Pops's. Once I tried to tell Ethel, but I backed down when I realized it must be my fault. The last thing I wanted was to lose their love, so I kept my mouth shut.

"Then one day, she went after Andy. I don't know if she knew I was at home. I just know that I heard her screaming and Andy crying. I ran into his room. She was hunched over Andy's bed. Her back was turned to me. When she heard me, she wheeled around and dropped dead on the floor.

"God knows I wanted that bitch dead, but then when she was there on the floor, old dead-fish eyes staring up at me with a look of horror frozen on her face, a face that was so close in looks to my own mother's, I cried." Tears welled up in his eyes as he fought the years of dammed-up feelings that were now being tapped in his telling of the past. There wasn't a force on earth that could hold back his feelings now.

Sallee walked over to try to give him comfort, reaching to put an arm around his shoulders. He turned away, grabbed a pillow off of the gurney, put it up to his face, and howled into it with such ferocity that she backed away.

His wails subsided gradually to a sob. He shook himself, swallowed hard, and lifted his head. "I didn't know what to do. Andy was screaming. I was sure I had killed her. If wanting someone dead was enough, I was going to hang. I don't know what happened or how long we were there before Dad came in and found Andy and me in the room crying. I can remember saying, 'I'm sorry, I didn't mean to do it,' saying 'I'm sorry' over and over. I couldn't stop.

"I remember, Gran and Ethel came and got us and took us back to their house. I wet the bed every night until I went to boarding school, and not one person ever thought to wonder why except Ethel. By then I was too ashamed and too entrenched in my guilt to tell. She must have asked me a hundred different ways in that way of hers." He looked at Sallee. "You know, where she asks but doesn't— just somehow lets you know that whatever it is, she's still going to love you whether you tell her or not. I can't describe it. But I know you know what I'm talking about."

Sallee nodded her head in agreement, with tears streaming down her face.

❧

Peter appeared stunned by what he had just heard. He prided himself on that being one of his better talents—conjuring up the exact look people expected. More than anything, he wanted to go to sleep. His leg throbbed, but asking for pain meds at this particular juncture could be taken as inappropriate—like he didn't care, which he didn't. The last thing he wanted to do was give away his true feelings. Shame was not among his emotions presently, and as he thought about it, he wasn't even sure whether he had ever experienced the emotion firsthand. He presumed it was the feeling the other two were experiencing, unless they were just as good at faking it as he. He knew Sallee wasn't, but Trey—who knew? That could have just been him doing a great job of playing a role. A mighty fine job, if it was an act. Peter had to hand it to him. Other than possessing what mere mortals would probably see as a heart of stone and being what dear old Joe—that sanctimonious fool—would no doubt see as a monumental jerk, Peter had nothing to confess, and he certainly had no intention of confessing to these two. He happened to be living just the life he had planned. He'd married an extremely assured, accomplished woman, at the top of her law class and good-looking to boot, whom he had then systematically turned into a servile shadow of her former self. He had produced the perfect American family, a girl and a boy, both highly educated, both completely without charm, both losers. He didn't need his pompous prick of a father-in-law's pathetic impersonation of Werner Erhard to force him to see what kind of man he was or why. He knew.

What he didn't know was how to get through the rest of this fiasco without having to admit that he was a ruthless son of a bitch who enjoyed toying with people's lives. He smiled to himself sardonically. *Okay, pal, you need an Oscar performance. Nothing less will do. Go for it.*

"I'm glad I am going last. First, let me say, Trey, that was terrible, what you went through. Man, I don't know how you are able ..." He let the words just hang there, sure Sallee would supply just the right amount of pathos. When she didn't, and enough time had elapsed so that he appeared dutifully moved, he continued. "Man, how you just settled for porn ... I'd be on death row." He liked that jab—actually, he couldn't help himself—but it looked like G. S. Mackey III, who glowered sourly back at him, was not sufficiently pliant yet for Peter's kind of fun.

Sallee gave him a hard look. "Peter, if you want any sort of relationship with me in the future, you had better start taking this seriously," she quietly informed her husband, with enough steel in her voice to convince Trey, if not Peter.

What a bloody fucking bore Sallee is, Peter thought, *getting sucked into this crap*. Peter decided that the best way to proceed was to pretend to tell a story as near to the truth as he could make it without admitting that he'd had a perfect life, with perfect parents—he would just hint at the supposed perfection. So he started in on his embellished story, as far from the reality of his real life in foster care as was possible, while still in the same galaxy.

"My parents probably loved me just a little too much. They had struggled for years to have a child. When my mother found out she was pregnant, my father sold his manufacturing business and moved to Orange, Connecticut, so that Mother could live in a safe suburb while he taught engineering at Yale." So far this was easy. Sallee knew this much of the story. "Orange is just how you would imagine a typical New England town, complete with white clapboard churches and a town green—the perfect place to grow up.

"I can remember being so lonely as a child. If my mother could have wrapped me in cotton wool and put me on a shelf, she would have. She was so afraid that I might get hurt, or somehow be taken away from her, that I think you could say that her greatest fault was that she was overprotective." *Nice touch; this gives a hint of discontent without really admitting to any.*

"Like in all things, my father excelled as a professor. I couldn't hold a candle to his accomplishments, though I tried, graduating at the top of my class in high school and college. The man was a genius. I think it's hard for me to admit that my father was so much better at everything than I was. When I was accepted at Harvard Law, I was sure I had finally achieved something beyond my father. It was only after he died that I discovered that he too had been accepted at Harvard and turned it down, deciding that a career in engineering was more to his liking." *Careful, you don't want to lay it on too thick. You need something they can relate to, some suffering.* As he ran several scenarios around in his mind, he let his head hang, looking as if he were struggling not to blow the cover off a long-kept secret.

After he judged that sufficient time had elapsed and enough angst had played across his face, he said, "Sallee doesn't know this." He looked his wife straight in the eyes and said with an expressive sigh, "Forgive me. I've lied to you all of these years. My parents weren't happy. I know you think they died while vacationing in the Alps. It's not true. I was too ashamed to admit that my perfect father had an affair. My mother found out about it when he went to Switzerland, supposedly on business. She followed and confronted him. I was in law school at the time. I only know because she left a note. It was a murder–suicide. If I hadn't heard your stories, I never would have had the courage to admit to anyone the truth about my beloved parents." *Nice touch, even if I do say so myself.*

He felt like now was a good time to ask for a pain pill. His leg hurt like hell, and all of this mea culpa shit had gone beyond dull. If there was one thing he couldn't stand, it was dull. Without having to draw on any of his immense skills of deception, he begged Sallee to ask for some pain relief.

She more than happily left the room but at a languid pace, decidedly not her typical speed, to look for his doctor. *I am going have to do some work on getting her back in line*, he thought, *when all of this is over.*

♋

While Peter was fabricating his life story, Trey, new to this experience of allowing memories to flood, remembered a time when he was younger and heard Ethel and Gran talking about Sallee and Peter. Gran asked what Ethel thought had gotten into Sallee, to make her say and believe such hateful and untrue things about her life before Peter.

"It just breaks my heart," he remembered Gran saying, "to hear how much disdain she has for us and how oblivious she seems to be to the untrue and ugly things she says about her childhood. I would be the first one to agree that I acted horribly when the children were young. It hurts so much to think that those are her only memories. I certainly did everything I could to rectify things once I got myself in a better place. I know I wasn't a good mother. You made up for the kind of trauma she went through—we all went through—but you were … you were loving when I wasn't. It makes me so sad."

In memory now, Trey saw Ethel pull a dishtowel out of her apron string and start dusting the dining room table as she spoke, always a sure sign that she was upset. "I think Mista Peter done got int' Sallee, is what I think. He is slippery as a eel an' mean as a snake."

"Ethel," Ginny said, "I've never heard you dislike someone so much."

As if she were in the room with him, Trey heard Ethel's little snort. *"Well, Miz Ginny, you ain't been listenin' den. Dere be plenty o' people I doan like."* She attacked one spot on the table with more than her usual vigor. *"I doan trust him far as I can throw 'im. De thangs he say t' Sallee make me want t' haul off an' hit 'im upside de head most times. Den I want t' turn her over my knee fo' listenin' t' his foolishness. She know better'n dat."*

Ginny, sounding surprised, said, "Where do you hear these things? He seems reasonably polite when I'm around."

Ethel continued dusting with a vengeance. *"When dey is eatin' breakfast, an' any ol' where you ain't. He one o' dem kinda men dat think colored folk doan got no ears, I reckon, or maybe jest servants doan. He talk t' Sallee when I's around, different dan when you or Mista Joe be 'bout. Dey be a time or two it took everythang I had not smack 'im good. What I don't understand is why Sallee doan.*

"Don't what?" Ginny asked.

"*Haul off an' smack 'im int' de middle o' next week. Miz Ginny, dat man don't know what de truth is. I hear 'im say one thang t' y'all an' turn round an' tell a whole 'nother story t' someone else any number o' times.*"

Returning his attention to the present, Trey forced himself to turn his gray eyes on Peter and look right at him. "You know you really are a fucker." He was not going to let this worm intimidate him. There was no question in Trey's mind that the way he earned a living wasn't something he was proud of. Peter had made it abundantly clear he knew that too. But what he did, Trey thought, wasn't what he was. What he did could change. No, he didn't want his son to follow in his footsteps. Maybe that was a small point and maybe just a justification. But Trey knew in his heart that he still had some decency left in him. He was in touch with it for the first time in a long while, and more importantly, he liked the way it felt. It was clear that Peter didn't possess a shred. Trey wondered if he ever had.

Continuing to stare at Peter, Trey said, "I've never heard so much bullshit in my entire life. Don't worry, I'm not going to blow your cover as long as you agree to leave as soon as it's possible—and before you do leave, you offer Sallee a very amicable divorce. She deserves at least that for putting up with you for as long as she has.

"In the meantime, just one disagreeable word out of you, and I promise that chair will go for a ride that no one will question, leaving Sallee a bereaved widow—my preference, not that it matters." Trey's jaw tightened. He had operated for over ten years in one of the sleazier businesses imaginable, he thought, and had never encountered such a despicable creep. Hell, the people he worked with were Boy Scouts compared to this slimeball. *Poor Sallee. I bet she doesn't have a clue. Or she just can't admit it to herself if she does.*

10

After more time than Peter felt appropriate had passed, Sallee appeared with a nurse in tow.

"I was just coming to check on your vitals when I ran into your wife, who said that you are in a lot of pain?" The puffy-eyed nurse checked his blood pressure and temperature. She hadn't, Peter noted, succeeded in her effort to tidy up hair and uniform, rumpled from an apparent attempt at a quick nap. Weariness made her voice hoarse. "On a scale of one, being none, to ten, what kind of pain are you in?"

"Nine or ten," Peter grimaced. "It just started up really badly."

As much as Trey was suspicious of Peter so suddenly taking a decided turn for the worse, he had to admit that Peter's color had faded from his usual florid to a dull gray color. "He didn't look like this just a few minutes ago," Trey said to the nurse. "He was complaining of pain, but he still had color, not this"—he stopped and fumbled for a description—"fish belly. I mean just seconds ago; this just came on seconds ago."

The nurse pushed a call button above Peter's empty gurney before ushering Trey and Sallee out. As medical staff flowed into the room, the nurse drew the curtain and kicked the doorstop out of the way, leaving Trey and Sallee alone in the hall.

"Wow, that was fast. Jesus, one minute, he was his usual"—Trey stopped himself from saying "prick of a self"—"and then out of nowhere he turns that sickly gray." He looked over to see that that his observations were not having the best effect on Sallee, who was looking a bit peaked herself.

"Come on, you and I need to get something to eat." Trey took his aunt's arm solicitously. "I don't know about you, but I haven't had a thing since breakfast yesterday. I'm so hungry I could even eat hospital food." Seeing Sallee hesitate, he reassured her. "Peter is in the right hands. There is nothing we can do here but get in the way."

Sallee yielded, and he escorted her down the hall past Joe's room, where they stopped to look in. Seeing that he was asleep, they moved on.

The hospital, usually a hive of activity, was eerily quiet, populated by exhausted personnel whose normal bustle and rush had slowed to a numb slog. In the elevator, two nurses in scrubs leaned in the corners, too tired to stand. The few staff members at tables in the cafeteria looked like marionettes abandoned by their puppeteers.

Sallee, uncharacteristically subdued, allowed Trey to lead her to a table and absently nodded when he asked her if she wanted coffee. He pulled out a chair for her, making sure she sat before hurrying off to find coffee. When he returned, she too had slumped over the table, with her head on her arm. "Try some of this," he urged, promising to return in minutes with food.

She shrugged, more tired than she could remember ever feeling and somewhere beyond hungry.

Trey, buoyed by his newly unburdened soul, picked up a tray, put two plates on it, and proceeded to pile them both high with assorted breakfast offerings. When he placed the two brimming plates on the table between them, along with silverware and smaller plates for both, Sallee looked even paler, if that was possible.

Sallee smiled up at him. "You must have been a waiter once."

"Once, once, only once." He shuddered. "There is not enough money on the planet to make me do that again. Even we pornographers have our limits." He laughed at the easy joke as he sat down in his chair and started helping himself to eggs, bacon, toast, and hash browns. "Really, you should eat. You'll feel better, I promise. You know, it's funny. I feel better than I have in years. Pops has been kind of working on me, trying to get me to talk about what was bothering me, since we were back at the barn last night. The idea of telling anybody what I told you today was so repulsive to me. What I just did, I didn't think was possible. If I had known how good I would feel afterward, I would have told that story a long, long time ago."

He paused over his full but still untouched plate. "Thank you for your part in allowing me to see the fear and horror that has been driving me all these years. I know that sounds cheesy, but it's true. I was too ashamed to look at all of it, ever."

"It's a terrible story," Sallee agreed. "I can imagine it must have been a horrifying thing to have to deal with. What a burden. I have to ask, and I suppose if you don't want to talk about it, you don't have to. How in the world did you get into the pornography business?"

Trey quickly corrected her. "Please, it's adult entertainment. I know it sounds like hairsplitting, and I'm sure, from your perspective, it really still is pornography, but the fact remains that what FlyBy produces is in the category of erotic adult entertainment."

"And the difference is?" Sallee asked.

Trey laughed. "The difference is subjective. First and foremost, how you view sex defines the difference between what you see as porn and erotica in a big way." His tone became more earnest as he punctuated his points with a wave of the fork. "What I find pornographic, you might find artistic, and vice versa. Sex is such a hot topic emotionally. As a country, we are so sexually repressed. Believe it or not, there is a lot of artistic thought—"

"I wouldn't wait for a call from the National Endowment for the Arts anytime soon," Sallee broke in, scoffing gently.

"I don't mind talking to you about the industry or even why I got into it, but I have to say, I would much prefer to get to know you a little better first," he replied. "Find out what drives you, makes you tick, how you see your life in ten years."

Sallee raised her eyebrows, half-questioning, half-dismissive.

"Having heard myself tell my story earlier," he continued, "I know that it doesn't take Sigmund Freud or Carl Jung to see that I'd likely have some pretty conflicted feelings about sex and women—so no surprise that I'm in the business of sex. Ya think?" He shoved a slice of bacon in his mouth. "I have to tell you, this conversation would not have taken place yesterday."

"No kidding," Sallee snorted.

"Right. If Pops had not forced the issue, I never would have told you about what my grandmother did. And the shame would have kept me from talking to you freely now about what I do. Your very astute husband pointed out how obvious my shame is, and I don't mind telling you I could've killed him for it."

He stabbed a bite of scrambled egg and then looked up. "But right now I'm so grateful for what Pops pushed us into. I feel like a new man. Does that mean I'm going to go home and tell Dad and Mom what I do for a living? Hell no! They wouldn't understand and would probably think it was their fault. I guess to a degree it was, but I'm the one who made the choice. I'm the one who got a great education and used it to make a lot of money in a less than acceptable industry. There's a good chance at this point, thanks to Pops again, that I might start thinking about changing what I do. It's a tough world, and I don't want my son following me into it."

He paused and smiled. "It makes me laugh to think about what brought me here— Virginia's wedding, I mean. Reunions—college, high school, or family—are not places where you would tend to find many people in the *industry*."

"I don't suppose so," Sallee laughed. She next took Trey completely by surprise. With her elbow on the table and her chin casually cupped in her hand, she asked him what he thought of Peter's story.

His brain whispered, *Caution, buddy. This could be a trap.* So rather than answer honestly, he shook his head. "It's tough to say." Then he reconsidered. "No, actually, it isn't. I didn't believe one word of it. Felt like I was having lines delivered to me … and badly."

"Do you know how many times I have heard that story?"

Trey again shook his head and leaned in, pulling his chair closer.

"I've known Peter since I was in my midtwenties, I guess—just out of law school—so that's way over half my life. Do you know, I've never heard him tell another story about his youth, only that one. It's as if he grew up in witness protection, which I know he didn't. He has one story, and he can't even tell that story consistently, although he thinks he does. By the way, I have never seen his law school diploma. Don'tcha think he, of all people, if he had gone to Harvard Law School, would have his diploma displayed front and center?"

"I don't get it." Trey shook his head. "If you know he's been lying to you all this time, why in God's name would you have stayed with him?"

"That, young man, is a great question, one I have asked myself for, I don't know, the last thirty years. I think you and I have more in common than it would appear at first blush."

Trey, confused, tilted his head to one side. "Go on?"

Sallee sat up straight and took a gulp of coffee to fortify herself. "Oh dear, how do people drink this stuff? Ghastly! Ugh." She put the cup down on the table, wrapping her hands around the mug just to salvage its warmth. "Look," she said, nodding toward the window, "it stopped snowing." Above the new parking garage, blue sky peeked out around dove-gray clouds. "Bet there are a lot of folks here who will be glad to go home," she said, looking around the room filled with exhausted people and then down at her hands leaching the warmth from the dreadful coffee.

"I hate waste," she said. "I remember my fourth-grade teacher told a story about a woman, very rich, who had a party. Lots of the details of this story escape me." She smiled a sad half smile. "But when people were cleaning up, rather than give the leftovers to the help or save them for herself, the woman commanded that they throw it all away. I vividly remember the teacher going into detail over a pan of good unbaked rolls that were tossed in the trash. I can still see her, quintessential stern-faced spinster that she was, scowling: 'Such waste!'"

"Yeah?" Trey said, perplexed as to where Sallee was heading. He wished she would get on with it.

"Clearly, a cautionary tale for our impressionable little minds," Sallee continued, "and so, of course, there had to be a moral to drive home the point. According to Miss …" She paused as the name refused to appear and then gave up with a dismissive wave. "What's-her-name, I don't remember—according to my teacher, the very rich woman lost all of her money and died a pauper. Hands down, that was a more terrifying tale than the banshees in *Darby O'Gill and the Little People*. Think what that old biddy of a teacher would have done with Disney behind her." Sallee laughed a mirthless laugh.

"By the time I figured out that Peter was totally full of shit, I had invested so much of my life's energy in my own tale of 'oh poor me' that I had forgotten how to find my way home. I forgot that I had ruby slippers in the back of my closet. There was so much stuffed on top of them. Life with Peter became 'the devil I know is better than …' well, you know." She shrugged. "You make one wrongheaded decision and then a few more on top of that, and before you know it, more than half your life has gone by, and what do you do then?"

She picked up her cup. "It's sort of like this coffee. I hate the coffee, but I have to find something to redeem it because I hate waste more, so I wrap my hands around it to at least get that much out of it; otherwise, it's a total waste. You keep that sort of decision-making process up, and the next thing you know, you have heard the same story told ten different ways from Sunday, as Ethel would put it, and it doesn't faze you in the slightest.

"Dad has done us both a huge favor today. I can't say I applaud his methods, but I'm not sure anything else would have sufficed. I am going to ask Peter for a divorce. I'm going to move back home to Virginia, and I am going to let the chips fall where they may. By the way, I don't blame Peter, although I can only imagine his hell. It must be pretty awful for him to be as mendacious as he is."

The pair soon finished their breakfast and started back toward Joe's room. Trey had thought to gather some food for Joe, though the partitioned foam container gave the appearance of a doggie bag rather than breakfast.

Joe, dressed in his street clothes now, waved from his gurney as the two came around the corner with big smiles on their faces. "You two look like fast friends," he said, trying hard not to gloat.

Trey pulled the ubiquitous cantilevered table over and placed breakfast on it before leaning over and kissing the old man on the cheek. "Thanks," he said with tear-filled eyes. "Thanks." He blinked away his tears. "Sorry the food isn't a little more appealing."

Joe winked at his grandson as he pulled the table up to himself and opened the box. "Yum, powdered scrambled eggs, fake bacon, and cold toast. My favorites. How did you know? As my old daddy was so fond of saying, hunger is a great sauce."

Trey smiled at his granddad, pulled out his phone, and stepped out of the room.

Meanwhile, Joe efficiently stripped the plastic sheath off his fork and began stuffing food into his mouth with gusto. "Nice to see you back, Sallee girl. Been a long time." He winked and grinned, despite a mouth full of eggs.

"Dad," Sallee groaned. "Gross!" She laughed. "We spared you the coffee, although if I remember correctly, you would drink all kinds of dreadful brews back in the day."

"Yeah, you gotta watch those memories. They don't always serve you," Joe cautioned with a momentary point of his fork and another big grin.

"Don't I know that," Sallee agreed.

Trey popped back into the room. "Dad's on his way," Trey had popped back in, he said, sounding as if he were six and referring to Santa instead of his father. "Cell phone's working. Anyone you want to call?"

"Would you mind calling the house?" Joe smiled. "I would like to assure my bride that I am hale enough for her to plan how she is going to dismember me for my stunt last night."

They laughed in unison.

"While you do that, I am going to see if there's an update on Peter," Sallee said. "Give everyone my love. Oh, and tell Virginia to stop, whatever it is she's doing."

"Sorry, honey. That is not a job for us," Joe said with a wink. "It's all yours, and I have no doubt it's one of those jobs that will be waiting for you whenever you are ready. What happened with Peter?"

"I don't know. I thought he just had a broken leg or ankle. But about an hour ago he turned a horrible shade of—what was that phrase?—fish belly. I think that's how Trey described it. He's the artist, you know." She grinned at her nephew. "Suddenly, Peter was in a lot of pain. The nurse sent us out of the room, so we decided to get something to eat. So to answer your question, I don't know. I have to go find out."

Sallee returned a few minutes later. "He wasn't in the room. The room's a wreck. There wasn't anyone manning the nurses' station. I couldn't find his doctor—or anybody for that matter—to talk to. Finally, I went to the admitting desk and asked the nurse there. She said, 'It's unclear.'" Sallee sighed, hung her head, and then continued. "On the way back, I ran into the nurse that kicked us out of the room. She didn't know if he's in emergency surgery or the ICU awaiting surgery or what. I think she said he had an embolism, or maybe she said it was a something-or-other thrombosis, and they caught it before it burst. I'm a dunce when it comes to medical terminology. What is an embolism, anyway? And why did he turn that horrible color and so fast?" She looked on the verge of panic. "I don't know … I … God, I think I'm going to throw up."

Again she sighed, closed her eyes, and then blew out a long stream of air, leaning up against the glass wall with her arms wrapped around her torso. "This place is crazy today. People have been on duty for way too long. Nobody seems to know anything. I have had

more than my fair share of drama, and I have no idea what to do."
She walked over and draped herself over the foot of her father's cot.

On his way out of the room, Trey said, "Let me go see if I can
get any information."

Joe rubbed Sallee's back. "Do you want to lie down and maybe
take a nap? It might do you some good."

"I don't think I could possibly sleep right now." She rolled on her
side and took his hand. "Excepting your Machiavellian scheming,
I am very grateful that you forced me to take a look at my life this
morning. I don't know what kind of state I would be in now if this
had happened before I got my head screwed on a little straighter. I
don't want him to die. I am pretty sure I don't want to be married
to him. But we've shared a lot of our lives together, and that has to
count for something." She unashamedly allowed the tears to stream
down her face.

"I am proud of you. He's a lucky man to have found you." Joe
smiled down at his daughter.

෧

Early and Burt were giving Gordon a look that was the canine
equivalent of *Do you honestly believe you can leave us here? You go, we
go, and that's that!*

Alex found Gordon there at the truck, arguing apologetically
with the two Jack Russell terriers. "It's gonna be crowded with all
of us in the truck. I'd take you, but Alex can help out if we get in
trouble, and you guys—think about it—just can't."

"Do you always talk to your dogs like that?" Alex inquired.

"Only when they start it. Otherwise, I don't need to," Gordy
said, as if Alex had asked him whether snow fell up. "Don't you?"

"What, argue with my dog? I don't have one, but even if I did,
I doubt I would. I don't know. I've never thought about it. Does
arguing with my fiancée count?" He laughed. "I do that a lot, especially these days."

"Decidedly not. Arguing with your fiancée does not count, nor is it a very good sign for happily ever after, now that you mention it." Gordon moved on as they climbed in the truck, not one to linger on dubious ground. "I would have figured you for a dog man. I'm sort of surprised that you don't have one, but then I'm sorta surprised you live in New York City too. What a cesspool. What do you do up there anyway?"

Alex didn't consider himself a wizard at reading people, but since Gordon had just dismissed all of New York as a cesspool, he surmised that his present occupation might not sit very well and changed the subject. "Where's Bill?"

"Gone over to plow out his place. I don't think he wants to spend another night on the floor. I hear you and Virginia had the guest room last night." It was clear from his tone that Gordon didn't approve.

"Hey, it's her family, her rules," Alex said with a shrug. "What was I supposed to do? Pick her up and move her? I'd rather disturb a rattler."

"I see your point," Gordon laughed. "What did you say you did up there in the city?"

Alex groaned inwardly. This was going to be just a great little trip. "Wait tables and model some."

Gordy laughed and beat the steering wheel. "I thought all those male models were pansy boys? You're no pansy, are you?"

"You know that's offensive, don't you?" Alex couldn't believe he'd just said that to Virginia's uncle. "It is."

"You are a queer then?"

"What difference would it make?"

"None, other than you are marrying my sister's daughter is all. Don't get your panties in a twist. I was just making conversation. Suit yourself. I don't give a damn, not really."

They were setting off for the hospital before the storm finally packed it in. Alex, a one-man snowplow, had dug a path to the barn and instructed Eric to follow up as soon as it stopped snowing. "Grab a broom and brush off the rest of the snow, would ya? We don't want any of the old'uns to slip and fall. This stuff is gonna be slipperier than snot on a doorknob."

He had begun to slip back into his native Rocky Mountains twang, yet another thing that irritated Virginia. Now that he thought of it, he was getting a little fed up with always being on the outs with her. Maybe before it was too late, he ought to give this marriage thing another look, he thought as he scratched his day-old stubble. *Maybe I'll grow a beard.*

❧

For most of the morning, Virginia and Mackey had been circling each other like sumo wrestlers looking for an opening. Mackey's plan was to unnerve Virginia with kindness, whereas Virginia was looking to take Mackey down. She was fed up with this Miss Goody Two-Shoes persona Mackey had adopted of late.

After breakfast, Eric grabbed his wife's hand, pulling her aside. "Come on, while the kids are busy playing. Let's go into the other room and meditate. I'm thinking today would be an especially good day for it. There are so many emotional traps at play."

"What do you mean, emotional traps?"

"It's Christmas—is there a day more about expectations, mostly unmet ones? And then there is all of this stuff with your granddad and Virginia's dad."

"There is nothing for me about Virginia's dad other than that he is an idiot. I've never liked him."

"Okay, well there is that then. Anyway, do I really need to convince you that meditating today would be a good idea?"

"I guess not." She kissed him on the cheek, wrapped her arms around him, and then ran her tongue quickly around his ear, whispering, "We could do more than meditate if you want."

"You don't have to twist my arm." He sneaked a peek at Joey, who was engrossed along with his cousins in putting together a racetrack while making ferrous motor noises. "He looks occupied for the time being. I never thought I would say this, but meditation first, okay?"

"Yeah, okay. I haven't lost my touch, have I?"

"No, not in the least." He shot her a lascivious grin. "But I think sex after meditation would be awesome, don't you?"

"Don't know, but I am eager to find out. I love you, Eric." She kissed him hard. "Thank you for taking such good care of me and for helping me learn to meditate. Do we have to report the sex?"

They both laughed.

"What are you two whispering about?" Virginia smirked.

"We're going to meditate. Want to join us?" Mackey asked, meaning it.

"Oh please, I'd rather help with the cooking. You certainly didn't look like you had meditation on your minds a second ago. Is it some sort of tantric sexual meditation? I might be interested in that." She looked at Eric and licked her lips suggestively.

Mackey forced herself to laugh. "Nope, plain old boring meditation. Eric and I have been doing it every day for the last six weeks. It's—"

Virginia cut her off. "Yeah, yeah, I know. You are so Zen now. I get it. I'm so impressed. Go on, go do your little Buddha deal. Now that my cell is working again, I have a wedding to cancel."

"I'm sorry, Virginia. I really am. Do you want some help?" Mackey asked. "We'll only be about fifteen minutes, and I'd be happy to help."

"There's nothing to do but write one message and mass e-mail it. You go ahead and do your thing. It's not like anyone is going to be surprised or is planning to come in this mess." She swept her hands around.

Eric followed Mackey into Joe's office and shut the door. "That was sweet of you to offer, but thanks for blowing me off along the way!"

"Sorry. I thought she needed me more than you did. That's all. Will you forgive me?"

He came up to her, took her in his arms, whispered, "Yes," and kissed her until her toes curled. "Now, let's get to meditating," he said as he sat down on the floor and deftly folded his legs into a half-lotus position.

"Now?" she moaned.

11

Bill had come back from plowing as excited as any ten-year-old, with much to report. The electricity was on at his house, he had cleared a path so that the entire group could walk over easily, and—the best news—he would sleep in his own bed tonight. Best of all for the rest of the crew, he had made—to use a Joey word—an *awesome* sled run just off the drive. "Get the sleds out!" he whooped. "We've got some serious sledding to get to!"

The conditions were perfect. He had to admit, the run he had spent the last two hours crafting was a thing of beauty, complete with banked curves and a disembarking spot equal to none. As he helped Joey and Potts climb into their snow gear, he eagerly described his morning project, to which he had applied his entire store of architectural knowledge.

"Best part is no trudging uphill afterward. I made it so the sled comes to an easy stop at the bottom by the pool. All you do is step onto the pool deck—all snow blown off, thank you very much," he added, with a mock bow. "You take the steps to the front of the house and go from there to the driveway. The most civilized sledding you'll ever experience. It's an easy walk back up to the start. It's perfect, if I do say so myself."

He was as eager as his grandson and great-nephew to try it out. "Come on, let's go! But wait, before we do …" He paused the process of helping the boys with snow pants and boots. "Does anybody have to go to the bathroom?" He started to laugh. "I remember that a certain little girl would let me bundle her all up, boots and all, and then say, 'Daddy, I gotta go potty.'" He winked at Mackey, who winked back.

"What's so funny about that?" Joey asked Potts.

Potts shrugged. "Beats me."

Mackey and Eric helped Josh and Sally get ready. Kids and grown-ups alike piled out of the house in a flurry of excited burbling. Mackey headed to the barn with the older kids to gather up the sleds while Bill, Eric, and the little boys went to survey Bill's masterwork.

Six dogs sat at the door, patiently waiting and watching for the crowd to make up their minds about which way they were headed, before finally deciding that the barn held the most interest, so with three resonant *ba-roo-oos* and two yaps, the canine majority followed Mackey and the kids, tails wagging expectantly. Rusty, however, delighted to be homeward bound, followed Bill to his own house, where he spent the rest of the morning snoozing by the kitchen door. The other five escorted every sled down the track, ears flapping and tongues lolling as they cavorted like mayflies around the careening sledders.

"They're going to get run over!" Sally yelled over their baying. "Can't we make them stop?"

Mackey yelled back over the din, "They are having way too much fun. Don't worry. They can get out of the way, and they'll stop when they get tired." She had to jump out of the way herself as Joey and Potts, giggling, came roaring by with two canine escorts galumphing ahead.

❧

After a brief powwow in Ginny's kitchen, the remainder of the household decided that cooking such a large meal would be easier in Stuart's bigger and better-equipped kitchen. Susan and Andy volunteered to pack up the dinner fixings while Ginny and Stuart would go ahead to prepare a room for Peter. Ginny, so thrilled to get her house back, almost buzzed audibly with excitement. The idea of taking hemlock, as Joe had suggested just a few nights earlier, had started to intrude on her to-do list for that day. She was happy to dismiss that recourse with a laugh. *It's the little things*, she thought. Ethel immediately came to mind.

She remembered the day of the wreck, almost eighty years ago, that had so changed her life. Had hemlock been available, she gladly would have taken it. She went over to the kitchen table and sat down, overcome with the memory of that time long ago.

"What are you not telling me, Ethel?" she remembered asking. The memories of that time in her bedroom whirled around her like smoke curling from burning leaves on a misty day. It was hard to tell the smoke from the mist, all mixed together.

"Something is going on, I know it," Ginny had said. "You are not normally this jumpy. The whole place has that feeling like something is wrong. Pansy doesn't ever move that fast."

Ethel just stood there, looking like a kid about to wet herself as she shifted onto one foot and then the other. "Miz Ginny, you needs t' stay righ' he'ah. Momma say I is t' keep you righ' …"

Ginny snapped out of her reverie for a moment. *Oh, and then I broke my promise to her too. Did Bertha punish her, I wonder?*

Ginny remembered running, running toward the uproar and then seeing all of that black acrid smoke. She could still hear Ethel panting behind her, trying for all she was worth to gather enough wind to yell, "Stop, stop, Miz Ginny!" What it must have taken, poor soul! She was so right. Going out there and seeing all of that carnage, smelling the blood, oil, and sweat of men and mules, had been terrible. It was so horribly heady, such a waste.

Ginny started to swoon and caught herself only barely. No one in the kitchen noticed, so busy were they with their appointed tasks. No one had noticed her back then either, at first. Then there was that dreadful C. L. *What was his last name?* she wondered. *He used to live next door. God, life is funny that way.* Ethel, bless her heart, cut *him off, whatever his name was, and practically got run down by mules in the bargain. Dabney! That was it.*

She quaked as the memories continued. Losing Cy had been heartbreaking. Losing Ethel would have been catastrophic. She shuddered. *I should have listened to you, Ethel, and stayed put, but oh no, not me.* Ginny shook her head. *How she put up with me, I'll never know, but I thank God every day that she did.* She shook her head again as if to clear it. "Ohhh, what a day that was!"

"Did you say something, Mom?" Stuart looked over at her mother, her eyes filled with concern. "Are you feeling all right?"

Ginny waved off Stuart's concern. "Just thinking about old times. I'm ready to go when you are. Not that I think I'll be much help."

Once they were dressed for the outdoors, Stuart took her mother by the arm, gingerly leading her down the hill at a snail's pace.

"We can go faster than this," Ginny carped.

"Not on my watch, we can't," Stuart said. "I'm not putting you in jeopardy. It's beautiful out. Enjoy the fresh air."

"If I sign a waiver, can we go a little faster?" Ginny giggled.

Stuart patted her mother's arm. "Humor me. I'm no spring chicken and am not interested in a broken hip. Okay?"

❧

Virginia felt like the walls were closing in on her. There were people everywhere. Not even the view through the windows offered relief—there was only a prison-gray landscape when she could see out, and when she couldn't, it was like staring at a blank computer screen. As far as calling off the wedding, she was glad to do it. Alex had turned, it seemed overnight, into Grizzly Adams. "If he grows a beard, I am outta here. It's over, no hope!" she muttered.

Lying on the bed and staring up at the wooden ceiling, she tried to stave off the intrusion of a rare moment of introspection. *What is up with this primitive wood thing around here?* she mused. The place looked to her like a Wild West–Japanese tearoom combination—decidedly not the look she would have gone for. *Why does everyone think Gran has such great taste? This place is an abomination.*

Unbidden, a deeper question arose, despite her attempt at distraction: what was it about Alex that had gotten her so keyed up about getting married? She was almost certain at this point that love didn't have much to do with it. He was good in the sack—she'd give him that much—and he was funny. The latter probably had more to do with his stupidity than his wit. Could it be because he was just good-looking? Was she that shallow?

Crossing one leg over the other, she slipped off a pink sock to inspect her pedicure while allowing herself to wonder briefly how her father was doing. He'd pretty much iced the deal for her. How was he going to walk her down the aisle with a broken leg?

Enough of this, she scoffed. Quickly, she wrote a terse e-mail explaining that the wedding had been canceled—not postponed. She thought for a minute about changing the wording to "postponed" and then, with a what-the-hell flick of her wrist, went with "canceled" and dragged the guest list folder to the "To" line. She applauded herself for having made sure that she had everyone's e-mail address and for having taken the time to organize the addresses in a folder titled "Wedding Guests." As she was about to push the "send" button, she stopped. *I don't want to do that.* She grabbed the guest list folder and dragged it to the "Bcc" line, typed her own e-mail address in the "To" field, and pushed "send." Done, done, and done.

Now what am I going to do? she wondered, as it occurred to her, not for the first time, that her last few months had been completely and utterly devoted to wedding planning. "I'm certainly not going to sit in here for however long it takes this shit to melt," she said out loud as she glared out the window at the offending weather.

Allowing her thoughts to drift about on their own had never been an occupation that served Virginia well. From early on, she had developed a habit of keeping very, very busy. Keeping busy, experience had taught her, was vital; otherwise, things could go very wrong, very fast. Meditating was anathema to her. Even thinking about it made her stomach hurt.

She wondered what she could do with her wedding dress and congratulated herself for having picked the backless one. A good dye job, maybe fuchsia or black—long, slinky black, yeah—and no one would know it was a never-worn bridal gown. Or maybe she should just throw it away. Bad karma and all.

Mackey's invitation to meditate irritated her. She was even more irritated, she was sure, because she couldn't find anything else to think about. She hated this place. How had she come up with the idea to have her wedding here? It must have been her mother's idea. That trapped feeling descended on her again. This time it threatened to take up residence permanently.

I can't believe Alex went off with Uncle Gordy to the hospital. We could have gone sledding. Maybe those little hellions in the other room might be interested. She rummaged around the room, looking for enough layers to keep her warm without making her look fat. Finally ready for her next adventure, she opened the door and strode out into the living room to organize a sledding party.

To her utter dismay, there was no one to be seen. "Gran, are you here? Aunt Stuart? Mackey? Aunt Susan? Is anybody here? Hello!" she called. She went over to the window and looked out. There was nothing to see other than a world of blinding white and startling blue. Removing her hat to hear better, she called again and then stood still, listening to a clock tick with insistent clarity, despite the omnipresent hum of the generator and her own heartbeat.

"Where in the hell did everybody go?" she whined, willing herself to shut out the maddeningly repetitious, almost mocking sounds of clock and heartbeat. She stripped off her outerwear, leaving it where each piece fell, plunked herself on the sofa in front of the fire, and plugged herself into Facebook.

❦

Gordon congratulated himself for having put the chains on his four-wheel-drive crew cab dually. By the time he and Alex rolled into the hospital, they had slid off the road twice and had needed to use the snowplow once to slow down their forward momentum. He didn't bother to cut off the rumbling diesel engine when he stopped in the half-circle drive at the entrance to the new University of Virginia hospital. As he jumped out and walked around the front of the truck, Alex looked a bit askance at him.

"We won't be here long enough," said Gordy. "Besides, where in the hell would they find a tow truck today? And who is going steal it?"

"I don't know, but I sure as hell would, equipped like it is for this kind of weather."

"Okay, I'll turn it off. But I don't think we are going to be here that long."

"Never underestimate the power of a hospital to slow time to a crawl," Alex muttered, with what sounded to Gordy like real-time experience.

Gordy looked around. "Man, this place has grown like a bad cancer. Jesus, it is huge."

"Yeah, hospitals for sure are in the cancer business, and it's a big one. Lots of cash."

"You sound like you have had some experience in that department?"

"I have," Alex admitted.

Gordy waited for more details to come. Nothing did. "You aren't exactly free with information, are you?"

"Can't see any particular reason to be."

"There is the small item of how we are about to be family."

"I guess," Alex said with a shrug. "Do you know where we are supposed to go?"

"Stuart said they were still in emergency. How she got information out of anyone in a hospital is more than I know. They are about as good at providing information as …" He cast about for a simile and then whipped out his best grin. "You!"

Alex scanned the signage. "Emergency this way." He headed off, not waiting for Gordy.

Gordon hustled to catch up. "I didn't piss you off, about the hospital thing, did I?"

"Nope. Just forgot how much I don't like hospitals. In here." He stepped through the door before it had fully swished open.

Gordy followed close behind. The normally teeming waiting room was empty. Two seemingly sleep-deprived nurses were staffing the check-in desk.

"Mackey?" Gordy asked. "Came in last night. And Barstead?"

One of the two nurses snapped to attention like a too-stretched rubber band. She perused the computer screen for several seconds before speaking. "Mackey is through the door," she said, indicating the direction with her head, "and to the left. Barstead … it's unclear."

"What do you mean, it's unclear?" Gordon asked, while Alex exhaled a long sigh that Gordon interpreted as *Told ya so*. "Is he here or not? He was admitted last night with a broken ankle."

"I see that." The exhausted nurse gazed red-eyed up at Gordy. "It's not clear where he is now is what I am trying to say. I am sorry if I didn't make myself clear. It's been a long night."

"Can we go to my father's room then? Mackey? We've come to pick him up. Well, both of them. But he can go home, right?"

"He hasn't been discharged yet." Her voice was flat.

"So can we go in?"

The nurse pulled herself wearily up out of her seat and pointed toward the door.

Gordon and Alex headed in that direction. "Jeez, would a few more words have killed her?" Gordon grumbled.

༄

Sallee greeted the two with mixed emotions. She wanted to stand up to celebrate their arrival and her impending liberation from the hospital. But the continued uncertainty surrounding Peter's fate held her immobilized at the end of her father's bed.

Joe was not going to let a little thing like where in the hell Peter Barstead was curb his enthusiasm. "Merry Christmas," he boomed. "You two are a sight for sore eyes. Get me outta here, would ya?"

"Merry Christmas to you too, Dad," Gordy laughed. "And you too, Sal." He felt like he was in some alternate universe where emotions bounced up and down like a basketball. "Umm ..." He hesitated, afraid to ask. "Is everything okay?"

Sallee burst into tears.

Damn, he thought. *Wish I hadn't asked.*

Joe quickly brought the two newcomers up to speed—or his speed at least. "Trey's gone to see if he can find out more. The place is discombobulated by the storm. How did you get here?" He laughed. "Like it is a big surprise. You and the post office—how does that go? Neither rain nor snow, nor something-something of night, can, um, huh, stay Gordy from his appointed rounds." He chortled. "I think the PO has moved on from there. I am glad you haven't."

Sallee laughed for the first time since learning of Peter's plight. "I'm not sure that is exactly how it goes." Then she sighed. "And I don't know if I should stay here or go home with you."

"Absolutely, you need to go home, at least to eat, get a change of clothes, and take a nap," her father urged. "I'm sure it will be easier to find out what is going on later. If Gordy can get through, other shifts will be able to make it in here and relieve our exhausted staff." He reached out and took her hand. "There isn't anything you can do here."

Sallee was gearing up to protest when Trey walked in and spotted Gordon.

"Dad, man, it is good to see you." He laughed heartily. "It only took a blizzard and a wild, crazy night with Pops to get me to say that." He threw his arms around his startled father. "Merry Christmas."

Gordy, looking dumbstruck, turned back to Joe. "Can you leave now?"

"Let them try to stop me," Joe retorted, as he slipped his still-sodden shoes on and headed for the door.

Trey followed behind with his coat. "Did you forget something?"

"You've turned into an old woman," Joe chuckled. "Gimme that coat." On his way out the door, he gave Alex a hearty slap on the back. "Good to see ya, son, and it was nice of you to accompany old Sasquatch here out to get us."

"No problem," Alex replied. "Nice to see that you are better."

Trey had forgotten all about Alex and his perceived threat until now. Fighting the old familiar urge to flee, he walked up and shook the younger man's hand. "Hey, Trey Mackey. Nice to meet you, Alex."

As they made their way to the truck, Trey—with one arm wrapped around his aunt's shoulder—told her that he hadn't been able to find out anything further about Peter. He gave her a reassuring squeeze. "It will all work out. I am sure of it," he said, surprised to hear himself repeat a phrase he'd always hated when someone used it on him. Things *had* worked out for him, and what hadn't would—he knew that now for sure. That surety was more precious than gold, he thought, as he escorted his conflicted aunt, new friend, and granddad to his father's truck.

The sky, such a brilliant blue, must surely be the backdrop for a movie set. Had he ever seen a color in nature so intense? Nature, in his mind, had always been drab and muted. Now, as he realized that he was looking at the world with different eyes, he wanted to skip; he wanted to sweep Sallee off her feet and dance with her down Jefferson Park Avenue, or at least to his father's truck. Had it taken that much energy to suppress his childhood horrors? If walking outside after a blizzard was such a rush, he wondered, what else was in store for a man with a new life? He eagerly looked forward to the answers.

When they got to the truck, Trey asked with a laugh, "What, no dogs?"

"They asked," Gordon said. "I told them they couldn't come unless they sat in your lap. All three of them suddenly had better things to do."

Gordon and Trey laughed at the joke, to the surprise of both of them.

Debate ensued now, as they milled around beside the truck. Under no circumstances was Gordy going to relinquish the driver's seat in this mess. After much insistence that since Joe was the eldest, he should sit up front, consensus emerged: Trey—his father's own son—needed the leg room, leaving Sallee, Joe, and Alex to squeeze into the back seat.

Cheek by jowl in the back, Joe remarked, "What kind of *crew* did they use to spec this thing out? Munchkins? What is this, a Ford? Sallee and I hardly make up one normal-sized man, so in effect there are two normal-sized people back here, and one of them is unable to speak because he has both knees shoved up in his face. Where would big, hulking workmen sit? If I want to scratch my nose, I have to alert Alex; otherwise, I risk giving him a black eye." He grinned at Alex, who smiled back.

"You aren't complaining back there, are you?" Gordy asked. "I can stop and let you out if you want."

"Just saying," Joe laughed. *How the tables have turned*, he thought. "Reminds me of years gone by when a certain boy and certain girl would vie for shotgun, and the loser would carp in the back."

"I'll get back there if you want," Trey said. "I don't mind. Sallee can sit on my lap if it's too crowded."

"Not on your life, pal." Sallee laughed as she too thought of how far the tables had turned, but from not longer ago than this morning. She was surprised at how much lighter she felt. Was that really because of the confrontation her father had instigated with his horrible threat? She allowed her mind to play with the notion of how different she would have felt had Peter died.

12

The drive homeward would prove to be much more complicated than the trip to the hospital had been. The roads hardly looked as if they had been cleared, thanks to the wind and the drifting snow. The layer underneath was hard-packed and icy. Road crews' chemicals had melted it, and dropping temperatures had refrozen portions, making it—as Alex pointed out again—"slippery as snot on a doorknob."

As soon as they left the hospital, Gordy misjudged just how icy it was as he made a tight right turn out of the hospital and did a one-eighty smack in the middle of the deserted road. "Wow, man, this stuff sure *is* slippery." Chuckling as he remembered Alex's remark, he righted their course. "I'm going to have to go a whole lot slower. Hope you guys like each other. It could take a while to get home. It's a good thing Peter …" He let that thought drop.

They narrowly escaped catastrophe again when a plow came barreling at them from the other direction. "Is he going to move over? Jesus!" Gordy shouted, following up with a torrent of blue invectives that made even Sallee blush, no stranger as she was to such talk.

Gordon cut the steering wheel hard, narrowly missing the snowplow's big blade as it continued on down the snow-covered road, leaving them to slam deep into a snowbank. "That son of a bitch almost killed us and didn't even check back to see," he shouted, more from fear than anger. "You all okay?" He scanned the cab's passengers to check that everyone was still in once piece. "Good night, that idiot must have been doing sixty."

"I bet he's been at it since last night too. Poor guy is probably exhausted," Joe added. "We're okay."

"Poor guy, my ass. He almost killed us," Gordy snapped.

"Do you think you can get us out of this mess?" Joe looked around at the variations of gray slush, ice, and snow surrounding them. "We sorta went right in it, didn't we?"

"I didn't have a choice. It was going here or pushing up daisies." Gordy was clearly shaken.

"I'm not criticizing. Actually, I am very grateful that you saved our bacon. Thanks, son. Great job. Really," Joe exclaimed with an unexpected burst of emotion. He was surprised at how much gratitude he felt. How many times did he need the point made, to be reminded how happy he was to be alive? He tried to catch his breath, which had been knocked out of him at the impact.

Gordy, Trey, and Alex were attempting to wedge their way out of the truck. As Joe made a move to try the same, Sallee grabbed his hand. "Don't even think about it," she commanded. "You sit here with me and let those guys do the heavy lifting."

It took several minutes of Alex banging and pushing, scratching, and working his fingers, and then his arm, around the edge of his passenger-side back door to scrape the snow away and free the door enough for him to squeeze out. He stepped out into waist-deep snow and waded through the stuff, shouting in his observations of their predicament from his vantage point. It was decided that Gordy and Trey were going to have to climb out of Alex's door because both of theirs were too blocked to open.

Much grunting and groaning ensued as they began attempting this. Sallee and Trey had to perform a little do-si-do to exchange places from front to back while Joe smashed himself up against his side of the cab to give them more room to maneuver. He laughed when he found Sallee's backside perched on his shoulder. "It's been a while since I've had this vantage point."

"Would you shut up?" She started to laugh so hard that her forward momentum had to stop.

"Shall I push?"

"Thank you, no." With a great burst of energy, she catapulted herself into the front seat, narrowly missing kicking Gordy in the head as she landed head-first in the passenger-seat footwell.

Trey slithered into the back seat over the top of her to give her room to turn around. Once righted, Sallee exclaimed, "Well, that was quite something!"

Just before throwing himself into the bank of snow, Trey looked down at his designer boots. "I don't think these are going to be much good out there," he said ruefully.

Gordy rummaged around under papers—of which there were many—in the center console, then under more papers, and finally under Sallee's seat to produce a spare pair of winter work boots and gloves. "Here," he said, tossing them back to Trey. "See if these work."

Sallee laughed to see her brother pull so many necessities out of seemingly thin air. "Your truck is a regular magician's hat," she giggled as Gordy climbed over the seat to extricate himself.

Finally disgorged from the truck, the three men lunged through the waist-high snow and gained the road. With much pointing and removing of hats, followed by head scratching and the replacing of hats, along with varying degrees of scowling, they tried formulating a plan to disengage the truck from what appeared to be a hopeless situation. Its front was buried in the bank, canted decidedly to the left. The right back dual wheels were barely off the ground, but enough so that they would provide no traction.

Trey would be next to worthless or so Gordy thought as he and Alex debated their course of action. Alex climbed on the truck bed and began digging through the snow, finally coming up with a thick piece of chain. "This'll help—if someone comes along, we can get 'em to pull us out."

"Hey, Alex. Can you see the front of the truck?" Trey yelled. "See if the plow's buried completely?"

"No, it's pushed up against the snow. Why?"

"Dad, do you have a come-along in the truck?" Trey was remembering the tool with which his father had been able to work miracles in Trey's youth. "If you do, we could hook it to that tree over there and use it to at least right the truck enough to get the wheels under it, on the ground. Then they can pull us out of this mess."

Surprised and delighted by his son's innovative idea and feeling more pride than he could remember feeling in a long time, Gordy crowed, "I think there's one in there." He directed Alex on where to dig.

Giving a thumbs-up to Trey for the idea, Alex attacked the snow with fervor and soon had uncovered the truck's tool chest and extracted a well-used come-along and a long lead pipe. "Okay, guys, time to put some muscle in it." He laughed as he jumped out of the truckbed.

They set about rigging the come-along to the tree and the chain to the truck, using the pipe to lengthen the handle for more leverage. "Good thing this tree wasn't any farther away," Alex said as they stretched the chain to its full length and attached it to the come-along.

"It's a good thing it wasn't much closer, or we would have been wrapped around it," Gordy observed.

ॐ

There was an awkward silence when the two were left alone for the first time in a long time. For so many years, Andy had gone out of his way not to see his mother, and when he did, it was always in the company of his father or former wife. His ex-wife had asked on a number of occasions if he was afraid of his mother. "No," he'd say. "I just can't stand talking to her. Either she's drunk, or we get in a fight, or she's drunk, and we fight about that." The only communication they had had for at least as long as Sally had been alive was on the phone, where he could hang up without much of a scene if things got too contentious.

"This is an enormous turkey. It will take all day to cook," Susan said as she wrestled the bird into the sink. "I guess we'd better make stuffing before we start doing anything else."

Andy rummaged around for bread while she scoured the boxes of food they had brought from Ginny's house for onions, parsley, and celery.

"Do you see any oysters?" she asked.

"No, it looks like we have the makings for plain old stuffing. I did find bread already cubed, so why don't I chop onions? You can give the gobbler a bath in the meantime." He smiled at his mother for the first time in so long that it was noteworthy.

"Okay. Did we bring pans over, or do I need to hunt one down?" She laughed a little nervous laugh that struck Andy as so full of longing and hope.

"It's nice that you and I are here together fixing Christmas dinner," she said. "I am so glad that you were able to come and bring the children." *Don't talk too much. Don't blather. He hates blathering*, she reminded herself, leaving another awkward moment of silence to loom between them.

Since Andy had elected to chop onions, it was impossible for Susan to tell what was causing the tears to stream down her son's face when he said, "Mom, you look fantastic. Thank you—a thousand times, thank you for quitting. I think this time you got it. *Happy* doesn't begin to cover how I feel about it. I'm so proud of you."

Andy wanted to put the knife down, take her in his arms, and hug her. But this felt stupid and contrived, so he continued to chop onions and hide his tears of joy.

"Joe has been such a help," she replied. "We look at things together—things that up until now have terrified me so much that I literally couldn't think about them, much less look at them." She handed Andy the celery. "Will you chop this too, please?"

While Andy chopped, she dumped the bread cubes into a bowl, melted butter, and located the stock, reassuring herself that she was fine. It was all fine; nothing more need happen. Suddenly, she was compelled to say, "My mother was a very disturbed person, so I understand how you might have felt when I was drinking. I am so sorry."

Andy smiled at his mother and nodded as he kept chopping, afraid that if he stopped, he might melt into a puddle on the floor or disappear. He wished that he could be just a little more like his demonstrative relatives. If ever there were a time, now would be it.

Since Susan had never been loquacious like Ginny with her children, the two attended to their various tasks in silence, each delighting in their newfound peace with one another, while wishing for the courage to show it. After a few minutes, Andy quietly stopped chopping, walked over to his mother, and—tentatively at first—embraced her for the very first time that he could remember.

℘

At the truck, Sallee watched the proceedings for a while until it seemed that the plan was going to take some working out. She leaned up against the door so that she and Joe could see one another. "Conversation is so much better when you see each other, don't you think?" she asked before suddenly erupting into tears.

"Daddy, what have I done?" she gasped through her sobs. "All morning long, I have been worried about seeing Virginia, not"—she hiccupped—"not because I am concerned … in any way … for *her*," she said, with sobs and hiccups continuing to interrupt her speech. "I am … terrified … of her anger." Sallee stopped, trying to get control of herself. "Ohh," she sniffled, "she … she blames me for everything that goes wrong in her life, everything …and just today … just today, a huge lot of things have gone terribly, terribly wrong." Sallee's voice rose to a wail. "Peter, for example … oh … and the wedding for another!" As the truck rocked in response to the men's efforts outside, she cried out in frustration and rage, rearing back against the door and kicking both feet like a two-year-old in a tantrum.

Joe waited for a full minute. "Are you through?" he asked patiently.

"Not yet." Sallee's sobs had subsided, and she spoke a little more calmly but with despair. "I feel like B. F. Skinner was possibly a better, more loving parent than I. If I had tried, I don't think I could have made more mistakes as a parent."

Joe suppressed a chuckle. "Last time I checked, the little buggers don't show up with instructions. You did what you thought was best. Didn't you?"

"That seems so lame. Skinner did too, and look where that went."

"I don't know about what was going on in Skinner's head. I do know how you feel about my worldview, so I won't bore you with it, but I will instead take a page from your mother's book: I'm all ears. It sounds like you are blaming yourself."

"Well, duh! I am the one that chose to see myself as a hapless, pathetic victim of sad, dysfunctional parenting."

"Believing you were a victim of sad, dysfunctional parenting, you made a choice to look for a better way to raise your own children? That sounds like something a good parent would decide."

Sallee's eyes narrowed. "What are you up to? You don't think I'm a good parent. I am almost positive of that."

"It makes not a tinker's damn what I think of your parenting. That is not the issue at hand. You have stated what you thought of my parenting, and I can't disagree with some of your conclusions. What I know is that I did the best I could with what I had available to me at the time. I believe you did too."

"Isn't that a cop-out?"

"Not for me. If I could have done it differently, better, I would have, but I wouldn't have been me. Here's the rub. You wouldn't have been you, either. You would have been someone else—not an improved, brighter, healthier version of Sallee. There is no such thing. You would have been somebody entirely different—same for Virginia. If you had done it differently, she wouldn't be Virginia-improved. There is no improvement on Virginia or you or me. As our old buddy Ethel would say, 'We is what we is.' Damn it, I said wasn't going to give you my worldview. Here I am, doing just that. Sorry." He smiled. "Proves my point." He gave her another lopsided smile as the truck jerked and lurched backward.

Minutes later, Gordy clambered in through the same door he'd climbed out of an hour before. "I'm going to back it out," he said as he climbed into the driver's seat. Out his window, he shouted to Alex and Trey, "You two get over on those right back wheels and hang on. It might be a rough ride!" For what seemed an interminable time, Gordy rocked the big truck forward and back, forward and back, shouting instructions as to which way Alex and Trey should push, lean, or apply weight, until finally they were free.

He bounded out of the driver's door, and the three men walked around the truck, assessing the damage.

Meanwhile, Sallee turned again to her father. "I want you to tell me what you really think of how Virginia turned out. I want to know what you think."

"I might try, but I'm not man enough to jump at that bait. You wanting to know what I think is something I have waited for for a long time. I think Virginia is perfect."

Sallee rolled her eyes. "Please don't feed me a line of crap."

"You asked. I'm telling you. She is a sweet girl."

Sallee rolled her eyes again.

"She has a sweet heart."

"Oh, he's a beaut, all right, no doubt about it."

"Not sweetheart, *sweet heart*. I wasn't speaking of Alex, although now that you bring him up, I think he is an excellent fellow. I for one am very grateful he was here. Need I remind you, from the little I've heard he more than likely saved your husband's life last night?"

With a big sigh, she agreed that he "maybe was okay."

"When I say that Virginia has a sweet heart, I am referring to the fact that she is responsible for all of us getting together. You weren't the one who suggested a wedding here, were you? Over Christmas? And inviting the whole family?"

"No," she pouted. "I was against the whole idea. So was Peter." She gave a sick little giggle. "I don't guess that's news to you."

"She was remarkably perceptive, then, to have come up with this idea—wouldn't you agree?"

"I'm not sure I would go so far as to say perceptive. I honestly don't know why she wanted to get married here. And I'm not sure she does either."

"Good has come of it, though, don't you think? A lot of family rifts have been healed. Look at Helen's letter, for example. That by itself was a wonderful by-product of your perceptive daughter's wedding plans. And if you need more proof, check out the Gordon Mackey elder and younger right there." Joe pointed to Gordy and Trey standing outside, their arms clapped over each other's shoulders, drinking a beer. "I know for a fact they have never had their arms around each other like that." He turned back to his daughter. "Have you ever asked Virginia if she thinks she had bad parents?"

"No," Sallee said uncertainly.

"What if she doesn't think she did? What if you are the only one who thinks Virginia is a mess? Then she is perfect as a bludgeon for you to use to beat yourself up. Mind, I don't believe a well-placed *no* here or there would be a terrible disservice to her." He rolled the window down and shouted, "Boy, that beer looks good. Got two more?"

When they were finally on the road and under way again, Sallee was feeling remarkably buoyant. "Gordy—oh, excuuuse me, *Gordon*. What's up with that, anyway? Never mind. Do you know what ever happened to Lil' Early? I think he might have been my first real crush," she laughed.

"I don't know. I was surprised that he wasn't at Early's funeral, so I only half-expected to see him at Ethel's. I asked Ethel's sister, Roberta—man, you ought to see her." He laughed. "She came up to my elbow but looked just like their mother, Bertha. I didn't remember that she was so short. I guess when you're a kid, every grown person is tall."

"Except … what was that woman's name? You know, the babysitter that I called a cab for, to take her away?" Sallee giggled.

"Mattie Bruce," Gordy yelped, laughing. "Yeah, I was taller than she was when I was six. By the way, the Gordon thing was me taking myself too seriously." He laughed again, hard, as did his son, his father, and his sister.

"Imagine that," Sallee chortled, "you taking yourself too seriously. Hey, Trey, did that ever happen that you can remember?"

"Dad or me? I certainly have. I think I'm going to take the fifth on whether Dad did or not." He gave his father a playful wink.

"Hey, sis, I think we have a serious case of the pot and kettle going on here," Gordy chided Sallee.

"I stand convicted," Sallee said with her hands in the air. "Guilty as charged."

"He was a nice kid, Lil' Early," said Joe. "Falling in love with black men seems to be a family trait." Joe patted Sallee on the knee.

"My family too, kind of," Alex suddenly said. "My mother was black. I wasn't going to say anything because I wasn't sure how it would play out in the South. Besides, your family is so perfect, and mine isn't anywhere close."

"Perfect?" Sallee exclaimed. She and the others roared with laughter at how far from the truth that word was in their view of their family.

"I don't think so, son," Gordy said, catching his breath. "We are a lot of things. Perfect isn't one of them. I don't think the word is meant to apply to families, unless we are perfect in our imperfection." He laughed again. "You're rubbing off, Dad. That sounded like something you'd say."

Sallee, a little shocked at Alex's news, asked without thinking, "Does Virginia know?"

"No, I guess I need to tell her."

"Ya think?" Sallee regretted her snarky tone as soon as it was out of her mouth. She reached out and put a hand gently on Alex's arm. "You know, I think this snowstorm might have given you and my daughter a chance at true happiness—whether together or apart, I don't know. Seems like there are a lot of things you two need to talk about." She smiled. "I know how terrifying that can be. My suggestion, and you can take it for whatever it's worth, is to say what needs to be said before you tie yourselves to each other. Going into a marriage with secrets is a recipe for misery." She gave a little nervous titter. "That is the voice of experience."

Simultaneously, all three of the Mackey men said, "Amen to that."

"Everything?" Alex asked.

"Everything that matters," Gordy answered from the front seat.

Trey, sitting across from his father, hoped that the kid wouldn't necessarily feel the need to unburden himself at this particular moment. He had been debating how to break the news of his chosen profession to his father before this came up. Having so recently come to this sense of belonging, he was loath to jeopardize it just yet, even though he knew that he needed to come clean. He was also keenly aware that his grandfather and his aunt must be thinking similar thoughts. He stole a glance at the back seat's occupants with a look of fear on his face.

Joe caught his eye. Ever so slightly, as if reading Trey's mind, the old man shook his head and mouthed, "Not now," to Trey's utter relief.

છ

Ginny did little other than watch Stuart ready a room for Peter. Since the bed already had clean linens, readying consisted mostly of pushing things out of the way that might impede Peter on the way to the bathroom. "I wonder what is taking them so long?" Ginny said as she picked absentmindedly at a frayed cuticle on her thumb. "Gordy—blast, Gordon—left hours ago."

"I imagine it's slow going in these conditions. We got well over three feet of snow, so much more than they were expecting." Stuart stopped pushing a table for a minute. "Do you ever wonder who *they* are? I am always saying '*they* this' and '*they* that.'"

Ginny laughed. "Trying to distract me, are you? Foiled again. Your scheming won't work."

"Actually, I wasn't. I catch myself referring to *they* all the time and wondered if you do too." She sat down across from Ginny and looked into her eyes. "Just wondering how much we are alike. I guess I like the idea that we are." She started to laugh. "Although I remember hating it when I was young. The words 'You are so like your mother' were absolute fighting words back then, enough to make me lop off my hair or perform some other atrocity on my body. No one was better at utilizing that fact than Sallee."

They both smiled.

"It is funny how we change," Stuart said.

"Poor Sallee," her mother interjected. "She is going to have her hands full with Peter laid up and with Virginia now that she doesn't have the distraction of wedding plans. Do you think they will marry?"

"I have no idea. I have to say, I have never seen a more unlikely pair," Stuart said. "Marriage makes strange bedfellows, though, doesn't it? So who knows! Look at Sallee and Peter. Could anyone ever have figured those two would end up together?" She stood up and leaned over to smooth out the bedspread and then went back to moving furniture. "I want so much to connect with Sallee. Everything I say pushes her farther and farther away. I envy those people who have such easy relationships with their siblings. I wish our family wasn't so complicated."

"Life's a complicated proposition sometimes," Ginny said with a little laugh. "Not sure, but I think you are referring to *they* again. Honey, *they* and *those people* don't exist. There is an expression in AA that warns against comparing your insides to other people's outsides. There is quite a bit of difference in the view, you know."

"Hmm." Stuart was silent for a moment "What do you suppose Dad was doing with Trey last night?"

"Oh, you know how he ferrets out lost sheep. He's like a border collie, always trying to round up the herd." She snickered. "Trey's a good-looking man, isn't he? A little too reserved. Maybe he is just shy. Those two boys are so different. Andy is such an old shoe."

Stuart looked down at her mother quizzically. "Old shoe?"

"You know what I mean. You know him the instant you meet. There is no artifice, no subplot, and then there's Trey, so aloof, mysterious, such a mystique. We'd make a good novel, this family—so many interesting characters. You should write it."

"I'll get right on it," Stuart laughed. She moved to the window. "Look at the kids out there, having the time of their lives. Joey and Potts are like peas in a pod, inseparable. I'm so glad Trey brought him."

"Is that what that was? I heard shrieking and whooping. I thought it was a television set. Yes, children at play—it has been a long time since I have heard that sound. It is glorious." She walked over to the window and stood shoulder to shoulder with Stuart. "Potts is the image of his father at that age." She shivered. "Oh! I just had the worst feeling—like someone walking over my grave, as Ethel used to say."

She moved slowly back to her seat by the bed and sank into the armchair. "Trey's other grandmother took care of him when he was that age. Susan, I think, was in treatment at the time. Ethel really disliked Susan's mother, possibly because the woman had such a thick brogue that it was nearly impossible to understand her. Now that I think about it, Susan's mother was as broadminded as a blade of grass—such an endearing trait. If I remember correctly, she had been a nun. She had to leave the convent for some reason. Um ..." Ginny stopped, dropped her head, and put her hand to her forehead, obviously thinking. "Let's see ... her oldest sister died. She left to take care of her sister's children, eventually marrying her brother-in-law. Susan was her only child. I don't know if I dreamed this or not, but it seems there was something odd about her husband's death. He either killed himself or was killed by her or one of his sons. What was her name? Um … oh, I don't know. It'll come to me. Anyway, her name may have been why Ethel didn't like her too. You know how she could be at times … Morga!" Ginny almost shouted. "That's it! Morga."

Ginny wagged her head. "Lord, she was a sour old lady. No wonder Susan drank. I think Morga was mean. She had that old-world Catholic superstition, not that Ethel wasn't superstitious too, but mixed up with Celtic charms, it was weird, too weird for me. She saw fairies, sprites, all sorts of fey things—and charms. If you said this prayer or that, your children wouldn't burn up in a house fire … that sort of stuff."

She shuddered and then continued. "Trey had started wetting his pants. It worried Ethel. She was sure it meant something terrible had happened to him, especially since he begged us not to tell. I remember she came to me, saying, 'Miz Ginny, I don't mean t' alarm you, but I think somebody been abusin' little Trey. I helped him change his wet pants jest now. Dere was bruises all over his arms like somebody been yankin' on him. When I took his pants off, I seen more bruises on his gentles.' I had forgotten that Ethel used to say 'gentles' rather than 'genitals.' Isn't that sweet?"

"Did she think that someone was sexually abusing Trey?" Stuart looked horrified. "Poor little guy. What did you do?"

"Well, child abuse is a pretty big accusation, not something you want to race into. I talked to your father about it. We certainly didn't think it was Gordy, and Susan was at a treatment facility, so that could only mean Morga. Poor Gordy had more than enough on his plate. We decided we would invite Trey to come stay with us until we could figure out exactly what could be done—what authorities needed to be contacted, that sort of thing." She sighed. "I feel awful about it now, but back then we just didn't feel like marching in and pointing fingers would be helpful. We were meeting with a social worker when Morga died. We got the call just as we got home.

Morga had dropped dead while Gordy was out. He didn't have any idea how long the boys had been there with her dead. Ethel and I went to pick up the boys, and Joe drove over to help Gordy deal with the aftermath. What I feel terrible about is, after Morga died, no one did a thing for little Trey."

"What? You just dropped it? I can't believe that you … really?" Stuart's shock left her slack-jawed.

"Stuart, it was a terrible time for all of them. We didn't know then what we know now. We did our best. It just wasn't very good. I have no doubt that is why your father was with Trey last night. I'm sure he still remembers."

Stuart shook her head. "Even if the grandmother wasn't abusing him—to have those little children alone with the dead grandmother for God only knows how long and for no one to talk to about it?"

"We tried. Ethel and I gave them both every opportunity to talk about it."

"Mother, professional help—they needed professional help."

"What would you have me do? I can't go back and change what happened. I obviously would have gotten them help if I had known what I know now."

"Poor Trey," Stuart said. "That kind of stuff can really mess you up. It's so unfair."

Unfair. The word reverberated in Stuart's head like a hammer hitting steel. The echo took her back to a time long before.

∓

"Ethel, it's not fair. It's just so unfair. They were babies. They were just little tiny babies." Stuart looked at Ethel with such pain in her red swollen eyes that it was all Ethel could do not to cry herself as she held her, rocking her gently.

"Darlin', I know." She tenderly brushed Stuart's hair away from her tear-streaked face. "I know. You right. It ain't right fo' dem babies t' die, or fo' Mista Frank t' have t' suffer so long afore he die too. It

hard t' tell why de Lord give what he give. I know one thang. It ain't
got nothin' t' do wit' deservin'."

Stuart, who had been holding up for the last seven days, dissolved into another fit of weeping. She had staved off tears for as long
as she could, afraid that if she ever started, she might never stop. The
constant recurring memory of the policeman at her door with his hat
in hand, looking so young and awkward as he delivered the dreadful
news, was driving her mad. "There's been an accident. I am sorry
to have to tell you, ma'am. The, uh … the babies, ma'am, well …
they, um, didn't survive the crash. Mr. … um … your husband has
been taken to the University Hospital. He is in critical condition,
ma'am …"

It wasn't enough horror that, as she would later learn, her two
precious six-month-old babies, the twins, had been burned to death
in the ghastly wreck, the product of a drunk driver. Then there was
her husband, her beloved Frank, lingering at death's door for so
long, suffering, with god-awful pain in his eyes—so much of him
unrecognizable. She helplessly watched the fear spread throughout
his wracked body as he anticipated the agony of having his wounds
redressed and hydrated. Finally, Stuart had prevailed upon the doctors—or had she?—to put him in a forced coma, even though she
knew this risked death. Maybe they told her that was what they were
going to do. Maybe that is what they did, and he didn't suffer; there
was no anguish in his eyes. His body was not wracked with pain.
She made it all up. Or maybe they were alive. Were they? Was this
a horrible dream? Would she wake soon? She couldn't remember.
The only memory was that absurdly young policeman at the door
droning on. "There's been an accident. I am sorry to have to tell you,
ma'am. The, uh … the babies …" On and on.

She didn't feel guilty when Frank did die. She had been praying
for it for what seemed forever, although in reality the time could have
been measured in hours rather than days.

She felt guilty only that she had lived—that she hadn't been
driving and that it had been her idea to drive the girls around to get

them to sleep. With a fresh onslaught of guilt, she wailed, "If I had been a normal mother, a good mother, I would have let them cry themselves to sleep at home in their beds."

Ethel cradled Stuart, cooing to her like when she was a baby. "Honey, doan do dis t' yo'self. It ain't gon' t' help nothin'. You done de best you could do fo' little Maggie an' Ginger. You was a good momma an' a good wife t' Mista Frank. Blamin' yo'self ain't gonna brang 'em back. I know."

The thing was, Ethel did know. Not the exact pain, but close enough. She knew that for Stuart to heal, she was going to have to go through this suffering. There was no easy way around this—pills and bottles and all of the rest might make it bearable for a time, but just for a time. If Ethel and Ginny had learned anything about life, it was that the most efficient and healthiest way for Stuart to heal was just to live through the suffering until she could get to the other side. Ethel and Ginny were able to bear listening to Stuart's suffering because they both knew from their own experience that the suffering would pass, if allowed. As long as they could help Stuart feel her feelings, the pain would subside.

After months of listening, silently loving, praying, and nurturing Stuart's sad, aching soul, Ethel felt it was time to share her thoughts on "fair." "Darlin', let me tell you somethin' 'bout fair. Dere ain't no such thang. Fair is an idea man came up wit', or ol' slew foot whispered in his ear. Makes no sense t' me dat people be sayin' dis he'ah fair an' dis ain't, den tryin' t' make it so. How you gonna make it fair?

"I don't know 'bout you, but I ain't got no idea how t' even go 'bout sayin' what is fair. I 'member when I lost my baby. I felt like de world had come t' de end. I was mournin' a baby I didn't know I was even carryin'. You woulda thought de way I carried on dat I had been anticipatin' dat baby fo'ever. Thang is I was. I knew de color o' his eyes an' de way he smile afore I even knew he was on de way.

"If I was gon' t' be talkin' 'bout fair, I could say ain't fair dat my baby die 'fore I could even hold 'em while you got two, an' you got t' hold 'em fo' six months, an' Miz Ginny got four, an' dey all alive today."

Ethel delivered her words as evenly and free of recrimination as if she were saying, "Have a nice day." She sighed and continued. "We gits what we gits. Our job, de way I see it, be not t' argue wit' what we gits, but t' live wit' what we gits, de best we can. Comparin' what I got wit' what you got be a surefire way t' make dat nigh unt' impossible."

She turned and looked into Stuart's swollen eyes with great compassion. "I don't know how it woulda been had my baby lived. I know dat losin' 'im made it possible fo' me to help you get through dis he'ah pain an' sufferin'. It makes me happy dat I can do dat fo' you. I don't know dat wasn't what de Lord had in mind all along. But I is happy He use me t' help you through dis he'ah, an' yo' momma too. I know she feel de same as me, 'cause we done talked 'bout it mo' dan once."

Stuart gave Ethel a sad smile. "I hate the idea that you had to suffer to help me. But I do love that you were able to transform your pain into a force for good. I am so grateful to have you and Mother in my life. I just don't understand why we have to suffer so." She patted Ethel on the arm. "You or me or anybody."

"I don't know either. I have to suspect it has t' do wit' expectin' life owed us anythin' other dan we is. If we didn' expect life t' be a certain way an' took it like it come t' us, I 'spect dere be a lot less sufferin'."

"I'm going to have to think on that, Ethel. No expectations? Pretty tall order."

ᕲᕲ

"Did Ethel ever tell you—expound on—her theory on suffering, why she thought we suffered?" Stuart asked her mother as they left Peter's newly prepared room and headed toward the kitchen.

Ginny, never taken by surprise when Ethel was brought up

seemingly out of the blue, answered, "I have to think about it for a minute. I remember it was pretty radical, and I wasn't sure I could go along with it. Do you know?"

"Yeah, expecting life owed us anything other than what we are. I'd say radical, and I'm not sure she wasn't one hundred percent right, although I wouldn't have been able to say that until now. God, she was smart. How did she know so much?"

"I think Ethel was a gift. I don't know how she knew what she knew. What I do know is, we would not be where we are if it hadn't been for that sweet soul and all of her wisdom that she shared so freely." A tear sparkled in the corner of Ginny's eye. "I've never been all that religious, as you know. Ethel's rock-solid faith was as close as I got to believing in anything religious."

"She wasn't about religion," Stuart said. "It was her faith that sustained her, not her religion. I don't even know what religion she was. I imagine Baptist, but I don't know, nor do I think it matters. It was her faith that was so inspiring. That was what made her who she was."

To lighten the mood a bit, Ginny said, "You know what else I miss about Ethel? Her marmalade tarts. You don't know how to make them, do you?"

"No, but I think Sallee put together a cookbook years ago with lots of Ethel's recipes." Stuart started to smile as she remembered Sallee badgering Ethel with questions. "I remember she followed her around, pestering her to tell her how to make this and that. She even spent a day measuring Ethel's handfuls of flour and her pinches of salt so that she could re-create the recipes. I bet she knows."

13

Five exhausted dogs barely lifted their heads from the living room floor as they heard Gordy's big truck rumbling up the driveway outside. Even Burt and Early put their noses back down on the carpet, eyes closed.

"Looks like they're all at Stuart's house," Gordy said, turning into that drive. "Dad, do you want me to take you home?"

"I don't know. Let's see where your mother is because that is where I want to be. Besides, there's a good chance there'll be some food here." Joe chuckled. "I could eat an entire side of beef, I think."

"Wow," Trey whooped, "look at that sled run. I bet Potts has had the most fun of his entire life." He felt like a kid himself. He couldn't wait to get out of the truck and grab a sled. He knew he had some serious soul-searching ahead, but not just now, and the truck had barely come to a stop when he leapt out. Potts and Joey were wobbling from fatigue as they made their way toward the house. He called out to Potts, "Think you could go for one more run with your old man?"

The little boy's face lit up. Despite his apparent exhaustion, he ran over to his father and then turned back to his cousin, yelling, "Come on, Joey. Just one more, this time with my dad."

"I can't. My legs won't work," Joey said, and he indeed looked like he was about to topple over.

Eric snatched up his tired son, tossed him over his shoulder, and marched into Bill and Stuart's house, waving for Potts and Trey to go ahead without them. "He's completely done in," he laughed. "We all are. Been at it all morning."

"Son, are you all right to go downhill with me?" Trey asked Potts.

It was clear from the expression on his son's face that Potts would have followed him to the moon—all he need do was ask.

In a move completely alien to the two of them, Trey bundled the boy up in his arms, plopped himself down on the sled, and with a whoop of delight set off, both of them giggling as they whooshed down the run.

"That was fantastic," Trey exclaimed at the bottom of the hill. He picked up his exhausted son, pulled the sled behind him, and trudged up the steps. He couldn't remember when he had been so happy. "That was so much fun. Have you been doing this all day?"

Before reading the joy on his father's face, Potts looked a little nervous. "Yes, sir, with Joey, Mackey, Eric, Josh, and Sally." His voice lightened with each name he listed. "Merry Christmas, Dad." He wrapped his arms around his father's neck and gave him his first spontaneous kiss.

"Merry Christmas to you too, son." Trey stopped his climb, let go of the sled, and held his son close, burying his face in the child's snowsuit and absorbing his sweet scent. "Merry Christmas," he murmured again, with just the slightest awkwardness as he felt tears of utter joy welling up in his eyes.

As they continued making their way up the hill, Trey chattered to Potts about everything he could think of—sledding, the encounter with the snowplow, what might be for dinner—which was a departure of such magnitude from his usual briskness that it finally occurred to Trey that he might be frightening the child, especially since Potts had not responded since somewhere around "Merry Christmas." At the top of the hill, he looked down to find the child dead asleep. "Good that he doesn't take me too seriously," he said to no one in particular. "Potts, old boy, you can teach me a thing or two." He laughed as he carried the sleeping child into the house.

The smell of roasting turkey made him almost weep from hunger. In the kitchen, the din of a hastily prepared lunch and the clucking of mothers and grandmothers over exhausted children sounded sweeter than anything he could remember hearing.

Susan came right over to him and lifted Potts out of her son's arms. She carried her grandson to a nearby chair, sat with him on her lap, and started undoing boots and zippers—the whole process so simple, so natural, and so completely foreign to Trey. *Where have I been?* he wondered. *Look at all this life I've missed out on.* He knelt down in front of his mother and helped slip the child out of boots and snowsuit.

Susan, surprised at his aid, looked up at him. He smiled at her, his eyes so filled with love that they both burst into tears. "Merry Christmas, Mom," he said before he kissed her on her tear-streaked cheek.

"Oh, your boots are soaked," Susan said.

He looked down at his father's work boots and grimaced, although he was grateful he had them on rather than his own boots. Nothing was dry, nor was most of it appropriate for the weather.

"You must be half frozen," Susan said. "Quick, get out of those wet clothes before you take sick," she instructed. Instinctively, she started to admonish herself for her motherly concern. She knew how much Trey had always hated any maternal attention directed at him. But she swallowed the habitual "sorry" that had sprung unbidden to her lips, sensing the change and reveling in it. "Merry Christmas, son." She looked up at the others. "Mackey, do you think you could find some dry clothes for Trey?" she asked, not stopping to check with her son.

Once Potts was laid abed and Trey had been outfitted in drier gear, he headed back to the kitchen and grabbed a sandwich, which he stuffed into his mouth with much more gusto than his usual contained self would have allowed. Mackey, watching, commented with a chuckle, "Been a while?"

"You know, powdered eggs just don't have much staying power," he mumbled with his mouth full. "And that's all I've had to eat since I don't even know when. God, that turkey smells like heaven. Thanks for taking care of Potts."

Mackey nodded. "Thanks for taking PopPop to the hospital. I would imagine you could have worked up a pretty sizable appetite just trying to convince that stubborn old goat to do what's best for him for a change." She laughed hard. "I love that man so much. If anything had happened to him, I don't ..."

"Yeah, me too, more than I could even imagine."

Andy showed up with another plate of sandwiches, of which his brother snagged two.

"Are you feeling better?" Andy asked.

"Yeah, great, thanks. Merry Christmas, bro, and thanks for taking Potts in last night. He looks like he has had the time of his life."

Mackey said, "Joey and Potts have been inseparable. You might have to leave him here, although I wouldn't think his mother would be too keen on that. Eww, sorry ... I didn't mean ..."

"No worries. I am way too grateful to let anything upset me. Besides, who knows? Anna might like Virginia. She grew up on a farm, so ..."

Mackey and Andy exchanged surprised looks as Trey laughed.

❧

The dinner preparations were winding up to a frenzied climax, and Alex said he was heading over to the other house to look for Virginia since he certainly wouldn't be any help in the kitchen. Trey saw this as his opportunity to talk with him. This was not a conversation he was exactly looking forward to, but he felt it was only fair to come clean with the kid. Alex was on his way out the door when Trey caught him.

"Before you go, can we talk?" he asked.

"Sure."

"On second thought," Trey said, gesturing in the direction of his grandparents' house with his head, "if you're headed up to Pops and Gran's, can I walk with you?"

"Yeah, sure," Alex said with a shrug, and he waited at the door for Trey to get his coat and his father's work boots back on.

Once they were outside and making their way toward the other house, Alex asked, "What's up?"

"I wanted to talk about the conversation we all had earlier in the truck." Rather than beat around the bush, Trey decided to get the whole issue out there. They didn't have that much time to talk, and he knew that Alex was set on telling Virginia everything. "You know, they said in the truck you should tell Virginia all of it, all of the dirty little secrets. I'm not saying you shouldn't, but ..." *Thought you were coming clean, and here you are asking this guy to help you out of a jam,* Trey thought. *Nice!* "I'm just asking if maybe you could hold off on giving too many details about your acting job. Your role as ..." Trey was having a hard time even saying the name. *Who the hell had thought up that name anyway? How had he allowed himself to sink so low and get hooked up in such a smarmy business? Man!* "Your role as Angus LeBoeuf ..."

Alex swung around like a discus thrower. "How do you know about that?" He looked at Trey from under brows more hooded than usual.

"I, uh, own the company," Trey admitted, though not proudly.

"Oh man, what the f— Dude! Whoa. Shit, really? Damn. Son of a bitch. I never would've figured," Alex spluttered.

"Yeah, what are the chances?" Trey laughed without mirth.

"So I'm guessing nobody in the family knows what you do," said Alex. "Hmm, that's a bitch, isn't it? I can see why you want to talk. What do you have in mind?"

"My plan is to tell my dad. I'm not sure I want my mother to know, but I'll leave that up to Dad. My thinking is, if you tell Virginia about your job before I get a chance to tell Dad, things could get ugly fast. I'm not down with my son knowing."

Alex shook his head. "You know, I never really thought about all the complications of being in *the business*." He put air quotes around the last two words. "You have to lie a lot, huh?"

"Tell me about it. Or you have to have the *business*"—Trey mimicked the air quotes—"be the entirety of your life. I am here to tell you, that doesn't work so well."

"I can see that. Shit, man, you've got stones to be able to even come down here. What was up with that?"

"Good question. I don't know, but I think there was a big part of me that wanted this to end. It's not like if we had met in the city over drinks, I would've said, 'Hey, Alex, I want to quit this life.' It wasn't like that at all. I thought I was super cool. Slick as shit." Trey snorted. "Jeez, the last to know." He shook his head. "So anyway, I am not asking you not to tell Virginia. I think you need to be as honest as you can be. I'm just asking for a little time to get Dad on board. Who knows, he might banish me from the family. I don't know."

"It's weird that you are asking me this," Alex said, taking off a glove and scratching his head. "I didn't know you had anything to do with the film or Angus LeBoeuf." He looked awkward as it dawned on him for the first time how stupid the name was. "It's terrible, the name, isn't it?"

Trey agreed with a nod.

"Anyway, like I said, I wouldn't have known about you if you hadn't said so. So how would Virginia put it together?"

"I don't know. I have found …" Trey stopped and tried to gather his thoughts. "There is something here I've been looking for … my whole life. I don't want to mess it up. If this information came out before I had a chance to lay my case before my dad … I guess I didn't really think about it." He shrugged. "You know, I'm tired of lying and living this lie. I want a different kind of life, for me and Potts."

Alex nodded. "Man, what a mess. Shit, I don't have a clue what's up with V. A. For all I know, she's skipped out." He looked around at the snow-covered landscape and laughed. "Well, maybe not skipped out. But shit, you can't tell with her. She blows so hot and cold. I hadn't even decided what I was going to tell her. I guess I'll tell her about my mom. Beyond that, I don't know. They said in the truck the *important* stuff, and if I'm not going to do the movie anymore, maybe she doesn't need to know?"

He stopped at the door of the house. "I'm not even sure I want to get married. Having hung out down here, I've gotten a little homesick. I can't see V. A. living on a ranch in the mountains of Colorado—not a lot of shit to look at if the big city lights are what turns you on. Dude, I won't say anything to her about the porn. As for the rest, huh … Rocky Mountain high? Dunno. I can't see …" Lost in thought, he let his sentence trail off.

❦

Alex found Virginia amid a large, neat pile of Christmas wrappings and opened boxes, crying. Her crying was something Alex just couldn't handle. She could yell and scream all day, and it wouldn't bother him like her crying did. It reminded him of lying in his bed as a child, listening to his mom cry and feeling so helpless. It ate him up just like the cancer had eaten her up. "V. A., what's the matter? Did something happen?" He rushed over to his fiancée, gathering her up in his arms. "Are you okay?"

She held up her red, tear-streaked face to his and looked at him for a long time before blubbering, "I didn't get what I wanted for Christmas."

Alex had thought he'd readied himself for her answer, certain that it had to do with the wedding and how her plans had gone so awry. But her answer floored him. "You are crying because you didn't get what you wanted for Christmas?" he repeated as he looked slowly around at the mound of rolled paper and neatly arranged ribbons. *Jesus Christ*, he thought as he knelt there holding the woman he had thought he wanted to spend the rest of his life with. *What kind of shit is this?*

Several seconds crawled by before he was able to cobble some sort of sentence together. "Gee, that's too bad. What did you want?"

"I don't know," she blurted out, "but I'll know it when I see it."

Alex fought the urge to jump up and run. If he hadn't liked Virginia's relatives so much, he might have. Mustering all of his will, he said evenly, "I came up to get you. Dinner is almost ready. You want to eat, don't you?"

She nodded yes, pulled herself up off the floor, and headed for the guest room bathroom.

Alex sat on the sofa in front of a fireplace filled with the morning's ashes. To take his mind off Virginia's strange behavior—was it strange?—he considered starting a fire but decided against it. They wouldn't be there to enjoy it. While weighing his options, he wondered, *How have I not seen what Virginia really is?* Had she always been this self-absorbed? He rubbed his palm over his forehead and up into his hair, doing his best to remain calm. He didn't want to hurt her—that wouldn't help, especially in this strange condition. That was clear. But he sure as hell didn't want to marry her either. *How did I miss it?* "Talk about having your head up your ass. What the hell have I been doing?" he said out loud.

As he rehearsed scenarios for the best way to call off the impending nuptials, Virginia emerged from the guest room looking radiant, bubbling as if nothing had happened. "Did you say something?" she asked, fresh-faced and doe-eyed.

"No, I was just thinking out loud," Alex murmured. "Are you ready to go? You'd better bundle up. It's cold out there." He found himself a little frightened, like he was dealing with a coiled rattler. Did she know that her father was still in the hospital? He didn't think so. She hadn't bothered to ask either.

"Where were you all day?" she asked. "Everybody left."

Choosing his words with as much care as a bomb squad might use when choosing which wire to start on, he said, "I was … um, I went … uh … you know, uh, to the hospital … with your Uncle

Gordon?" He finally got it out as he hurriedly put on his boots and coat in case he had crossed a wire. "You are feeling okay, right?"

"Yeah, why?"

"You know your dad went to the hospital last night, right?"

A cloud crossed her face, and he steeled himself.

"Yeah," she said, "you didn't bother to tell me this morning." Indignant, she sniffed as she tied a scarf around her neck and pulled a knit cap on her head. Checking the effect in the mirror, she turned and asked, "How do you think this looks?"

"V. A., don't you want to know how your dad is?"

She looked up at him and waited and then finally said in a flat voice, "He has a broken leg. What else is there to know?" Then with an uninterested shrug as she went out the door, she said, "I guess it hurts?"

They walked to Stuart and Bill's house in silence. Alex's mind was in overdrive, trying to come up with a way to end this relationship without the whole thing blowing up in his face. Several times he was on the verge of saying, *V. A., you know, I think maybe ... maybe we ought to put off ... what do you think about ...?* Finally he gave up, taking the disjointed silence as likely the best option for now.

҈

During dinner, the conversation waxed and waned. The sledders, though ravenous, were exhausted. Ginny and Stuart, subdued by their earlier conversation, were not up to making the effort. Sallee fought with her emotions throughout the meal. First, she felt relief that so many stuffed emotions had been excised, then she fretted about Peter, and then she felt depleted.

"Sallee, do you have Ethel's recipe for marmalade tarts?" Stuart remembered to ask as dessert was being served.

"I'm not sure. I used to," Sallee said. The effort of remembering felt too overwhelming. She shook her head, shrugged, and smiled a sad smile.

Stuart opted to let it drop.

"You know," Bill announced, looking at the four children, "tomorrow we have some work we have to do."

"I know … put the sleds away," Josh lamented.

Bill shook his head. "Nope, as a matter of fact, I think we need to get out the toboggan for more sledding—that is, if y'all are up to it."

Four eager faces affirmed that they were.

"Then what is it we have to do tomorrow?" Sally asked.

"Open our Christmas presents," Bill bleated, waving his hands in mock dismay. "We were so busy today, we never got back to them. So I vote that tomorrow when Peter gets home, we open those presents."

Sallee gave Bill a cautionary look that seemed to say, *We don't know if he's coming home tomorrow.*

Bill acknowledged Sallee with a warm smile and a wink and looked back to the children. "And if he has to stay another day, we will just go on without him. Okay?"

"Yay! Presents and sledding! This is the best Christmas ever!" Sally shrieked and then checked herself with an apologetic look in her Aunt Sallee's direction.

Alex hardly spoke through the meal. Virginia chatted with Susan and Andy. Trey watched Alex, worried that he had inadvertently given Virginia more information than he should have.

Before dinner concluded, Gordy announced, "It's cold as hell out there, which means that all of the snow that melted today in the sun will have turned to ice tonight. So I think we should all stay here overnight." He looked at Bill and his older sister. "Assuming that is okay with our hosts. There is no point in any of the rest of us going to the hospital."

Virginia replied that she and Alex were going to risk the ice and stay at PopPop and Gran's. She didn't bother to ask if that was acceptable to her grandparents or Alex, but then why would she? Alex debated countering but let it drop. *What are you so worked up about?* he admonished himself. *It's not like she can hurt you.*

Andy said he was going to take his little ones back to the barn right after dinner. "I think we are—well, they are—young enough that a tumble on some ice won't hurt."

His mother gave him a concerned look, and he answered, "And I promise I will go very, very slowly. No need to worry, Mother."

Ginny groaned inwardly, for what she wanted most was for everyone to go home and to have her life back. Since it was clear that wasn't going to happen, she wanted to be back in her own bed. She smiled a weak smile at Joe before excusing herself.

After the kitchen had been cleaned up, Joe—nearly in a food coma and so tired that holding up his head challenged him—said, "I don't think I have what it takes to make it to my bed, seein' as how it's so far away. Where's my bride?"

Trey laughed. "I heard her ask Stuart if she'd mind if she lay down in the guest room. It's not as far as your bed. Want me to carry you?"

Joe chuckled. "Nope, if I can't make it under my own steam, I'll live with the consequences. Besides, if Ginny has already retired, I won't be disappointing her." He winked at his grandson.

"Good. Glad to hear I don't have to lug you off to bed. I am done in as well. That barn seems a long way off. And once again, Eric and Mackey have taken Captains Joey and Potts under their wing. I think Mackey said something about bedding down in her mother's old room?"

Joe laughed as he and Trey sat on the sofa in front of the fire and propped their stocking feet up on the table in front of them. "Ethel would take a dim view of us here. She never was one to "cotton to" feet anywhere but on the floor." They both laughed, and Joe continued quietly. "I know you want to tell your father, to make a clean slate of it, but before you do, think long and hard about who it will serve. That is all I am saying. Sometimes the kindest thing isn't … you know. I don't need to tell you what to do." He took in the whole of his grandson and smiled, pleased with what he saw. "You look about thirty years younger, ya know?"

"Pops, I feel like you gave me my life back. I am going to follow your wisdom in this. I don't have a clue what is the right thing to do. I sure as hell don't want to cause my parents any more pain. That I know." He leaned back into the sofa cushions. "You know, I think I could fall asleep right now, right here. That is something that would never have happened in the past." He punched the older man gently on his arm. "This sounds corny as all hell, but I can't help it. I love you." He had lost count of how many times he had cried that day, and here he was doing it yet again, and the very strange thing was, he was loving it. "Has anybody heard anything about Peter?" he asked, surprised that he cared.

"Sallee had called the hospital a few minutes before I came in here. I don't think she knows anything new. Virginia, it seems, was missing most of the day. The cooks thought she was sledding, and the sledders thought she was cooking. I imagine she was at our house, more than likely plugged into one of those infernal pads or pods or phones, I don't know." Joe threw up his hands theatrically and shook his head.

"I imagine we are a strange lot to you and Gran, always plugged in as we all are."

Joe winked. "Well, whatever she was plugged into, Alex is going up with her to the house now, and considering what we heard in the truck, I think we're all wise to leave them alone." He yawned and stretched carefully. "The very good news is, all of this drama with Peter's turn for the worse has taken Ginny's focus off my little stint in the hospital. She is clucking around Sallee, which is just fine with me."

Trey chortled. "Methinks thou doth protest too much. If I remember correctly, you said just a while ago that you wanted to be wherever Gran was." He cocked an eyebrow and grinned.

"It's true." Joe chuckled. "I've lived to regret those words."

"You wouldn't know what to do without her. You are one lucky man. It's what I want."

"Truer words have never been spoken, and I do hope the same for you." Within minutes, both men were snoring softly, side by side.

Ↄↄ

Before she and Alex left, Virginia had kissed Ginny and Joe on the cheek and then wished everyone a Merry Christmas, happily waving as Alex shut the door. He trailed behind her on their way back to Ginny and Joe's house, close enough to catch her if she slipped, but not close enough to make conversation easy. He needed to think. His mind was working at warp speed, trying to come up with an exit strategy and then figure out how to implement it. He was certain that marrying Virginia was not remotely in his best interest. Yet he really liked her family—well, at least the southern part of the family. They didn't strike him as the kind of people who would give him a cold shoulder if he and V. A. parted ways, assuming he was gentlemanly about it.

Twice, Virginia slipped on the ice, and twice he caught her before she fell. Gentlemanly wouldn't be a problem, assuming V. A. went along with the breakup. If she didn't––that expression, what was that expression? Hell hath no fury like a woman's something? That was it. So the trick was to make it V. A.'s choice to end the relationship. That could be quite a trick, considering she was as predictable as a green mustang in heat.

I could tell her I've been working in a porn movie. That might do the trick, he thought. *But then, Trey did ask me not to tell her that. Hmm. Maybe just telling her the truth about my mother being black would do it. I'm pretty sure she wouldn't be exactly down with that—or that I kept it from her.* As they neared the house, he made up his mind that he would tell the truth about his parentage, sure that if the plain facts of the matter didn't make her mad enough to call the whole thing off, the fact that he had kept it from her would.

Feeling better about life, he moved up beside her and attempted to take her arm. She snatched it away, growling, "What do you want?"

"I just thought I'd …" Alex stopped. "Is something the matter?"

"You are. Take your grimy mitts off me," she yelled as she scurried forward.

"V. A., what are you talking about? What did I do?" This change in attitude had come on so quickly that he didn't know whether to be angry or afraid.

She stopped, turned around, and started beating her gloved hands on his chest, shrieking, "You didn't say a single word to me at dinner! I had to talk to those two hayseeds, Susan and her dumbass son, the whole time."

He grabbed both hands and held them. She jerked them away, not checking her diatribe in the process. "No one else will speak to me. I'm everybody's *bestie* when everything is going along perfectly, but one little glitch, and all of a sudden, nobody has time for Virginia. Mackey, the bitch, hardly looked at me. I have half a mind to take back those curlers I gave her. And speaking of gifts, do you know what she had the audacity to give me for Christmas?"

Alex shook his head, not in answer to her question but in stunned dismay at this display.

"She gave me a fucking child's toy, a *used* child's toy at that. Can you imagine?" She sneered, her curled lip almost doubled over. With that out of her system, she turned away from him and stomped the rest of the way to the house.

Alex, flabbergasted by the vileness of what he had just experienced, stood rooted on the spot. "Jesus, she is crazy." *Has she always been like this? How did I miss this? What the hell is wrong with me?* Suddenly, he was overcome by the notion that he had almost signed up for happily ever after with this maniac. He felt faint.

When he got to the house, the front door was wide open, Virginia's coat was thrown in a heap next to it, and her boots looked to have been thrown from where she had taken them off. She was nowhere to be seen. He debated going back to Bill and Stuart's place. This whole thing was beginning to creep him out.

As he entered the living room, Virginia suddenly appeared from the kitchen with an open bottle of wine and two glasses. She casually asked, "Are you going to close the door? Take all of that snow stuff off and come sit." She curled her legs under herself as she sat down on the sofa. "Honey, could you start a fire and turn the lights down please?" she purred.

The hairs on the back of his neck had begun to stand on end. *What in the hell is going on here?* Emboldened by his proximity to the door, he asked, "Didn't you just scream at me to take my filthy—I believe was the word you used—mitts off of you? Didn't you tell me that *I* was what was the matter?"

"I didn't say that. I was a little upset because I was stuck talking with Andy and his mother during dinner, that's all. Will you start a fire please? I'll make it worth your while, promise." She gave him a lascivious look that turned his stomach and at the same time spread her legs, revealing a decided lack of undergarments. She poured two glasses of wine and then sat back on the sofa, looked him in the eye, let her legs fall apart, and started stroking herself. This was not something she had ever done before—not that she was a prude, but this was something far beyond prudish.

"What is the matter with you?" he yelled. "Would you stop this?" *Is she making fun of the porn stuff?* he wondered. *But how could she know?* This erratic behavior worried him. If he was honest, it scared the hell out of him. *Get control of yourself,* he told himself, attempting to calm down. Yelling at her was not going to help the situation, so as gently as possible, he rephrased and repeated his request. "Would you please stop that?" Her eyes weren't right. Were they unfocused or intensely focused? He couldn't tell. Whatever they were, looking at them gave him the creeps.

"Hey, how about I call your mom and ask her to come up and hang out?" he asked, realizing the absurdity of the question before he finished it.

"Do you want a three-way with my mom?" she asked.

"Uh, no. Um … I'm going to go get some stuff. I'll be back in a minute, okay?" He was desperate for help. Whatever was going on with her, it was way beyond his skill set. "You stay here," he stammered. Should he call down to the other house and ask someone to come up? Should he run down? He wanted to run and get as far away as possible. The longer he spent with Virginia like this, the more terrified he became. *Maybe she found out about the porn stuff, and this is just her sick way of embarrassing me*, he thought.

"I'm going to the bathroom. I'll be right back." Patting his pockets to check for his phone, he ran out of the room, stopping once he was out of her sight. He couldn't decide whether to call or run down to the house. Still in his coat and boots, he decided to run.

He quietly opened the door and slipped through it, closing it just as quietly after him. He took off in the direction of Stuart and Bill's like a shot.

❧

Bill was outside when Alex arrived. Alex quickly filled him in on what was going on. Bill's immediate response startled Alex. "Go back up there. If she tries to hurt herself or you, lock yourself in a room and call 911. I'll get Stuart, and we'll be right behind you. I'm going to keep this quiet. Sallee has had a hell of a couple of days. At this point, there is no reason to get other people involved."

Alex didn't move but looked at Bill, stunned.

"Go! Don't leave her alone. We'll be right there."

"No offense, but what is Stuart going to do?" Alex asked.

"She's a psychotherapist. From what little I know about it, this sounds like something we could well need her to handle."

"What if this is a joke? What if she's just coming on to me in a funky new way and I overreacted?" Alex was starting to doubt his report now that Bill was jumping to such far-fetched conclusions. "I'm sure I must have overreacted. I … she's … um …"

"Look, kid, you strike me as a pretty normal guy. If a woman was doing what you described, and it made the hair on your neck stand on end and scared you like you are, I'm pretty sure there is a whole lot not right. I'm in no position to be making diagnoses, but you don't look like somebody who has spent much time with a person in a psychotic state. So don't be a hero. She could be dangerous. We'll be right there."

Alex turned around and charged back up the slippery slope. A few minutes later, he burst into the house to find Virginia in the same place on the sofa, but with a broken wine glass in her hand and surrounded by a huge pool of blood—more blood than Alex had ever seen. "Oh shit!" he screamed. He ran to her, and she listlessly lifted the glass up as if to attack.

He stepped back, found his phone, and dialed 911. As calmly as possible, never taking his eyes off Virginia, he said, "I want to report an attempted suicide. Hurry, she's bleeding pretty bad … With a broken wine glass … I don't know the address—the Mackeys … With a wine glass! She cut her thighs, her wrists, all up her arms. Hurry … I don't know, it's the Mackeys' farm. Please! Hurry."

Bill rushed through the still-open door with Stuart at his heels. He took the phone from Alex and gave their address while Stuart gently but firmly approached Virginia.

"Virginia, give me the glass," said Stuart. "Virginia, give me the glass."

Alex could see that she was losing consciousness and prayed that it would come soon so that they could attempt to stop the bleeding. "Oh, this fucking snow. It'll take them hours to get here," he moaned.

Virginia had become so weak that she wasn't able to hold the glass up. Stuart moved so quickly that Alex hardly saw how. She was suddenly standing in front of Virginia one moment and then was kneeling beside her, checking her wounds, the next. "Get some towels, sheets, quick. Alex, do you know how to tie a tourniquet?"

Alex nodded and hurried forward. As he knelt by Virginia, Bill was already back with the sheets, ripping one in strips and handing the strips to his wife.

Stuart gave Alex several pieces of the fabric. "On her arm here and the other there, yeah. And then on that thigh, here," she said, indicating the spots with her nose and her elbow as she applied pressure to the girl's wrists. "Bill, press here and here, where my hands are. I want to check her vitals, so you apply pressure, okay?" She moved to allow Bill room. Wiping the blood from her hands on a spare strip, she gently pried the girl's closed eyes open and then checked for a pulse in her neck. "Keep it up. She's lost a lot of blood, very weak."

Alex tried to focus on what was going on in front of him as a voice in his head screamed, *If she dies, it's on you. You left her!*

Stuart calmly sat down to check the tourniquets. "You are good at this stuff. Were you trained as an EMT?"

What the fuck, lady? Alex wanted to scream. *Virginia is dying, and you are asking me dumbass questions?* But instead he said, "No, I just watched and learned."

"Alex, this is not your fault." Stuart touched him on the arm, causing him to almost jump over the sofa. "No matter what happens, this is not your fault. You did everything humanly possible. Do you hear me? Alex?"

Alex dissolved into tears as he realized that Stuart was saying that Virginia was gone.

The EMTs showed up in a remarkably short period of time. Alex didn't understand why, after checking her, they put her on the gurney and quickly wheeled her away, sirens screaming in their wake. "Why the sirens? Isn't she dead?"

Stuart shook her head. "No, and you are probably the reason why. So don't allow yourself to listen to that voice in your head."

"But you said …" He stopped and thought for a minute. *What did she say?* "You said it wasn't my fault. I thought you were saying she was dead, and it wasn't my fault. Do you think she'll make it?"

"I don't know. She was pretty weak. What I do know is that this is not anything you could have anticipated, nor did you cause it by

anything you said or did. She had a lot of pressure …" She left it at
that. "Wow. Let's not do this again. Three people whisked off to the
hospital in less than twenty-four hours? No, thanks! I am going to
make an executive decision here, so if you guys don't agree, please
say so. I'm not telling Sallee until morning. She can't do anything
tonight but worry, and she's already done enough of that. Besides,
I'm almost positive that they won't let her visit on the psych unit
anyway."

"Absolutely," said Bill.

Alex nodded wearily.

"Alex," Bill said, "I'm going to walk Stuart back, and then I'll
come help you with this." He waved his arm, encompassing the
room. Bill thought about taking some presents back with him but
quickly dismissed the idea. The last thing he wanted was for Stuart
to fall, with him laden down and unable to catch her.

Outside, as Bill and Stuart started the walk back to their house,
Bill said, "Jeez, didn't see that coming."

Stuart had been very quiet as Alex and Bill had hatched a plan
to keep this event on the down-low. Now she said, "I think I could
have, had I been more attentive."

"Don't go there. I just heard you tell Alex this wasn't his fault.
Don't you be picking up that guilt. You've had enough on your plate.
You hardly know the girl, and from what I've heard, she has acted
pretty true to type until tonight, so stop, now." He pulled his wife
around to face him. "I mean it. Look at me, Stuart Amos. You can't
save the world. So quit trying." He wrapped her in his arms and held
her as she slowly unwound.

"Poor Sallee. I just wish there was something I could do for her."

"Ahem, I think you did something already for her. You saved
her daughter's life."

"That remains to be seen. I hope so. Underneath all of that anger
and bravado is a sweet, frightened kid."

"I'm going to have to take your word on that," Bill said. "You,
my dear wife, are a better man than I, to see it," he added, hoping

for a smile. It worked, garnering a smile from his wife, though only a small and tired one.

As they carefully returned home, they held hands. "Boy, this stuff is slick as snot on a door handle," Bill observed.

"I have always found that saying to be such a remarkably unattractive misstatement. Snot on a door handle would be sticky, not slippery, besides gross. Is it Southern? Or did you make it up?"

"I didn't make it up. I don't know where it hails from. I never really thought about it. Watch your step, 'cause no matter what snot is, this ice is slippery. And sheesh, now I'll have to think of another metaphor, I reckon. I surely had no intention of offending your delicate sensibilities, ma'am. Guess that's what comes when beauty marries a beast of a country boy!"

They both laughed.

"Since I reminded the kids about the presents," Bill said, "I'm going to bring them all down to the house tonight, so that no one has to come up here until we get it presentable. It's going be hard to keep Ginny and Joe away."

"I know, and they have already been through so much. I hate for them to be more stressed with this Virginia thing. But I don't see any way around it. Mother will tar and feather me if she finds out later and I didn't tell her. I don't see how she won't hear eventually."

"It will certainly be easier on her if she doesn't see her living room covered in blood. Alex and I will take care of as much of that as we can tonight. I think you are going to have to tell her, but wait until tomorrow and let me be there with you, okay?"

Stuart nodded.

After depositing Stuart at home safely, Bill hightailed it back to the scene. Alex had turned out to be a wunderkind in any number of ways. By the time Bill returned, he had packed and boxed all of the Christmas presents, arranging the large boxes by the door, and had scrubbed most of the blood off the sofa. The area rug had taken the brunt of the gore, and it was nowhere to be seen.

"If I didn't know better, I would think you were a former

crime-scene cleaner-upper." Bill chuckled nervously. "That was awful, wasn't it? And look at it now—and at you, kid. You can hardly tell. I suppose we could say the stain on the sofa is wine."

"Actually, most of it is," Alex said. "I took the rug to the basement and washed it with a hose and brush. I left it down there to dry. It's nice that they have a drain in the floor down there. It made cleaning the rug a breeze. I hope washing it like that didn't hurt it. It looked to be a pretty fine rug."

"I don't think water'll hurt it as much as blood. 'Sides, I'm sure Ginny and Joe will be grateful not to have to see the carnage. How did you get all of this accomplished so fast?"

Alex shook his head. "I don't know. When something needs to get done, I was raised to get 'er done, I guess. My father was not one to accept shoddy work, so I learned early to get 'er done and do it right or get smacked upside the head, hard. Growing up on a ranch a million miles from nowhere, you pick up a lot of skills. I can't say those skills have done me much good in New York."

"It's funny that way," Bill said, heaving a heavy box to his shoulder. "You work hard to develop a set of skills that suit ya, and then you go off and live in a place where those skills aren't worth a plug nickel. I did the same thing when I was about your age. Stuart doesn't know this about me, so don't tell her." He winked at Alex to let him know that this was not going to amount to a dark secret. "She might never stop laughing, and I know for damn sure she'd never let me hear the end of it. And God, if Gordy ever got a hold of it …" He shook his head. "So, as for me, I was a male model in the city for about a minute and a half, when I was around your age. Me, a model? Needless to say, that didn't work out too good. I went back to school and never looked back." He laughed as he headed out the door with his load. "I'll be back in a minute to help tote the rest of this down to the house." With that he was gone.

Alex stood with a dustpan filled with broken glass, shaking his head. "No shit. What a family."

14

Potts and Joey awoke before Mackey and Eric, so they stayed snuggled in their warm makeshift bed on the floor, whispering. "That sled run Granddad Bill made was awesome," Joey exclaimed in a loud whisper. "This has been the best Christmas. That was so fun, going down the hill on top of Dad."

"Yeah," Potts agreed. "My dad and I never sledded before. I don't think they have sleds in New York. I don't have one. You are so lucky to have such a fun dad and mom." The admission surprised him. One thing Potts had always been was stoutly loyal to his parents. Never had he entertained the thought that someone else might have better parents. His friend Elliot may have had an easier time with the family tree, but Potts knew Elliot didn't see his dad any more than Potts did. It wasn't so much that he thought his were so great. He knew they weren't. And it wasn't that he wanted his dad to be different, to be like Eric, though that sure would be fun. What he wanted was just for his dad to be around. He couldn't decide if he was angry or sad or both. Here he was with a family he had never met before, and he had spent only—was it even twenty minutes?—with his dad. He was pretty sure that was what he meant when he told Joey he was so lucky.

Joey had fallen back asleep while Potts was thinking, so Potts crawled out from under the covers and went in search of his dad. Since arriving in Virginia, he had yet to sleep in the same house, much less bed, twice. As he tiptoed around Stuart and Bill's house, quietly looking for his snow clothes, he tried to conjure his way back to the first room, the room his father had said was theirs. He knew it wasn't in this house, and he was sure it wasn't in Gran's house. It was fuzzy, that other place. It was already dark when they'd arrived, and he had been so excited to meet Sally and Josh that he hadn't paid any attention to which way they went after they came to get him.

Having managed to collect all of his belongings, Potts zipped up his jacket and put on his boots but decided to forego the snow pants since he wasn't sure he could manage them on his own. As he crept to the front door, he wished he had paid more attention and chided himself for not having made the effort to take in his surroundings. His mother had drilled into him the need to be aware at all times because they lived in the city. It would not sit well with her if he got lost, he knew.

He tiptoed past the living room. At the front door he reached for the knob, only to find that it would not turn. "Darn," he mumbled quietly. There was no deadbolt like at home and no slide lock, so he tried the knob again. The knob was too big for him to manage with one hand, so he wrestled with both. His height worked against him. Just as he was looking around for a chair to pull up to the door, to put him at a more advantageous level, he heard snoring coming from the living room.

Creeping around the edge of the doorway, he peeped in to find his father and great-grandfather sitting up and leaning against one another on the sofa, snoring contentedly. Quickly, he shed all of his outer garments. With great stealth and care, he inserted himself between the two snoring men and fell almost immediately into a peaceful sleep.

Hours later, when Mackey awoke and missed Potts, she scurried out of bed in search of him. She found the three still sleeping on the couch. Potts had wrapped himself around his father in what had to be an extremely uncomfortable position, but he was sleeping as if on a cloud.

Trey was the first to wake. Finding his son sandwiched between himself and Joe and wrapped around him almost brought Trey to tears. He cradled the child's dark brown head and kissed it. *What have I done to you? I am so sorry.* Tears welled up in his eyes, and when he moved to wipe them away, Potts stirred awake.

"Hi, Dad," the little boy said, rubbing his eyes.

"What are you doing here? I thought you had a nice comfortable spot with cousin Joey," Trey whispered so as not to wake his grandfather.

"I did. But I wanted to find you. I wanted to ask you something."

"What is it, son?" Trey felt himself tense up from a reflex that he was suddenly recognizing all too well. But how had it become so entrenched? This was his *son*.

"I want you to stop being a spy." Potts looked at his dad so earnestly that it made Trey's heart ache.

"A spy?"

"Yeah," Potts said with pride. "Elliot—you know, my friend from home? We figured it out." He lay back with his hands behind his head, pleased with his deductive skills.

"A spy," Trey repeated. "Hmm, guess I'm busted." He laughed. "You want me to stop, eh?"

"Yep, I want to live like Joey does, with a dad that comes home all of the time and plays."

"Hmm, a dad that comes home *and* plays? Do you think I could do that? You want me to come home?"

"Of course I want you to." The child scrabbled to prop himself up on an elbow. Placing his head in his hand, he looked at his father earnestly, not bothering to hide his incredulity. "You don't think you can play?"

"I don't know. I'm not sure I ever have."

"Dad," the little boy said with a shake of his tousled head, "it's easy. I'll teach you."

❧

Since Trey hadn't gotten a read on Alex at dinner the night before, he decided that speaking with his father should be first up in the morning. What Joe had said made sense. Maybe he had a point. If Gordy heard from someone else the truth of what Trey was, any hope of a relationship could be irrevocably damaged. It's not like it was in the best of shape just now, but it was certainly better than it ever had been.

Potts and Joey had made plans at breakfast to play in Joey's parents' room until it was time to go sledding. Mackey assured Trey that she would be happy to keep an eye on the boys. So he was clear to talk with his dad; he just needed to get him alone.

Gordy was in the mudroom feeding the dogs when Trey approached him.

"Hey, hand me the bucket of scraps, won't you?" Gordy asked as Trey stood by, watching his father dole out food for all six dogs. "Daisyduke, get outta his bowl, ya big pig." Gordy extended a foot to push Daisy away from Six's bowl.

Trey tried his damnedest not to show his irritation. The man couldn't help it. He loved dogs. There was nothing to be done about it. Trey picked up the bucket like it was going to bite.

"Son, just hand me the damn bucket," Gordy snapped.

Miffed, the younger man quickly handed over the bucket, fighting with himself not to give up with a "screw it" attitude. *Things are never going to change*, he thought, but he willed himself to stay put.

"Sorry about snapping," Gordy volunteered. "It's a bad habit. It didn't serve us when you were young, and I can't believe it will now either."

Trey grabbed the counter for support, bowled over by his father's turnabout. "I, uh … it, umm, wasn't … a big deal," he stammered, surprised to find that he was on the verge of tears again. "Thanks for that," he finally managed to say.

"It was a big deal. I am sorry. I have bullied you most of your life, and I'm sorry about that too. I'm not going to make excuses. I was a pretty shitty dad, and I would like to make that up to you—if you'll let me and there is still time."

Trey had to check to see if his mouth was hanging open. He couldn't trust any feelings at this point, even the less subtle ones. Finally, after debating any number of things he might say, he managed to croak, "Umm, I don't know what to say." Surprisingly, the fact that his father had handed him this admission of guilt, out of the blue, infuriated him.

Here he had planned to bare his soul and ask for his father's forgiveness, and the old bastard had beaten him to it. *What in the hell is the matter with you? So what? Isn't this what you wanted—a relationship with your father as an equal?* The internal struggle he felt threatened to tear him in two. He wanted more than he had ever realized to bury the hatchet with his father. The man was handing him an olive branch, taking responsibility for his bad parenting without excuses or equivocation, and Trey couldn't feel anything but rage. Had he completely lost his mind?

He stood silent, shaking with anger, unable to respond. Gordy waited without speaking, not pushing his agenda, just waiting. They must have stood there an hour, Trey was sure—at least an hour with this hulking silence and unforgiveness between them. In reality, less than a few minutes passed before Trey heard Ethel say, as clear as if she were standing next to him, *I oughta tan yer hide, stubborn as you is.* Trey laughed and moved toward his father to embrace him. "Thanks, Dad. I love you." The two men stood locked together, tears running down their cheeks.

Finally, wiping his eyes with the back of his hands, Trey stepped back and laughed out loud. "I don't know if now is the time, but I can't think of a better one. I have to tell you something." He hated the risk of breaking this magic spell, but he had to take it. "I have to …" The words wouldn't come.

"You don't have to tell me a thing. I think I know what you want to say."

"No, Dad, you don't. I wish I didn't have to …"

"Tell me about FlyBy Productions?" Gordy guessed.

"You know?"

His father nodded. "I know. I know why too. Ethel and I talked about it."

"Ethel?" Trey looked around for a place to sit as his knees started to cave. He pulled up a trash can and perched on the edge of it. "What did Ethel know? How in the hell … What are you talking about?"

"If you'd shut up long enough for me to tell you …" Gordy laughed, and Trey joined him.

Gordy continued, "She asked me how you were doing a couple of years ago. I grumbled and growled, trying to change the subject. You know how she was, like a bird dog at point." They both laughed again at Gordy's inevitable choice of image. "You know what I mean. She just kept on it. Finally, I gave up—like I had a choice. This is Ethel I'm talking about. I said that I didn't understand what had gone so wrong in our relationship. I didn't know what changed or why you hated me so much." He let out a big sigh. "Ethel reared back and gave it to me with both barrels."

Gordy began to tell the story, slipping into an Ethel speech pattern. "'Gordon,' she said, 'dat boy been 'bused—an' bad—by dat old bat, Miz Susan's momma. Early an' me done talked 'bout it. I tol' him what I 'spected. Tol' him 'bout de bruises too.'

"'What bruises?' I asked.

"'All round his gentles,' Ethel said. 'Early say he bet his bottom dollar dat woman done dat to 'im. He say dat we ought t' tell you so dat you could put a stop t' it. I tol' him I tried t' tell you, but you was in no mind t' hear. He say he would see what he could do.'

"The long and short of it is that as usual, Ethel was right—I was in no mind to hear. I will regret that the rest of my life." Gordy wiped away tears.

"You had a lot of things going on. I know that now. Life is never as simple as it seems from a child's perspective."

"Maybe so, but when your child is being assaulted, and you

stand by and do nothing ... and continue to do nothing? I ought to be drawn and quartered."

Trey stood up and reached out to his father.

Gordy put his head down on his son's shoulder, stifling a sob. "I am so sorry, son. You don't know."

"I think I do, Dad. I think I do. And so am I." They stood in the embrace for some time before Trey summoned the courage to ask the question on his mind. "Ethel didn't know about FlyBy, did she?"

"No," Gordy said with a laugh. "Can you picture her reaction? I can't even imagine what that would have looked like. I did some snooping recently, after the invitation arrived. I got a ... um, I don't know how to say this ..." He sputtered a little before finally continuing, "Oh hell, I'll just say it. Early made a visit."

Trey looked only slightly askance.

"You look like Dad when you do that," Gordy said.

Trey smiled. "I know the look. You mean his askance glance?"

"The very one. Anyway, Early impressed upon me that there was another way of going, and I needed to take it. So I got somebody to look around. Found out what you were about to tell me just now, and pieces of the puzzle fell into place in such a way I couldn't deny the truth of what Ethel had said to me. By the way, your mother doesn't know this, and I want to keep it that way."

"She might be the only one who doesn't know." Trey gave Gordy an abbreviated rundown of what had transpired in the hospital.

"He is a cagey old goat, I'll give him that," Gordy replied. "I swear, he would have done it too. I'm glad you realized that. Explains Sallee's turnaround too. Hell, on the trip home from the hospital, she was as human as she has been since she was a kid. I never did like that bastard she married. Hmm, some family!"

"Yeah, some family," Trey agreed.

"So what are you going to do now?"

"I want to move back home," Trey said.

Gordy gave his son a wicked grin. "I don't think people are gonna take to having movies like that made around here."

"It's a little more complicated," Trey said.

Gordy raised an inquisitive eyebrow.

"Umm, Alex works as an actor in one of my productions."

"Is that work?" Gordy joked.

Trey gave him another Joe-inspired glance.

"Yes, it is complicated," Gordy acknowledged. "Does Virginia know?"

Trey shrugged.

"Her parents?"

Trey nodded that they did.

"That's just swell. Only a matter of Peter getting back here before he throws that at a wall to see what sticks." Gordy looked as if he would explode. "Virginia doesn't impress me as the most, umm … I don't even know what to say … uh, reliable confidant. Didn't we just tell Alex to come clean with everything? Shit."

"I had a chat with Alex last night about that. I think he realizes the implications," Trey said.

"Yeah, but Peter—he's a loose cannon," Gordy warned.

"He didn't seem so interested in bringing it to the light before he got sick," Trey said. "We can hope he won't be inclined to afterward. Sallee appreciated how upsetting the news would be for you and Mother." Trey now heard himself speaking with his father about his choice of career as dispassionately as if the subject were someone else. The changes a few days had wrought were mind-blowing. "You know, keeping secrets is such a heavy burden. I don't really care if it does come out. I think Mother could handle it. She's not made of glass, you know?" He held up his hand, forestalling comment. "We don't have to tell her. I'm just saying, let the cards fall where they may. If Peter wants to be a prick, let him be. He'll only end up hurting himself in the long run." He stopped as if finished, thought for a minute, and then added, "He *is* a king-sized prick, by the way!"

"No kidding! Sallee would be well shed of him," Gordy said. "What in God's name was she thinking when she married that asshole?"

Trey smiled. "Love, Dad, in case you haven't heard, is blind."

⁊

As it turned out, no one in the sleeping family at Bill and Stuart's had heard the sirens from the night before. Not a soul, they would discover, suspected there was anything amiss. Alex and Bill had managed to arrange the gifts under Bill and Stuart's somewhat smaller Christmas tree without disturbing the sleepers on the sofa, although they had come close. Bill had bumbled into the room with his armful of unwieldy boxes and tripped over a chair that had been moved earlier to create a fort. A masterful juggling act on his part had averted a fall. He had started to swear lustily before he heard a snort from the sofa and saw the two sleeping men. "What a family," he had whispered, chuckling to himself all the way back to Alex.

Come morning, Stuart had lain in bed, dreading the task that lay ahead while waiting for Bill to wake. She decided that she could stretch the bounds of truth a bit and call the hospital to check on Virginia before informing Sallee of last night's events. She imagined the alternative of telling Sallee first: *Sister dear, your daughter tried to commit suicide last night. No, I don't know if she was successful. We could call the hospital, but I'm not sure they can or will tell you anything. You know, patient confidentiality and all that.*

Under the circumstances, Stuart decided, a white lie was in order, and she reached for the phone. The nurse who answered was a diehard HIPAA advocate and repeated that she was not able to confirm or deny the existence of a patient by that name.

"I am her attending therapist," Stuart fibbed.

"I'm sorry. We can't discuss this with you in a telephone call. You could be anyone," the nurse said, stubbornly sticking to her guns.

"Let me speak to the attending physician," Stuart demanded.

Fortunately, Stuart had worked with the doctor on duty, who told her that Virginia had survived. She was heavily sedated and in restraints so she couldn't remove her stitches. She was not allowed visitors for the time being under any circumstances.

After ending the call with the doctor, Stuart reconnected her phone to the charger and sat back up in the bed. "Well, that's good at least," she said.

Bill, one eye just barely open, pulled himself groggily up to lean on an elbow. "What's good at least? Virginia?"

"Yes, she's alive, sedated, and still assumed to be psychotic, they said. That's a relief."

"That she's crazy as bat shit?" He crossed his eyes, looking comically confused or crazy, Stuart couldn't decide.

"No!" She smacked him playfully on the shoulder. "That she's alive, you idiot. That's so much nicer a lead than *Oh, your daughter committed suicide last night.* Don't you think?"

"So now what?"

"I don't know. I guess I need to tell Sallee."

Just then Mackey knocked and pushed into her parents' bedroom without waiting. She waved good morning. "Tell Sallee what?"

"That habit is going to get you in trouble one of these days," Bill reprimanded cheerily, "when you come face to bare ass with your father and mother engaged in events you don't want to be privy to, miss. It is a wonder that it hasn't happened yet, considering how active we are sexually."

Stuart smacked him with the pad she had been writing on.

"Eeew," Mackey cringed. "You are so disgusting."

"Since when is sex disgusting?"

"When your dad is talking about doing it is when," Mackey shot back.

"Then knock and wait to be invited in," he replied, lounging back on his pillow.

"Moving on ... what do you have to tell Sallee?" Mackey asked again.

"None of your business, nosy pants," her father replied.

Mackey stuck out her tongue.

"What do you want?" Stuart asked, interrupting their banter.

"Just came in to say I love you and ask how you want this day to play out. Breakfast, sledding, presents? Presents, breakfast, sledding? I didn't want to presume anything. Sallee, I know, didn't hear anything substantive last night, so my guess is that Peter isn't coming home today. My vote is for breakfast, presents, sledding." She spread her hands, inviting comment. Then, getting no immediate reply, she added, "What was up with Virginia last night? She was bitchier than usual and a lot weirder."

Stuart sank back into the pillow. *You'd have to ask, wouldn't you? No chance that my daughter could miss a clue. No damn chance in the world.* As she lay propped up in bed, debating whether she should spill the beans to Mackey, someone tapped softly on the door.

"Can I come in?" Ginny called from the other side.

Bill jumped out of bed and pulled his pants on. "See, that is how it's done," he said with a nod toward the door. "Sure, Ginny, come on in. You won't catch a peek this time. I'm all covered up."

Mackey and Stuart rolled their eyes.

"Do you think you'll ever be able to housebreak that husband of yours?" Ginny chuckled as she opened the door. "Did anybody see the scene in the living room a little while ago?"

Stuart and Bill simultaneously flinched. "What scene?" they both asked a little too fast, and Mackey and her grandmother both noticed.

Ginny cocked a glance at Stuart. "In the living room. Are you all right? I was going to suggest you go see. It was adorable, but it's too la—"

Stuart and Bill shot out of the room before she completed her sentence.

"We didn't give those two hounds anything to track, did we? Can't keep a secret in this house, no way, no how," Bill said with a grimace. "We might as well tell them."

"A secret? Tell them what?" Gordy asked, coming from his talk with Trey and feeling a little too sensitive to the word at the moment.

Jeez, what a family! Stuart sighed. "Nothing. Good morning."

By the time they got to the living room, they had attracted as many followers as a teen idol on Twitter.

Joe blinked awake as most of his family stared down at him. "What? Can't a man sleep on the sofa if he wants? Jesus, what a family."

Just then Sallee emerged from her room. "Well, this is quite a little gathering. What's going on?"

Joe grumbled, "I slept on the sofa last night. There is so little to do around here that waking me seems to be the morning's entertainment. Go watch television or something, the lot of you! Get."

"Peter called," Sallee said, ignoring him. "He's going to have to stay in the hospital for a day or two and possibly have to go to a nursing home until his leg heals. You can imagine how well he took *that* news. Apparently, he had a …" Trey walked in as she was delivering Peter's news. "Hi, Trey … a blood clot that had traveled to his lung. They had to do some procedure with a catheter to break up the clot. I don't know. I think he's lucky to be alive. If you had gotten to the hospital sooner, Gordy, and we had taken Peter home, there's no telling what might have happened." She looked distressed for an instant, and then her good humor returned.

"Dad and I will take you to the hospital if you want to go visit him," Trey volunteered.

Sallee shook her head. "Thanks, but no thanks. He can cool his heels there on his own. Lucky for him, he has to stay in the hospital. He was so disagreeable on the phone, you would have thought that I broke his leg and caused the blood clots all by myself. If he came back in his present frame of mind, I might just consider wringing his neck. So it's just as well he is where he is." She laughed. "Is there any coffee?"

Mackey darted to the kitchen to get her some.

"Bring me some too," Joe called after her.

Stuart debated about what to do. If she had to receive the sort of news she was about to give Sallee, would she want to have it delivered quietly, just the two of them, or right here, right now? Her choice would be to have it delivered privately. *Just relax*, Stuart told herself. *She doesn't need to know this instant. You can wait for the right time. She can't do anything now anyway.* She sighed as she tried to talk herself out of the mounting anxiety that delivering bad news caused her.

Ginny accepted Joe's coffee from Mackey and took it over to him on the sofa. Sitting down next to him, she said, "Here, Grumpy. Drink this, and then I want you to take me home."

Stuart looked for Bill, panicked.

He nodded at her with two thumbs up, mouthing, "It's okay." Bill looked around. "Where are all the children?" he bellowed. "Santa is going to get his feelings hurt if these presents don't get opened." He'd done a very neat job of arranging presents so that the children's were front and center. He figured the news would put most of the adults off unwrapping gifts, so he'd left theirs behind the tree, tucked away in the boxes Alex had packed.

It took every ounce of patience Ginny possessed to get through the second round of present opening. "I want to go home," she whined in Joe's ear as they sat side by side on the sofa.

He patted her thigh. "Soon, sweetie."

As the children unwrapped their gifts, Bill and Stuart decided that while she was telling Sallee, he would tell Ginny and Joe. After all the presents were unwrapped and snowsuits, boots, and mittens were tracked down and donned, Sallee went into the kitchen. Stuart followed while Bill walked over and sat down next to his in-laws on the sofa.

❧

Sallee absorbed the news of Virginia's suicide attempt with surprising equanimity. "You know, I'm not surprised. Hindsight and all that, you know? I thought she was becoming more antisocial and self-absorbed—but mind you, that was a matter of degree, since that daughter of mine has been both since she showed up. Peter and I certainly didn't help the situation, doting on her the way we did."

Stuart was surprised to hear Sallee take responsibility for her part in Virginia's problems without guilt or blame. But she soon discovered that telling her sister, the lawyer, that the law was currently not working to her advantage was another matter entirely. It wasn't until Stuart explained how little she knew and how she knew it that Sallee turned rabid.

"What? You're telling me that had you not known the doctor on duty, you wouldn't be able to tell me if Virginia had even survived the night? Despite you being, as far as they knew, her therapist? That's just not right! That makes my blood boil." She was on her feet now, eyes flashing with indignation. "We'll just see about this." With that she marched out of the room, leaving Stuart to surmise what her sister's plans might be.

Ginny and Joe took the news much as Bill had anticipated—with concern, anxiety for Sallee and her burdens, and relief that Virginia had failed in her attempt. They, too, were not greatly surprised by the turn of events. After expressing their gratitude to Bill and sharing a brief conversation about the rest of the night's events, Ginny repeated her need to go home.

"What else could go wrong?" she asked as they were putting on their coats.

"Oh, don't go there! Plenty. After all, we're all still alive," Joe replied, not missing the irony of his statement as he shrugged on his jacket.

"Yeah, no thanks to you!" his wife shot back.

"Now, now, I've come to see the insanity of my ways," he rejoined. "That lesson has come back on me more than once in the past forty-eight hours, thanks," he added without the slightest bit of defensiveness. "And I'm sorry, you know. I truly am, Ginny. I was a horse's ass."

"Okay, as long as you remember that, I'll forgive you," she said with a twinkle in her eye and a peck on his cheek. "Let's go home. I guess the hemlock ship has sailed for now, huh?"

They both laughed as they headed out into the snowy landscape.

"Where are you two going?" a grinning Trey asked as he came up the hill, pulling a toboggan with four giggling children attached. "A little alone time?"

"That's exactly it, pal. Don't call, don't send a card, and definitely don't visit," Joe laughed.

"Message received loud and clear. Are you going to be all right, walking up there on your own?"

Joe looked at his grandson like he had three heads.

"The ice, man. It's dangerous. We don't need to have you guys take a tumble, now do we?"

"We're okay. Ginny's armed with her cane."

Ginny lifted the cane in the air as proof.

"And I have the steady-as-she-goes gait down pat."

"All the same, I think we should take extreme care of our most precious commodities." He turned to the kids. "Let's give the g-rents a ride to their house. Whaddya say?"

The children tumbled off the big sled. "Yeah!"

Trey stood there with both hands out, palms open, indicating the toboggan. "Okay, climb on. We'll pull you up."

"You *are* trying to do us in, right?" Joe laughed. "There is no way Ginny and I could get down onto that thing, much less back up."

"We're going to help. Aren't we, guys?"

It took a good ten minutes, first to talk the elders into the scheme and then to get them situated. Once that was done, and Ginny was sufficiently assured of their safety, they set off up the slight incline toward the house amid shrieks of laughter. Trey had enlisted Eric and Andy's aid in the pulling effort. Joe made a snowball and tossed it playfully at Josh, who reciprocated.

"Hold it," Ginny whooped as she ducked her head, covering it with both arms. "Throwing snowballs at me is strictly off-limits, and don't you hide behind me, you old fool. You started it." She laughed until her sides ached, as children ran alongside, tossing snowballs at each other, and as the dogs cavorted after them.

When they finally reached the house, the three-man team was exhausted, the children were breathless, the dogs were clamoring for more fun, and the g-rents were exhilarated. "Thank you for that. It was such fun," Ginny said. She couldn't stop giggling. "I feel like a kid again. Thank you." She rolled off into the snow and held her hands up to the children. Joey and Potts each grabbed a hand while Trey came around back and gently lifted his grandmother to her feet.

Joe, of course, couldn't allow anyone to help, wallowing around in the snow until Eric took pity on him and grabbed him under the arms from behind. With far less grace than his wife, he was finally righted.

The children and Andy waved goodbye, piled on the toboggan atop one another, and sped down the slope, shrieking with joy. On the way, one after another tumbled off.

As Eric and Trey accompanied Ginny and Joe the rest of the way to the house, Alex emerged, looking lost and forlorn. "Any news about Virginia?"

"She's going to be okay," Joe said quickly. "She's going to have to stay in the hospital for a while, but she's going to be fine. It actually might be the best thing that could have happened to her." Standing at the door, Joe turned to Eric and Trey, both of whom looked thoroughly confused, and said, "I'll let Alex fill you in." With that, he and Ginny went into the house and closed the door.

∾

There was one positive thing about Peter: he was true to his nature. Shortly after calming down enough to function, Sallee had called him, only to discover that neither his forced stay in a hospital bed nor the three feet of snow outside his window had impeded his ability to make things happen. "As soon as the airport is open, I've got a flight out on a private air ambulance service. I'll be damned if I'm going to rot in this backwater," he snapped immediately upon answering, not even giving Sallee a chance to say hello, much less tell him the news.

"You might want to rethink that," she snapped back, not pausing to soften the blow. "Virginia attempted suicide last night and is there in the psych ward as we speak."

"For Christ's sake! What, over that damn wedding? Well, if she's psychotic over a wedding," he said, "this doesn't change my plans."

"So happy to hear your concern for your daughter," Sallee retorted. "I'll be sure to tell her you send your love." She hung up without another word.

She returned to the now-deserted living room to regroup and then went in search of Gordy. Not finding him after a trip through the kitchen to the mudroom, she quickly pulled out her phone. "Hey, it's me. Can you give me a ride to the hospital? … Oh, okay … No, don't worry about it. I can drive. I'm sure Bill won't mind lending me his truck. I just thought if you were here … No, *he* is okay. Flying out as soon as the airport opens, as a matter of fact. I'm going to see Virginia … It's a long story. Suicide. She's, um … alive. I'm going to have a chat with the hospital administration face-to-face … Yeah, good to see you too. I'll let you know. I love you. Give my love to Susan. Bye."

❧

"Stuart, do you know where Bill is?" Sallee bellowed as she turned to head back into the kitchen and almost bumped into her sister.

"He's outside, putzing around. Do you need something?"

"Yeah, I wanted to borrow his truck, run to the hospital. Do you think he'll let me?"

"I'm sure he'll be happy to drive you. Going to see Peter?" she said, assuming that Virginia was still off-limits to visitors.

"Decidedly not. If I never see him again, it might be too soon. He's arranged for an air ambulance to take him home as soon as the airport opens."

"What about Virginia?"

"What about Virginia? Has she ever impacted his plans, really? He sees this as an irritation for me to deal with. He's too important, too busy, too much of an ass …"

"Oh, Sallee, I'm so sorry." Stuart moved to hug her sister, but Sallee waved her off.

"No, this is good. I want to stay mad right now. I'm going to have a chat with the hospital administrators and, if need be, the president of the university and the entirety of the board of visitors. It's not right that they don't train their people to have more regard for humanity than this asinine letter-of-the-law bullshit."

"Go get 'em, tiger," Stuart laughed. "The keys are in the truck."

Hours later, Sallee left the hospital administrator's office beaming. *Nothing feels better than striking a blow for the little people*, she thought as she pumped her fist in the air. She had been assured by the powers that be that there would be immediate and ongoing training to teach hospital employees how to stay within the bounds of the law while treating patients and their relatives in a respectful, humane manner.

Riding the wave of her success, she thought she was up to a final meeting with Peter. As she opened the door to the unit, she heard Peter's voice rising in his most imperial tone. "You tell that son-of-a-bitch doctor to get down here, now! I have a chopper on standby. If he doesn't sign my release papers now, he will be staring down the barrel of a …"

She turned and retraced her steps, chuckling to herself. *Yes, no need to look back. Thank you for that, Peter. Thank you for being true to type.* As she stood at the elevator, pondering whether she was up to visiting the psych unit, the elevator door opened. A handsome man about her age, his white coat unbuttoned over street clothes and a clipboard in his hand, was the only occupant. She laughed at herself as she furtively admired him. *A little early to be checking out other men, isn't it?* she thought as she pushed the button for the fifth floor and stepped away from the controls. Rather than turn to face the door, as she would normally, she stayed facing the center of the elevator. There was something familiar about this man, very intriguing. She was lost in her thoughts as they rode up two floors in silence. As they stepped off the elevator, the man spoke.

"Sallee … Mackey?" he asked.

She turned back in surprise.

"Early Thompson," he said. "I would have known you anywhere."

Sallee's head buzzed as she tried to put together his words. Finally, she exclaimed, "Lil' Early? I can't believe it!" She laughed. "Is that you, all growed up? I mean … what are you doing here?" She stammered, trying to get her tongue and brain to cooperate. "Do you work here?" She held out a hand to him. "It is so good to see you."

"Yes, and this is my domain, the psych unit. Do you still live in town?" He was rushing, hoping to engage her before she had time to run off.

"I'm on my way there too. My daughter tried to commit suicide last night. Are you a psychiatrist?"

"Yes." His deep brown eyes filled with concern. "I'm so sorry … your daughter …"

She shrugged and bit her lip. "It's a long story. We're hoping for the best. Hoping for the best." She nodded, looking down at the floor for a moment. Then she smiled just slightly and looked up. "And well, you know what Ethel would've said: 'If it ain't one thing …'"

CPSIA information can be obtained
at www.ICGtesting.com
Printed in the USA
LVOW11s1305060618
579805LV00001B/42/P

9 781480 849396